Praise for

## STING OF THE DRONE

"*Sting of the Drone* explores a premise that members of the intelligence community have been kicking around for years: What would happen if the targets on the receiving end of a killer drone decided to strike back? As you read *Sting of the Drone* you get the sense that it isn't fiction at all. Clarke has written a classic in the genre of what is known as insider fiction—a novel or, more often, a thriller inspired by real episodes . . . *Sting of the Drone* stands above the rest . . . This is riveting reading." —*The Washington Post*

"What Tom Clancy did for submarines, Richard A. Clarke does for drones. Fascinating and frightening, *Sting of the Drone* moves as fast as the new kind of warfare that it depicts, with authentic details that only someone with the author's impressive insider credentials could know. This first-rate thriller . . . a cross between a techno-thriller and a docu-thriller, ought to be required reading for anyone who wants to know the current status of the battle against terrorism."

—David Morrell

"*Sting of the Drone* is a jet-fueled race through a world where the sky itself can be your worst enemy."

—*Seattle Post-Intelligencer*

"Insider knowledge of politics paired with amazing state-of-the-art technical details fuel this realistic nonstop action thriller . . . [Clarke] has set the standard by which all such titles in this growing subgenre will be measured." —*Publishers Weekly* (starred review)

"On rare occasions a thriller comes along that turns out to be prophecy: *Sting of the Drone* is one of them. This rip-snorting thriller may be the best unclassified peek you will ever get on the new high-tech offensive in the war against terrorism. A seminal, prophetic, troubling must-read." —Stephen Coonts

"Clarke does a terrific job showcasing how the drone program works and revealing something about the men and women behind the scenes who use the machines."

—*Booklist*

"This one smacks so much of reality you'll swear it's real. Written in a deft hand, by a man who knows what he's talking about, the take-no-prisoners plot serves up a banquet of high drama, action, and adventure. A great read." —Steve Berry

"It's rare a novel is written *ahead* of the headlines, but the plot of *Sting of the Drone* is just that book. If you've wondered what it's like to be inside the U.S. Predator drone program, your wait is over. Prepare for your hand to take hold of the joystick, your heart to lodge firmly in your throat. Tom Clancy takes to the air. Put this book on your radar." —Ridley Pearson

"Exciting and disturbing . . . There may be no better person to write this story than Clarke, who brings his deep subject knowledge to the pages."

—*Kirkus Reviews*

"*Sting of the Drone* is a riveting page-turner that goes deep into the complex world of those who hunt with, and are hunted by, military drones. Rich with detail and informed by his expertise in national security, Richard Clarke brings this hidden world to vivid life."

—Jeff Abbott

## ALSO BY RICHARD A. CLARKE

### NONFICTION

*Against All Enemies: Inside America's War on Terror*

*Your Government Failed You: Breaking the Cycle of National Security Disasters*

*Cyber War: The Next Threat to National Security and What to Do About It*

### FICTION

*The Scorpion's Gate*

*Breakpoint*

# STING OF THE DRONE

RICHARD A. CLARKE

St. Martin's Paperbacks

This is a work of fiction. All of the characters, organizations, and events portrayed in this novel are either products of the author's imagination or are used fictitiously.

STING OF THE DRONE



For information address St. Martin's Press, 175 Fifth Avenue, New York, NY 10010.

Library of Congress Catalog Card Number: 2014008828

ISBN: 978-1-250-06768-5

Printed in the United States of America

St. Martin's Press hardcover edition / May 2014
St. Martin's Paperbacks edition / May 2015

St. Martin's Paperbacks are published by St. Martin's Press, 175 Fifth Avenue, New York, NY 10010.

10 9 8 7 6 5 4 3 2 1

*Dedicated to*
*Michael W. Lower,*
*who loved thrillers only slightly*
*less than crossword puzzles*

# 1

SATURDAY, JUNE 27
PAKTIKA PROVINCE
AFGHANISTAN

The man they called Skander had come this way. It was over a hundred generations ago, but the watcher on the hill knew the story. Everyone did. The long column, pounding down the dirt, kicking up the dust, had passed through the canyon below. Then he had built the city in the south and named it after himself. Finally, he and his men had gone, as they all eventually do, as these new ones would.

Now the hardpack road below was rutted, studded with rocks, seldom driven. The lead Pajero SUV sent up a cloud of dry sand, which settled back down on the road before the second vehicle came along. They had learned to keep a distance between their vehicles, but not because of the dust clouds. After two hours on the road, the men noticed that the searing sun covered only half of the narrow path. The high, steep walls in the canyon limited full sun to a few hours a day. The two faded

Pajeros maneuvered slowly around a boulder where the road turned north.

Then they saw the goats. The animals on the canyon floor were spread around a few stunted trees and a small green pool fed by a stream falling from the rocks above. Scattering the baying goats, passing the pond, the drivers accelerated as the road straightened out for almost a hundred meters. Then the lead driver hit the horn, three short bursts, although he knew the watchers had announced their approach. The flaps in the netting against the canyon wall parted as the vehicle drove toward the gray camouflage. Under the cover, with the engines off, it was cooler, darker, quiet.

The men in the tent welcomed the new arrivals, kissing them on both cheeks, their bushy beards brushing together. Then they showed the guests to the low table on which the roasted goat lay surrounded by piles of its meat, sliced, spiced, shredded. Bowls held the mezza of lentils and pomegranates. Pitchers held cool water and lemons. Seated on the worn rugs with their rifles behind them, the men began to break off pieces of the flat bread, folding it in their right hands into scoops to pick up the meat. Few of the men spoke. Business could not be discussed before the guests accepted the hospitality. It was tradition.

Although the guests were Pakistanis from the big city of Karachi, they were ethnically Pashtuns, as were the Afghan Taliban who now welcomed them. For the Pashtuns, there was no Afghanistan-Pakistan border. The visitors had come, as they often did, to review the reports of poppy production and arrange for shipments. The beautiful red flower grew so easily in Afghanistan and from it came the paste that the men from Pakistan sold throughout the world as heroin. The Afghans and Pakistanis did other business as well. The Pakistani crime cartel, the Qazzanis, helped their Afghan cousins fight the latest invaders and their Afghan stooges, helped in all sorts of ways. The Qazzanis had many friends in Rawalpindi, home of the Pakistan Army, and in Islamabad, where the intelligence agencies had their headquarters.

Mohsin Qazzani finished his meal. As deputy to his older brother, Mohsin was the heir apparent to the vast Qazzani crime empire, but he liked getting out of the city, seeing the operations. He felt safe here, off the road, hidden beneath the new camouflage. It was sad that the Afghans had to live like this, but it was better than being in the open where the killing birds could see you. There were so many of the birds now, and they had killed so many, on both sides of the border. His hosts now brought boys with bowls of water to wash the feet of the guests. They lit aromatic wood in small braziers to honor the guests. More tradition. Business would have to wait a bit longer.

FRIDAY, JUNE 26
GLOBAL COORDINATION CENTER
CREECH AIR FORCE BASE, NEVADA

The room five thousand miles to the east was also cool, dark, quiet. Lit by the glow of the screen in front of him, the red-haired Air Force pilot suddenly sat straight up in his specially designed ergonomic chair. He was one of thirty Air Force pilots in the room, each remotely flying a drone somewhere in the world. Each wore an olive-drab one-piece flight suit emblazoned with colorful unit patches and symbols.

In front of him were two large and six small screens, ten analog dials, and two sticks. The two large screens provided the live image feeds from two of the cameras onboard his drone, one a high-definition televisionlike video, the other an infrared or synthetic aperture radar image for night operations. One stick directed the aircraft, up and down, right and left. Thumb dials on the side of the stick allowed the pilot to precisely control ailerons and wing flaps. The other stick armed weapons, launched them, and guided them to the target. For weapon release a small, red metal cover on the side of the stick had to be lifted and a button physically depressed before the selected missile launched or the chosen bomb dropped. Despite all of the on-screen controls, a hand had to touch metal before the death from above could be unleashed.

Next to the pilot a similar cockpit could be staffed by a noncommissioned officer to assist the pilot when needed on complicated missions, providing a second set of eyes to look at sensors, or perhaps to steer the aircraft while the pilot guided a missile to the target. Today, the second seat was empty. The pilot was on his own.

"Got somethin' here, boss," the pilot called out.

Colonel Erik Parsons spun around in his chair above and behind the pilots. Parsons was the squadron commander for the drone pilots at Creech Air Force Base, where there were more Unmanned Aerial Vehicle pilots than at any other of the twelve bases from which Americans directed their worldwide fleet of drones. If pilots were supposed to look like the cartoon hero Steve Canyon, tall and blond, Erik Parsons looked more like a wrestling coach, short, stocky, with closely cropped black hair.

Erik got out of his chair and walked purposefully, quickly down the row of pilot cubicles toward the pilot who had called out, Major Bruce Dougherty.

"Whatchya got there, Carrot Top?"

"Goats, boss. I got goats. But I don't have goat herders. Water, but no people."

"Bruce, there is water all over the world without people nearby."

"Yes, sir, but not in these arid mountains in the summer. Besides, that was just the tell. I made a second pass with the synthetic aperture radar imager turned on and . . . presto . . . two SUVs sitting under a camo tarp about a football field up the road from the water. Three more and a couple of pickups under netting farther up the canyon. Now, with the infrared on you can see a whole complex of shit nestled up against the canyon wall, hiding from view under the netting. Or so they thought."

Erik Parsons leaned over the pilot for a better look at the screen. "Throw it up on the Big Board, Bruce." As a series of green blobs flashed onto the main video screen, covering two hundred square feet on the front wall, Parsons picked up a red handset. "Sandy, we got any HVIs likely to be up in grid square A-08? I think I got a live one."

In the glass-walled room behind the pilots' cubicles, Sandra Vittonelli consulted her own small screen. "Maybe. We lost signals from a guy guarding a High

Value Individual almost three hours ago in sector A-17. That's not too far away, he could be in A-08 by now. But that's hardly reason enough to get excited."

"Well, Sandy, even without a named target on screen, I am looking at enough suspicious activity here to designate this a signature-based strike. I think we got us a terrorist camp." As Erik Parsons spoke he patted Bruce Dougherty's shoulder.

Sandra Vittonelli stood and squinted through the glass at the Big Board in the next room. "I'll be right out to the floor."

Since she was far away from Washington, Sandra wore jeans, but in deference to standards she had learned at Headquarters over the years, she also wore a blue blazer. It helped to make clear the authority relationships. Sexism was officially taboo, but some of these jocks needed reminders sometimes. They were not all used to taking orders from a short, civilian woman in blue jeans. Although she was a CIA employee, as Director of the Joint Global Coordination Center for the program, she owned the pilots. There had been a single, integrated drone program for both the Pentagon and the Agency planes now for three months. When Erik had asked her about the blazer once, she had told him that she wore it because the air-conditioning was set too low in the Center and, moreover, the jacket also gave her lots of pockets for her "stuff." Then she had changed the subject to why the pilots felt the need to wear jumpsuits when their airplanes were thousands of miles away.

As she stood at Bruce's cubicle, she was aware that all the other pilots were watching her and not focusing on the video feeds from their aircraft. "I gotta admit, it does fit a signature," she told Erik and Bruce, "but how long you been looking at it?"

Bruce looked at the digital elapse clock running in his console. "I've been loitering for seventy-three minutes now. I've run electro-optical, infrared, and synthetic aperture radar passes. This is one of the new birds with all three types of sensors. The analysis software has located thirty-two human life-forms, identified all of them as adults. Except for seven guys on the hills, all of them are under the camouflage. No signatures of women or kids."

She looked at Erik, who shook his head in affirmation. "It's a good one, Sandy."

Vittonelli put on her poker face. "Let's loiter some more. And pull up any imagery of the place from past missions. Somebody must have passed over it before en route to somewhere else." Then she picked up the handset of a red phone. "This is the Director, GCC. Let's wake up the boys and girls in DC. I'm initiating a Kill Call."

SATURDAY, JUNE 27
ABOVE PAKTIKA PROVINCE
AFGHANISTAN

The mechanical extension of Major Bruce Dougherty, the thing that moved in the air when Bruce's hand made adjustments with the joystick in his cubicle, was pressing ahead at only eighty-five miles per hour against the cold wind two miles above the canyon. Up there the sound of the propeller at the rear of the plane, twenty-seven feet from the nose, might have seemed loud, but there was no space on board for a human, nobody up there to hear the constant buzzing. No one was there to notice that the bottom of its fuselage and its forty-eight-foot-long main wings were a light blue like the sky above it, while the top of the aircraft was a dark gray. There was no one to see the three mechanical eyes of the sensors twisting, adjusting, focusing. The pump quietly kept the fuel flowing steadily to the little engine. The seven onboard computers hummed softly. The blister antenna, inside the bump on the top of the plane, moved silently to keep pointed at the satellite, while sending a steady stream of data up to space and capturing the constant flow coming down.

In response to Bruce's slight pressure to the control, the bird now banked, its left wing moving up, causing the aircraft to move to the right, back toward the men below the nets.

In the canyon, shadows now covered all of the road and much of the rock wall. Some goats were still in the sun, higher up, near the watcher, hunting for grass and little stubbly shrubs among the rocks. The air had been still, but then the wind shifted and the watcher heard buzzing. His eyes darted back and forth, scanning the bright sky. He saw just the blue, nothing else, the blue. Then the buzzing came again, louder, closer. He unbuckled the radio from his belt and hit the push-to-talk panel. "Drone."

As he spoke the word, which meant the same thing in Pashtu as it did in English, the watcher on the hill was bowled over by the blast from the first of the four Hellfire missiles hitting the canyon floor below. The missiles hit ten meters apart in a tight pattern, each puncturing camouflage netting and canvas, bursting into orange-yellow balls of flame and then into black plumes of fast climbing, churning, thick smoke. Sections of the rock wall broke off and fell to the canyon floor, kicking up brown clouds of dust. The concussive sound rolled down the canyon, overwhelming and persistent. The goats on the hill tripped and faltered as they ran higher up. Over a mile above them, the blue-tinted drone nosed up and banked right into a tight turn.

Another watcher on the road near the big boulder to the south saw the flashes in the distance before he heard the sound. Then it took him almost twenty minutes to climb higher, enough out of the canyon so that the satellite phone could pick up a signal. He knew the call could only last thirty seconds so he thought of what he would say before he hit Call. "Mohsin Qazzani. Droned."

The unmanned aircraft circled for a few minutes more, recording the BDA, the Bomb Damage Assessment, waiting to see if others would arrive to help the injured. If others showed up, they could be hit by the two Hellfire missiles left on the Predators.

No one came.

SATURDAY, JUNE 27
GLOBAL COORDINATION CENTER
CREECH AFB, NEVADA

Erik Parsons pointed to Bruce Dougherty. "Okay, bring the bird home."

Standing next to him, Sandra Vittonelli turned toward the two men in flight suits and read aloud the message on her secure iPad. "NCTC reports Mohsin

Qazzani was at the camp. He's the younger brother and chief deputy to the head of the Qazzani clan, the Pakistani drug cartel and designated terrorist group. Righteous shoot. Big Kill."

"Way to go, Brucey." Erik high-fived his pilot.

"Righteous kill, man! That's what I'm talkin' 'bout," the Major called out as he stood in his cubicle. A ripple of hoots and applause arose in the darkened room. On the Big Board the image from the drone showed the smoldering fire in the blackened mounds on the canyon floor. Then the image jerked and shifted to the tops of mountains, beautiful in the early afternoon sun, set against the cloudless blue.

But when he later left the room full of pilots and walked into the fresh air, Erik Parsons found himself in a place where it was still dark, hours before the dawn. He stretched and sucked in the air, stared at the stars, then walked to the car parked in the Squadron Commander's space.

Erik turned on the radio in his black Camaro as he drove past the guards at the gate, moving out into what the pilots called "Civilian World." He passed Indian Springs and headed south on 95 toward the city.

"It's all-you-can-eat at Las Vegas's best Fancy Seafood night at the Galaxy Club Wednesday with Maine lobster, Alaska King Crab, and Louisiana crawfish. . . ."

He switched the Bose sound system from the local FM radio station to Sirius satellite radio and '90s Pop Hits. Although it was four in the morning the lights from the Strip glared on the horizon from the billion-dollar casinos, the re-creations of Manhattan, Paris, Venice, ancient Rome, and even more ancient Egypt. As incongruous as it all was, he loved it, the dancing fountains, the erupting volcano, the clashing pirate ships. Leave it to the Air Force, he thought, to put a complex of air bases in the desert outside of Las Vegas, Creech Air Force Base to the northwest for special operations and the huge Nellis Air Force Base to the east where they flew the fighter-plane contests, force on force.

He hit "Home" on the Camaro's communications screen and he heard her voice after two rings.

"Hey, hon. You on your way home already?" Jennifer Parsons was a night owl who preferred to see her patients after dark and then stayed up writing her reports until Erik came home near dawn. In nocturnal Vegas, it didn't seem that odd.

"Five minutes out. It's been a good night." Erik accelerated the car at the thought of seeing his wife. "Meet you in the pool?" He pushed the speedometer past ninety as he headed down route 95 toward their North Las Vegas housing development.

"I'm beginning to see some advantages to this whole Empty Nest syndrome," she replied. "I'll bring the brewskies, Flyboy." With that, Dr. Jennifer Parsons rose from her desk, unbuttoned Erik's old shirt, let it drop to the floor of her home office, and then walked naked down the hall to the kitchen. She slid back the glass door to the patio and, beers in hand, stepped from the barbecue area down to the pool and the hot tub. She did three laps before she heard his car and finished the fourth while watching him climb out of his flight suit and dive toward her.

Fifteen minutes later they got around to the Heinekens in the hot tub. Erik looked again at the stars. "He was a big one, Jen. Well hidden. Bruce found him. Another guy would have missed it."

"Good, Bruce needed a lift."

"We're finding them, Jen. We're winning." Erik threw his two arms up in the air, mimicking a monster, moving across the hot tub toward his wife. "We're gonna get them all, ha, ha, ha."

Jennifer Parsons ran her fingers through the thinning black hair on his head and then through the graying hair on his still firm pecs. He kissed her breast, then moved his head lower. She threw her head back. She thought the sky in the east seemed pink; maybe daybreak was approaching. Or maybe it was the glow from the Strip, maybe just a false dawn. She had lost all track of time.

# 2

## TUESDAY, JUNE 30
## THE SITUATION ROOM
## THE WEST WING, THE WHITE HOUSE
## WASHINGTON, DC

Winston Burrell was late. His chair, at the head of the table that filled the room, was empty. The Seal of the President of the United States hung on the wall behind his chair, giving the room an aura. This was not a corporate boardroom, not a Congressional committee room. It was a place where power was the currency. Meetings in this space had saved lives and taken lives. Today's meeting was about taking lives.

The old chair had been replaced with one that better fit Burrell's height and weight. He was not of average build. He was not average in many ways. For a man who had started his professional life as an international relations academic, he had become the quintessential behind-the-scenes operator, making things happen first in state government, then in the corporate world, and then in national politics as the White House National Security Advisor. While he could recite the details of almost any national security issue, it was in understanding their domestic political relevance that he excelled. The President was focused on domestic policy challenges. Burrell was intent on not letting national security get in the way or take up too much of the leader's time. He saw his job as preventing disasters, promoting those causes that bought the President domestic support.

The men and women who waited were far from displeased to have some time together without the National Security Advisor. This was when the number twos and number threes from the departments and agencies got to meet, gossip, ask each other for favors, trade and deal, complain and bargain, with only one aide each looking on. This time, before the meeting started, was where the wheels were greased and coordination accomplished, without rhetoric or pretense.

"Sorry to be late," Burrell said as he entered the room and plopped down in the big chair. He wasn't sorry, of course, and everyone knew it. "Sorry, too, that we haven't been able to have this meeting sooner," he said. Most of those around the table doubted that, too. They knew he found these sessions distasteful. He disliked having to decide who lived and who died.

Winston Burrell looked around the table. The two highest ranking representatives were the Under Secretaries from State and Defense, both women. Nancy Schneidman from Defense might be the first female Secretary of Defense in a few years. Her opposite number from State, Liz Watson, was a career Foreign Service officer. She had been ambassador to Turkey.

Admiral Harlan Johnston was a SEAL assigned to

the Joint Staff at the Pentagon. Like many of the "Special Operations community," he did not look the part. Slightly shorter than average, he probably weighed less than anyone in the room. As he opened his briefing book, he donned a pair of black glasses that would have made his social life difficult had he still been in high school. He had served in combat in Somalia, Kosovo, Iraq, Afghanistan, and places where the Pentagon never acknowledged the presence of U.S. military personnel. Then they had made him an admiral and assigned him to Special Operations Command headquarters in Tampa, where the endless PowerPoint slides and bullet papers had caused him to see the optometrist.

Ron Darden from Justice was probably the wealthiest person at the table. He had been managing partner of a Los Angeles law firm before joining the Administration as Associate Attorney General. He was also the only person of color at the table.

The Intelligence Community was two headed. Seth Kaplan was the number two at CIA, but he was accompanied by Todd Hill, who ran the National Counter Terrorism Center. Hill frequently, awkwardly, made the point that the NCTC did not report to CIA. Both men sat at the table.

"I know the requests have been piling up. So let's get started. You all have the files. Let's start with the Pentagon nominations. Admiral?"

"We have six nominations," Admiral Johnston began. "Two in Afghanistan, one each in Yemen, the Philippines, Algeria, and Chad. All are AUMF cleared by the Pentagon."

The Under Secretary of Defense, Nancy Schneidman,

representing the civilian control of the military, concurred. "Right, Winston, we believe all of these six men pose an ongoing, continuous, or imminent threat to U.S. military personnel and/or are senior officials of AQ or an al Qaeda affiliated group. As such, they are all eligible under the criteria for Authorized Use of Military Force." She had said the magic words, chanted the incantation that would place a hex on and doom men probably then asleep, thousands of miles away.

Two rows of three squares appeared on the large screen at the other end of the table from Burrell. Each square had a photograph of the intended victim, a code name, his real name, and some words in a font too small to read.

"Everyone has had these noms for a while now," Burrell observed. "Any questions or objections?"

"I have a question about the guy in the Philippines," Liz Watson, the Under Secretary of State, began. "Explain to me how a guy in the jungles of Mindanao is a threat to U.S. forces. And is the civilian government aware of this? I mean, at what level have the civilians signed off on this in Manila? Their President know?"

Burrell nodded to the Admiral to answer.

"You would be speaking about Rambler," he said, pulling a green file folder out from a stack he had placed on the table. Each folder was covered with a red and black striped paper with the words TOP SECRET in a large font size at the top and bottom.

"Rambler?" Burrell asked.

"We're using old car names now as code words,"

Under Secretary Schneidman explained. "Someone objected to our using Native American tribe names."

"Rambler," the Admiral began, reading aloud from his file, "is known to be planning the kidnapping or assassination of American military personnel acting as advisors to the Philippine Armed Forces engaged in counterinsurgency operations in Mindanao against an AQ affiliated offshoot of the indigenous Islamist militant movement."

"And we briefed the civilian Defense Minister and the President's Chief of Staff in Manila," Nancy Schneidman added. "They concur. It was actually the Philippine military that first suggested we drone this guy. He's holed up in a mountainous, jungle area where any attack force would just be slaughtered. Fact is this guy's invulnerable except to drones."

"See, this is exactly what I was talking about last time," the Justice Department representative interjected. Ron Darden often felt like an outsider in the acronym punctuated interagency discussions. He was more at home in corporate boardrooms. "This guy didn't bother our military so much, our guys weren't so threatened by him that they nominated him. The local government asked us to go after him because they can't do it without maybe losing a few guys in the operation. If he's not really a threat to Americans, we should not be going after him."

The Admiral removed his glasses, turned to stare at Darden, and then used his baritone voice to note, "We have solid intelligence that Rambler is planning to kidnap or assassinate American military personnel. And yes, we don't want to, what did you say, lose some guys, to get him. But we also want to get him before he gets us. Okay?"

"These are U.S. troops we are talking about, at risk," Nancy Schneidman added. "I don't want to have to go to Dover one more time to welcome back a coffin or go to Arlington to meet one more widow if we don't have to."

Burrell looked at the Defense Under Secretary as he might have regarded a disappointing student in an honors seminar. "We don't need to go there, Nancy. We have all been to Dover and Arlington too often. Everyone at this table has a right, indeed a duty, to question the nominations that come before us." The room was silent for a moment.

"All right, then. Does any agency object to any of the Defense nominations?" Burrell asked.

"I'm okay with the guy in the Philippines, assuming we do the usual Pattern of Life thing to make sure there will be no collateral damage," Watson, State's Under Secretary, interjected. Behind her, in one of the "back-bench" seats against the wall, her "plus one," an Assistant Secretary of State, squirmed and frowned. He had clearly put her up to complaining about the Philippines target and now she had withdrawn her complaint. "But tell me why the guy in Yemen is a Defense Department target and not a CIA target. I thought the strikes in Yemen were supposed to be covert operations done by CIA."

Admiral Harlan Johnston was ready for that question. Without consulting his notes, the Admiral replied, "Studebaker is known to be plotting an attack on the

U.S. Embassy in Sana'a. That constitutes a direct threat to U.S. forces, our military mission in the embassy, as well as the Foreign Service and Other Government Agency personnel."

"In that case, Harlan, fry his ass," Liz Watson replied. Before she was in Turkey, Under Secretary Liz Watson had been ambassador to Yemen six years ago.

"All right then, shall we consider the six Defense nominations approved, subject to the rules of engagement on collateral damage?" Burrell asked. No one dissented. "Now, let's move on to the Agency nominations, Todd and Seth."

Todd Hill was the Director of the National Counter Terrorism Center, an independent intelligence organization that reported to the Director of National Intelligence. Seth Kaplan was the Deputy Director of CIA, which had its own large Counterterrorism Center. The White House budget staff had suggested merging the two groups, but Burrell was reluctant. Even though he also thought having two big Centers was ridiculous, he also knew that if there were another significant terrorist attack after the White House had "downsized" the counterterrorism intelligence staffs, the CIA and its friends on the Hill would blame the President. Better to waste a billion or so a year than to put the President at risk of appearing soft on terrorism.

In reality, the President was very far from soft on terrorism. He had given Burrell broad but extremely clear guidance: "Winston, I don't want to micromanage this stuff. Just make sure we do not get attacked again. Do what you have to do. Minimize the negative press, no torture, and hold down the collateral damage to an acceptable level, but err on the side of killing the bad guys. If we fuck up trying to kill bad guys, I will be fine. If we fuck up because we didn't kill the right bad guy and he then kills a bunch of Americans, particularly in the homeland, then I get in trouble. Understood?" Burrell had already understood that, intuitively.

Todd Hill from the National Counter Terrorism Center flashed a similar set of mug shots onto the screen, three rows of four. These faces had only code names attached to them on the graphic. They were named after fish.

"Flounder is the head of the Qazzani group's European operations, drug distribution," Hill began. "Not normally an offense that would get him on the Kill List, but we have a very sensitive source that has informed us that the Qazzanis have signed a contract with AQ to conduct attacks on targets in Europe, specifically U-Bahns, German subway trains."

"Where is our attack to take place?" the Under Secretary of State asked.

"Probably Austria. We have a technical source that says Flounder is meeting with his subordinates in Vienna to go over the plans," Seth Kaplan, the CIA number two explained.

"Jesus Christ, what is wrong with you people?" Under Secretary Watson responded. "Austria is a friendly state. They are cooperative on counterterrorism. You can't go bombing Austria like it was 1944 again. It's in the heart of Europe."

"She has a point," Winston Burrell observed. "Why can't we just ask their *Polizei* to round these guys up when they are having their little meeting?"

"They don't have a legal basis for arresting them. No evidence we can give them," the CIA man, Seth Kaplan, said. "Our source is too sensitive to tell anyone about."

"Including me?" Burrell asked.

"We can give you a little bit more detail in private, but this source is way too valuable to risk more broadly," the CIA man replied.

"So, let me get this straight, we can't have the Austrians arrest this guy because we can't give them the evidence against him. So we have to kill him? What if we were able to kidnap him and bring him to the U.S. and indict him here?" Darden from Justice asked. "Under a 1992 Supreme Court ruling, the U.S. courts do not care how a person arrives before a U.S. court as long as he was not tortured along the way. It's legal under U.S. law to kidnap him. It may violate Austrian law, but . . ."

Seth Kaplan looked uncomfortable. His staff at CIA had predicted this Kill Nomination would not go down well with Justice. "I appreciate your flexibility, Ron, but even if he were standing outside the White House fence, we could not arrest this guy. The evidence we have against him is far too sensitive to share with a U.S. judge or jury, let alone a defense attorney. So it's actually a good thing he is not in the U.S., because I am not sure we could do anything to him here."

"But because he is overseas, we can kill him?" Darden asked.

"Yes, of course," Kaplan replied. "That is what we have been doing, using the President's Covert Action authority under the Intelligence Act to remove terrorists from the battlefield in other countries. His Covert Action authority has no legal basis inside the U.S."

"Well, thank goodness for that, Seth, or you would be coming after me I suspect," Under Secretary Liz Watson intervened. "I'm half joking, Seth, but this is a serious problem. You are asking us to approve killing a guy in a friendly European country and you won't tell the Austrians, or even this committee, who the source is so that we can judge for ourselves whether to believe that there is a risk that justifies this action. You have only one source? No corroboration? What is this source's motivation? What is this source's past record of reporting? How long has he been reporting?"

Again, the room fell silent.

"I've said all I can say. We have good reason to believe the source," the CIA man finally replied, looking down at the tabletop.

Normally backbenchers were quiet, but the man sitting behind Winston Burrell spoke up. Raymond Bowman was the Director of the Policy Evaluation Group, a small, unconventional unit that theoretically reported to the Director of National Intelligence, but really worked directly for Burrell. PEG was his "second opinion" team, his independent, low-profile unit that trolled through the other agencies' intelligence, but also mastered open sources. They talked to subject matter experts no one else had found, and had a track record for prediction that consistently beat the rest of the gigantic Intelligence Community. Although they all knew him, it was Bowman's first time attending the Kill Committee, as some of the participants had taken to calling the meeting.

"Putting aside the sourcing for the minute," Ray began, "how exactly are we planning to fly a drone into

Austrian airspace and then cause an explosion somewhere in their country without them figuring out that we violated their sovereignty?"

Burrell intervened before Bowman's question could be answered. "You all know Ray. I have asked him to serve as my, sort of, informal deputy on all things drones. So, in the future, when you hear from him on these issues, he is me. Good question, Ray. Goes to the operational risk assessment. Seth?"

The two Intelligence Community men looked at each other, both clearly upset that they would now have another intelligence professional second-guessing them. Bowman's PEG already did that to their analysis on a regular basis. Now that group of odd balls was going to start questioning their operational judgment? It seemed that neither Intelligence representative wanted to be the one to get into the operational risk details. Todd Hill from the National Counter Terrorism Center, however, grudgingly explained, "We will be using new, covert drones. They will be launched from a rural area inside Austria at night. The attack ordnance will self-incinerate, leaving no forensic signature. We will provide the Austrians with information that leads them to conclude that a rival drug gang did the attack using a hidden parcel type bomb."

"Oh, shit. This just gets better and better," Liz Watson said. "I can tell you, Winston, that the Secretary of State will not support this. You are going to secretly smuggle drones into Austria. You are going to convert some Austrian farm into a secret U.S. drone base. You are going to lie to the Austrians about what happened. And you are going to blame some other group for the attack, probably leading to them being killed in retaliation for something they did not do. Beautiful, just beautiful."

"I'm afraid the Attorney General will join in that dissent," Ron Darden added.

The Admiral and the Under Secretary of Defense sat silently.

"Well, I will have to discuss this with my boss," Burrell said. There was no indication what he would recommend to that boss. "There are eleven more IC noms, Mackerel, Salmon, a whole sushi bar here. Has everyone had time to go over the rest? Any comments or questions on those?"

"I do," Ron Darden from Justice answered.

Burrell slumped back in his chair. He had clearly been hoping that this session was nearly over. He could not help but think of himself and the others as Roman senators in purple-trimmed togas, sitting in the Coliseum and holding out their arms with their thumbs up or down, signaling which of the Christians and slaves would be killed. Only none of these victims were Christians.

"Pike and Pickerel," Darden began, "they are both Mexican drug kingpins. How is it that they are being put on the Kill List? I thought that the Finding only authorized us to go after al Qaeda and its affiliates. Since when is the Rico Martinez cartel an AQ affiliate? And again, why can't the Mexican authorities get them? Or do you have an ultrasecret source you can't tell us or the Mexicans about there, too?"

"Good questions," Burrell commented. "CIA, Dr. Kaplan?"

Todd Hill replied instead. "I've got the brief on this one. Hezbollah has approached both the Martinez and the Montevilla drug gangs. The leaders of both groups, Mister Pike and Mister Pickerel, have agreed to smuggle terrorists into the United States in return for a lot of money from Hezbollah, meaning ultimately Iran. Hezbollah is also on the list of terrorist groups we can peremptorily attack."

Liz Watson returned to the fray, on behalf of the State Department. "So, since you can kill Hezbollah guys if they are planning to kill Americans, therefore Hezbollah guys being smuggled into the U.S. are automatically assumed to be planning to conduct terrorist attacks in the U.S. and Mexicans who have agreed to help them with the human trafficking are therefore assumed to be affiliated Hezbollah terrorists and subject to death by drone. And the reason you can't tell the Mexicans is again some sensitive source bullshit?"

"No, Ms. Watson," Todd Hill began slowly, "we actually have told the Mexicans. They asked us to use UAVs against these two gentlemen because the Mexican authorities said that they are too well guarded for the Mexicans to arrest or attack, even if they used the Mexican Marines."

"Have we used drones in Mexico before?" Ron Darden asked.

"Homeland does, but they are unarmed," the Admiral chimed in.

"Now may not be the time to open up another theater of operations for lethal drone attacks, particularly so close to U.S. territory," Winston Burrell noted, sitting up straight and folding his fingers together on the table, forming a little tent above his papers. "Seth, Todd, maybe you could come back to us with an alternative to the Hezbollah Mexican human trafficking caper?"

The two Intelligence Community men nodded.

"Anything else for the good of the order?" Burrell asked. "Good, then we are adjourned."

As he left the Situation Room and walked down the hall to the take-out window of the White House Mess, Burrell wondered how it had happened. He had just signed the death certificates for sixteen more men, plus however many others who would have the misfortune of standing nearby them. On average that number was four. So, he had just ordered sixty-four executions and, he thought, he wasn't even the Governor of Texas.

He ordered a large coffee, black, from the young sailor at the take-out window. It would take a while, he knew, maybe a few months, but based on past practice, the targets would all be found at a place and time when they could be killed without unacceptable collateral damage. Some would probably die tomorrow. How had he ended up doing this? When they had started using the drones to kill, right after 9/11, it had seemed like a welcome way of finally stopping terrorist attacks on Americans. Somehow, it had grown into an industry, and he was the CEO of the industry leader.

Burrell looked up and saw Raymond Bowman exiting the Situation Room with Admiral Johnston. He signaled Ray to join him upstairs.

"Well, you too are now indictable by the War Crimes court," Burrell started when Ray walked into the National Security Advisor's office carrying his own large coffee. Burrell dropped into a large, wing-backed chair. Ray sat in another one opposite him.

"That's what I was just thinking," Ray replied. "Why me?"

"Who else? You saw the way they are all playing their games down there. I need somebody I can trust, somebody with no agency agenda," Burrell said. "You realize, of course, that the Mexican thing was a ruse. They nominate a few every month for me to reject. Makes the other agencies think I am being tough on the CIA."

Ray laughed. "I thought that might be happening. And the Austrian thing. Think the President is going to go for that?"

"We're not going to ask him. Too risky. We need to insulate him. Deniability. Protect the Principal," Burrell explained.

"So you tell them no?" Ray asked.

"Quite the contrary. You are going to tell them to go ahead. And you are going to imply that it has gone up to The Man, but you are never actually going to say that. It will get you off on the right foot with CIA, giving them the go ahead."

"Do I also have to tell State and Justice?" Ray asked.

"No, they'll read about it in the papers when it happens," Burrell replied.

"Okay then," Ray said. "And you're not overly concerned about the operational risk?"

"No, we've done this kind of thing before. A lot, actually. They never get caught. It's the one thing the CIA seems to be able to do well, fly drones," Burrell said. "And actually, it's not even CIA that flies the Goddamn things, it's Air Force officers seconded to CIA. We've got this joint CIA-DOD coordination center that flies the sensitive missions and coordinates all the others. In fact, the new director of it is coming in to see me. You ought to join me in the meeting. Let me see here," he said looking at his schedule. "Ms. Sandra Vittonelli."

"Sandy?" Ray said, spilling some of his coffee.

"You know her? Is she good?" Burrell asked.

"She was when I knew her," Ray smiled. "She is one tough cookie."

"Good, that's what we need in that job." Burrell got up and walked back to his desk, signaling the meeting was over. As Ray was getting near the door Burrell added, "Oh, and Raymond, now that you are a member of the Kill Committee . . ."

"Yes sir?"

Burrell looked across the wide office at him. "Don't call it the Kill Committee. And we don't call them drones."

"Why not?" Bowman asked.

"Because that implies that they are autonomous and they're not."

"Really, what do you call drones then?"

"Now, we say RPAs," the National Security Advisor explained.

"What's that stand for?"

"Remotely Piloted Aircraft. Reminds people that there is a human in the loop, if not actually inside the aircraft."

"I thought they were UAVs, Unmanned Aerial Vehicles," Bowman said.

"They were, but now they're RPAs. The human involvement wasn't clear with the use of UAV. See, actually they are not unmanned. It's just that the man, or woman, is on the ground."

"Okay, but I hear that the pilots call them Fuckers."

"I've never heard that. Why would they say that?" Burrell asked.

"FKRs, Flying Killer Robots. The Predators are the Little Fuckers and the Global Reach are the Big Fuckers."

"No, don't call them Fuckers. I don't want that to spread. Very bad messaging."

Bowman nodded and left the room.

# 3

## TUESDAY, JULY 2
## THE RINGSTRASSE
## VIENNA, AUSTRIA

It was a summer rain, from clouds that had moved quickly across the plain and then hit the foothills, dropping a cooling spray on the stones and asphalt of the old city on the Donau.

The black BMW had been maneuvering through a series of narrow side streets, known well to the driver who also served as a concierge at the palace hotel. He edged the car onto the slickened Ringstrasse, across the wet trolley tracks, and then turned in to the tree-lined road. The short street was blocked at the end by the stone ruins of the city's old wall. Rising out of the remnants of that battlement, a modern glass façade reached up for three floors. Above and behind the glass and stones were the whitewashed walls and windows of the eighteenth-century Palais, now one of Vienna's most exclusive hotels.

The passenger emerged from the back seat of the car under an umbrella held by one of the hotel's doormen. Another doorman took his bags. The guest appeared to be perhaps a wealthy Italian, Greek, or Spaniard, in a fine dark suit. The gray speckles in his hair suggested he was in his late forties or early fifties. He looked up at the grand façade of the yellow and white Palais, lit by a string of flood lamps on top of the high, gray rock wall in front of it. Between him and the old town wall was the lobby of the hotel, a large expanse enclosed in glass. Inside, he could see a bar area and a grand piano and lights shining up at the rocks and stones that had once defended this old city from the men on horses who came from the East, from lands near where his people now lived.

Once inside, a doorman led him to a modern leather seat in front of a low registration desk.

"Coffee, sir?" the registration clerk asked.

"*Ja, inder Tat. Einen grossen schwarzen, bitte,*" the man replied with a Berlin accent, *Hochdeutsch,* not the lilting Viennese version. He passed the clerk a Turkish passport. "Mustafa Gulkkon." He checked his watch, which was made from a reddish gold. Then he switched to English. "My office made a reservation for two nights, I believe." His English sounded British accented, perhaps slightly Indian.

The thick Viennese coffee appeared quickly from the Lobby Bar. "I have it here, *mein Herr,*" said the clerk. "A beautiful suite on the fifth floor. You will be staying with us for two nights, yes? And, let me see here, I also have a message waiting for you from your colleagues;

they are up in the Cigar Bar. If you like, we can have your bags taken up to the suite and I can have Wilhelm show you to the Cigar Bar."

Led by the young bell clerk, Herr Gulkkon walked through a glass door in part of the stone ruins and up a glass, spiral stair. The indirect lighting made the ruins' stone walls seem warm and comforting. The Cigar Bar, a small room on the second floor, had a large window that looked across a narrow corridor to the outer glass wall. The bar's door was covered by a black shade on the inside. A small sign hung on a chain outside, GESCHLOSSEN.

Wilhelm was not deterred by the "Closed" sign. "Your colleagues have reserved the Cigar Bar for just themselves this evening, yes?" he said in American-accented English. As he pushed open the door with his right hand, Herr Gulkkon slipped a five-euro note into his left.

"*Danke, mein Herr.* There is a bar set up, but if there is anything else you would like, please just ring the Lobby Bar."

Now there were three men in the dark, wood-paneled room. Like Gulkkon, they were clean-shaven, in expensive, dark suits, probably from Saville Row. They sat in large, red leather chairs around a low table. Only one man was smoking a cigar, but that was enough to fill the small room with the rich fragrance from Cuba. Behind glass doors on the walls, boxes of many varieties of Cuba's crop were on offer. On the low table in the middle of the armchairs were half-empty glasses and opened bottles from three of the Permanent Member states of the UN Security Council, Cristal champagne from France, Johnnie Walker Blue Label scotch whisky, and Kauffman vodka from Russia. All that was missing, Gulkkon thought, was baijiu and bourbon. This was his version of Islam, one modified by years living in Canada and Europe.

The three men, who had been seated, stood and shook hands warmly with Gulkkon, who appeared to be somewhat older than the others. "Perhaps we could raise the curtains," he suggested. "Meeting with them down looks suspicious and we are, after all, just businessmen with nothing to hide."

As the curtains were raised, Gulkkon fiddled with his mobile, quickly removing the back panel, pulling the battery, and slipping them both into a side pocket of his jacket. The others had already done the same. "So, now we are all good here, yes?"

The men nodded. The youngest looking of them offered, "I have been here three days. No problems, no sign of interest from anyone." Gulkkon noticed that the line leading into the telephone on the bar had been unplugged. "And we reserved this room just an hour ago and then went right into it, so no time for anyone to leave anything behind," the younger man said.

"Good, then let's discuss the state of our project," Gulkkon began. "As you know, our organization has been hired by our friends to run it, since they themselves now have little infrastructure and staff left in Europe."

Before he could continue, he was interrupted by the man to his right. "Omar . . . I am sorry, I mean Mustafa . . . if we do this project, it may be very hard for us to sell our product in this market for a while. It will be very hot here. The people who take our gifts now may no longer be able to continue to look away."

The man who now called himself Gulkkon twisted in his chair. As he poured from the Johnny Walker bottle, the room was silent. Then he looked to the man on his right. "Our leader knows the risks. Believe me, we are being very well paid for this project, very well. Our friends must have many sheiks behind them."

Outside the Palais, the rain was letting up, passing to the west. In the dark, above the building across the street, the small, black object hovered quietly, emitting only a soft humming. Without the interference caused by the falling rain, its invisible laser could now beam through the glass outer wall and through to the glass interior window of the Cigar Bar. The laser beam could now carry an uninterrupted audio signal from the vibrations on the window of the Cigar Bar.

". . . the U-Bahn in Munich, the U-Bahn and the S-Bahn here and in Berlin, all at the same time. . . ."

On the hovering black oval a lens whirred, refocused, clicked, and moved slightly to the left, zooming in on the face of the man next to Gulkkon.

THURSDAY, JULY 2
SPECIAL OPERATIONS ROOM
CREECH AFB, NEVADA

Bruce Dougherty heard the voices from the Kill Call in his earpiece, coming from Washington, Virginia, Maryland, and Germany. "Positive facial ID on number four," said the voice from Virginia. "True name Omar Faqir

Nawarz, traveling on a Turkish passport as Mustafa Gulkkon."

"Roger that," a voice in Washington replied. "That gives us positive audio and facial on all of them."

Dougherty was sitting in a smaller room, down the corridor from the GCC Operations Center from which he normally flew his aircraft. The sign outside said simply ROOM 103. Inside was a second door, on which a red sign said RESTRICTED ACCESS AREA. Around the GCC, Room 103 was known as Spook Ops, the place from which special CIA missions were managed. Bruce Dougherty did not want to read too much into it, but he had been chosen by Erik and Sandra not only to fly a Spook Ops mission, but also to do so with two new CIA-only stealth mini-drones. He was feeling good, but he also knew a lot of high-level eyes were on him tonight as he flew their first European mission, the least of whom were seated next to him, Erik Parsons and Sandra Vittonelli.

"Collateral check?" another Washington voice asked.

"Collateral good. Just the four targets in the room. No one else within the planned blast range," Erik Parsons responded.

"Bird Two check?" Sandra Vittonelli asked.

The images on the screen were of the Palais Hotel, seen from several different angles, from traffic cameras across the street, security cameras in the lobby, and on the hovering oval above and across the street. This was Bruce's first operational mission with the small hover-capable drone. The Agency called it the Hummingbird. Tonight, he had designated it simply Bird One, the little one that listened and watched while its bigger brother waited to strike. Bruce was also piloting the armed drone, another new, covert, short-range model. They called it the Myotis, the bat.

Now it was Bruce's turn to speak. "Bird Two is circling two blocks away over the Hotel Imperial. All systems nominal."

He looked up at Colonel Erik Parsons and Sandra Vittonelli standing just outside his cubicle. They both had headsets on, listening to the conference call. Erik raised a thumb. Sandra spoke into her headset for the benefit of the others on the call. "Bring her in. Clear to strike, repeat clear to strike."

"Roger, clear to strike," Bruce replied.

The Red Army had been headquartered in the Hotel Imperial during the Allied Occupation that ended in 1950. Its now elegant white and gold façade was bright and looked cleansed by the rain. Two hundred feet above a black triangle lurched quickly forward, banking left, and proceeding west above the Ringstrasse, picking up speed. Myotis, the black triangle, was three meters across at its base and two meters long on its sides. The back corners curved slightly upward, making it seem almost like a piece of paper folded into the shape of a paper airplane.

Fans spun on the bottom and rear of the triangle, providing lift or forward motion. The entire triangle was made of material that would quickly incinerate, leaving only black and gray ash. It turned off the Ring into the airspace above the trees on the block-long Coburgstrasse.

"Target acquired," Bruce spoke into the mouthpiece of his headset.

"Target confirmed," he heard from Erik Parsons.

"Switching guidance to the laser designator from Bird One," Bruce replied.

"Roger, laser designator."

In the Lobby Bar a zither player was setting up, unrushed. There were only two couples on the couches, only three men sitting at the bar rail. Maybe more people would stop in later, the zither player thought, now that the rain had passed by. Twenty-five feet away the clerk at the registration desk waved over the bell clerk. "Wilhelm, please bring Herr Gulkkon his room key and return his passport. Tell him his bags have all been brought up to his suite, 593." Wilhelm Stroeder dropped his medical textbook on the bell desk and strode quickly across the lobby for the key and passport and then began with his long legs to take the glass stairs two at a time.

The black triangle stopped in midair, vibrating slightly up and down as it hovered.

"Booster check?" Bruce heard Erik in his ear.

He looked down on his virtual control panel. There was the indicator for the small, solid fuel packs that, when initiated, would briefly propel the triangle forward at a speed greater than Mach 1, the speed of sound. The fuel would burn fast, but enough would be left when combined with the plastic explosives along both sides of the airframe to cause a miniature fireball that would totally destroy any trace of the black triangle. Sitting just above the long tubes of explosives were the little pieces of razor sharp steel that would act as antipersonnel shrapnel, slicing everything and everyone for twenty-five to thirty feet. The indicator light on the booster was green.

"Booster good," Bruce said.

"Engage booster."

"Engaging booster, aye."

The triangle had been blending into the black sky. Probably no one would have seen it had anyone on Coburgstrasse been looking up. No one was. But they could have seen the brief orange flame when the booster initiated, then maybe have seen the blur of black streaking forward and down. No one did.

A few people heard a bang, when the triangle hit Mach 1, but it was so soon followed by the crash of the glass façade when the triangle hit it, and then by the muffled thump when the triangle exploded in the Cigar Bar. Wilhelm actually saw the triangle as it came through the outer glass façade, less than a second before it went through the Cigar Bar door where he was headed. His eyes registered the flash of light when the triangle exploded in the bar, but his brain did not have enough time to process what his eyes had seen before the steel shards sliced his eyes and his brain and all the rest of him into a bloodied pulp on the burning carpet.

The visual feed from the Myotis triangle, Bird Two, had looked blurred, incomprehensible shapes on the screen as the aircraft had hurtled toward the narrow laser beam projected from Bird One. Then the camera feed from Bird Two, the black triangle, had stopped.

"Target hit. Warhead ignited. No secondary. Fire seems contained," Bruce reported into his mouthpiece after he turned his attention back to the image from Bird One.

"Fire alarm has gone off in the building, automatically signaling to the Feuer Brigade around the corner," said a voice from Maryland.

"Zoom Bird One's camera in on the room, please," someone in Virginia said, and Bruce adjusted the view. "Thanks. Not much left there."

Bruce switched the camera back to wide angle and the image on the screen showed the hotel guests filing out of the front door in orderly fashion, guided by hotel staff, as two fire trucks rolled to a stop at the curb.

"Congratulations. This has been a team effort, HUMINT, SIGINT, and the kinetic element, identifying and stopping an advanced plot." The voice was from Washington. "You are all reminded that this was structured as a Special Op, so it would be completely deniable. No evidence of drone usage. Let's keep it that way. No bragging. No spiking the football. No leaks."

More fire trucks and ambulances appeared on the live image of the Palais projected on the screen.

Bruce felt Erik's hand clamping on his shoulder. "Nice work, Major. Now let's fly Bird One to the Safe House and call it a day."

The small black oval stopped its hover, gained altitude quickly to four hundred meters, and headed out toward the Wiener Wald at the edge of the city. There, in a clearing on a wooded estate, a team waited for Bird One to gently set down on the grass. They would then pack it into a truck and drive it to Germany and a U.S. Air Force base.

The bird was on autopilot until it got near the Landing Zone. Then Bruce took control and, using a joystick in his right hand and a sliding throttle in his left, he delicately brought the aircraft down in the clearing for a soft impact touchdown. He had stopped listening in on the Kill Call conference bridge.

The voice from Maryland came over the speakers, "Wien Feuer Brigade Zwei commander reporting to his headquarters five bodies recovered, a few minor injuries from flying glass. Fire is out. He's thinking someone placed a bomb in the bar."

Sandra Vittonelli and Erik Parsons left Spook Ops and moved back to her glass-walled office just behind the row of pilots in the GCC Operations Room. Erik was seated on the couch looking out at the Ops Floor, at the images pouring in from above five countries. Sandra was getting two bottles of Pilsner Urquell from her mini fridge in the closet off her office.

"Well, you were right about Bruce," she called out. "The first time we fly the new stealth, covert birds in a real operation and he did it like a pro. I just wish those new birds had longer loiter, longer range." She looked at Erik, who did not appear to be listening to her. "Hey, Colonel, wake up. We just got Omar Nawarz, the head of the Qazzani narcoterrorist group's European operations, plus three of his lieutenants."

Sandra was looking for the beer bottle opener inside the cooler. "And, while I am not supposed to tell you this, the reason for this as a Special Op was that we had a sensitive HUMINT source inside al Qaeda, one we could not share with the Austrians or anybody else. So we could not tell the Austrians to pick these guys up. The Stapo would want to know why, they'd want to see some evidence."

She had popped the beers and was walking back into

her office. “If we told the truth, that these guys were going to bomb subway systems in Vienna and Germany, that word would leak out fast. And our guy on the inside in AQ would get discovered and killed. So, as far as the Austrians will know, this was a bomb planted by a rival drug gang.

“Hey, you listening, Colonel? We just stopped another 7/7 attack, only bigger. Well done.” She thrust out her right arm toward Erik, with the open bottle of Pilsner.

Erik did not take the beer. “NSA said the fire chief reported finding five bodies. Who was number five?”

# 4

MONDAY, JULY 13
THE CITY OF DERA GHAZI KHAN
THE PUNJAB, PAKISTAN

He gave up and dismounted from the Kawasaki. There were just too many people walking in the street to try to drive. Sunset and Iftar had been four hours ago and now, with the heat breaking, everyone seemed to have left their homes and gone for a walk to the market street. After living for years in Canada, surviving this kind of heat was not something that came easily to him. It had been 42 degrees Celsius during the day as he had driven down from Multan. Someday, they said, there would be the new M5 motorway connecting to Multan. But someday had not come.

And so he had dodged trucks in the heat for hours. He knew that Dera Ghazi Khan was now a city of more than two million people, but it was not exactly Karachi or Islamabad. It was not even Multan. Of course, that is exactly why the old man had chosen it to be his latest base of operation. Karachi had become too violent, even for him, and there were too many spies in Islamabad. But here in the heart of the Punjab, white spies stood out.

He had never been to this city, although his father had joked that he had named his son after the town. Although his father had enjoyed a Canadian and then a European lifestyle for years, this kind of place was where his roots were. It was his father who brought him here now, his late father. The thought of him brought waves of emotion, the joy he knew when they were together, the sadness that he was gone, the anger at those who had killed him in Vienna. And he now knew who had killed his father.

The fast would not resume until sunrise. He pushed the bike past groups of young men walking together in the street, taunting each other and laughing. Some families strolled together, the father in the lead. Merchants were reopening their stalls, filled with what they had sold for centuries: spices, incense, and rugs. The street had been closed to vehicles for the evening hours during Ramadan. Stalls and shops on the crowded street sold the twenty-first century additions: mobile phones, tablets, DVDs, T-shirts. One stand sold both leather-bound Korans and cloned Xbox video games, two reflections of Pakistan's soul.

To snare the nocturnal Ramadan walkers, vendors were setting up outside of their shops with hookahs, sweets, figs, dates, and chai. Ghazi Faqir Nawarz ignored their beseeching and pushed the bike forward through the crowd. They had sent him convoluted directions, but he also had his handheld GPS. The coordinates read 30°3'27.61" N and 70°38'22.66" E. He was close.

After he passed the third mobile phone store on the right side of the street, he saw the alley and the boy, as he had been told he would. Just inside the alley, he removed his pack from the bike and let the boy push the Kawasaki into the alley. From a chain hanging under his shirt, the boy produced a key, opened a wooden hatch door in the wall, crouched, and disappeared into the hole in the wall, pushing the bike ahead of him. In seconds, he was back in the alley, relocking the hatch. Then he spoke for the first time to Ghazi, "Up that stair, at the top." He turned and walked back to resume his place at the head of the alley.

The alley was narrow, all the more so for the bags and barrels. The stair was metal and attached to the outside of a building halfway down the passageway. As he climbed the steps, Ghazi saw that the bolts were showing signs of detaching themselves from the stucco wall some day soon. The door on the second floor landing was locked. At the third floor, the door was already open and two men stood just inside. They exchanged mumbled Salams. The first man patted Ghazi down, then the second grunted out an order to follow him, "*Mere saath aaiyd,*" and then led the way to an interior door off the dimly lit corridor.

"*Salam Alekhem, Khush Aamdeed.*" The old man sitting on the pile of rugs offered warm greetings to Ghazi. Rashid Bakri Qazzani, the leader of his tribal clan, had become so much more. Now men from many tribes worked for him, Punjabis, Baluchis. His international network bought and sold weapons, heroin, vehicles, land, electronics, gold, currencies, and fuel on both sides of the Pakistan-Afghanistan border and, in the case of heroin, well beyond into Asia and Europe. He did not rise, but did grasp both of Ghazi's hands and offered his cheeks to be kissed. "My regrets, that your father has gone to Allah before his time," he whispered in Ghazi's ear.

"*Ramadan Kareem,*" Ghazi offered as he joined the circle of five others who sat on rugs in a semicircle around Qazzani. Two boys appeared with chai and dates. When they left, Rashid Bakri Qazzani began.

"Mohsin, as you know, was droned by the Americans. My youngest brother, my brother for fifty-five years. My right arm." The men in the circle looked at the rugs below them and offered brief words of prayer.

"Now, all of our chiefs in Europe, including Omar Nawarz, your father, Ghazi. Four men from the villages here who years ago we sent to schools in Australia, Canada, Turkey. For decades they built our operations in Europe. Now, gone."

The men in the circle, Ghazi realized, were of his generation. They could all be in their thirties. One looked maybe younger. Were these the people who would take over now? Was that what this was about?

"But do not doubt that our operations continue, even now. They were designed to withstand deaths. We anticipate deaths in this business. Men have moved up, good men, men trained by those who have been killed.

"But before we move on, we must avenge their deaths." The old man looked down at the carpet and when his head rose, his voice did, too, and the anger within him. "Who bombs luxury hotels now, in Europe? Who did this?"

The room was silent. No one would say what they were all thinking: the leaders of the European branch of the Qazzani crime cartel were killed because the man sitting in front of them had accepted a lucrative subcontract from the remnants of al Qaeda, had agreed to use Qazzani people to put Yemenis and Somalis into large suicide bombs and then have them explode on commuter railways in Berlin, Vienna, and Munich. Now, the Qazzani leaders in Europe were gone, their operations probably could not really be put back together, and the al Qaeda money would never show up.

Finally, Ghazi coughed. He addressed Qazzani with a deferential title. "*Janab,* with respect, it wasn't a bomb. It was a new kind of drone."

"The Austrians say it was a bomb," the man next to Ghazi offered. Like the others, except Rashid Qazzani, this was a man that Ghazi did not know. He had said his name, Bahadur, at the greetings. "They say it was Russians, guys in our business."

"Yes, but there are videos that Austrian Security Police have. They slowed them down and they see a drone like a big black arrow and another black drone watching nearby." No one asked how Ghazi knew. He was not really part of the clan, not like his father. His mother was a Canadian. He lived sometimes in Karachi but mainly in Vancouver, did his own business, whatever it was. Sometimes it had been special errands for Qazzani. He must have done them well. The old man trusted him, and now he had sent for him. "The Austrian Security Police work with the Americans. They will not tell their own people what they suspect," Ghazi concluded. "They will keep the Americans' secret, not tell the Ministers."

Qazzani threw his head back and looked at the ceiling. "Drones. American drones. They chased al Qaeda from here, but now, now they kill us, they kill my brother when he goes to Afghanistan, they kill the Taliban all the time." He returned his gaze to the men around him. "Where do they live, these drones, where is the hive?"

"There are many, *Janab,* around the world." Again it was Ahmed Bahadur, who ran operations in Asia and Australia. "They fly from bases in Afghanistan, Djibouti, Seychelles, other secret places in Europe and the Arabian peninsula. But their big hive, their television says, is in America, in their city for sin, Vegas."

"Sin. Yes, these flying robots are very sinful," Rashid Qazzani agreed. "But how do the robots . . . who tells them where to fly, and how do they know what to do?"

Bahadur deferred to Ghazi. "They are not really robots, *Janab.* Men fly them. These men are in Las Vegas and other places. They see what the drone sees, they fly it like an airplane, except their controls are in Las Vegas and what they do there is sent to the drone off a satellite in space using something like the Internet."

Rashid Qazzani stared at Ghazi. Was he trying to understand what Ghazi had just said? No one spoke for several minutes. It became clear that their leader was thinking, assessing his situation, his options. Some of them had seen this before. Soon there would be a pronouncement, a big decision.

"Ghazi, my friend, we must stop the drones, not just to get revenge for our people, but to save ourselves. If we do not do this now, they will breed. They will come for us one day.

"Flies can be swatted. Men can be killed. These drones can be stopped. Ghazi, I want you to do this. You will understand how and I will give you all that you need."

Ghazi bowed his head in respect. "Thank you for the honor, *Janab.* The men I work with in Kiev, they have some people who I have used before for special help. Computer men. They rent out these computer men for a high price."

"You will have all that you need, my friend," Qazzani promised. "As will you, Bahadur."

Ahmed Bahadur looked confused. "*Janab?*"

"You have a mission, too. We have a job to do, for the Arabs. I agreed we would do it. I gave my word. They paid us half, a big half. We will do it." Qazzani scanned the circle of men after his announcement, showing the palms of his hands, opening the floor for discussion.

The one who looked perhaps to be in his twenties spoke first. "Father, if the Americans were the ones who killed our people in Europe, it may be that they knew what we were planning. If we go ahead, won't they be looking for bombs in the metros?"

"Yes, they may be. That is why, son, we will not do the train operations where they were originally planned. I have told the Qaeda people we will do it in the heart of the beast, in America. It will be harder, riskier, more expensive." He let the thought sink in. "They have already sent the money. For a group that has so few of its own action men left, they still get the gold, from the secret *Ikhwan,* from the rich ones."

Bahadur examined his sandals, summoning courage. "*Janab,* I will do whatever you instruct, of course. My territory is the Pacific, Indonesia, Philippines. I live in Sydney. I do not know America. I do not know people who will do bombings there. And if we do the bombing in America, won't they come after us here?"

"I know, nephew, I know. Even an old man can learn from his mistakes. Al Qaeda will still provide you with the bombers, from their new groups in the Yemen, Nigeria, and Somalia. But Ghazi Nawarz and his Ukrainians will help you with their computers. If you and Ghazi both succeed, the Americans will think Qaeda did all of it. Or the Taliban. And yes, they will go after them, even more, for a while. But not us, not us. And then they will finally leave."

Qazzani signaled to Bahadur to help him stand up. The meeting was over. Rising, the older man pulled his nephew close and spoke into his ear in a whisper. "Tomorrow I will go to Iftar at your mother's house. After we break the fast, you and I will sit alone in your late father's diwan. We will discuss how you will do this. And your reward, Bahadur, your big reward."

Everyone stood.

"Friend, Ghazi, walk with me," Qazzani summoned as he headed for the door. The two men crowded into a small elevator with the guard who had patted Ghazi down earlier. In the basement garage a white step van waited, its rear doors open. Inside, Ghazi could see that the van had been converted into a little room of red carpets and green pillows. The guard lifted Qazzani into the van and strapped him into a seat on the floor. Ghazi sat next to him and the van began to move up a ramp and onto a street, one in which people were not walking, vendors were not selling, people not watching. The van had good suspension, but Ghazi could still feel the bumps through the rugs, through to the bones in his cheeks.

"Ghazi Faqir Nawarz, a man should always leave enough gold aside for his wives, for his boys, for dowries, in case he may be called by Allah. And Allah, he may call at any time. Your father left his gold with me for safekeeping. Now it is yours. I will understand if you just want to take it and go back to your life in Canada." Qazzani took hold of both of Ghazi's hands and squeezed them. "Are you sure you want to do this mission? If you do, I will add one rupee for every one your father left with me for you."

"*Janab,* the message I sent you was sincere. I asked for a mission to avenge my father. He gave me everything I have, everything I am," Ghazi replied. "I may seem like a Westerner to the others, but I still hold with many of the traditions. When a man murders my father, I must avenge the death. And with this way of revenge, I can also stop the drones, which are unnatural, a sin against Allah."

The old man stroked his beard, which he kept black with a dye that Ghazi could now see had clumped in places. "I make honey at my farm, Ghazi. I have many drones, but they do not sting. Drones in nature do not sting. These American drones sting with a lethal venom. They are unnatural. They must be stopped."

He placed his hand in the hand of the younger man as they sat together. "Ghazi, I know about these Ukrainians. Your father told me about them, what you have done with them. I don't understand it all, but I understand that with the computers, you have become a rich man. Tell the Ukrainians if they help you stop the American bees from buzzing us and if they help with the operation in America, they can take over the distribution of the poppy paste in Europe."

"That is a high price to pay for vengeance, *Janab,*" Ghazi replied.

"Ghazi, with your father gone, you are now my son and I can tell you things that I cannot share with the others," Qazzani said, no longer sounding like the old man in the meeting. His voice was different. No longer the sage who talked in riddles, he began to sound like the CEO he was. "Your father ran Europe for us, but the men killed with him, his deputies, were the ones who were trained to take over if something happened to him. The men I have there now are not up to the job. In time, the Russians will move in and take over our markets. So what we offer the Ukrainians is a wasting asset. They don't know that yet."

The truck began to pick up speed as they left the city. "By attacking their drones, you will distract the Americans and make us safer. Then when the bombs go off in their cities, Qaeda and the Taliban will tell them that the bombs will continue until the foreigners all leave Afghanistan completely. The American people will agree, they are weary of war. After they bomb Qaeda and the Taliban some more for revenge, they will go. This time, they will all actually leave."

Rashid Qazzani smiled for the first time since Ghazi had been with him that night. "And when the Americans finally leave, it will not really be the Taliban who take over, it will not be Qaeda. Ghazi, it will be us. We will have all the money we need to do it. We have all the growers. They do not want the Taliban in charge. When they were, last time, they stopped the farmers from making the paste from the poppies. But when the Americans finally leave, the drones must stop, too. We cannot have these pilots from their Sin City hitting our people here and in Afghanistan. So while Bahadur's operation will convince the Americans that the price of keeping their soldiers in our part of the world is too high, you will convince them that using the drones must also stop."

"I understand, *Janab,* and I will stop the drones. And I will help Bahadur. But, *Janab,* why did the Americans kill my father and his men in Europe? Not because of the drugs. They must have known what they were planning to do for al Qaeda."

Qazzani looked into Ghazi's eyes, probing them. "You are a wise man, Ghazi. Your father was very proud of all the money you made stealing with the computers. He wished you had brought him grandchildren, but he was very proud of his Canadian son."

The van stopped abruptly and one rear door opened. "Ghazi, this time there must be no connection to us. Make it look like the ISI is going after the drones. Some of the ISI will help you. And Bahadur will leave a trail from the bombings to Qaeda. Not to us. Not this time."

Ghazi stared back at the old man. "I will do this, *Janab,* but not for the extra money, for my father."

"I feel like the falconer who launches two birds to attack the target. You, Ghazi, and Bahadur are my two attack falcons. I trust you both and you may trust each other, but Ghazi, trust no one else. The Americans would not have killed your father in Vienna, of all places, unless they knew what he was planning. Somewhere, my son, there is a traitor. I will find him and he will die a slow death, but until then, be very careful."

"*Shab bakhair,*" Qazzani said in parting. Ghazi stepped out of the van onto an empty road. The van pulled away. In the dark, under the tree, Ghazi could see his Kawasaki. It had been moved from the alley while they were meeting. Qazzani was always thinking several steps ahead, moving pieces on the board while eyes were elsewhere.

Qazzani's bodyguard moved next to the old man on the floor of the van. "Tell them I will be there shortly and tonight I want a younger one, no hair," he admonished the guard. The bodyguard removed a mobile from his pocket and inserted a battery. In less than three minutes, he had placed the request, and then removed the battery again and slipped the mobile back into its leather case in his pocket. That was time enough.

Eight kilometers west and five kilometers up, the mobile's signal triggered a response in an unarmed black object flying quietly in the night. The caller's number was known. He was a man associated directly with Rashid Qazzani. The small drone dove, sped up, and activated its night vision camera. The onboard computer calculated that the mobile was moving at eighty kilometers an hour off to the east. Just before the mobile shut down, the computer targeted the camera to look at all vehicles heading north within a hundred-meter strip on the highway. There was only one. Its image was recorded. Its license plate imaged. Its route tracked.

The information was bounced to a satellite and then down to a server, for when it might be needed. Then the black bird resumed its patrol.

# 5

TUESDAY, JULY 14
THE NATIONAL SECURITY ADVISOR'S OFFICE
THE WEST WING, THE WHITE HOUSE
WASHINGTON, DC

She could no longer pretend. Sandra Vittonelli had to admit to herself that she could no longer wait until after the meeting. She would, after all, do better in the meeting with the National Security Advisor if she weren't squirming. Moreover, Burrell had not yet shown up.

His waiting area consisted of two chairs stuffed among three secretaries in his outer office. "We make most people wait in the West Wing lobby, but you can just sit here with us," one of his secretaries had said. "After all, you're one of us." Sandra vaguely remembered the woman, maybe Rhonda, from the seventh floor at CIA Headquarters, but now she was in the West Wing working for Dr. Winston Burrell, the President's alter ego on foreign policy, defense, and intelligence issues.

"It's that first little door on the right, dear," maybe-Rhonda said. "Just be sure to knock. It's a one seater. Unisex." As Sandra was about to knock, the narrow door opened and a man she thought was Vice President Menendez came charging out.

"Yes, he doesn't have his own bathroom in his West Wing office. Neither does the Chief of Staff or Dr. Burrell," maybe-Rhonda laughed when Sandra returned. "It really is a little old building, you know." Sandra had never thought of the White House West Wing that way before, a sort of Big Brother house with everyone living and working on top of one another. The few times she had been in the West Wing before it had always been downstairs, on the ground level, in the Situation Room meeting space. And she had always been "backbenching" for the CIA Director, or the Director of National Intelligence. Now she was here by herself, wondering if that meant she was being left out to hang by herself.

"Burrell just wants an informal, kind of off-the-record update," she had been told at Headquarters. "No PowerPoint, no Happy Snaps, no YouTube hits. Just walk him through it. You do it by yourself. You can do it in your sleep." She might have to do it in her sleep, she thought, since she had been largely unable to sleep the night before, her mind processing, planning, unable to shut down.

When she returned from the restroom, a man thrust out a hand. "Hey, Sandra, great to see you again. How've you been?" She recognized him immediately.

"Ray, are you working over here now?" Raymond Bowman, the last time Sandra had worked with him, had been Deputy Director of the Policy Evaluation

Group, a small and somewhat vaguely purposed, independent agency that sat above the Potomac on Navy Hill, across the street from the State Department.

"Same, same. Still at the PEG." Ray beamed his good mood, in a way that was rare among people in the intel business. "No, Winston asked me to come over to sit in on your meeting. I think it's just going to be the three of us."

"It is," Winston Burrell announced as he entered the cramped outer office. "Come on in." The National Security Advisor's office was spacious and bright, with a conference table on one side and a living room set on the other, a huge desk set in the back. Two walls had floor-to-ceiling windows, causing Sandra instant reflexive worry about snipers and laser beams linked to audio devices.

Burrell motioned her to the couch. The two men sat in the armchairs, one on each side of the lower couch. It did not look like a power group, more like a meeting of a prep school faculty. Winston Burrell was in his sixties, broad, balding, beefy. He was known for his rumpled look. He could have been mistaken for the prep school headmaster. Ray Bowman was two decades younger, six inches taller, and looked like he had escaped from a J.Crew catalogue. He might have been the crew team advisor or tennis coach. At five foot five, with short black hair, and businesslike manner, Sandra Vittonelli might have been the Dean of Students or head of the English Department. Rather than having power over a thousand adolescents, however, these three ran a global empire of killing machines.

Burrell began. "Hell, you've been running this

operation out in Nevada what, two months now? Figured it all out?"

"Four months now, sir. It's familiar in some ways. I was originating some of the Kill Requests when I was at Kabul Station and before that at Baghdad Station."

"Well, I just thought I should get to know you better, rather than just have you be a face on a television screen in the conference room," Burrell explained.

To know me better, or to know the program better? Sandra thought. She knew the National Security Advisor by reputation. He was a survivor, having worked in both the Pentagon and at State. He had done his cooling-off time in a think tank, and then come back in with the new President. He had been with the President early in his campaign, before anyone else in the national security business. They were said to be very close, the two meeting for drinks most nights up in the Residence after the President and First Lady put the twins to bed. Burrell must work very long days, she thought.

"Let me start with an admission that I will deny I ever said, but should explain why I want to know who is on the other end of the Kill Calls. The President has delegated the approvals to me," Burrell explained. "I only go to him with the rare ones that pose new issues or close calls. As far as the rest of the world knows, he is making every decision."

Burrell stared at her, looking for a sign that she understood the trust that he was giving her, the weight that was on his shoulders. "I understand," was all that she could think of saying.

"I knew when I took this job that it would involve life and death. I wanted to save the good guys and I was willing somehow to be a part of getting the bad guys," Burrell continued. "But now, I feel every day that if I mess up, if we mess up, if somebody I never met messes up, innocent people will die, and the bad guys will win. I know this sounds overly simplistic, but that is what it comes down to.

"But now, I am not just involved somehow. If I say yes when you call me, people die. If I say no, bad guys get away and may later kill innocent people, Americans, allies, people with families who I will have to meet with and console and explain things to."

There was an awkward silence. Sandra and Ray were both trying to figure out if the National Security Advisor was done baring his soul. He wasn't.

"All of which is to say, Sandra, that I am putting a lot of faith in you and your team to get it right. But I know that erring on the side of indecision, which means doing nothing, is sometimes not better than acting. You just have to maintain very high standards. No more Herr Stroeders."

Sandra shook her head and looked puzzled at the name. "Wilhelm Stroeder, age twenty, a premed student at the University of Vienna," Ray explained. "His mother is a doctor in Philadelphia, where he was born, making him an American citizen. He was the collateral fatality in the Palais attack. Officially, the Austrians have not figured out it was a drone attack. The new self-incinerating drone seems to have worked. A few people in their security service know, but they are looking the other way in return for some augmentations to their savings. The official After Action is that someone placed a bomb in the room, probably a rival drug gang. We have supplied the Austrians with intelligence that suggests that one of the Ukrainian drug cartels was possibly involved."

Sandra was seeing layers to her business that she had no idea existed. "Ray here, whom I gather you know, he is your unofficial Guardian Angel, so appointed by me," Burrell said. "He's had your back, even when you didn't know it. He's also been the biggest advocate of the program in the interagency."

Ray picked up where the National Security Advisor had left off, giving every impression to Sandra that they had planned the conversation. "Sandra, I remember before 9/11 when CIA and the Pentagon were fighting against the whole idea of the Predator and especially the armed Predator. But they had nothing that could find terrorists in real time, verify that there was no collateral at the site, and bring in an arrest team or a kill team. We had nothing. We were blindly sending cruise missiles at targets. Predator changed all that. It has almost completely eliminated al Qaeda Central in Af-Pak, it has been a huge force multiplier against the Taliban, it has kept AQAP in Yemen on the ropes, it has shattered al Shabab in Somalia, it helped to defeat Qadhafi in Libya. It has probably saved thousands of American lives. We need it."

The two men continued to finish each other's sentences. "And if we screw up in how we use it, people will demand we stop," Burrell continued. "I have the ACLU and half a dozen other groups trying every legal means to stop the program as a violation of international law, or as a criminal conspiracy to conduct extrajudicial murders. 'The President and Winston Burrell have set themselves up as prosecutors, judges, jury, and executioners.' That's what they say and the truth is, they're right. We are all of those things."

They seemed to have played out their script, so Sandra responded. "Dr. Burrell, we all feel personal responsibility for these life-and-death decisions. No one in the program thinks this is just another job; they are all acutely aware of how sensitive and important the work is, how necessary it is that we get it right, every day."

"Okay, Sandra," Burrell said. "What would you tell a Congressional Committee?"

"I'd tell them we do not initiate Kill Calls lightly. We track a target and spend days getting a Pattern of Life on him, what does he do every day, where does he go, when does he go there, who else is there. We work very hard to ensure that there are no women and children, no civilians anywhere nearby. We often wait until he is in a car alone or with another terrorist, off on a road by himself.

"If we are going after an HVI, we make sure it's him, through facial and voice recognition, through human assets on the ground. Then we act under Title 50, Intelligence Act authority, under the Presidential Finding. If we see a signature of an imminent terrorist threat or an opportunity to do irreparable damage to the terrorist organization, we go Authorized Use of Military Force, under Title 10, Defense authorities, under the Law of War standards. Lawyers pore over every strike before I initiate a Kill Call. We are very careful." Then she thought about the Viennese student. "We know how we missed the student in Vienna. We have run an After Action to figure out what went wrong. It won't happen again."

Burrell got up and walked over to his desk, picked something up and returned to the sitting area. He handed Sandra a picture of a handsome, young blond boy. "The President gave me this. It's Wilhelm Stroeder. I have no idea where he got it. He gave it to me. I'm giving it to you. I should be giving you a picture of the thousands you've saved, but we don't know who they are, so I am giving you Wilhelm to remind you and your team that this is about real people, not just HVIs and code names."

Burrell rose and offered Sandra a handshake. "You're doing a good job, but you have to keep it that way because there are people gunning for you, for me, for the program. And Ray's right: it's all we got."

Leaving the suite, Sandra Vittonelli felt that the already heavy weight on her shoulders had just doubled. "Got time for a coffee?" Ray asked as he followed her out. "Let's drop downstairs to the Mess." On the ground level, outside the Situation Room doors, Ray Bowman seemed to know everyone, even the enlisted sailors running the take-out window of the West Wing's little executive dining room. He talked them into opening a side dining room, where he and Sandra sat alone with big mugs of dark roast.

"Are you sure you don't work here?" Sandra asked when they had settled into the chairs in the dark, wood-paneled private dining area.

"I do have a Mess account," he admitted. "I am here a lot, doing special projects, off-the-books stuff sometimes, for Winston. He doesn't trust the Bureau or the Agency."

"But I'm Agency," Sandra noted.

"Yeah, but your program is closely identified with the

President. The program is a hybrid, half Intel, half DOD. And it's kind of a redheaded stepchild. The boys up the river keep a safe distance. Notice that you were the only Agency person here today. No Director, no Deputy. If it goes splat, they will be nowhere near it, and if it does go wrong, they will let it go splat all over the President and Burrell. If it works, they will take the credit."

Sandra laughed.

"What's funny about that?" Ray asked.

"I thought you were a redheaded stepchild once. Weren't you?"

It was Ray's turn to laugh. "Very good memory, Sandy. I was, when my mother got remarried. Now it's really darkened, kinda auburny brown," he said patting down his hair.

Sandra Vittonelli's secure mobile phone chirped. "I have to take this," she said to Bowman. After a short, cryptic conversation, she returned to the table.

"Ray, Erik is acting when I am on the road and he wants to initiate a Kill Call. Is there someplace here? Can you get me into the Sit Room?"

Three minutes later they were sitting together in a small conference room in the Situation Room suite. On the main screen was an image beamed from a drone in Pakistan, an image that seemed to be mainly clouds. Erik Parsons's face was on a smaller, side screen. "Ms. Vittonelli, we have been tracking an HVI code-named Packard for six days now. His Pattern of Life was that he kept to the house or the yard, receiving bad guys, but always with his wives and kids around, so No Joy. An hour ago he and two goons got in the SUV and they are driving south toward civilization. Right now they're still on a back road, pretty empty, but they are about ten minutes away from a main road that will have traffic."

Sandra muted the microphone and turned to Ray Bowman. "We give each targeted terrorist a code word name. Civil War battles. Whatever. Now we are on old cars."

Winston Burrell walked in and sat next down to Sandra, who remained at the head of the table. "Keep going, this is your show," he said.

"Erik, there is too much cloud cover in this image for me to authorize a shot," she said.

"If we go lower, they will hear the bird," the Colonel replied.

"Go lower."

The image on the screen showed the clouds disappearing and then a lone SUV moving slowly on a road. Two minutes later the Toyota pulled abruptly off the road and halted. Three men burst out of the vehicle, each running in a different direction, diving under the low scrub bushes that lined the road.

"They think they can hide," Erik's voice said over the speaker. As he spoke, the image on the screen changed to black and white with shades of gray. "The infrared cam has all three targets fixed."

Sandra looked at Burrell, who nodded, got up, and walked out of the room. She looked into the video camera above the flat screen. "I judge that we have located an HVI on the target list and two of his body guards. I have determined that there is no apparent risk of collateral damage. I have obtained the necessary clearances and I authorize weapons release."

Within seconds, the image on the screen was showing three explosions. "How much do each of those missiles cost?" Ray asked, after muting the microphone.

"You don't want to know. A lot more than a nine millimeter bullet," she replied. "But a lot less than the cost of a U.S. embassy blowing up."

The videoconference continued, as the operation went into the Bomb Damage Assessment phase and the wait for compatriots who might show up. Ray kept the microphone muted. "Sandy, Winston has asked me to watch out for you. That means intel support, being the political eyes and ears in this town, doing counterintel and force protection analysis, everything. In short, I got your back." He hesitated a moment. "It's been a few years, but, as I recall, it's quite a lovely back."

Sandra flashed on a night in London six years earlier. "Watch it, Ray."

Erik Parson's voice came out of the speaker on the wall, "Kill Conference closed."

# 6

FRIDAY, AUGUST 14
WORLD WIDE NEWS HEADQUARTERS
NEW YORK, NY

The bottom, again. She threw the ratings report in the waste bin under her desk, closed her eyes, and ran her left hand through her hair. Then Karen Rosen remembered that her office had a glass wall looking out onto the news floor. Everybody could see her, unless the curtain was pulled. And it wasn't. She had to look positive, give no signs of impending doom to further demoralize the team.

They really were the best news team left, the best international correspondents, the longest stories, in-depth coverage of issues. Yet, there they sat at the bottom of the cable ratings, getting little more than a million people in the United States in prime time. That meant three hundred and twenty million Americans watching something else, or worse yet, not watching at all, playing soldier on computer games or streaming pirated movies.

What passed for news on the legacy networks was

morning shows about diets and cooking, evening news about elderly people's medical problems, and once a week a "magazine" show that was often indistinguishable from reality TV or Hollywood gossip. She had thought about moving to print, but the scene there was worse. Magazines were disappearing, *Newsweek* and *U.S. News* gone. Newspapers were dropping like flies and those that were left were trying to figure out how to make money online, putting things behind a pay wall that nobody was paying to penetrate.

She looked across the newsroom, filled with a combination of grizzled veteran correspondents and editors and a bevy of young, enthusiastic twenty-somethings hoping to make a name for themselves while making the world better. Fred Garrison, the international editor, was standing, talking with the new Middle East rover kid, Brett something. She caught herself thinking that if that kid could look that sexy on camera, that would sell. She hit the intercom button to the International desk. "Fred, can you come in for a minute. And, is that Brett with you, bring him in for a second so I can just say hi to him."

"Hey, Karen, what's up?" Fred Garrison said, walking into her office. "You know Bryce, of course." He emphasized the name. "Bryce Duggan, our soon-to-be veteran war correspondent. How many combat assignments have you had in your first year on the job with us?"

"Just three. Pleased to meet you, ma'am," the young man beamed. He had three days of blond stubble, a build like that Olympic swimmer, and a shirt with too many buttons undone. Karen feigned disinterest. "Yes, of course, Duggan. You speak Arabic, if I recall correctly."

"Speak it, he majored in it at Toronto. Then a year at the Kennedy School before stringing for the FT in Cairo," Garrison said. "He's done great work so far. Just need to get him more airtime. And more money. He's back for his first year review. I'm trying to find some money in my budget for a raise for him." Duggan seemed to blush.

"Well, more airtime we can easily do," Karen smiled. "I've been thinking our viewers need to get to know our reporters better, see the same ones more regularly, build up a rapport with them. Maybe tie it in to some online stuff, like a reporter's blog."

Garrison scowled. "We do have the same ones on night after night when they're covering a persistent story, but most of the time stories only last a few days and then they don't get back on for a couple of weeks. We can experiment with the blog thing, as long as it doesn't take up too much of their time from the field reporting."

"Well, maybe a series. Get a topic, a theme, and travel around covering it from different places. Viewers could follow them, see how they have to travel, the backstory, get to know the reporter as well as the topic." Karen was thinking out loud.

"Got any ideas for a series, Bryce?" Garrison asked.

"Sure, lots." Duggan said. "How hard it is for millions of people to get drinkable water, the struggle young women are having challenging customs in the region, the growing gap in education—"

"Hard news, Bryce, wars. We want to make you into a war correspondent," Garrison countered.

"Right, the next SCUD stud. Who was that guy in the First Gulf War who was always standing outside while everyone ran into the shelters when the SCUD missiles were falling all around him?" Karen said. Garrison suppressed a smile.

"Well, we could do children made orphans by several different wars, we could try doing something on the drone strikes and how they are often counterproductive, or we could—" Bryce replied.

"Drones, that's it, drones. You go to each country where the U.S. is secretly flying drones. There was a great report on it from some university the other day, long thing, it's on my desk," Garrison said. "But, Karen, that would cost money. Eight, maybe ten, countries. Team of three, plus Bryce, some local security guys in some of these places, a little baksheesh, you know, walking-around money."

"I'll find the money, including the raise. Give me a budget tomorrow morning, Fred," she replied. "Nice to meet you, Bryce Duggan." She kept her eyes on him as he walked back into the newsroom.

# 7

SATURDAY, AUGUST 15
JAMSHED DISTRICT
KARACHI, PAKISTAN

"I hate this city," the older Arab said.

"You hate everything. That is why it is so difficult for you to recruit new followers," Bahadur replied.

"We love Islam and we have no problem recruiting. We have enough people in America to do the attacks," the younger Arab added.

"Then why do you need us?" Bahadur answered. "If al Qaeda is still so strong, why us? Why don't you do the attacks in America without us?"

The older Arab looked Bahadur in the eye for a moment before replying. "We have learned not to expose our men in America. Too many have been lured into thinking they were talking to brothers, getting an assignment, a mission, only to be arrested by the FBI. The new people we have do nothing to risk being identified. They do not visit Islamist Web sites. They go only to the regular mosques. They buy no guns, no bomb material. They do no planning of missions. They wait. Our men will do the missions, but we need someone else to be the controllers, to set up the operations."

Bahadur hoped no one had followed the Arabs to this small appliance store in the Jamshed district of the sprawling city. Qazzani gang spotters were out in the neighborhood looking for signs of surveillance.

"How did you find those people?" Bahadur asked.

"Our friends in the U.S., the Ikhwan, they are often teachers, or bankers, or doctors. They look for young men who want to do a special Jihad. They send them out of America for vacations, never an Islamic country. Trinidad, Brazil, Mexico. There we meet them. We test them. Those who pass, we instruct on how to wait without attracting attention. Then they go back."

The younger man looked to the older Arab for confirmation that he could give more detail and then added, "Some of them we appoint as a cell chief. Each cell chief knows five to ten other men. The men know only their cell chief, but each one of them we give a special code word of his own. We give it when they pledge loyalty to al Qaeda. If someone recruits them to do a mission, if he does not say the code word, the men know the recruiter is FBI."

"We need you to build the bombs, to survey the targets, to coordinate the attacks," the older Arab said, "but we have good people."

"These people, they are all Arabs?" Bahadur asked.

"No, very few. Some are Somalis. Some Nigerians, but my friend," the younger Arab smiled, "all are

Americans. Either they were born there or they became citizens. No visas needed. They all have American passports."

Bahadur was beginning to think that perhaps Rashid Qazzani was right to take this contract from al Qaeda. They did need help, but not for everything. In the decade after 9/11 al Qaeda had gone underground in America. They had used good security procedures, cells in which most members knew only a few others. They were long-term sleepers who did nothing to attract attention. The Qazzanis would activate some of the networks, give them explosives, assign them targets, and leave before anything happened. For this simple task, they would get most of the special reserve fund that AQ Central had been building over the years, three hundred million euros.

"And they will all die for you?" Bahadur asked.

"No, most will not," the older Arab admitted. "This is a new generation. They will not be suicides." He lowered his head and his voice. "And they will want some money, maybe one million dollars each."

Bahadur smiled. "That will be in addition to our fee. Unlike you, we do what we do for money, not for Allah." Suiciders were erratic, too much trouble, he thought. People who worked for one million dollars would be more reliable. And if they died in the blast anyway, or later when they came for the money, then that million might be something he could keep personally.

"Very well," the older Arab replied. "At least make *zakat* with some of the money."

"We do, but we have our own charities." Bahadur laughed.

The older Arab stared at him and then said, "I am told to offer you the names of some of our friends in the ISI, brothers who will assist you in fighting the drones. Some have quit the ISI, but still have connections; others are still on active service. We trust them. A few of them knew about Abbottabad."

He handed Bahadur a small notebook, code names and contact procedures. "Those at the beginning are the ones in the U.S. The ones in red at the end are the Pakistanis, the ISI. Loss of these names will mean men die."

Bahadur took the small green Moleskine. "For us, this is business, but do not worry. We are very good at business."

# 8

FRIDAY, AUGUST 14
DEGREES BISTRO
THE RITZ-CARLTON, GEORGETOWN
WASHINGTON, DC

She was already seated in the restaurant when Ray arrived, late. He had texted her to apologize that he was running behind schedule. He had left his car with the doorman, along with a big tip, and taken the big metal stairs, two at a time to the second floor. He worried she would take his tardiness as an insult. Instead, she seemed fully absorbed in her iPad, and a glass of Viognier. The bottle was on the table.

"So sorry. No excuses," Ray began.

"No problem. I'm reading the new Alan Furst novel," Sandra said, shutting down the iPad. "Hope you don't mind I ordered the wine. I wanted something a little sharper than Chardonnay." She poured him a glass. "Let me know what you think of it."

He sipped the tangy white wine and remembered

why he had hit it off with her so well when they first met at a U.S.-UK intelligence liaison conference in London. She did not defer to him in the least. She did not make a point of doing things to prove she was his professional equal, she knew she was and had entirely internalized that. "So does the Agency book you into the Ritz now?" he asked.

"Hell, no. I've just got so many Marriott points that I occasionally upgrade myself. The Agency had me in the Key Bridge over in Rosslyn, but this place is kind of funky. Red mood lights, high ceilings. Feels like a movie set from *Batman* or something. Big redbrick factory."

"It was a giant trash incinerator building that they, ah, repurposed as a hotel," Ray explained. "Hence the name of this restaurant, Degrees. It used to get very hot in here."

"So, is it really getting very hot in here, in DC, for the drone program? You're the big shot Washington insider," Sandra said with a smile. "So maybe you can answer a question that has been floating around in my head as I try to fall asleep at night."

"This doesn't sound good," Ray replied.

"No, really, it's about work. It's this: behind all the politicians posturing, why do you think so many regular Americans have a problem with drones? Because I just don't get it. They're just airplanes after all."

"Well, look, they aren't really just airplanes. They're different. I think they are less likely to hit the wrong guy or create a big blast on the ground, but people see them as Flying Killer Robots," Ray said. "And people have a deep fear of armed robots."

"Well, yeah. *Terminator.* Who saw that movie and identified with the Schwarzenegger character? No one. We all wanted the human to beat him," she said.

"Right and no one rooted for the Borg bots in *Star Trek.* They were terrifying and seemed unbeatable. There are a dozen or more movies over the decades, all of which have conditioned us to fear killer robots, and now you get told that the U.S. has Flying Killer Robots?" Ray was on a roll. "There are all sorts of legitimate concerns about our drone policy being counterproductive or precedent setting, but at root, for a lot of people, there is a subconscious fear of armed robots going crazy and killing humans."

Sandra shook her head in a combination of disgust and disbelief. "Well, let me assure you that my drones do not have minds of their own. They're not going to all gain consciousness one day, like in *The Singularity,* and start flying themselves and picking out their own targets."

"Maybe not, but I happen to know DARPA is funding some initial work on unmanned fighter planes that would shoot down enemy fighter planes with no human in the loop. Also bombers that would seek and destroy enemy tanks and missiles. Not quite minds of their own, but closer," Ray said, playing devil's advocate.

"I'd have a real problem with eliminating the human in the loop," Sandra replied.

Ray chuckled. "That's because you're that human who's in the loop. You just want job protection."

In an ever so delicate way, Sandra smiled and shot Raymond Bowman her middle finger.

Ray laughed. "Do we always have to talk about work?"

"You should talk," Sandra replied. "Mr. Workaholic. Speaking of which, I heard you split up. I'm sorry. Permanent?"

Ray nodded affirmatively. "Afraid so, but it wasn't just me who was more married to the job. She was always running off to refugee camps. First, it was the Horn of Africa, then Jordan. Last I heard from her she was in Chad. That's where she was when she signed the divorce agreement. Almost a year now."

"First year's the worst, trust me," she said. "Frankly, I am a workaholic and I admit it. It's what gives me pleasure. So without having to worry about Josh, I am a much happier little spook."

They were halfway through the main course when she realized they had emptied the bottle of white. She signaled to the waiter. "Can you bring us a bottle of the Papapietro?"

"Italian?" Ray asked.

"Yes, I am. Can't you tell? Vittonelli. But the wine is from the Russian River. Sorry, I should have consulted you."

"No, no. I defer to you. You seem to know about wine. I'm forty-three years old and still into beer. Arrested development," Ray replied.

"Shit. Are you really only forty-three? And now that Schwartz is retired you're running the PEG? Maybe I'm the one with the arrested development," she said, as the waiter brought the Pinot Noir.

"And you are an old lady at forty-five? Running the

joint DOD-CIA coordination center for all drone flights? Pretty damn important job. Better than station chief in Tunis."

Sandra Vittonelli stared into the deep purple fluid as she rolled it around in her glass. Still looking at the wine she said, "So you know my age and the job I was scheduled to take. Mr. Bowman, have you been illegally reading my personnel file?"

"Yes. I mean no, not illegally," he said as he felt himself blushing. "I had to go through the jackets on all the candidates for the drone Global Coordination Center's Director."

She tasted the wine and stared across the table at him. "You pick me for the job?"

"Burrell did," Ray lied.

"Winston Burrell wouldn't have known me from Madonna prior to today."

"You're wrong," Ray said. "He'd know Madonna. You were by far the best person for the job. And it is a big job. Lot better for your career than Tunis."

"Assuming I don't fuck it up," Sandra replied. "So I beat out all the boys on points, huh? It had nothing to do with our little fling at the You Suck talks?"

Ray choked on his wine. "Excuse me," he blurted out, coughing. "I suck at what?"

"The U.S.-UK conference. We call it the You Suck Talks. Don't tell me you never heard that."

Ray was laughing loudly, attracting looks from others in the restaurant. "I had a lot of fun that weekend," Ray replied. "But it had nothing to do with who got this job. I can compartmentalize work and play."

"Can you now?" Sandra asked. "Well, I wanted to ask

you upstairs, but because we're now supposed to be a team, professionally, I thought maybe not. But if you can compartmentalize. . . ."

Ray smiled broadly. "I was going to ask to see your room. After all, I'm not really in your organization or chain of command," he said.

She stared into the Pinot again. "Some understandings then? It's going to be just for fun. And we're both in the same business and we can't really do it with civilians. As long as it doesn't get in the way of our working together, and, of course, either one of us can say no to getting together anytime and either one of us can call it off with no hard feelings."

"Well, yes to all that," Ray answered. "But I am having some hard feelings right about now."

Sandra turned to look for the waiter. "Check, please."

# 9

SUNDAY, AUGUST 16
GLOBAL COORDINATION CENTER
CREECH AFB, NEVADA

"And dawn breaks over the FATA," Colonel Erik Parsons said as he walked onto the Operations Room floor, still carrying his coffee mug from the Camaro. "How's the night been so far?" Night in Vegas was day in the FATA, Pakistan's tribal border area. On the large video screen on the Big Board was the color image from a drone's camera, orange light coming up into the purple sky, the sun rising behind a mountain.

"Was routine until a few minutes ago, boss," Major Bruce Dougherty replied. "Remember this compound up in the Swat Valley we got tentative approval to hit next time we saw bad guys using it?" Bruce switched the image on the Big Board's main screen to a close-up of two small houses and a barn, isolated, surrounded by a wall.

"Yeah, Agency says it's associated with the Qazzanis. Kill Committee approved a strike if we see hostile activity in it and no one else nearby. We got that?" Erik asked.

"We do, boss. Been looking at it for twelve hours with a Pred. Then four guys show up in that Mitsubishi, all armed. No one greets them. They open the place up. Then, this is the kicker, one of the guys just called a number in Karachi that NSA says is associated with a senior Qazzani deputy. I say we met all the conditions."

Erik nodded and sat down at the empty pilot's chair in the cubicle next to Dougherty's. "Yeah, I can approve this shot, given what the Kill Committee authorized. Go for it, two Hellfires simultaneously. Then, we'll wait and see if anything is still moving or anyone comes to dig them out."

Bruce Dougherty pulled right on the joystick, causing the Predator twelve thousand miles away to bank to the right and begin an arc that would line it up for a firing position on the compound. One camera on the Predator stayed locked on the compound, even as the aircraft pulled around. Erik looked at the four men who were about to die. One had his head inside the hood of the SUV, working on the engine. Two were tending to a fire pit and the fourth leaned against the back of the Mitsubishi talking on a mobile phone. "Some guys never learn," Erik thought aloud.

Sergeant Rod Miller was sitting next to Dougherty, listening on a headset to an audio feed from NSA in Maryland. "Colonel, Maryland's finally got a Pashtu speaker on this. She's gisting what they're saying in real time. You may want to listen in, sir, it's on channel six."

Erik picked up a headset and dialed in. He heard someone speaking a foreign language in the background, hurried, excited, then in the foreground and louder the voice of a woman summarizing the conversation. "So, Karachi guy is saying around the end of Safar," she summarized and then paused. "Just before the Americans' Prophet's Birthday, the Americans will have Shock and Awe. He said that phrase in English, Shock and Awe. The guy in Swat is now saying he wished he could be part of the operation, he hopes they kill a lot of Americans. . . ."

Erik caught a flash on the Big Board in his peripheral vision and looked up in time to see the smoke from the two Hellfires' rocket engines filling the image on the screen, as the two missiles dropped from the Predator and ignited their propellant. They were instantly soaring toward the target. "Shit!" Erik almost yelled, as his fist came down on the thin four-foot-high wall between the cubicles. As he hit the divider, the screen showed the missiles impacting on the compound, creating a flash and then two columns of smoke rising above the dust storm where the buildings had been.

"Something wrong, Colonel?" Bruce Dougherty asked.

"Not with you, Bruce, with me," Erik Parsons said quietly, taking off his headset. "I should have listened to that call before I authorized the kill. We should have kept that guy alive so we could hear more, or better yet capture him and interrogate him."

"Good luck with that. CIA can't capture anybody in Pakistan and even the Pak Army won't go up into the Swat," Bruce shot back. "Killing them is all we can do. Hell, we didn't even interrogate bin Laden."

Erik Parsons put his headset back on and punched in

a number on the keypad to connect with the CIA analyst who had been watching the shoot and listening to the audio back in Virginia. "What was that guy saying before he got hit, about Shock and Awe? When was that supposed to happen?"

"That's what we were just trying to figure out here, Colonel. The Prophet's Birthday isn't in the month of Safar. Safar would be our December this year." Erik could hear the young man on the other end talking with others. "He said our prophet's birthday, America's. That would work because the religious birthday we celebrate is Christmas, which is in December, obviously."

Erik scowled, "I know when Christmas is. I was hoping that you bright CIA guys could tell me what you took from that conversation."

Another voice answered, maybe the first guy's supervisor. "Colonel, what we will be writing up in a report is that the Karachi guy, who is a senior in the Qazzani network, seemed aware of a large-scale plot to kill Americans around Christmastime. He didn't say where, over there, here, could be anywhere. He also didn't say who would be doing it, AQ, AQIM, AQAP. Could be any of the groups in the network.

"We'll probably go through Station Islamabad to ask the ISI to find the guy on the Karachi end of the call, the guy you didn't kill, thankfully."

"What are the chances they'll find him?" Erik asked.

"Not real good. NSA says that phone went off the grid after that call," the voice from Virginia replied.

Erik Parsons could see Sandra Vittonelli entering her office, separated from the Operations Room floor by a glass wall. His boss showed up at all times, day and night. He never knew when she would appear, but he knew her drop-ins would be frequent. He walked off the floor to brief her.

"Hey, what's up?" she said, apparently in a chipper, happy mood.

"I think you may want to give your friend in Washington a call so he hears it first from you," Erik began.

"Shit, what's wrong?"

"We just killed a guy who was talking to another guy about what your home office boys think is a plot to do a major terrorist attack on Americans around Christmas," Erik explained.

"Well, fuck, why did you kill him? We should have milked that source for more details," she said, sitting down behind her desk.

"We only killed the guy at one end of the call," Erik answered. "The guy who was being told about it, not the guy that knew about it. But we should have held off. We figured it out too late."

They sat looking at each other. Then she asked, "Where, how, who?"

"No idea."

"Great," she said.

"Just when."

" 'Round Christmas?" she asked.

Erik nodded his head.

"Just enough to get the big boys agitated, but not enough to do anything with it. Lovely."

# 10

SATURDAY, AUGUST 29
TSENTRALNI TORGOVI LAZNI
KIEV, UKRAINE

Ghazi Faqir Nawarz did not like being naked with other men. And even though they all had big, thick towels wrapped around them, the men in the steam room were naked, as were the men in the pools and the spa and the locker room. It made him uncomfortable, but that's what the men from the Merezha cartel had told him to do. Take the Turkish Airlines flight from Istanbul to Kiev, check in at the Hotel Slavutych, and then go to the baths in the park across the street. They would contact him within two hours. But they hadn't and he was done sitting in the steam room waiting.

He got up, tightened the towel around himself, and walked back to the locker room. He would dress quickly and shower back at the hotel. Then, suddenly, there was a bag over his head and hands grabbing at his towel. He went to swing, but his arms were pinned and then forced into something. They were putting a robe on him. Then in English, "Don't worry. We are not the Americans. Just walk with us. We aren't going to hurt you. We are taking you to the meeting."

He was aware that they had left the building, then that they were in a truck, and that, after what seemed like at least half an hour, he was escorted out of the truck and, suddenly, the bag was lifted quickly off of his head. As his eyes adjusted to the light, he saw that he was standing in a large garage or warehouse with bright overhead lamps forty feet above, shining down on the concrete floor. Two white trucks were behind him, one with the back door still open.

"Please accept our apologies, Mr. Nawarz," the slight, youngish man began. Dressed in blue jeans and a polo shirt, wearing glasses and a scruffy beard, he looked like a graduate student. The two men behind Ghazi were much bigger and in suits. "I hope my colleagues were not too unpleasant. We had to be sure that you were not followed and that you were not bugged. I'm sure you understand these things. Please, we have a changing room for you. And we have some of your clothes from the Slavutych. When you are ready, Dmitri Bayurak will see you."

Dmitri Bayurak looked like an older version of the man who greeted Ghazi. Older, heavier, with thinner hair, he wore a blue blazer with his jeans and polo shirt. His office, up a stairway from the warehouse floor, was decorated in a Scandinavian design, chrome, leather, and glass. Ghazi's quick initial scan caught two flat screens running television news, two desktop computers, and three telephone handsets. It was an executive's workplace.

"All is forgiven, I hope, for your arrival," Bayurak began. "You should worry if we brought you here any other way. Security is number one for us. Which is why you are here, *da?* You have had security issues, your organization? Vienna? We can help you." He thrust a shot glass of vodka at Ghazi. Ghazi took it, but only sipped from it. He did not empty it in one swallow, as the Ukrainian was doing.

"I have had a very useful relationship with you, hacking, stealing identities, credit cards, moving money from banks," Ghazi said. "But all of that has been my personal work. Now, as you know, I come to you representing the Qazzani organization."

Bayurak filled his own vodka glass, again. "Very lucrative for us both it has been. My favorite one is where we assume the identity of the company's comptroller, submit bills for services, and then pay ourselves into accounts in the Caymans. Works every time with these big American companies. They never even notice, two or three hundred thousand dollars."

Ghazi put down his glass, still half full. "What my organization wants from you is intelligence support from your cyber team. The Qazzanis need them for two special missions."

Bayurak gestured for Ghazi to go on.

"The drones. We have had enough of them. We are going to go after them. We are going to swat them dead."

"Well, my friend, we have some things that will help," Bayurak began. "We have SA-24s from Russia, like the American Stinger missiles only better. But they are expensive. Very high end. Not available on the international arms black market, but we can get them for your organization, given all that we have done together in the past, all that we want to do together in the future."

"We already have SA-24s, I just got them from Libyans. Remember Qadhafi left the doors unlocked?" Ghazi said. "What I said I want is intelligence support. I need answers to five questions: Where are the drone bases and what can we know about them? Who are the drone pilots and where do they live? How do they operate, their rules? Where is their technology vulnerable to disruptions? And, last, how do we get some drones of our own?"

Bayurak rose and walked to a window. He pulled back drapes and revealed a room below where perhaps thirty young men sat around computer screens, seemingly randomly scattered in clusters across the large open space. "These boys can get any information in the world, but what people do with that information can be a problem for them, for me. If what you do with that information gets the wrong people mad enough, maybe they come looking for me. Maybe they find me. Not good."

Ghazi ignored Bayurak's remarks and kept going. "The second special operation we need intelligence support for is a day of bombings in the subways, the metros, in America."

Bayurak laughed and closed the curtains. "You're mad, you people. You want to bring all the shit in the world on your heads? It's not enough you want to go after the drones, now you want to bomb their trains? What do you think the Americans will do if you succeed, run away and hide? They will hunt you down if it takes them a decade, like they did with Osama. And one of you will tell them, when they pour water up your nose, that you got all the help from me. And then they come after me and my family. Do you think I am crazy?"

Ghazi stood, crossed the room, carrying his vodka, and looked out between the curtain. "You do this and the Qazzani organization will make you its exclusive distributor of heroin throughout Europe."

Bayurak scratched his forehead. "The risks are too big even at that price."

"No, no they're not," Ghazi pushed back. "Nobody in our organization will know you are supporting us on these two operations, just me and our leader. You can take all the security precautions you want." Ghazi emptied his vodka. "Or, or, I can fly tonight to Moscow. I have some friends there who are very close to the Czar. The Czar also has people who are very good at getting information. And Czar Vladimir is not so happy with the Americans. He also knows how to keep his fingerprints off dead bodies. But then you have seen proof of that here in Kiev, haven't you?"

Bayurak walked to his desk and sat behind it. "You people are such bad businessmen. You let your crazy ideology cost you so much money." He opened a red leather folder and took out a Montblanc pen. "All of Europe, no competition. At the same price we buy it now for the Ukrainian market?"

"Yes," Ghazi replied. "And let me assure you, this is not about ideology. For us, this is good business. For you, it will be, too. You will make a lot of money."

Bayurak nodded. "All right, now what were those five questions you wanted answers to?"

SATURDAY, AUGUST 29
GLOBAL COORDINATION CENTER
CREECH AFB, NEVADA

Bruce Dougherty hated sleeping during the daytime in Vegas and flying the birds in the daytime in AfPak. It upset his body clock and he didn't sleep well as a result. He had been using Ambien for so long that it didn't seem to help much anymore. It just put him into a strange, waking, trance-like state while he tossed and turned, twisting the sheets and blankets. Then when it was time to get up and go to the base, he needed lots of strong coffee. Then Red Bull at work. This had been a bad week. He kept wondering about the boy in the hotel in Vienna, kept thinking of what his life was like, what it would have been like, if he had only seen him earlier, if he had not killed him. He knew it was crazy, after all of the other deaths, but he could not clear it from his mind.

Today, it was a recce mission, unarmed. HUMINT had reported an HVI holed up in a high perch just inside Afghanistan. No one had ever flown a mission to look up there before, but from the maps and the satellite images, it made sense that someone would hide there, at least in the summer. It was pretty inaccessible and you could surely see anyone coming. Anything that looked like a road ended ten miles away, then the goat path went up, and up, and up. The sheer mountain faces on either side of the wide valley formed a box canyon that ran for almost six miles before it ended in another mountain wall, with a little flat space, high up near a small waterfall.

Bruce could not help but think that it must have been

really beautiful at the end of the box canyon, on that cliff, just below the top, in the cool shade, with a natural shower and pool, and a view of the mountains and the valley. He would see it up close fairly soon. The challenge was going to be flying through the box canyon without being seen, then maintaining an orbit long enough to start developing the Pattern of Life on the HVI, the data that would be needed to support an attack decision later on. The chameleon software would help, electronically changing the color of the skin on the bottom side of the bird to what the sky above it would look like from the ground below. But first, even though the HUMINT source was supposed to be good, he had to see if there were any signs of human life up there at all.

It had been ten days for the men in the rocks, ten days in the thin atmosphere at twelve thousand feet. That did not bother them, since they had lived at altitude for years. What bothered them was trying to figure out the electronic equipment they had been given, the short-range line of sight radios, the heat detecting binoculars, and the Russian Stingers with their precious batteries. Finally, that day when they turned on the Thuraya satellite phone for the one minute at a time they used it, there was the text message, "Storm front moving generally north." It meant a drone had taken off and been tracked by the Pakistani radar moving toward their general location. Before they could alert the others, farther up the canyon, they saw it approaching from the south. As they had been told it might be, the drone was below them and its dark gray fuselage stood out. The electronic chameleon skin was only on the bottom of the drone. They were above it.

As the bird passed below them and made its way slowly up the canyon, they could hear the buzzing. They hit the alarm on their special radio. Three men farther up the canyon, sitting on the high edge of the canyon wall, grabbed for the SA-24. They flipped all of the switches to "on" and to "arm." The long tube started to make noises, beeps and whines. The gunner saw the drone head on through the optical sight and hit the Target Designator button. He threw off the safety. The tones coming from the tube changed into one long, high beep. As the drone passed by them, he pulled the launch trigger. The tube jumped and shook. A flame leaped from the back of the tube as the missile shot out into the sky and after the drone, now ahead and below.

The image on Bruce Dougherty's screen dissolved into a bright blue rectangle. "Jesus! This is no time for the blue screen of death, man." He stood up in his cubicle and screamed at the computer support contractor who sat toward the front of the room. "IT, I need connectivity back to my bird, now, or she will just turn around and fly home in a few minutes."

"Dude," the civilian contractor yelled back, "chill. There ain't no signal coming from your bird. The link shut down just as that flash started."

"What flash? What are you talking about? I didn't—" Bruce stopped, wondering if he had missed something on the video feed while he was watching the instruments, or rubbing his eyes to stay awake. "Listen, just reboot or whatever you do."

There was still a smudge of smoke hanging in the high, thin air above the canyon and a dozen small fires in the grass and scrub bushes on the canyon floor below where the fuel and the pieces of the drone had fallen, scattered across a wide area.

The men on the top of the canyon wall packed up. They did not call in. They would tell their story in person. It was safer that way.

Dougherty filed an incident report, unexplained loss of connectivity to UAV, probable crash. The drones crashed far more often than the public was aware. The Predators especially were fairly fragile, underpowered aircraft. At the end of his shift, he went to his boss, Colonel Parsons, to discuss his suspicions that maybe something unusual had happened. Before he could raise his hunch, however, Parsons stood up on a chair and asked the other pilots and support team to gather around.

"What we do is secret, you all know. Therefore, we can't have the big, public ceremonies that they do in the rest of the Air Force. But that does not mean that the Pentagon leadership or the President is unaware of what we do or who we are. Nor does it mean that they are ungrateful, quite the opposite." Erik scanned the group, making eye contact with as many as he could.

"In fact, they have created a special honor for UAV pilots and team members, the Distinguished Warfare Award. It can only be given to those of us in the UAV units and to our nation's new cyber warriors. It recognizes what we do is warfare and it is the new way of war.

"I am pleased today, on behalf of the Secretary of the Air Force, to present the Distinguished Warfare Award to Major Bruce Dougherty for his essential role in a recent classified mission." Erik jumped off the chair and handed a folder to Sergeant Miller, who read the citation aloud to the group.

"Attention to Orders," Miller began and then read a brief, uninformative script while Erik placed a medal on Bruce Dougherty's flight suit. There was a brief round of applause and handshaking.

"All right, everyone back to work. We got birds to fly," Erik ordered. He then walked Bruce Dougherty out of the building and to his car in the parking lot. Bruce sat up on the hood of his Mustang.

"You know what they call those medals in the real Air Force? The Desk Warfare Award, for guys who go to war without ever leaving their desks. Cyber geeks and Xbox gamers, us. It says right in the regs that the medal cannot ever be given for valor in combat," Bruce explained.

"You wanna give it back?" Erik asked.

"No, boss, I want to fly again, like you and I used to do. F-16s. What I'd really like is a crack at an F-22."

"Bruce, we have had the few F-22s we got for how many years now? And not one has ever flown in combat. You fly in combat every day. How many enemy have you killed so far? Bruce, the era of manned aircraft is over. We are the future of military aircraft. You want to be in something that goes fast? Take your Mustang out on the back road. Never any sheriffs out here."

Dougherty laughed. "That's the way I go home every day. Zero to a hundred in nine seconds."

"Great," Erik Parsons said, patting his friend on the shoulder. "And, Bruce, keep the Desk Warrior medal. You saved a lot of lives by the mission you flew in Vienna. We just can never tell anyone, about the bad stuff, or even the good."

# 11

SUNDAY, AUGUST 30
PODILSKY DISTRICT
KIEV, UKRAINE

"You look better today," Dmitri Bayurak said, thrusting his hand forward.

"Yesterday you kidnapped me from a steam bath and threw me in the back of a truck. Today I was picked up at my hotel in a Range Rover," Ghazi Nawarz replied. "I look better. I also feel better. And you?"

"Your money hit my account overnight," Bayurak said. "So I feel better, too. Let me introduce you to Yuri and Mykola. They have also been at work overnight. I will leave you three to talk about ones and zeroes. I have bigger numbers to deal with."

The two Ukrainians led the way downstairs to the computer operations floor where over twenty young men hovered over computer screens. It could have been a control room for a bank, but these men seemed all to be in jeans and T-shirts, and looked like they had not been to a shower or a barber in a long time. Yuri and

Mykola led him to a conference room with the same modern, Scandinavian design feel that had been present upstairs in Bayurak's office. There were large flat screens on each of three walls. The fourth was glass, looking out at the computer operations floor.

Yuri pressed a button next to the door. The floor-to-ceiling glass wall went from clear to opaque, a milky white barrier suddenly appearing inside the glass. "Polymer dispersed liquid crystal," Mykola said.

"Of course," Ghazi said and sat down at the conference table. "So what exactly did you do overnight?"

"Hacked AAFI," Mykola replied.

"Go on," Ghazi said.

"The American Armed Forces Insurance company in Texas. Almost all the U.S. military, and ex-military, insure their cars, sometimes their houses, with AAFI. They give low rates and give good service," Mykola continued.

"Why do I care? Am I looking to insure my car?" Ghazi asked.

"No, your Jaguar XS in Vancouver is already insured with Royal Canadian Sun," Mykola smiled. "As is your condo."

"You have been investigating me?" Ghazi said. "You are supposed to be investigating the American drones."

"Enough fun, Mykola," Yuri said. "We did. The main American drone control facility is at Creech Air Force Base, outside of Las Vegas. It's a shit hole. People like to live off base. So we look in AAFI to see what Air Force pilots live nearby. Then we see which ones came there from Langley Air Force base in Virginia, where they train the drone pilots. Here's your list of drone pilots now living near Creech, their street addresses, their height, weight, eye color, hair color, and what cars they drive."

Ghazi began flipping through the printouts. "The pictures. They look very young," he said.

"Some are old pictures. From the college yearbooks. And driver's licenses. Some from Facebook," Mykola explained. "But none of them are on Facebook now. For security, ha!"

"We also cracked Dominion Federal Credit Union, it's like a bank. CIA employees use it," Yuri added. "Here are active duty CIA people living in Las Vegas area. This one just bought an expensive condo, in a nice building downtown."

"We want to go to Vegas," Mykola interjected. "Is necessary to help with operation. More secure. You can't be calling us from there, besides time differences. You'd be waking us up all the time."

"Too risky. Too hard to get a visa," Ghazi replied. "No, you can't go."

"No visas, we have American passports," Yuri replied. "Already these passports are on file with the State Department. Such bad network security these people have. It's a wonder everyone doesn't have an American passport by now."

Ghazi did not reply. "What about the drones themselves. Can we get at them?"

"You just did," Yuri said. "Wasn't that your people who used the Stinger yesterday?"

"SA-24," Ghazi replied.

"Same thing. Russians copied the Stingers they got in Afghanistan years ago," Yuri said.

"The drones are networked. Anything networked is vulnerable," Mykola added. "We have plans. You'll see. We have some boxes we need to ship your guys. And we'll need an Executive Jet."

"I want to kill these people, the drone people, not just hack them," Ghazi said.

"Yeah, yeah, we got that. Not a problem," Yuri replied. "Lots of ways to die."

"Can we kill them with their own drones?" Ghazi asked.

The two Ukrainians looked at each other and exchanged a few quick words in their language. "Maybe," Yuri replied in English. "With drones, for sure. Maybe not with their Predators or Reapers, but with drones, maybe. Easier to do if we are both in Vegas."

"Before I left Kiev your boss told me he had seen a videotape the Austrian security service has, showing the special black drone that killed my father, do you have that?" Ghazi asked.

"Is not good, you watching your father die, but yes we have it, of course," Mykola answered.

"I don't want to watch it," Ghazi replied. "I want you to send it to someone. With a letter. Make it look like you sent it from Vienna, like maybe you work for the Austrian government and stole it from them."

"Done," Yuri said. "What else?"

"The metros, subways. Did you start looking at them yet?" Ghazi asked.

"Mykola loves metro. He takes metro every day, rubs up against girls. Never asks them out, just rubs up against them and gets slapped, am I right?" Yuri teased his colleague.

Mykola blushed. He hit his laptop and began showing images on one of the large flat screens. "American metros come in two types: old and very old. The very old ones are harder to hack, no network controls. They use people to drive them, like in Kiev. Primitive. So, Boston, New York, Philadelphia are like that. The newer ones, Atlanta, Washington, San Francisco, we have hacked those. Piece of cake."

Ghazi watched the maps and photographs as Mykola flipped through them in slideshow mode. "I need to know where we should put the bombs for maximum effect, how we get around security," Ghazi said.

"Bombs. Always it's bombs with you people. It's the digital age man, you can kill with bits and bytes," Yuri replied, "at least in the newer metros. The older ones you can bomb. We can do some surveillance through their own cameras. New York has a lot of cameras, easy to hack. Maybe have to send some people in to look around, too. Your people, not us."

"We will have people ready, soon," Ghazi said, wondering how Bahadur was doing with that part of the plan.

"Bayurak doesn't want what we do traceable back to Kiev, back to him," Mykola announced.

"Well, you know how to anonymize, bounce through servers in Saudi, make it look like it's al Qaeda in Yemen," Ghazi said.

"The Americans can figure that shit out now. Fort Meade, NSA, Cyber Command, those guys," Yuri said.

"So?" Ghazi asked.

"So, we got to be in Vegas," the two Ukrainians replied in unison.

"Fucking Christ, all right, you can go to Vegas," Ghazi exclaimed.

Mykola high-fived Yuri. Then Yuri turned back to Ghazi. "Fucking Christ? I thought you were Muslim."

"I was, as a child," Ghazi replied. "Now I am a global citizen. I believe in what works."

# 12

THURSDAY, SEPTEMBER 17
MANDALAY HOTEL
LAS VEGAS, NEVADA

The Peter Michael "Pointe Rouge" Chardonnay flew through the air. It was carried by the sommelier's attractive assistant, who had attached herself to a wire, touched a control pad, and had been pulled rapidly fifty feet above the restaurant floor. There she had opened one of the many glass enclosures that held the extensive wine collection in temperature-controlled environments, a series of wine rooms that composed not a wine cellar, but a wine attic soaring above the diners.

Descending to tableside, the acrobatic wine steward announced, "So, we did have the 2009. You're in luck, because it really is the best available year. Would you like it chilled?"

"No, no that will suppress the taste," Colonel Erik Parsons replied. "Just leave it on the table, thanks."

"You knew that wine was in the top case, didn't you?"

Jennifer Parsons said, smiling and simultaneously shaking her head. "Did you pick it just for the show?"

"I don't know why you say things like that. This is the best California Chardonnay on the list," Erik replied.

"So what is the occasion? This is not our anniversary and it's not my birthday, which I think was the last time you took me to a fancy Vegas casino restaurant."

"Do we need an occasion? It's my night off. We live ten miles from some of the best restaurants in America. With our combined incomes, we can afford to live better than we do, especially now that we have the last of the tuition payments behind us."

She looked at him as he tasted the wine. "Honey, we have been together for twenty-five years. I know you. And I am a working psychiatrist, so don't tell me we have come here just because it's Monday. Talk to me. What's on your mind, GI?"

"Well, see, doctor, I have this friend," Erik began. "And he has been having fantasies of flying through the air above a restaurant and hooking up with his wife, who is also in the air, and they do it somewhere between the Shiraz and the Merlot. But in the dream, they knock over this whole wall of Pinot Noir."

Jennifer laughed and touched her glass to his. "That is an easy diagnosis. Your friend is probably a former fighter pilot who commanded a squadron of F-16s and is frustrated because now his squadron is a bunch of flying killer robots and neither he nor his pilots ever get to fly themselves through the air . . . which for them, when they were flying their F-16s, was better than sex."

"Jeez, Jen, that was such a classical Freudian interpretation, I'm surprised you didn't go for the F-16s are phalluses thing."

"Ha!" she laughed. "Goes without saying."

"Going supersonic, the high G turn, all that stuff was never better than what we've done together, really," Erik said softly.

"Bullshit, now really, what's bothering you?"

They had ordered the six-course "Degustation" tasting menu and the courses began to appear.

"I think some of the guys are getting ragged. Two days ago one guy clipped the wing of a UN 737 over Mogadishu. He says he never saw the plane. The Reaper spun out and hit a refugee camp, exploded. Amazingly, no one got killed. And the 737 continued on in and landed. Lucky.

"Another guy, Bruce, you know him, says he never saw the civilian walk right into the kill zone, just before he fired. Fried the guy, as well as the four bad guys.

"Then one of Bruce's birds just seemed to disappear. We later found it on satellite imagery in pieces on the ground. Still trying to figure out whether he clipped the mountain or what happened.

"Out of seventy-five pilots, eleven have asked for early transfer, I dismissed three for DUIs, and eight have filed for divorce since they got here. Those are not normal numbers, Jennie. I am supposed to be a leader, inspire them, keep them happy, act like a team. That ain't happening. Washington has suggested having chaplains and shrinks just outside the Ops Center, in case the pilots need immediate counseling. "

Jennifer Parsons had followed her husband around

the world, moving ten times since they married. There had always been Air Force hospitals or off-base clinics where she could practice. She knew the stresses the military placed on most families and she had always felt blessed that she and Erik had maintained such a real partnership, that they and the two girls had always been such a team together.

"I can't see any of the guys in your unit or their spouses because of the conflict of interest rules, but I do consults with my colleagues, so I hear things, always without names, but nonetheless . . .

"There is a lot of stress in the program. Let's face it, they kill people fairly often and then they walk out of their dark game-boy room and they're in the blazing Las Vegas sun, where it's perfectly safe, fun is all around. It's hard to live in those two worlds simultaneously," Dr. Parsons observed. "You don't want them to think of their job as just a computer game. You want them to know there are real people at the other end. But then when you achieve that they also know that those real people are killed like fish in a barrel, they can't fight back. It's not really a fair fight, so your guys get guilty."

"It's not supposed to be a fair fight," Erik shot back. "That's the whole point. We have found a way of eliminating our enemies that does not put our people at risk. Military leaders have wanted that forever. That's why they put men inside big metal tanks or had them fly overhead in bombers, but then those things got vulnerable, too. I don't want it to be fair and to have one out of ten of my guys killed. I want none out of ten killed. And that's what I got with the drones."

They stopped talking as the waiter explained the next course. They were used to editing their remarks when others were within hearing distance, when civilians were around. Erik hoped that, to the waiters, they looked like a couple in from Columbus for the medical equipment show that was filling up the casino's giant convention hall.

"Trouble is, you got a bunch of your young pilots who spent their high school years killing pretend people on their computer games," Jennifer said when the waiter had left. "They have to constantly remind themselves that this is not a game. And they're not supposed to go home and talk about it with their husbands and wives. It's an abnormal environment."

"Truth is they know that we don't really need highly trained pilots who can drive an F-16 to do this stuff," Erik admitted. "And they know they may never get to fly a real fighter, one that they get to sit in. We're buying fewer and fewer fighter planes and more and more drones. The days of the fighter pilot are dwindling fast. They've gone from being highly select, well-trained jocks to being, what'd you call them, game-boys?"

"You got it, Colonel. Game-boys with blood on their hands, who don't always see how the sucker they just evaporated, who never saw it coming, in Yemen, or Somalia, or Pakistan, or Mali has anything to do with keeping the Homeland safe. Game-boys who sit up in bed in the middle of the night, let out a scream, and wake their partners, who find them covered in sweat. That's what's happening to some of them."

With a thud, the wine steward landed tableside. She

was attached to a wire and holding a bottle. "Is now a good time for the Pinot? Foxen from their Bien Nacido vineyard. Fantastic."

Seven blocks away, they opened the champagne. "I always pop a bottle of the bubbly when a client finds just the right place for them and gives me their check," the real estate agent said to Ghazi. "And I just know, Mr. Romano, that this is the right place for you. Completely furnished, ready to move in, thirty-three floors above everything. You can see the Strip out the bedroom windows and the mountains from the living room."

Ghazi clinked glasses and sipped the celebratory drink. "It's very nice. And the Internet speeds seem to be very fast. I need that to keep in touch with my business in New York." He walked over to the floor-to-ceiling window. "Is that the airport out there?"

"No, sir, the airport is over here. That's the Air Force base way out there, but I guess you can see things taking off from there because you are so high up. Just a fabulous view. And because you are paying cash you can move in less than a week from tonight."

After locking the condominium, Ghazi and his real estate agent walked down the brightly decorated hall to the elevator, passing a woman dragging a wheelie with a large computer bag strapped on top of it. "G'evening," Sandra Vittonelli muttered as she passed them on the way to her apartment. Even though she was doing it every two weeks now, it had been a long flight from Washington.

As she unlocked the door to her unit, she could hear the landline ringing. Entering the living room, she felt the secure Blackberry on her hip vibrating. She reached the landline in the study while it was still ringing. "Please authenticate," a man's voice said.

She placed the four fingers of her right hand onto the phone's small screen, then removed a card from a pouch that was hanging around her neck and inserted it into the side of the phone. Finally, she spoke into the handset, "Vittonelli, Sandra. I am code blue, repeat code blue." With that, she had completed three-factor authentication and the phone began receiving encrypted voice traffic from the Global Coordination Center, forty-three kilometers away in the desert, on the airbase.

"Ms. Vittonelli, we have a potential signature strike pending."

She lifted the computer bag off the wheelie and placed it on the floor next to her desk. The little study was still dark, she hadn't had time to turn on any lights in the apartment. "Is it on the HPTL?"

"No, ma'am, not yet on the High Payoff Target List, but it sure fits the signature and we think we have two HVIs there."

"You think you have two High Value Individuals? Do you or don't you?" she asked.

"We are waiting confirmation from Maryland, but what we appear to have is a meeting of two of the Qazzani group leaders. We're not sure how long it will continue. We're afraid that if we don't take the shot, the meeting will break up and the HVIs will leave."

She knew what this probably meant. She would have to try to get out to the base as fast as possible. "Have you done a collateral scan?"

"Yes, ma'am, collateral damage potential is currently scored at zero."

"How long have you had eyes on?" she asked.

"We followed the first possible-HVI there almost six hours ago. HVI two arrived about an hour later," the voice from the GCC said. "But we have gone back and looked at historical images of this site from satellites and from our own birds passing by. Never seen anything but guys with guns around."

"Where is Colonel Parsons?" she asked. Maybe he could handle this one, so she could get into a hot shower and then sleep in her own bed.

"Colonel Parsons said to inform you, ma'am, that he is on his way over to pick you up at your location. He was downtown. He should be there in about five mics." Sandra groaned, there was no way that she could avoid driving out to the base now, but at least she would not have to drive herself.

She quickly changed out of the clothes that she had worn on the flight and into a tracksuit. She put her Yankees hat on to hide the disarray of her hair. When Erik called to say that he was downstairs, she was waiting for the Nespresso machine to finish pumping out an intensity ten demitasse of eye-opening caffeine.

It could be a long night.

# 13

SATURDAY, SEPTEMBER 19
KUNAR PROVINCE
AFGHANISTAN

"How will you kill your cousin's husband?" the older man asked, as the two men sat beneath an undercut rock, amid the boulders on a hillside three kilometers from their vehicles.

"Just shoot him," the younger man replied. "I am not one for the torture. It takes time and then there is the cleaning."

"But he has been placing these little radios on your Toyota for money, money from the Americans. You should use your knives first."

"Fadl, if he had not been placing the beacons on my Toyota, do you think that we would have that drone circling up there? This is a good plan Ghazi gave us."

The two men squinted up at the blue sky, looking for the drone that they had heard almost an hour earlier. Both men were reluctant to move out from under the overhanging rock, to look around the boulders, to expose themselves to the all-seeing eye above them. They were also tired from the walking, alone, from the tunnel exit, up the hill.

"It will be a good plan if it works, but we have been here for many hours. The drugs will be wearing off soon."

SATURDAY, SEPTEMBER 19
OUTSIDE LAS VEGAS, NEVADA

Erik drove the black Camaro only slightly above the speed limit. He did not want to be delayed by the Highway Patrol pulling him over, even if they would probably buy his excuse that he was an Air Force officer who had just been called and told to report to base urgently. For the first part of the ride, neither Erik nor Sandra spoke. He was still angry that he had to leave his wife when there were still two courses left to be served, when their "date night" had only just started. He wondered if he would get back to her in time to enjoy the suite they had taken for the night as part of the casino's "Dinner and Sleepover" package, designed to lure in locals. Sandra, fighting fatigue, was going over the meetings she had the past two days in Washington.

Erik read her mind. "So how was our Nation's Capital? Inspiring, efficient, focused on the things that matter?"

"None of the above," she replied. "You know what struck me on this trip? The briefings I got at Headquarters about the extent of the problem. Sure, al Qaeda in AfPak is almost gone, but we still have the various

Taliban groups on both sides of the border and now the narcoterrorist criminal cartels like the Qazzanis.

"But in Yemen we have al Qaeda in the Arabian Peninsula taking over towns, in Nigeria it's the Boko Haram offshoot burning down Christian churches with people in them, in Mali it's al Qaeda in the Maghreb that runs half the country, like the Shabab affiliate that has a swath of Somalia. Bin Laden is still dead, but this thing has just metastasized."

Erik turned the car into the base, flashing his identification to the Air Force policewoman at the gate. "Well, we are flying in all of those places. It's a target rich environment. And it's employment for the likes of us well into the future, no matter the other budget cuts."

"Remember that intercept last month about something happening around Christmas?" she asked.

"Yeah, whatever happened to that?" Erik said.

"This is why these trips back to DC are essential, even though they take a lot out of me. You'd never know it on the outside, but people on the seventh floor at Headquarters, people downtown, are all trying to figure out how to stop the Christmas Bombings. That's what they're calling it, but they don't want it to leak to the press, especially since there may be nothing to it."

"Nothing to it?" Erik replied. "That just means they haven't been able to develop any leads."

"That's exactly what it means." She looked out at the variety of drones on the runway and in the hangars as they drove down the flight line. There were some of the older Predator and the larger Reaper drones based there for the pilots to use in training flights, some of the large Global Reach drones that went anywhere in the world from the United States, and some of the newly arrived Homeland Security drones to patrol the Mexican border, on both sides.

"That's what struck me, Erik. We are the only thing that they have that works. We shoot at the bad guys and keep them so they can't really set up shop and start training thousands of terrorists the way they used to do in Afghanistan before 9/11. But we can't drone every guy who gets radicalized on the Internet in his dorm room. And we can't shoot Hellfires into houses in the U.S. where they may be planning the next one. All we can do is get some small fraction of the guys overseas."

Erik pulled up to the single-story, windowless white building that was the Global Coordination Center. "Maybe, but let's go kill a few more of them," he said, thinking about Jennifer alone in the hotel suite.

Walking onto the floor of the GCC gave Sandra all of the adrenaline rush the coffee had failed to deliver. She felt at home here, like she had a purpose. She strapped on her wireless headset and began the drill. "Okay, what have we got here? Let's start with Virginia. CIA, what's your story?"

"We have a HUMINT source with excellent access and substantiated previous reporting on the Qazzanis. He beaconed the vehicle of Musuhan, number three in the group. They're meeting just over the Pak border inside Afghanistan, so the strike won't raise concerns in Islamabad."

Then the voice from Maryland came over the speakers, "NSA here. We geolocated the beacon at the coordinates of this compound that you are looking at on screen."

Bruce Dougherty continued the story from his cockpit cubicle on the floor of the GCC. "We found the compound at those coordinates. Checked the plates on the vehicles parked outside. One is the vehicle we associate with Musuhan and the other is a vehicle of another HVT named Fadl Kaprani." Bruce zoomed the camera in on vehicles parked outside a high-walled compound of one large and two smaller buildings. "They have been inside for hours. Some sort of cartel board meeting maybe. The usual smattering of guards on the roads in and up in the hills, one-zees and two-zees."

"And you said the collateral score was zero?" Sandra asked.

"Yes, ma'am, we have imaged the area for seven hours now and there is no sign of any civilian activity. We have looked back at historical images from satellite sweeps and never any women or children. They had some guys there recently erecting that outbuilding there at the top. We think it's a new, private hooch for a senior guy, so he doesn't have to stay in the big house with the guards and cooks."

Erik was flipping through the supporting documents on his iPad. "Legal has signed off on it. Pentagon and Agency have cleared the shot. The White House has been notified to stand by."

"Okay, patch me in to Dr. Burrell," Sandra agreed, looking up at the image of the isolated compound on the Big Board. "That's a hell of a long meeting they're having. Let's get the shot off before it breaks up."

SATURDAY, SEPTEMBER 19
KUNAR PROVINCE
AFGHANISTAN

The children were mainly Tajiks. The man who took them from the orphan school had promised that they would be resettled in a new school for Islamic orphans in Saudi Arabia, a beautiful new campus funded by a Prince. The man had also made a generous gift to the orphan school, so that even those children who could not yet go to Saudi Arabia would live in better conditions. No doubt some of that gift actually made its way to fixing the dilapidated building, buying some food. Most of it probably went into the personal bank account of the headmaster.

The seventeen boys, the oldest of whom was ten, had been thrilled by the bus ride, at first. The trip, however, had taken eighteen hours and the snacks they were given were not enough to quench their hunger. Thus, when they got to the compound, they gorged themselves on the hot food that had been prepared for them. There were sleeping rolls for twenty and soon, tired from the bus ride and drugged by what was in the food, all of the children were settled quietly in their bedrolls.

As the first of the boys began to wake, to try through the fog of the remaining sedative coursing through their systems to figure out where they were, they discovered that they could not open the doors to go out. One boy found a hatch door on the floor, the one that led to the tunnel, but that, too, was locked from the other side. The men who had fed them were gone. They were alone.

The three boys who woke first learned this and began to be afraid.

The others never knew that fear. They had gone to sleep with full stomachs for the first time in months. They had settled happily into new, clean bedrolls, thinking of the ride in the airplane that the men had promised would take them to their new home.

The Reaper was circling at twelve thousand feet in a light ten-knot wind from the north. A Predator was two thousand feet above it to provide a second set of eyes. Occasionally, the Predator's pilot would use its camera to scan the skies for any other aircraft. There were none in the area. The antennae on board the Predator scanned frequencies for mobile telephones, handheld radios, any electromagnetic signatures emanating from the valley below. There was only silence.

At Creech, the Reaper pilot's control panel showed all systems nominal. On the Reaper's underside, toward the front of the thirty-six-foot fuselage, inside a protective dome, the multispectral camera moved slowly, always pointing at the target below. The camera could zoom in close and provide High Definition images in daylight or zoom back and show the entire valley. At night, the Low Lite camera would flip into place, providing green or gray images as clearly as in midday. Toward the back of the aircraft, inside a four-foot blister, a synthetic aperture radar scanned the ground below, feeding data to an onboard computer that generated photographic quality images from the radar's return, day or night. Below each of the thirty-six-foot wings, hanging from the weapons racks were two laser-guided 250-pound bombs and two Hellfire missiles.

The first Hellfire penetrated the roof of the house where the boys slept, and then it exploded. It had an antipersonnel warhead, one that spread smaller balls of explosives and razor sharp metal. The second Hellfire had a high-explosive warhead, designed to knock over walls from the overpressure created by its blast wave. Hellfires three and four hit each of the two smaller outbuildings inside the compound wall with high-explosive detonations. All four hit in less than a minute. Each impacted within eighteen inches of their designated aim point. The wooden gate in the compound's wall was blown open from the blast. An alarm on one of the SUVs outside the wall began to wail.

SATURDAY, SEPTEMBER 19
GLOBAL COORDINATION CENTER
OPERATIONS ROOM
CREECH AFB, NEVADA

"No secondary," Bruce Dougherty observed. Normally terrorist camps were filled with enough of their own explosives that the Hellfires triggered additional detonations. "And no rescue party from the watchers in the hills."

"Yeah, well they've all learned by now that we wait around and pop the rescue parties, too," Erik Parsons observed. "Nothing's going to happen. Might as well bring the birds home and call it a night."

As they walked to the door of the GCC, Erik asked Sandra, "So we killed the number three in the Qazzani group. How long 'til they have another number three? And why don't we like the Qazzanis again, remind me?"

As they walked to the car, Sandra wearily replied. "The Qazzanis support al Qaeda and the Taliban. They have set up their own little country that spans the two sides of the AfPak border. They sell heroin all over Europe and the Middle East," she paused. "And they killed three senior Agency people last year in an ambush they set up because they wanted to kill CIA officers."

"Ah, so it's personal?" Erik asked.

"We don't do revenge killings, they do," Sandra replied. "But for me, for the guys at Headquarters that set the priorities, yes, it's personal. I went to two of those Agency funerals, saw the kids. We may sit back here in CONUS perfectly safe, but what we do here only works because we have some guys out there on the ground, in the shit."

As they drove down the flight line, a large Global Reach drone was taxiing into launch position. Erik stopped the car to watch it take off into the night for its thirty-six-hour mission. "Where is that big boy going?" he asked.

"That guy is flying to Mali tonight to take out a big camp AQIM has set up just north or Timbuktu," she replied as they watched the 737-sized drone lumber down the runway loaded up with both bombs and missiles. "I got the mission approved in DC. Quote: The several hundred casualties expected will do irreparable damage to al Qaeda in the Islamic Maghreb. Unquote."

Erik resumed driving the Camaro toward the base gate. "Well, yeah. Death is kind of irreparable."

# 14

SUNDAY, SEPTEMBER 20
SIND CLUB
KARACHI, PAKISTAN

"Over here," Fares called out as Bryce Duggan entered the bar at the Sind Club. Fares Sorhari was the reporter's traveling producer, the guy who made things happen no matter where in the Middle East and South Asia. "We're drinking to the new little Princess, born this morning in London."

The Sind Club had been the elegant retreat of the Colonial era. It was now where elite Pakistanis and expat Brits wined and dined. It was the place Fares had said they had to go, perhaps because he had reciprocal rights from his club in Dubai. The club was a relief from the crowds, the noise, the traffic, the knife's edge of madness that was Karachi.

"This is Duncan Cameron from *The Guardian*. Duncan, Bryce Duggan from WWN," Fares made the introductions. Cameron did not look the type who could make the transition from the print world to television,

Bryce thought. The guy would have to stop sleeping in his suit. Bryce guessed that the Brit was thirty years older, but the older man could well be the type that had really gotten to know the place. Bryce had learned in Cairo, in Aleppo, in Benghazi, from the old hands.

"Welcome to the most violent city in the world," Cameron said, raising his glass of Balvenie. "Fares, here, tells me you are in search of drones. Well, go north, my friend, go north. Plenty of droning going on up in Waziristan. You could get lots of pretty pictures of bombed-out houses, if they let you in, or rather, if they let you leave."

"That's our hope," Bryce began. "But I want to get behind the pretty pictures, tell some of the stuff that you've done in *The Guardian*. How the Pak military is playing both sides, letting the U.S. fly the drones, but complaining publicly when they do, having them strike the Pakistani Taliban but helping the al Qaeda remnants and the Afghan Taliban."

"You've read my stories on that?" Cameron smiled. "Well, you and two dons in Oxford. I didn't know that my readership had grown to three."

"I'd also like to talk to some villagers. Get their reaction, maybe contrast it to a more modern, secular type, maybe in Islamabad, who may think it's a good thing that the Americans are keeping the radicals from the gates," Bryce said. "Do you think that works?"

"Let's sit at a table," Cameron suggested. "Afik, give us that bottle of the Balvenie, will you now."

They sat in a corner, well apart from the few others in the room. "Never know who else tips Afik," Cameron began. "Listen, my friend, if you are going to do stories on what the Pak mil are doing, especially their intel people, the ISI, you have to be very careful. Reporters die out here."

"We know," Fares replied. "But, unlike you, we don't live here. They won't see our story until we leave country."

"Well, if that's the plan, let me suggest that you do the voiceover after you leave. They will hear what you say on camera when you are shooting here, and what people say to you." Cameron refilled the three glasses. "Got myself lectured to up in Rawalpindi by the ISI when I suggested that they were playing both sides. Truth is that they are, of course. They want the Taliban to succeed somewhat in Afghanistan, but the local variant, the Pak Taliban, they see them as a threat. Okay to have the crazies running the asylum next door, but not here."

Bryce was not used to straight Scotch, but he knew better than to ask for a mixer, or even a chaser. "Isn't it true that some of what we think is ISI activity is actually some retired intel guys who are more Islamist than the people now running the service?" Bryce asked.

"That's what they put out. They'd like you to think that," Cameron replied. "It's only partially true."

"Like all things," Fares said. "Excuse me one second, I'm going to get us some waters from our man Afik. I have a feeling we may get fairly deep, and deep into the bottle."

"Duncan, if I am reading between the lines in your stories, you don't just have ISI sources, you're talking straight to the Lashkar guys, Pak Taliban, the Qazzanis, AQ. How the hell do you do it?" Bryce asked.

"Remember what I said, you can get killed out here for talking to the wrong people or being in the wrong places. You really want to go there?" the Scot replied.

"Tell me how."

"I can put you in touch with some people, but not with all of them. Maybe one or two. Qazzanis are businessmen. AQ are media savvy. Stay away from the others. They won't even hostage you, just leave you in a drainage ditch." Cameron rested his chin in his hand, partially covering his mouth with fingers that looked like they had been battered in rugby years ago. "But these boys need to be lubricated and not with the Balvenie. They like U.S. dollars, cash. Give me twenty-five K to pass to them and you'll get some pretty pictures no one else has seen and some guy in the shadows to talk on camera, but he will be the real deal, or damn close to it."

"I can do ten," Bryce quickly replied.

"Then it will just be the Qazzanis. They actually want some coverage right now for some reason. Give me a few days," Cameron said.

# 15

MONDAY, SEPTEMBER 21
TERMINAL E
LOGAN AIRPORT
BOSTON, MASSACHUSETTS

He had been standing in the line for over an hour. The lines for Americans were short, but they were making the wogs wait, he thought. Already he could see the way they treated the brown people. The Air India 747 had disgorged a lot of them into Logan's Terminal E, International Arrivals.

He watched as people at the head of the line moved up to the booths where the policemen sat. The policemen asked them questions. Some went through quickly, but most were asked many questions. The policemen typed into computers, searching for any indication that the person standing before them should be barred from entry into the country. He noticed that the policemen were wearing pistols on their belts. Once, he noticed that a man was taken away from a booth and escorted by two policemen to a door on the sidewall. He wondered if that would happen to him. He worried, but he did not want to sweat. That, they had told him, would be a sign for the police to look more carefully. He should not look nervous.

He told himself there was no reason to worry. He was now Birbal Malhotra, Indian citizen, born in Delhi. Three months ago he had obtained the new Indian identity card, one of over three hundred million that they had issued so far. Only a billion left to issue, he thought. It had his picture and a computer chip with his fingerprints and iris scan. It had cost a lot to get from the Indian civil servant who worked in the Identity office, but it was real. He was now in the Indian government database. He was Hindi.

And as a Hindi with one of the new ID cards, he had had little difficulty getting the visa from the American embassy in Delhi. His mother needed special long-term cancer treatment in America. He needed to go in advance to get them an apartment. More money had created a Mrs. Malhotra, a letter from a real doctor in Delhi, and a real Indian-American doctor in Boston. The American doctor had family in Mumbai, now they were a more wealthy family. It was a solid legend. It would withstand scrutiny. He hoped.

Was it really necessary for him to be here? It would have been safer to send others, but he wanted to be sure. He needed to meet the men who would carry the bombs, look them in the eye, take their measure. Would they panic? Would they fuck up? He could have met them in Europe, but he did not want a record of them traveling abroad. It was a risk coming here, but he saw no other way.

"Next."

The policeman yelling at him woke him from his daydream. He moved up to booth 8 and presented his passport and the I-94 form he had filled out on the airplane. He was surprised to see the police officer was a black man.

"What is the purpose of your visit?"

"I am here to prepare for my mother coming to get cancer treatment." He knew that would be the first question.

"Where?"

He felt the sweat running down his back. "Dana-Farber," he replied. "It is part of Harvard."

"I know what it is," the black man replied. "Where will you be staying?"

"Hotel Essex, long-term stay, in Back Bay."

"How long will you be in the country?"

"They said the treatment could take two months for her. The visa is good for a year, but I will not be here that long, sir. I will probably leave before Christmas."

"You know you can't work while you are here? No employment here. What do you do in India, what is your occupation?"

"I am a solicitor, what you call a lawyer." Could the policeman detect the Australian accented English? He had tried to sound like he was from Delhi, but he knew it did not work.

"Put your right hand on this screen. We are going to take your fingerprints. Look up, we are taking your picture. Do not smile."

The policeman returned his passport to him. "Do not lose this I-94 stub. You have to turn it in when you leave the country. Now collect your bags and give this blue form to the officer at the exit. Good luck with your mother's treatments."

Good luck? Maybe he had worried too much. He had no luggage to collect. He had shipped it on ahead to the Essex. There was only his carry-on wheelie. Would they look through that? They could. They would find nothing.

They did not look in his bag. He could have had anything in it, but how was he to know they would not inspect it? He handed in the blue form to the last of the policemen and walked through a door, following the sign to Ground Transportation.

He found the right bus stop and took it to the blue train, the T they called it. T for target, he thought. He wanted to see it right away, so what better way to get to the hotel? Take the blue line to the green line, they had told him. Get off at Copley, walk two blocks to the hotel. It was beginning for Ahmed Bahadur. He was starting to think it would work.

MONDAY, SEPTEMBER 21
2700 LAS VEGAS BOULEVARD
LAS VEGAS, NEVADA

Her mobile must have rung when she was in the shower, she thought, as she stood, drying herself off and deciding what to wear. The little voice mail light was blinking. Instinctively, she picked up the device to hear the message even before dressing.

"Hey, Sandy. It's Ray. I'm in town for Black Hat, the hacker convention over at Caesar's. But I see there's a drone exhibition and conference at Mandalay. Wanna go? Call me."

A drone exhibition? She tapped "drone, Mandalay" into the search engine on the MacBook Air on her coffee table. "No shit," she muttered aloud as the Web page for the Unmanned Aerial Vehicle Exhibition and Conference popped on the screen. UAVEC. "Well, why not?" She picked the mobile back up and scanned for Ray's number.

Ninety minutes later they were wandering together on the floor of the Mandalay Hotel and Casino Convention Center, which was packed with exhibits and displays about drones. "This is the fifth Israeli company I have seen so far," Ray observed as they stood in front of a scale model of a bright, white drone that seemed no bigger than three meters in length and about two in wingspan. The word SHERIFF in blue letters was painted on each side of the short fuselage.

"Interested in our Police Patroller?" a chubby man said as he emerged from around the wall of television screens showing videos of the UAV in action. "Take a precinct where you now use ten police cars and you can reduce that to two. And with Police Patroller you will know before you dispatch a car that it's worth doing. And for tactical response, we can beam live shots to the police cars, so they know what kind of situation they are driving into before they get there." He walked over to the scale model and began pointing things out with a handheld laser. "It comes standard with a forty million candlepower spotlight and a loudspeaker."

"Does it come with a shotgun capability?" Ray asked.

Sandra Vittonelli looked at him with incredulity apparent on her face.

"That is an option, not in the standard config," the salesman replied. "But you have to check to see whether that option is street legal in the U.S. I don't think it is yet, but we hope it will be soon. Lotta interest in that."

Sandra began to move on. "Are you the buyer, sir?" the salesman asked Ray. "City police? County?"

Ray pointed at the retreating Vittonelli, "Actually, she's the sheriff of Jefferson County. I'm just a deputy. . . ." He smiled at the salesman. "Got to catch up with her. You know that kind of boss. . . ."

She stood in front of a four-meter-tall circular device that appeared to be a helicopter drone. The sign in front of it said THE PERFECT HOVERING SURVEILLANCE PLATFORM. It was from Canada. "Where the hell is this Jefferson County where I'm sheriff?" she asked Ray as he caught up to her.

"Oh, you heard that," Ray replied. "There must be half a dozen Jefferson Counties around the U.S. Do you have any helicopter drones?"

She gave him a look that suggested she did not quite share his sense of humor. "I don't," she said. "Homeland Security might. They're buying all sorts of stuff like that."

"We have a much larger model coming out next year that can shoot suppressant foam under high pressure right down into the heart of a fire. Are you from a fire department?" the Canadian saleswoman asked.

"I am the sheriff of Jefferson County." Sandra replied, "Do we look like firemen?"

"Oh, sorry. No, of course not. No you don't," the Canadian reassured. "But the Hovering Fire Truck model also comes in a crowd control and dispersal version, too, with tear gas, slippery solution spray nozzle, even an option for a noise generator that operates at a frequency and power that makes people void."

"Void?" Sandra asked.

"Shit themselves," Ray offered.

"Yes, that's right," the Canadian woman agreed. "We don't make that piece of equipment ourselves, but we can add it. The Hovering Fire Truck model is designed for the Crowd Control Sound System to be just plug and play." She smiled broadly.

"I guess that would make rioting difficult," Sandra observed as she started to walk away. "Lovely. We'll think about it."

"We have a whole range of nonlethal options. . . ." the Canadian called after the short woman and the tall man as they moved on down the aisle of display booths. Sandra spotted a coffee bar and café in the corner of the sprawling exhibit hall and moved to it.

Sitting with her Caramel Macchiato, Sandra looked at the ingredients list on the energy drink bottle that Ray put down on the small round table. "Careful with this stuff," she said, "there's enough five-syllable chemicals in it to make you short-circuit."

"You mean void?" he asked as he sat down.

"That, too. So what are you really doing here? Did you come all the way to Vegas to make the point that the use of drones is getting out of control? Because I still disagree with you."

"Actually, no. I didn't even know that there was a

drone show until I checked in last night at the hotel," he said. "I'm here for the hacker convention. My chief hacker, Dugout, has been on my case for a couple of years now to come. He says he always learns new tricks here. And he reconnects with the hacker underworld types he uses sometimes."

"Dugout?" she asked.

"It's his hacker handle. His real name is Douglas Carter the third, so in prep school they called him Trip. He hated it. But he's a big Red Sox fan and he's helped them with a software program, so they let him sit in the dugout once. Hence, Dugout."

"I won't even ask how you gave a hacker a security clearance. You guys at PEG clearly have different standards than we do at the Agency," she said.

"He's a national asset, helped us a bundle already. But you're right, we look for the iconoclasts, the force multiplier geniuses. Want to avoid groupthink. That's how we can have such great analytical capability with fewer than a hundred staff. We beat the pants off the Agency analysts every time, even though we are way outnumbered," Ray said. "I've had Dugout create some software to look for patterns on the thousands of hours of video you guys collect from your birds."

A small, round drone with four rotors flew up and hovered above the café. Three others quickly followed. Then the formation of four mini-helicopters formed into a line and began slowly to move down the length of the exhibit hall like a flock of ducks in a line abreast. Sandra and Ray watched and then, without commenting on the flying flock, resumed their conversation.

"Here's what he has found so far. He's detected four

new patterns. First, the HVIs don't seem to be meeting in buildings anymore. He thinks they know we look for meetings and then we blow up the buildings. So they are meeting in cars. One car goes to a meeting spot and an HVI gets out, the car keeps going. Then another car with the second HVI comes along and the first guy hops in. The meet occurs in a car in a crowded neighborhood with lots of potential collateral damage if we strike. This way the classical signature of a meeting that you look for never happens."

"We do have a fixation on blowing up buildings," she admitted. "But we also pick off HVIs in cars if they are alone on a road. Meetings in cars parked in crowded market streets will give us a problem. What else?"

"The second thing is related. He thinks that now when HVIs do go into huts or houses, they seem to exit from a nearby house. He thinks they are using tunnels. They know we are watching them and we like to blow up the buildings they are in, so they go in one building then walk through a tunnel to a building nearby but beyond the blast range if we detonate the first building," Ray said.

"Okay, we can look for signs of that, maybe use our multispectral cameras to look for indications of tunnels," Sandra replied. "Sometimes a tunnel under a dirt field will show up as a different color, a line, on a multispectral image. We don't have a lot of birds with cameras like that, but . . ."

Ray continued. "Dugout also thinks that the terrorists aren't afraid of single Predators anymore. They seem to have figured out that we fly a lot of solo missions that are just recce, just looking for targets. When we are going to strike, there are two or even more birds circling. One to attack and one to film the strike, or a backup to fire missiles at anybody that shows up to rescue people from the rubble."

"That's an easy fix," she said, "we start running a few lethal solo flights so we're not so predictable."

"Yeah, well if you kill the targets, how are they going to spread the word that solo drone flights can be lethal, too?" Ray asked.

"Not a problem," she replied. "There are always squirters."

"Squirters?" he asked.

"That's what we call the guys who survive the detonation and run out of the rubble. That happens a lot. We usually pick them off on the run, but we can let a few go," Sandra suggested. "Dugout sounds like he's good. What's his fourth idea?"

Ray casually looked around to confirm that they were still the only ones at the little round tables in the café. "He thinks that the bird that you lost recently was lured into an ambush, shot down by a Stingerlike missile fired from a mountaintop above the Predator."

Sandra drained her cup. "Yeah, Colonel Parsons came to that conclusion, too, about the Stinger. Actually, probably a Russian knockoff like the SA-24. But Erik didn't suggest it was a setup, a lure. That would indicate a level of sophistication, of premeditation."

"That's the point. My analysts think it could be indicative of a terrorist response to the drones that is not just smarter defensive tactics, but going on the offense against them."

Sandra laughed. "Yeah, well good luck with that.

That's the beauty of drones. There's not a lot you can do to fight back against them and even if you get off a lucky shot like that one . . . the pilot, Major Dougherty, went out and played a round of golf after his plane was shot down. Let's go over to the Homeland Security Department display. I want to see what Coast Guard and Border Patrol are showing off."

As they moved down the aisle, they passed a scale model of what looked like the large Reaper drone made by the U.S. firm General Atomics. The sixty-five-foot-long giant had a jet engine mounted on top of the fuselage, just in front of a V-shaped tail. The sign in front read CHINA AVIATION CORPORATION UCAV MODEL 7. Four Arab-looking men in military uniforms stood looking at the mock-up and talking with two Chinese salesmen. "This is the submarine-hunter version. It can drop sonar buoys and torpedoes," one of the salesman said. "Also comes in an air-to-air fighter aircraft version with missiles to shoot down fighter planes, or other drones."

"That's a U.S. Reaper D the Chinese are selling," Sandra said to Ray as they walked by.

"Yeah, they hacked in and got the plans for the modified Reaper," Ray replied. "But it looks like they have improved upon it."

A flat screen at one of the booth displays was showing WWN. The BREAKING NEWS logo appeared and both Sandra and Ray instinctively walked closer to hear the newscaster. ". . . exclusive film of the orphanage blown up by the American drone inside Afghanistan three days ago. We warn you that this report from WWN war correspondent Bryce Duggan is disturbing."

The screen switched to a young American standing in front of the charred ruin of a house. "We have been told this building used to be an orphanage. What is clear is that children lived here, or rather died here. This video, provided to WWN by a local tribal elder, shows what is definitely this same building still smoking after a fire and here, inside, on the video are what appear to be the partially burned bodies of little boys, many of whom appeared to be in their sleeping bags when they died.

"We arrived two days ago in time to see the burials, which took place at sunset hours after what several of the locals told us was a drone attack. The tribal elder also gave us a video of what appears to be a U.S. drone firing missiles into what is almost certainly this area. We cannot account for the authenticity of these tapes, but we interviewed numerous villagers, including some we chose at random, all of whom confirm that they heard and then saw a drone overhead prior to what they say was a missile attack on this house. They say there are no al Qaeda people here, no terrorists, but they do say that they themselves would do harm to the Americans who did this attack on them, what they call this unprovoked attack. The American Embassy in Islamabad would not comment to this reporter, saying only that they do not discuss intelligence, and referring us to Washington. Bryce Duggan, World Wide News, reporting tonight from Waziristan."

Sandra Vittonelli's secure mobile phone vibrated in the left pocket of her jeans. It was Erik. "Boss, sorry to bug you on your day off. We have a problem. Looks like we may have had some collateral on that strike against those Qazzani HVIs on the AfPak border. And Dr. Burrell's office just called to say he wants you and Mr. Bowman on a videoconference with him at noon our time. Where are you now?"

# 16

TUESDAY, OCTOBER 13
U.S. CAPITOL BUILDING
WASHINGTON, DC

They were up high, inside the dome of the Capitol. Ray Bowman's legislative liaison officer had arranged for their black Chevy Suburban to be cleared through two gatehouses, allowed to drive onto the Capitol Plaza and then to park behind the main exterior staircase just below the Rotunda. He then escorted Ray and Sandra Vittonelli quickly through the magnetometer and the Capitol Police, past a tour group, to a small elevator door behind a velvet rope. The tiny elevator had shot them from the ground level of the cavernous U.S. Capitol building to the most secure hearing room on Capitol Hill, and the highest, built into the side of Bulfinch's great dome.

The hearing room was used for briefings, but not public ones, only secret and top secret. There were no seats for the press or public, no television cameras from C-SPAN. Before Ray and Sandra were allowed into the room, Capitol Police took their phones and then ran wands over them to make sure there were no other mobile devices in their pockets. Inside, there were only Members and staff of the House Permanent Select Committee on Intelligence (HPSCI), or as it was known around town, "hipsy." The committee were Members of the House of Representatives, elected to Congress from across the nation and sworn to secrecy about the workings of the U.S. intelligence agencies that they monitored on behalf of the House.

All the Members of the House were running for re-election in three weeks, but instead of campaigning back home, they were still in session because the President and Congress had not yet come to an agreement on a budget to fund the government in the fiscal year that had begun two weeks earlier. While the Congressional leaders tried to work out a compromise, some Members held hearings hoping to get media attention back in their districts. Unfortunately for the Intelligence Committee, its hearings were not televised. That combination of facts made the Members of the Committee somewhat out of sorts.

The Chair was Roberta Levinson, a liberal Democrat from Massachusetts. The legislative liaison officer had called her "Bobbie the Bitch" during his prebrief in the Suburban as they had driven up to Capitol Hill from Ray's offices in Foggy Bottom on the banks of the Potomac. Ray had told him that was an inappropriate comment. Levinson may have come from the same party as the President, but she was a bit further to the left of the political spectrum than the Commander-in-Chief.

As soon as Bowman and Vittonelli were seated, Congresswoman Levinson opened the hearing with a gavel.

"We're here today as part of our ongoing oversight function on the use of armed Unmanned Aerial Vehicles by the U.S. Intelligence Community." Some Members were still drifting in and getting seated. "We requested two senior officials with responsibility for the operation of the program and we have with us today Raymond Bowman, Director of the Policy Evaluation Group, and Sandra Vittonelli, a CIA officer assigned to the multiagency Global Coordination Center for UAV Operations. Welcome."

Ray's staff had set up video screens on which he intended to show the Members some film of recent attacks. "Madame Chairwoman, thank you for inviting us to brief you. I thought perhaps the best way to reveal what the program is like on a day-to-day basis would be to show you a short video, condensing into a few minutes the days of careful reconnaissance and consideration that go into a decision to attack a High Value Individual or a signature-based facility on the High Payoff Target List."

The Chair cut him off. "Thank you, Mr. Bowman, if you will leave the video, staff can watch it later, obviously only in the vault." Ray did not like the way this briefing was going and it had only just begun. "I think our time can be more effectively used by getting answers to some of the questions I know my colleagues on the Committee have, and I know I have. Let me start by calling on Congressman O'Connell, the gentleman from California."

Sandra Vittonelli had never been at a Congressional briefing or hearing before. She found herself both charmed and intimidated by the formality of it, the wood paneling, the gavel, the formal language, and the fact that the Members sat behind a long curved, wooden dais raised three feet above the witness table. But the formality and courtesy quickly ended.

"Thank you, Madam Chairwoman," Paul O'Connell began. "I want to start with how it was possible, if you actually do all this reconnaissance and review before killing people, how it was possible that you bombed an orphanage and killed over a dozen little boys. Can you explain that to us? Do you want us to show you a video, the WWN video of their charred, little bodies?" The legislative liaison officer sitting behind Sandra slipped her a handwritten note, "From Napa Valley, and overly fond of the wine."

Ray took the incoming spear. "Congressman, we have investigated the incident you refer to, including an independent examination by our Inspector General. We do not believe it was an orphanage. We believe it was a trap designed to discredit the UAV program."

Congressman O'Connell leaned forward, his chin almost touching the microphone in front of him. "Well, it certainly did discredit the program. You didn't have checks and balances, internal controls in place to notice that there were a bunch of little boys in the building?"

"Congressman, our review indicates that there was a tunnel leading out from the compound," Ray began. "That tunnel was undoubtedly used by the terrorists to smuggle the children in without our seeing them and to permit the terrorists to leave without being detected. We discovered that tunnel after the attack using one of the few drones we have with a multispectral camera and ground-penetrating radar. It was not flyable when the attack occurred. Our requests for funding for such UAVs were severely reduced."

The Chair interrupted. "Mr. Bowman, do not attempt to blame the failure of the program to do its due diligence on this target on some funding decision that the Congress made."

Ray regretted his response, but did not reveal it. "Congresswoman, if I may, we believe that this heinous, despicable act by the terrorists demonstrates both the depths to which they will go to discredit the UAV program and, therefore, how much they fear the program, how effective it is against them."

Congressman O'Connell tapped his microphone to resume his questioning. "It's effective, all right. Effective in alienating the very population we have been trying to influence, trying to turn away from terrorists. Your attack on the orphanage caused days of mass street demonstrations and protests in Afghanistan, Tajikistan, and Pakistan, attempts to storm our diplomatic missions, probably led to some of the suicide bomber attacks and roadside bombs that have killed our troops. This is what happens when you are not on the scene, when you are observing from thousands of miles away."

Sandra felt a need to respond welling up inside her. She was there to provide Ray with technical details, but she thought she was coming under personal attack. "Congressman, no unit of Special Forces hiding up in the hills nearby and helicoptering in to raid that compound could have seen better than the UAVs. From above, we had a complete view of the compound that no one on the ground could have achieved. We were able to follow two separate targets as they drove to the compound. We confirmed through High Definition Imagery and Facial Recognition Software that both men were on the HVI list approved by senior level policy, intelligence, and legal officials from six departments and agencies. They were there."

"Not when you fired missiles at that compound," O'Connell shot back, almost screaming into the microphone. "Not when you murdered those boys."

"Congressman, we learned a lesson from that attack," Sandra replied, her face reddening. "We knew there was always a risk that the targets might escape through tunnels. We were willing to accept that. It did not occur to us that they would kidnap children and sneak them into a compound and then lure us to attack it. Maybe our minds were just not perverted enough to think of that. All of us involved in the program deeply regret the deaths of those innocent kids, but while it may have been our missiles that killed them, it was the terrorists who were the murderers, not us. If you want to yell at murderers, I think you are going to have to go to Afghanistan."

The hearing room fell silent. O'Connell pushed away from the dais and leaned back in his chair glaring down at Vittonelli. "The Chair calls upon the Ranking Minority member, Mr. Scott of Virginia," Levinson said.

"We are all, of course, in agreement that we have to deal with these terrorists," Congressman Scott began. "But I think we are all a little concerned that this new technology may have made it just a little too easy to kill.

So easy that you have stopped trying to apprehend them and put them on trial. And when you capture terrorists, you can collect all sorts of useful documents, as we saw with the raid on bin Laden's house. And you can get them to talk, as we saw with the advanced interrogation techniques used on Khalid Sheik Mohammad, the mastermind of 9/11."

Ray looked at Sandra, like a baseball player indicating that this was his ball to catch. "Congressman Scott, we have not abandoned arresting terrorists. Certainly in this country or any cooperating country which has control of its territory, we prefer to do arrests. But there are nations who will not cooperate and there are nations who would, but they do not control all of their own territory sufficiently to give us an environment in which it would be safe to try to perform arrests without placing an American arrest team at unacceptable risk."

Congressman Scott looked unconvinced. "Well, I just can't remember the last time when the United States actually staged an arrest raid to get a big terrorist target. See the thing is, when you say that it's too risky, the result is that you have decided to implement the death penalty instead. And you do that without any kind of trial, any kind of defense, any kind of transparent, public process. It's just the kind of government activity that the Founding Fathers, many of them from my state, opposed and tried to prevent through the Constitution. Now I know you two aren't lawyers and while I am, I am no Constitutional scholar, but this worries me."

After her last intervention, Sandra looked to Ray for a nod before commenting. She got it. "Well, actually, Congressman, I am a lawyer, graduate of the University of Virginia Law School, as I believe you are." She waited for that remark to hit home. "But also like you, I do not pretend to be a Constitutional scholar. We do have them, however, in the Justice Department and the White House General Counsel's office, and they have examined this question in great detail. Their view, which we can provide in writing, is that the Supreme Court has held that killing enemy combatants is not a part of the criminal justice system. On the traditional battlefield, there are no lawyers reviewing things before they happen. In our program, there are."

The Chairwoman seemed agitated. "Ms. Vittonelli, I think you have put your finger on part of the problem that makes so many of us up here uneasy. For you, the whole world is the battlefield and anyone is an enemy combatant. And as a lawyer, a graduate of Harvard Law, I think that you and the Justice Department have overconstrued the Supreme Court case about the Nazi soldiers in World War II."

Before she could respond, Congressman O'Connell was waving his hand at the Chair for recognition. "Madam Chairwoman, I think you are exactly on point. They not only can declare anyone an enemy combatant, they have declared American citizens as enemy combatants and killed them without a grand jury, a defense lawyer, a judge, a jury of peers, or an appeals court."

Ray put his right hand on Sandy's arm to indicate she should not respond. He did. "Congressman, to the best of our knowledge only four American citizens have been killed by the program and they were self-declared members of al Qaeda. They were engaged in planning the killing of Americans. They had been involved in terrorist attacks that did kill Americans. If we waited to the day when we could arrest them and give them their Miranda rights, there would be more Americans dead now.

"If an American in 1943 moved to Germany and put on the Nazi uniform and fought U.S. troops, no one would think his American citizenship should make him invulnerable to U.S. bombing raids, or that our troops should have tried to separate him out from the Wehrmacht and arrest him during a battle. With Americans who join al Qaeda and then scheme to kill their fellow citizens, they are a threat in being. Our first responsibility is to defend the other Americans they are trying to kill. And the best way to do that under current circumstances is often to use the UAV program. If we did otherwise, this Committee would, rightly, be criticizing us for not doing enough to protect Americans from terrorists."

Sandra was wondering if there were any Members on the committee who supported the program. If there were, they were being quiet, or absent. The Chair resumed her questioning. "This battlefield you keep referring to, Mr. Bowman, where is it? What countries are you operating in today? How many aircraft do you fly a day?"

Ray asked Sandra to respond. "On a given day, like today, we have probably fifty UAVs take off. We are flying UAVs over Afghanistan, Pakistan, Iran, Somalia, Yemen, Libya, Mali, Turkey, Iraq, the Philippines, and parts of the Indian Ocean. Some of those are armed, some are reconnaissance," she said.

"What about Mexico and the Caribbean?" another Congresswoman asked.

"There are UAV flights there, for counternarcotics purposes, but they are run by the Coast Guard and Customs under a separate Homeland Security program," Ray replied. "They are not under the Intelligence Finding signed by the President."

"What about Vienna?" Congressman O'Connell asked. "Are you trying, Ms. Vittonelli, to hide from the Committee the fact that you staged an attack in downtown Vienna, in the capital of a friendly country, where an arrest would have been possible? Where instead you killed and injured innocent civilians and destroyed a five-star hotel?"

How does he know that? Sandra asked herself. The Vienna attack was under a special Presidential authority and only eight of the leaders of Congress had been briefed. Besides, the question was where are you flying today. "Congressman, I answered the question that was asked, truthfully."

"Madam Chairwoman, I ask that we dismiss the witnesses and go into Executive Session to discuss whether we have had a case of perjury here, an intentional attempt to mislead the Congress," O'Connell hissed.

Ray looked at the Chair. She was one of the eight leaders who had been informed of the Vienna operation, in advance of its being carried out. They exchanged nods.

"I think this briefing is over," the Chair intoned. "But I want to leave the Administration in no doubt that there is concern up here. When you are launching fifty killer drones every day over a dozen countries, you are going to make mistakes. You are going to get America in trouble. And you are slipping into something potentially dangerous, where it is all too easy to kill and killing becomes like a computer game. Think about what our attitude will be when other nations do this. What would we think about a North Korean drone killing somebody in Seoul or a Chinese drone killing a Chinese dissident in San Francisco? Be very, very careful with this program. We will be watching. Meeting adjourned." She dropped the gavel.

Ray's legislative liaison officer moved the two witnesses quickly out of the room and to the elevator, avoiding any opportunity for Congressman O'Connell to say something more to Sandra Vittonelli, or vice versa. "Next time we are going to Little Big Horn, can you give me a better heads-up?" Ray said as the elevator descended. As the doors of the elevator parted, a bright light shone in. A television news camera crew had been waiting, along with a gaggle of about six reporters. Somebody on the Committee had leaked the fact of the top secret hearing. They had set up a press ambush. Sensing from the camera crew's presence that somebody important might be coming out of the slightly hidden elevator, a crowd of tourists had gathered.

Ray whispered to Sandra, "disappear" and then he pushed out into the mob scene and began to talk to a reporter to draw the media attention to him. Sandra Vittonelli, hoping to avoid her picture being taken and her identity being made public, put her head down, brought her papers up close to her face and slipped into the crowd on the opposite side from Bowman. She found the Suburban still parked under the staircase. Inside, feeling secure behind the darkened windows, she turned on her secret level Blackberry. There was an e-mail from Colonel Erik Parsons. “We need a Kill Call this afternoon. The sooner the better.”

# 17

TUESDAY, OCTOBER 13
THE POLICY EVALUATION GROUP
NAVY HILL
WASHINGTON, DC

"We had been following the truck for four days, since it crossed the border from Kenya. Kenyan police gave us a tip," Erik spoke, looking into the video camera in Las Vegas. His image appeared on the central screen of the Policy Evaluation Group's conference room wall.

Raymond Bowman sat in the conference room where "Wild Bill" Donovan had met every day with his deputies during World War II. Donovan had run the first real American intelligence agency, the Office of Strategic Services, from the same building. Back then it took hours to send a cable to an office in Europe. Ray and Sandra had driven straight down Constitution Avenue, from the Capitol to Foggy Bottom's Navy Hill at the end of that broad boulevard, in less than five minutes and were now sitting in Donovan's old OSS conference room watching a live image of a truck near Mogadishu,

Somalia. Erik Parsons in Vegas was on a screen-in screen.

"Then we lost it two days ago," Erik continued. "Just found it again yesterday, close to Mog."

"How the hell did we lose it?" Sandra Vittonelli asked. She sat next to Ray looking at half a dozen flat screens beaming in images from UAVs and from the operations centers of other U.S. departments and agencies on the videoconference call.

"We think they did a switch on us when it stopped for the night at one of the Shabab rebel camps. We followed the wrong truck when it left in the morning," Erik admitted.

"What makes us think it's a truck bomb?" Ray asked.

The face on the screen showing CIA headquarters fielded the question. "The Kenyans raided a warehouse up near the Somali border, found it full of bomb-making material. One of the Shabab guys they arrested gave up about the truck, ah, under questioning. Gave us the plate and the names of the drivers. Two of them, alternating."

The red light came on next to the Justice Department screen. Ray hit the control so that the lawyer from Justice could be heard next by everyone on the videoconference. "That's not going to be good enough for us. You admit you have a confusion about which truck is which. Besides, we are just not sure over here how this qualifies. There is no HVI identified as a driver or passenger of the truck. We don't see how destroying the truck would irreparably harm the Shabab."

"It qualifies," Erik responded from the Global Coordination Center in Las Vegas, "because it is an imminent terrorist attack. They didn't pack that truck full of ammonium nitrate and fuel oil to heat their house or fertilize a field."

The one-star General at the Pentagon signaled he wanted to contribute. "We have a JSOC team in Mog advising the Ugandan Army peacekeepers from the African Union. The Ugandans snuck a guy into that camp last night and he swiped the truck with a kit that our guys gave him. Came back this morning, definitely a truck bomb. This truck that we are looking at, no confusion with some other truck, this one that is on the screen now."

The State Department member of the meeting wanted to ask a question. "If we got somebody inside who confirmed that it was a truck bomb, why didn't he leave a timed charge on the thing to blow it up after he got out of camp?"

"Collateral damage," the General replied. "You see where it is parked now. That may be a pro-Shabab village there on the outskirts of Mog, but it is a village. With women and children and possibly noncombatant adult males. We can't strike while it is in the village."

"I don't understand something," the Justice Department lawyer said. "Why are we talking about using a Predator strike? Why don't you shoot the tires out? Why don't we just tell the Ugandan peacekeepers or the Somali government forces to go get the thing or set up a roadblock?"

"Our estimate is that if the drivers think that they are about to be stopped, they will detonate. If we ask the Ugandans to shoot at it, the thing might go off. That would wipe out the troops at the road block and probably everything else around," the General answered.

"That's why we want to wait until it is back on a road and then strike it when it is in the middle of nowhere."

Ray and Sandra were examining a hard copy map of the area around the war-riddled Somali capital of Mogadishu. They had found the village where the truck was about fifty kilometers outside of the city. "Looks like there is a fairly open stretch of highway between the village and where the urban sprawl begins," Sandra observed.

"That's where we suggest you hit it," the General replied.

As they watched the screen, the truck was clearly visible in the early morning light. It began to move out of the village and onto the road. In front of and behind it were open pickups. "Erik, zoom in on the pickups," Sandra ordered. Everyone on the conference call was watching the same video feed, which was being sent to all of the departments on the Kill Call.

"Oh, shit," Sandra said into an open microphone. The image on the screen was of a flatbed truck filled with at least four women and perhaps as many as eight children. As the image panned to the lead vehicle, they saw an identical image, a dozen more civilians.

"Can't hit that," the Justice lawyer announced. "If that truck bomb is as big as you think, if you hit the truck, it's taking out all those civilians in the trucks in front and behind it."

"He's got that right," Ray said to Sandra with his microphone on mute so that the other sites could not hear him. "Looks like the bad guys have figured out our rules and are using human shields."

The small convoy turned onto the main road for Mogadishu and began to pick up speed. "We've only got about twenty minutes or so before they get into built-up areas. If we are going to hit it, we need to do so when it's on this road," the General announced.

With the microphone still off, Ray said, "We better call Winston." He picked up a handset and hit a button for the office of the National Security Advisor. Sandra saw his expression change when someone at the other end answered. "Then could you please ask him to step out of the dinner for a minute. We're on a Kill Call." He hit the Speaker button so that Sandra could hear when Dr. Burrell came on the line.

"Ray, I hear you two got slaughtered this afternoon at hipsy. Not good," Burrell began. "We better be extra careful on these strikes. What's this one look like?"

Ray let the remark about the House Intel Committee go, for now. "We have a large truck bomb on the road into Mogadishu. It was made by Shabab, the local al Qaeda affiliate. In a few minutes it will be driving into a built-up area where we won't be able to take it out without causing all sorts of collateral damage from our missile and the truck bomb itself going off as a secondary explosion.

"Right now it's on an open road in the middle of nowhere, but the trouble is that it's being escorted by two trucks, each of which has about a dozen women and children."

"Well, sounds like you are out of Schlitz, Ray," Burrell replied.

"Well, sir, it's a matter of what is worse, killing

people who seem to be escorting this bomb to its destination or allowing it to go off and killing maybe ten times more innocent people," Sandra interjected.

"Yes, but it won't be us who will have killed the people when the bomb goes off and it would be us if we strike the truck. And after the orphanage fiasco . . ." Burrell replied. "Besides, it doesn't sound to me like there is an imminent threat of a terrorist attack *against Americans*."

"There is a UN compound at the other end of this road," Ray replied. "You remember how many people were killed at the UN headquarters in Baghdad by a truck bomb just like this. Not sure how we explain that we just sat by and watched. May even be some Americans there. There's also the African Union compound and the Somali government buildings, a big marketplace, lots of possible targets."

"Ray, I have to get back to this dinner with the Israelis. Here's what I suggest, you warn the UN and the others and suggest they evacuate possible targets. You do what you think best after that, but under no circumstances are we using the Predators in any strike that kills civilians. Not now. It's getting way too hot. Gotta go."

"Schlitz?" Sandra asked when Burrell had signed off. Ray rolled his eyes. He hit the microphone on button. "We're back." He glanced up at the image of the trucks moving down the road. "Doesn't look like anything has changed. CIA, State, DOD, can you all go through your channels to warn the UN, Somalia, African Union? We are not authorized to fire because of the risk of the civilians being killed. Anybody got any ideas?"

The conference link was silent except for the humming from the microphones' static. "If we don't do something, some of the guys on our side of this fight are going to get killed pretty soon. I don't know that they can evacuate everything that is a possible target, not fast enough," the General replied.

The red light came on next to Erik Parson's screen. Ray hit a button that connected his audio feed from Las Vegas to the group. "I want to confirm my orders," Erik began. "I am not authorized to fire where there is a risk of hitting civilians?"

"That is correct," Sandra answered.

"Is there any rule against scaring civilians or bombing dirt?" Erik asked.

"Nice," Ray replied. "No, Colonel, you may scare civilians and you may bomb nothingness. Just do not strike anywhere that could cause civilian casualties from our missiles."

TUESDAY, OCTOBER 13
THE GLOBAL COORDINATION CENTER
OPERATIONS ROOM
CREECH AFB, NEVADA

In the GCC, Erik Parsons walked about five meters from the videoconference site to the cubicle in which Sergeant Rod Miller and Major Bud Walker were flying the two Predators over Somalia. "Sergeant, step aside. Let me fly that baby for a minute," Erik said, replacing the pilot. He grabbed the joystick and put the first Predator into a steep dive from ten thousand feet.

The image on the screen showed the ground rushing up at the camera. Then the road quickly appeared on the screen and the three-truck convoy ahead. The Predator flew low over the convoy and banked right. The faces of the women and children on the truck showed clearly in high definition, faces of surprise and horror. "Christ, Colonel, you got that sucker down to one thousand feet off the ground. They'll shoot you down," Sergeant Miller said from behind him.

"Can't shoot me down. I'm not in Somalia. I'm in Vegas," Erik replied as he hit the toggle switch on the side of the joystick to arm the Hellfire missiles on the Predator. "Bud, look at the image from Bird Two. What's in front of these three trucks?"

Bird Two was the second Predator, operating as a reconnaissance spotter, flying at twelve thousand feet, above Stinger range. Major Walker panned the camera out ahead of the convoy. "Nothing on the road this early. I can see three or four clicks ahead. Nothing on the road or on either side of it but dirt, sir."

Erik quickly brought the Predator around for a second pass. The trucks had stopped. People were jumping out, running. Four men were standing still shooting rifles, probably AK-47s, up toward the incoming Predator. Erik hit the Launch button on the joystick once, moved the Predator slightly left and fired again, again to the left and fired, and a fourth time. He then pulled the joystick back hard, forcing the Predator into a steep upward climb to the right of the road.

"Give me the video feed from Bird Two on the Big Board!" Erik yelled.

The image on the screen showed four smoke trails as

Hellfire missiles from Bird One streaked over the convoy. In seconds, the missiles hit less than a kilometer ahead of the trucks. Two hit the road, two others hit just off the pavement, one on either side. A wide wall of brown smoke and dust rose up across the path of the convoy. Erik brought Bird One around and began another dive toward the now stationary trucks. It was out of missiles as it passed overhead, this time at fifteen hundred feet. The camera showed that the trucks in front and back were empty of their earlier passengers. What looked like as many as eight men were shooting upward, but even they were running away from the road as they shot. The images from Bird Two showed a cluster of people, the women and children passengers from the trucks, hunkering down in a dry river bed about four meters below the level of the road and about six hundred meters to the north of it.

In Washington, Ray watched with a broad smile spread across his face. He turned to the Pentagon screen. "Are those people, those civilians now a safe distance away from the target, General?"

"Safe enough for us to strike? I don't think we need to. That road ahead is so badly cratered, that truck isn't going to get through. Besides, when we told the African Union about the convoy just now, they dispatched a squad on a Hip helicopter. Now that the bad guys have abandoned the trucks, the Ugandans ought to be able to land nearby and render safe the bomb."

As the General spoke, the camera from Bird Two zoomed out toward the horizon and focused in on a helicopter moving slowly toward the scene of the explosions. The armed men running from the trucks heard the noise of the old helicopter and also looked in its direction. One of the men stopped running, took a small black box from his backpack, and lay down in the dirt. Erik was bringing Bird One around again to further scare the shooters away from the vehicles, as the truck bomb detonated, sending an orange flame and then a thick black column of smoke rushing into the air above the convoy. On the two screens showing images from the two Predators, one at two thousand and one at twelve thousand feet, the explosion erupted violently, silently.

Erik struggled to pull the Predator up quickly enough that it would not fly into the concussive wave sweeping out from the truck. The aircraft rocked violently, but began to climb. Then it shook and dove quickly down and to the right. "I think you lost a chunk of the left wing, sir," Sergeant Miller said. "Going down."

Erik still had video feed and he looked ahead of the path of the aircraft, hoping to bring it down where the impact would do no damage to anyone on the ground. There was nothing but sand and rock in the view screen. A lone tree stood in the distance, but the aircraft was not going to make it that far. The camera showed dirt rising up quickly just before the screen went blank.

Erik stood up and turned to Major Walker. "Bud, blow up my aircraft, or what's left of it."

On the Big Board, there was now only one image, from Bird Two. What it showed on close up was that Bird One had had a rough landing, with both wings breaking off, but remarkably, the fuel tank had not yet exploded. Then the image zoomed out. A Hellfire zoomed off the left wing of Bird Two, soaring ahead of the Predator, the smoke briefly clouding the image from the camera. In seconds, the wreck of Bird One exploded, leaving nothing large enough to salvage, nothing of value to anyone trying to learn about the aircraft.

"Well done, Colonel," Sandra's voice from Washington boomed over the speakers in the GCC. A cheer rose up from the twenty pilots on the floor.

Erik had walked back to his desk and placed the conference call headset back on. He spoke into it. "Kill Call Closed."

# 18

TUESDAY, OCTOBER 13
CAMINO AL NORTE BUSINESS CENTER
NORTH LAS VEGAS, NEVADA

"I'm afraid the doctor does not take walk-ins," the receptionist said. "You will have to have a referral and then request an appointment."

"Tell her Mustang is here," he said. "Go ahead. Ask her if she wants to ride a Mustang."

The receptionist was a temp and clearly uncomfortable. She thought that taking a job in a psychiatrist's office at night was going to be strange and it had been ever since she sat down.

"Doctor," she said into the telephone, "a man named Mustang is here and wants to see you and he won't go away."

"Oh, dear," Jennifer Parsons replied on the telephone, from inside her office. "Well, then ask him if I can ride him."

Hearing that, the receptionist hung up the telephone,

picked up her bag, and walked quickly out of the office. "You people are just not good Christians," she said as she slammed the door to the suite.

"You know, she's right," Jennifer said, standing in the doorframe of her office. "We're not. And I do need to find a new temp agency."

"Or a more devout husband," Erik Parsons replied.

"Never," Jennifer replied, putting her arms around his waist. "I like my Mustang, my horse." She gave him one of her long, slow kisses. "How was your day at the office, dear? Did you push lots of pieces of paper?"

"It was good. I think we saved some lives today," he said as he lifted her up and then sat her on the receptionist's desk. "But I crashed and burned, destroyed my airplane."

Jennifer folded her legs behind him. "That's okay, Mustang, they'll give you a new toy tomorrow."

The door flew open. "I forgot my cell phone," the ex-receptionist said. Jennifer and Erik leaped off the desk. "You people don't need a shrink, you need a preacher. And a cold shower," she said as she stormed out a second time.

"Buzzkill," Erik said to her on her way out.

"Let's go downstairs," Jen replied. "Le Croupier is still open. They make great mojitos."

"If that's what the doctor is prescribing for my condition," he replied.

"It's part one of a two-part therapy," she said. "The second part requires you to get in a hot tub. Later."

They took a booth in the back of the bar and grille on the first floor of the office building. Despite the half-off prices, the crowd was thin. Most people still preferred to go to the casinos for their drinking, free drinking if they were gambling.

"Did you really crash and burn?" Jennifer asked.

"Yeah, but these things only run around four million. It's not like I crashed a B-2, or even an F-16," he said, sipping his mojito. "You're right. They will give me a new one tomorrow. Several."

"So what's the problem? What brings you to the shrink's office today?" she asked. "Or were you just feeling horny because you were a hero?" She knew not to ask how he had saved people's lives, but she did not doubt it.

Erik laughed. "No, I'm okay. It's just that after the orphanage, things are a little different. More tense. We actually got turned down by the White House for the first time today."

"But you went ahead anyway?" she asked.

"Well, kinda. Let's just say I found a way of proceeding that was consistent with the Commander's Intent," he said. "But I am a little worried about Bruce. He thinks it's his fault those kids got killed. I think he's drinking too much, but I don't want to put him on report. That would tank his shot at promotion to O-5."

"But you can counsel him, can't you, without it going in his jacket?" she asked.

"Sure, and I have," he replied. "It's just, it's more than Bruce. It's like something's shifted. Like the bad guys are figuring us out, like we're not quite invulnerable anymore."

"Look, honey, you always said you had to fight against this whole idea that you all are the Avenging

Angels who can throw lightning bolts down from your home in the sky," Jennifer said. "You're not invulnerable and you do fly real weapons that can hurt real people. You may have to remind your guys of that every once in a while, but I am still much happier having you fly your drones than when you were flying the F-16. If you crashed and burned one of those, you might have been a crispy critter."

"Yeah, well, I miss the real cockpit," he replied.

A young man in a blue blazer, sitting at the bar by himself, finished his 7 and 7, put down a ten, and walked out. Jen watched him through the bar's window as he got into a Cadillac XTS. "I'm thinking about looking at the new Caddy to replace my Ford," Jennifer said to her husband. "Have you seen it?"

"No, I love my Camaro and I'm gonna take you back to my place in it, with the top down. Let's go check out the hot tub."

TUESDAY, OCTOBER 13
COPPER HILLS RANCH
KYLE CANYON, NEVADA

Yuri Poderev did not like the sun. He was happier now that it had set. Bright sunlight made it hard for him to think clearly. It distracted him. He liked the night, when it was as if a noise went away. To deal with the Nevada sun, he had bought black-out shades and curtains for the rooms where he and Mykola Zatonsky had set up their equipment. The rest of the house they had left largely untouched. It was isolated, well off the Kyle Canyon Road, slightly more than an hour's drive north from the

Las Vegas Strip. There was a large pool in the backyard inside the fence, and beyond that a horse barn twenty meters away. There were no horses.

There were satellite dishes, a T3 high capacity Internet connection from the phone company, and a separate fiber line from the cable company. Running the lines from the road had been costly, but there did not appear to be any budget constraints on this operation. The Pakistanis had money, apparently from some Arab supporters. The only Pakistani Yuri had met so far in the operation, the one who had just moved into a high-rise condominium in Las Vegas, was Ghazi Narwaz. And Ghazi appeared to be a very Westernized, global operator who seemed to be somewhat computer literate. He could not follow all that Yuri and Mykola had explained to him, but he seemed to have a far better understanding than most "tourists," as the two computer experts referred to the millions of Internet users who had no idea how either their computer or the networks worked.

Ghazi had been vague about his background, but he seemed to have operated in international businesses. Yuri knew that this operation was not the first time Ghazi had hired the Merezha organization, but the earlier projects were small, safe, profitable, personal. This thing now was huge and hugely dangerous. It was also bold and potentially fun, the sort of thing that Yuri and Mykola had always talked about doing. The thrill of it made them think less about the danger. And then there was the money. The Merezha was being handsomely paid for supporting Ghazi and his people. Yuri and Mykola would see a small portion of that, but even that portion was considerably more than they had ever made before and both men already had over ten million in dollars and gold scattered in banks around the world.

The beeping indicated a car had started down the long driveway. Mykola looked at the video monitor and then hit the control to open the gate that was set back where it could not be seen from the road. Ghazi appeared to be alone in the Cadillac XTS.

After he freshened up and poured himself a coffee, the two young Ukrainians showed Ghazi the Op Room, as they called the bedroom that they had converted into the computer war game playroom for this day's mission. "The Hawker took off over two hours ago from Karachi, allegedly bound for Almaty," Yuri explained. "And your guys say the Predator left Bagram almost three hours ago, so the two should be in the same general area by now."

"Yes, but this will only work if we know exactly what the Predator's target is so we can circle above it while it is circling below looking at the target for a while," Mykola added.

Ghazi looked over the two unkempt men, who looked like they had not washed or shaved or even changed clothes in days. He had noted the pizza crusts and Red Bull cans in the living room. He hoped they knew what they were doing. It had been expensive to lease the Hawker executive jet and even more costly to fit it out the way the Ukrainians had wanted. It was one thing for the Iranians to have done this kind of operation to get their hands on the RQ-170 U.S. stealth drone. Iran had a huge military and intelligence apparatus. The Qazzani Group and the Ukrainian Merezha were highly successful at complex criminal enterprises, but capturing a

U.S. drone was something few nation states could accomplish. "We are fairly sure we have lured them to the target. We fed them enough information that they should have sent one of their Predators out for a look and our source in the Pakistan Air Force says the flight is today."

TUESDAY, OCTOBER 13
GLOBAL COORDINATION CENTER,
OPERATIONS ROOM
CREECH AFB, NEVADA

The lone Predator was being flown by a senior noncommissioned officer. Officers flew strike missions and released weapons. Sometimes noncommissioned officers would fly the armed aircraft to the target zone and then hand it off to an officer. On unarmed reconnaissance flights the pilot for the entire mission was often someone like Sergeant Rod Miller, a twenty-six-year veteran of the U.S. Air Force. This flight seemed fairly routine to Miller. Take off out of Bagram in Afghanistan, fly over the Pakistani border into Northern Waziristan, and patrol an area where CIA sources said the Lashkar-e-Taiba had recently set up a training center.

The target was said to be an isolated cluster of about six buildings with a rifle range and an obstacle course. The mission was simply to find it and then circle it for several hours to develop a Pattern of Life, including whether there were women, children, or obvious civilians who could be considered collateral damage casualties. The presence of such potential casualties usually caused the target to be put on hold, even if it otherwise fit the pattern of a terrorist base sufficiently that it qualified for a possible future Signature Strike.

Once in the area, it took Miller only twenty minutes to find a remote cluster of buildings that seemed to fit the source's description. There were a few vehicles and some men wandering around the yards, but Miller also saw clothing drying on a line near what could be the living quarters. Maybe there were families staying there. Sergeant Miller kept the main electro-optical imaging camera staring at the target as he programmed the Predator autopilot to fly a wide circle ten thousand feet above. At that height, the small prop engine could usually not be heard and the chameleon electrostatic panels on the bottom of the wings and fuselage would appear the same color as the sky above, making visual identification difficult.

Miller asked Lieutenant Bill Wong, sitting next to him running a similar mission, to keep an eye on his screen while Miller went for a quick "bio break."

TUESDAY, OCTOBER 13
COPPER HILL RANCH
KYLE CANYON, NEVADA

"Better come in here, Nawarz," Yuri called out from the converted bedroom. "The Hawker has visual on the target."

Ghazi hurried down the hall from the kitchen, where he had been making coffee. "Yeah, they have also acquired the encrypted satellite links that the Pred is broadcasting, both the data streams and the video," Yuri said as Ghazi joined them. "We can't break the crypt though."

"Don't need to," Mykola said as he sat hunched over three screens. "Just have to jam the encrypted military grade Global Positioning System's signal from the satellite. And that we start to do now," he said as he hit the Enter/Return key on the Dell. "In two minutes, when the Pred still can't get the Military GPS signal, it will switch over to the public GPS channel. That's how they programmed it. And now we jam the data feed so that the pilot can't control the bird anymore. Zap!"

Yuri was standing behind Mykola, watching him and the screens. "The Hawker is circling at five thousand meters, so its radio signals are much more powerful than the commands on the same frequency coming down from the satellite in space. When the Pred can't communicate with its pilot, it will just circle. But after fifteen minutes, if it still can't phone home, it will break off the mission and fly home."

Ghazi looked at the computer screens, but could not understand the data that they were showing. "But we don't want it to go home. Home is the U.S. airbase at Bagram," he said.

"Don't worry," Mykola replied. "Fifteen minutes from now we will start beaming what looks like GPS data down from the Hawker, on the public GPS frequency, but much louder, much more power. We will drown out the real GPS signal and we will give the little Pred our own GPS data, which will be wrong, of course."

Ghazi sat down in an empty, ergonomic chair, webbed

and black. He was finally understanding the beauty of what the Ukrainians were doing, how it was that they guaranteed that they would capture a U.S. drone. "So, as of now that drone is not being controlled by its pilot? It's out of communications with him? And it's circling, trying to phone home? It can't get the military satellite signal to know where it is, so it is using the civilian GPS signal like my car gets from the satellites, right?"

"Exactly," Mykola. "Now we wait for when it decides to go home and then we make the west into the east."

TUESDAY, OCTOBER 13
GLOBAL COORDINATION CENTER,
OPERATIONS ROOM
CREECH AFB, NEVADA

"Miller, your bird's sick," Lieutenant Wong said to the sergeant as he returned from the bathroom. "Can't get through to it, but she's still circling and we're still getting the vid."

"What the fuck'd you do to it, sir?" Miller asked as he put his earphones back on. The sergeant was twenty-two years older than the officer and, despite the rank difference, tended to treat the younger man as he would his college-age son.

"I didn't touch it, Rod. Jeez man, this happens. The satellite radio for the control frequency died and the backup must have, too. So the bird will fly home. Without you doing shit. Just watch the camera feed, which you're still getting," Lieutenant Wong responded. "Chill, dude."

Sergeant Miller punched in an extension number on his keyboard and spoke into his headset. "Major Dougherty, I have a problem with my Pred. Data link is down and she will probably fly herself back to base here in a few minutes."

Bruce Dougherty was three rows above and behind him in the warren of cubicles. "Got it, Rod. Just keep an eye on her and alert Bagram. I got another problem on my hands right now. So, you handle it. It's unarmed."

"Roger that, sir," Sergeant Miller replied and leaned back in his chair to watch the Predator fly itself home. Exactly fifteen minutes after the command-control data link to the aircraft had been broken, the video images changed. The aircraft was no longer circling, staring at the camp below. The camera switched to a forward view of mountains lit by the last rays of the sun and the dark sky behind them.

"Wait a second," Miller said aloud. "The camera should be looking at the sunset, not mountains lit by it. This motherfucker is going the wrong direction."

WEDNESDAY, OCTOBER 14
MASHHAD AIRPORT
MASHHAD, PAKISTAN

The runway at Mashhad was only used a few times a day for the flights to Karachi. To get to Islamabad you had to go by bus. Occasionally a Pakistani Army helicopter or a Pak Air Force C-130 would land, but there was no military base at the airport. The local police and militia maintained security at the field, with a light hand.

The air traffic control tower was staffed twelve hours a day, but the workload was light.

By the time the on duty controller saw the Predator, it had already landed and was taxiing down the runway. He could not quite believe what he was seeing.

After taxiing to the end of the runway, the Predator just sat there, with its propeller spinning very slowly at the rear of the fuselage. Then the man in the tower noticed the cars and trucks driving across the grass toward the Predator and picked up his drop line to the police station. "We have a problem. There are vehicles on the runway that should not be there. And one of them is a drone."

He picked up his binoculars and focused in on the unmanned aircraft as its rotor slowed to a stop. Then he saw the bright light from the television cameraman standing near the little terminal building.

The young man in front of the camera was talking. "Behind me is what appears to be a U.S. drone. It has just landed at this civilian airport in Mashhad, Pakistan, apparently surprising local authorities. There were no Pakistani military or police here to greet it. In fact, at the moment, only WWN and some local people are at the scene. As you can see, the local men are hitting the drone with their shoes and look like they are getting ready to do some more serious damage.

"WWN was contacted by an anonymous source who suggested that we be here at Mashad airport today. When we got here we were given a piece of paper by a man who then drove away on a motorcycle. The paper said the Pakistani and Afghan people were fighting back against the drones that, they say, kill innocent people. It did not say how they were fighting the drones, but then this one landed and, well, it seems pretty clearly to have been taken out of service somehow, at least for now. Americans may not be the only ones who understand this new killing technology. Bryce Duggan, WWN, Mashhad, Pakistan."

# 19

WEDNESDAY, OCTOBER 14
828 NEW HAMPSHIRE AVENUE
FOGGY BOTTOM
WASHINGTON, DC

When Ray got up quietly from his bed, he saw on his Blackberry that it was almost four o'clock in the morning. It was about the only time of day when the neighborhood around his townhouse was quiet. When he came back to bed a few minutes later with two bottles of water, Sandra was awake. She had thrown off the sheet and the street lamp cast a soft orange light across her naked body. "You know we're crazy on all sorts of levels for doing this," Sandra whispered as he sat on the edge of the bed.

"No, I don't know that," Ray replied, as he slowly moved his hand along her leg. He spoke softly, slowly. "We're both single again. We work in different organizations. No rules broken, no harm, no foul. Just good conversation and great sex. Don't overthink it."

She sat up in the middle of the bed and leaned over

to kiss him, then moved behind him and put her head on his left shoulder and her legs around his waist. They sat there quietly for a moment looking together out of the second-story window at the quiet street below. She spoke into his ear, "It is great. And you're the only one who understands me, my job, where I am in life. It's all good, I just don't want . . ."

"Complications, I know. Look, I meant what I said that night at the Ritz. I like being single, too. I get that right now your career is central, mine is for me, too. Marriage didn't work for either of us and we don't need any more obligations than we've got. I'm fine with being in the moment, it's just that I've never been very good at it."

"You did a pretty good job of being in the moment a few hours ago," she laughed. "I like what we've got. We're so much alike, I mean aside from the fact that I'm short and Italian and you're tall and WASPy." She rolled over and sat on his stomach, straddling his wide frame, looking into his eyes. She slipped her fingers slowly through the hair on his chest. "It's good. We're a good pair. Neither one of us would ever have been happy breeding, raising kids in some dreadful suburban wasteland, punching clocks, sitting in commuter traffic. I'd have gone mad and become an axe murderer."

"Some people think we are murderers," Ray replied.

"Does that bother you still?" she sighed.

"No, never did," he said. "I know who the murderers are. The guys we go after." He took both of her breasts in his hands and buried his head in between them.

She felt behind her with her right hand until she found

it. "Seems like you're ready for me to show you something this time. In this one, I play the cowgirl and you play the horsey." He let out a loud neighing noise. The secure Blackberry on the bedside table replied with a shrill chirping. Sandra let go of him and reached for the Blackberry, handing him the mobile.

"Why did we land it at a civilian airport?" he asked whoever it was on the other end. "Then who did land it there?" He looked at Sandra as her eyes widened. "Goddamn it. I'll be right in. Give me fifteen minutes."

"What happened?" she asked when the call was over.

"We lost control of a Predator and someone else took over control. Landed it at some backwater airport in Pakistan where that pretty boy from WWN just happened to be waiting with a camera crew and a satellite uplink."

"Fuck!" Sandra exclaimed.

Ray laughed. "I will, just not now."

WEDNESDAY, OCTOBER 14
PEG HEADQUARTERS
NAVY HILL
WASHINGTON, DC

"I have to get back to Las Vegas," Sandra Vittonelli said as she sat down in Raymond Bowman's office.

"Well, gee, good morning. You finally roll in to work. I had a good time last night, too," he replied. "A night in bed with me again and you have to catch the next plane west."

"Keep it down," she said. "Last night was fun, but there is so much going on, I have to get back to the GCC. I am on the twelve thirty out of Reagan."

"National," he replied.

"All right, Reagan National," she said.

"DCA. Anyway, I want you to meet Dugout, my hacker who I went to Black Hat with," he said.

"Whom. With whom I went to Defcon," Dugout corrected, as he walked in, prying the top off of his Dunkin Donuts large black coffee, and sat down at the small table in Ray's office. "Pleasure to meet you, Sandra, when you are not on a video screen."

Ray walked from behind his desk to the small table and sat with Sandra and Dugout. "I asked Dug to run some artificial intelligence analytical programs on all our data from the program, see what he could spot." He turned to Dugout. "Why don't you run through it?"

"So, the overall observation is that this is not a static environment," Dugout said. "It's more like classic two-player game theory. We each learn about the other's behavior and adjust, but since we are both doing that at the same time, neither side is ever really optimized."

"Ah, yah. That's really helpful, I'm sure," Sandra said while looking at her Blackberry.

"So, there are more specifics. They realized that rifles aren't very useful against the drones, so some of them acquired Manpads."

Sandra looked up. "Whose pads?"

"Man portable air defense systems," Ray added.

"So, Stinger-class weapons. In response, you have kept most flights above ten thousand feet," Dugout continued. "They noticed that single aircraft are usually unarmed reconnaissance missions, so they do not run from them. In response, you have begun flying some solo weaponized flights and have been able to get some targets who might otherwise have gotten out of sight."

Sandra looked at Ray. "I know all this," she said. "We're putting infrared countermeasure boxes on the Preds to jam their missiles."

"See, action, reaction. So, did you know that they have greatly expanded the use of tunneling? It is not just a one-off at the fake orphanage. Using the multispectral imaging satellite, we have found over twenty houses associated with targets where they have tunneled between buildings. Enter one and then move to another.

"And, they are no longer meeting in buildings. They know you blow up buildings. So, now they meet in cars. One guy gets out of a car on a busy street and then another guy he's meeting with pulls up. Guy number one gets in and they drive around the crowded neighborhood, having their meeting."

Sandra looked at Ray in a way that said I'm bored with all of this.

"Tell her your theory about the drone hijacking last night," Ray suggested to Dugout.

"Okay, so they jammed the command data link from the satellite and then they jammed the military GPS signal. The bird switched to the commercial GPS signal, as programmed. Except they overpowered that signal from the satellite with their own phony data. When the aircraft couldn't phone home for fifteen minutes, it did as it was programmed and went home, or at least where it thought home was based on the phony GPS data. And it landed at Mashhad, Pakistan, thinking it was Bagram, Afghanistan," Dugout said rapidly.

"That's impossible. To do that, they'd have to be really close to the Pred all the time," Sandra replied.

"Yeah, like in an airplane maybe?" Dugout shot back.

"If they did that, that would indicate a level of planning and sophistication, aimed at the Program," Sandra suggested.

"Lady, what don't you get? They're after you. They started using Manpads. They knew enough to lure you to a target where they set you up to kill kids. Then they had WWN right there the next day. They know your Rules of Engagement so they use women and kids as human shields. They steal your drone and again WWN just happens to be there waiting. You think this is all just coincidence?" Dugout asked. "They're not just improving their defensive tactics. They're on offense against you."

Ray's eye was drawn to the cable news show running on the screen behind Dugout. He picked up the remote, to take it off mute.

It was Congressman O'Connell. "I'm here with Dr. Janet Stroeder of Philadelphia, who today filed a wrongful death suit in federal district court in Washington in connection with the death of her son Wilhelm Stroeder, an American citizen, whom we believe was killed by an American drone attack in Vienna, Austria, earlier this year. The suit names a series of individuals including the National Security Advisor and CIA officials as defendants. It also alleges that they engaged in a cover-up of the operation."

"That son of a bitch. That's classified information, top secret," Sandra said at the television.

O'Connell continued, "We have obtained surveillance camera video footage from across the street from the hotel that was attacked, clearly showing a drone." As he spoke MSNBC showed the grainy video. "This was not a terrorist bomb that went off in the hotel, not two drug gangs fighting each other as has been suggested, but a terrorist drone attack in the heart of a major European city. And the terrorists in question were CIA officers."

Ray hit Mute.

"So, as I was saying about adaptive behavior and two-person game theory," Dugout observed. "There is an organized, sophisticated, well-planned effort to attack the Program. And, it looks like, maybe you personally."

# 20

THURSDAY, OCTOBER 22
AL AMIRIYA MOSQUE
RADDA, YEMEN

"*Asalam Alekhem,*" Bryce said to the Imam. "May I enter your mosque?"

"Your Arabic is good, but you are not one of the faithful," the elder replied, "but all may pray here, if they show respect."

Bryce removed his shoes. "I was told that you might talk to a traveler."

"The Prophet, blessings and peace be upon him, taught us to give hospitality to the traveler." The Imam added, "But travelers from some places may not be safe outside of the mosque."

"I am from Canada," Bryce insisted.

"Welcome. What brings this traveler to this town?"

"I seek to learn, to know what has happened here," Bryce began. "There are stories one hears. Tales of death from the sky. I seek to learn who is dying and who is killing and why."

"This is not hard to learn, my friend. At first it was the fighters, mainly up in the hills. Some of them were not from our country, some were. Their camps were hit. Then when they were driving through the desert, their cars were hit. Then when they took over some villages, buildings in the villages were bombed. That's when the women and the children died."

Bryce had activated his digital voice recorder and was hoping it could hear the soft-spoken Imam. "And these attacks were from the Yemeni Air Force? That's what they tell me in Sana'a."

"*Pfft,*" the Imam spit. "Those fools could not hit one camel in a herd. It was your friends, the Americans. You know that. Their little white planes. You can hear them all the time. You can see them some days, here. They are flying here now, killing here now."

"Here? Could I see where? I would like to talk with the families," Bryce suggested.

"It would not be safe for you," the Imam replied. "Some people may not believe that you are Canadian. Some people may think you are American. And they are very mad at the Americans now, very mad." He pulled worry beads from his pocket and began to finger them.

"Imam, I have come to learn, but also to teach. I wish to teach people in North America, Canada, and the U.S. what is happening here. There are good people there, too. If they know what is happening, things may change. But if the suffering is a story that never leaves the places where it happens. . . ." Bryce spoke softly.

The Imam rose from the floor on which the two men had been sitting. "You will walk with me. You will not leave my side. You will not speak. You will listen. You will use no camera. You will learn. Come." Then the Imam turned and pointed at Fares, who was acting as Bryce's cameraman. "You, stay here. Stay in the mosque. Pray."

The streets were unpaved, packed sand and dust. The few people on the streets and in the doorways showed reverence to the Imam. The Imam turned off into an alley, and then another. The houses were close together, the smells of cooking and spices wafted out of some of the windows as they passed. Then the alley opened onto a little square. On the other side of the sandy square was an abandoned building, the roof gone, the signs of a fire around the empty windows.

They walked to a different building, on the left of the square. Two little girls ran to the Imam. "Ask your father to come out to meet me," the Imam instructed. After several minutes, a man appeared, sweating and wearing a work belt with carpenter tools. The Imam spoke to him in rapid Arabic, in the local dialect. Bryce captured only a few words.

"Tell him about that house," the Imam said more clearly.

"It was my brother's," the man said. "He lived there with his family, two wives only, seven children. He also rented rooms. Three months ago, it blew up, the house. Most of his family, thanks God, were at the marketplace and at the schools. My brother was working on the new rooms he was making on the roof. I have now taken his wives as my wives three and four. And the five of his children that survived, my children now. Maram and Munira, the beautiful girls, they died with my brother."

"How did the house explode, why? Tell him," the Iman spoke.

"It was a drone. I heard it twice, maybe more times, in the days before. Then I saw it again on that day. It was not just me. Others, they heard it and saw it on the day, firing its rockets at my brother's house. Why? I don't know. The Americans did not know my brother. He owned the house with me, the house they droned. He ran the supply store downstairs. We also rent rooms out to people. Maybe he rented to someone from the mountains, but only he died. He and the girls. I don't know why, only Allah knows now," the man seemed moved almost to tears to have to recount this story. Then he recovered and a wave of anger crossed his face. "But I do know that if I can ever find them, the Americans, Ibrahim will be revenged. And if I can't find an American, I will find one of the soldiers from Sana'a. At the right time, *inshallah*. Have you learned enough now? Have you?" The man stormed back into the house.

Fares emerged from the mosque when they returned. He quickly joined Bryce in the Toyota. Bryce thanked the Imam again, profusely. "Go now. You will be safe if you leave now and keep going. Keep going," the Imam said and then turned and went back into the little mosque.

Just outside the town Bryce told Fares to drive off road, up the hill overlooking the town. There they set up the camera and did a long-range zoom in on the burned-out house. Fares pulled the focus back, revealing Bryce standing on the edge of the cliff above the old town.

Bryce, looking into the camera, began, "In Yemen's

capital they told us about a recent success by the Yemeni Air Force, whose ancient MiG aircraft had destroyed a terrorist bomb factory in the town of Radda. Five terrorists, and only terrorists, were killed, they said.

"So we came to Radda and what we found here is very different. The villagers here tell us that the building was a family's home, the family business, a supply store, and some rooms to rent. They tell us that a drone fired rockets into the house, killing only its owner and his two young daughters, Maram and Munira.

"So, what we learn by coming out here is that the locals believe no terrorists were killed here and the Yemeni Air Force was not involved. Two young girls died, they say, killed by an American drone. What we can be sure of is that in this region, the people believe America is killing innocent people with drones and that is making Americans a lot more enemies. Bryce Duggan, WWN, Radda, Yemen."

Fares quickly folded the camera tripod. "All right, Bryce, that was good enough. One take. Let's get the hell out of here."

They drove back to the road and, one mile out of the town, as the path turned at the base of a hill, they saw the roadblock. It was two Hilux pickup trucks and an old Toyota SUV, not a government roadblock. It was too late to turn around, so Fares slowed down and turned on his blinkers. They counted eight men initially, all armed with AKs, all pointed at them.

"Get out," one of the men yelled in Arabic. "Hands on your heads." Once they stepped out, men stood in front of them with rifles. Others came up behind and pushed them down onto their knees. Quickly, deftly, the men behind them grabbed their hands and bound their wrists with plastic strips that cut into the flesh. Then Bryce and Fares were frisked, their wallets, mobile phones, and passports taken. Swiftly, they were carried to the old Land Cruiser, blindfolded, and thrown in the back of the SUV. Within three minutes of their seeing the roadblock, they had been taken and were being driven off. It had all happened very quickly.

FRIDAY, OCTOBER 23
OUTSIDE RADDA
YEMEN

They had each spent the night in a darkened room, alone, cold, hungry. Fares in one room, Bryce in another. Their hands had been unbound, but only after their feet were bound together at the ankles with heavy, old chain. The rooms had no windows and only the slightest ambient light near the high ceiling. Bryce thought maybe his room had been a storage closet of some sort. The walls were stucco, the floor dirt. He had heard talking in the distance, but could not discern a word he knew. Twice, since the time when he thought the sun had come up, he had heard a vehicle. His mind drifted, a result, he thought, of hunger, the low blood sugar.

He had told Fred Garrison in New York that they were driving out into the country. Garrison had expected a call in from them last night when they returned to the hotel. By now Garrison had probably called the embassy. Maybe the embassy could get someone in the Yemeni Security Service on the phone. Maybe Garrison would give someone in the U.S. Government their mobile phone numbers to track them. That would get them to where the roadblock had been, but they were at least an hour away from there now.

He tried to remember whether AQAP took ransom money when they kidnapped Westerners. Or did they just kill them? He thought of the pictures of Danny Pearl from *The Wall Street Journal* being decapitated in Pakistan. Bryce shuddered. He tried to take control of where his mind went. He willed himself to think of breakfast at the Tim Hortons near campus. He dozed again.

Bryce jolted awake as the door flew open and hit the wall. Bright light streamed in, as did the men, four of them with balaclavas hiding their faces. The leg irons came off and he was lifted. They were in a corridor, then a small, bright courtyard. Fares sat at a table with another man. Bryce was forcefully seated at the table. He made eye contact with Fares, who stared back, wide eyed.

"Wash your hands before you eat," the man at the table said in British-accented English. He pushed a bowl of water toward Bryce and handed him a small towel. Bryce noticed a second bowl, with fruit.

"You are CIA, yes?" the man asked. He looked to be in his forties, his bushy beard already speckled with gray.

Bryce tried to answer, but his throat cracked from the dryness. The man pushed a glass toward him and Bryce eagerly took it and swallowed the carrot juice.

"No, WWN. World Wide News," Bryce said. "I am a Canadian citizen."

The man nodded his head, agreeing. "Yes, yes. I saw the passport. And your bio on the WWN Web site says you went to the University of Toronto. Still, you could be CIA. They told us to expect you."

"I'm sorry, who told you what?" Bryce asked, reaching for a banana.

"We have mutual acquaintances in Pakistan, Mister Duggan, but I wanted to be sure for myself what you were doing here, what your report would say." The man rose from the table as a boy appeared with flat bread and a teapot. "I watched your videotape this morning. It tells the truth. But now you can say that you met with an AQAP leader, Mr. Duggan, and he told you that the drones are bringing us more brothers than anything we ever tried."

Two men with AKs appeared in the courtyard. "They will take you to your vehicle," the older man said as he left the courtyard. "The drones are working, CIA man. They are recruiting for us."

# 21

TUESDAY, OCTOBER 27
PEG HEADQUARTERS
NAVY HILL
WASHINGTON, DC

On the Big Board, they could see the speedboat. It was doing twenty-eight knots when the boat driver cut the engine and began to ease the boat toward the back of the yacht. From twelve thousand feet above, the camera on the Global Reach drone zoomed in on a face. "Facial Recognition Confirmation," the CIA officer said from Virginia, "Abu Yahya al Yemeni, the head of al Qaeda in the Arabian Peninsula. That means our source may be right. The heads of the two biggest al Qaeda affiliates, Somali Shabab and AQAP, al Qaeda in the Arabian Peninsula, meeting each other. This could be big."

Ray Bowman had just joined the Kill Call. "We've seen indications of those two AQ groups coordinating, doing mutual support, but if their two top guys are meeting, they must be planning something more. Have you seen any of the Shabab guys on the yacht yet?"

"No, we got here by following Abu Yahya's speedboat. Haven't been looking at the yacht," Erik responded. With Sandra Vittonelli in the air flying back to Las Vegas from Washington, Erik Parsons was running the Kill Call from the GCC.

"So we don't know whether there are civilians on the boat?" the Justice Department lawyer asked.

"Actually, we will shortly," the CIA officer said from Virginia. "Our source, and this is ultrasensitive, is actually the speedboat driver. He's supposed to go on board and check it out, then signal us. Can't do better than that. Human eyes on target."

"Okay, keep circling. Try to see through the windows on the yacht," Ray suggested.

"We can do better than that. Remember this is the big drone, Global Reach. It carries all sorts of tricks, including an audio collection mini-drone. We might be able to pick up conversation using its laser parabolic microphone," Erik said.

"Do it," Ray replied. "Have it drop its mini-drone."

Twelve thousand feet over the Indian Ocean, a panel slid back on the bottom of the large drone. A rotary launcher inside the aircraft spun, until the mini-drone was in position to be dropped. When it was released, the mini-drone fell toward the water, a small parachute opening at one thousand feet above the surface. As soon as the parachute had slowed the fall, a propeller on the rear of the fuselage started up. The parachute broke away from the drone, which pushed forward toward the yacht, twenty-two kilometers ahead.

"Let's hope they didn't see that," Ray said.

"Very unlikely," the Pentagon officer on the call replied.

On the Big Board, Erik could see the speedboat pulling away from the yacht. Only the boat driver appeared to be on board. A few minutes later, Erik heard the CIA voice on the speaker, "Just signaled us with a data burst on his cove comm. Four crew, six shooters, two principals. That's all he says are on the yacht." The source had gone on board, looked around, left on the speedboat, and used a CIA-provided covert communications device to beam an encrypted, data compressed message up to a satellite and down to CIA Headquarters.

"Does he say the Shabab guy is there?" Ray asked.

"That's all I got," the CIA answered.

"We've programmed the mini-drone to circle the yacht and throw its laser against windows and generally to search for conversation," Erik reported. "The laser beam is invisible to the human eye and the bird has the chameleon skin, so they shouldn't see it. Any audio will be fed from here straight to NSA for translation."

The minutes dragged. The image from the Global Reach drone stayed on the screens in each of the operation centers as the big drone flew circles over the ocean. It could stay up for two days from its base in Djibouti on the Red Sea, or from the airfield in Seychelles, in the Indian Ocean. What its sensors collected was beamed by radio up to a satellite in a stationary orbit above the Indian Ocean. From there it was relayed by laser beam to another satellite parked over the U.S. and then down to the GCC, outside of Las Vegas. The GCC then routed it out over a high-speed fiber-optic cable to NSA in Maryland, CIA in Virginia, and five offices in or near Washington: the White House, the State Department, the Justice Department, the Pentagon, and the Policy Evaluation Group.

"Okay, here's our analysis," the voice from NSA said. "We have detected four distinctly different adult male voices. We have detected no female voices, no children. It's difficult to maintain continuity on a conversation because the bird keeps moving, but we did hear one snippet between what we think is a Somali and the Yemeni. They're talking in English. Makes sense. The Somali probably doesn't speak Arabic. Here it is: 'At the same time as the Taliban hits, we go and you go.' That's all we caught of that."

The main camera on the Global Reach zoomed in on two men sitting on the fan deck on the yacht's stern. "Facial recognition of these two," the voice from the CIA said. "Abu Yahya from AQAP and Ibrahim Afrah from Shabab."

"Fascinating, both groups sent their top guys," Ray replied. "All right, we have two sources that indicate no collateral targets on board. We also have video from both the Global Reach and the mini-drone that only shows targets. Does anybody object to a strike on this ship?"

"State's good. Go."

"Justice clears off."

"DOD chops. Clean kill."

"CIA approves."

Ray Bowman had been on the secure phone to

Winston Burrell at the White House and obtained his approval.

"All right, GCC, execute the strike," Ray ordered.

TUESDAY, OCTOBER 27
GLOBAL COORDINATION CENTER
OPERATIONS ROOM
CREECH AFB, NEVADA

Erik indicated to the pilot to drop the two small torpedoes. Again, the panel on the bottom of the Global Reach opened and the rotary launcher spun about, until a torpedo was in position. When it detached and dropped, another one rotated into place and was then released. Like the mini-drone, they dove toward the water and then popped parachutes. Unlike the mini-drone, the torpedoes cut loose of their parachutes, fell below the surface of the water, and then fired up high-speed motors that sent them toward the yacht, their sensors programmed to detect the audio and magnetic signature of the large boat.

As the torpedoes sped ahead, Ray said to everyone on the circuit what they probably all were already thinking, "This is perhaps the biggest hit we have ever done. The leaders of the two most active AQ groups, and apparently planning some sort of simultaneous attacks, which we might just head off."

The video screens now showed images from two cameras on the Global Reach. One showed the white lines made in the water by the speeding torpedoes. The other showed a high-definition close-up of the two AQ leaders talking on the aft deck of the yacht. Erik, as Flight Controller, could also see the video feed from the mini-drone. It startled him. Erik saw that there was another speedboat headed toward the bow of the ship. In the boat were two men and four boys, and fishing poles.

Erik's eye darted to the many controls on his console. One of the buttons would detonate the torpedoes before they made contact with the yacht. Another would kill the video feed from the mini-drone. His left hand snapped out. He stopped the video feed.

The image on the Big Board from the Global Reach showed the water erupting, engulfing the rear of the yacht. Then a second explosion and then a third as the fuel tank erupted. What had been the yacht and the water around it was now a column of water and black smoke rising into the air, throwing pieces of metal and wood up and out.

Erik heard Ray over the headset, "Good job, guys. Big deal. And nice, clean kill."

Erik spoke into the microphone, "Kill Call closed." He flicked the switch that ended the videoconference.

# 22

THURSDAY, NOVEMBER 12
EXCHANGE STREET
PORTLAND, MAINE

"Have anotha?"

What was the question? Bahadur thought. He had struggled to learn English as spoken by the Australians, which had been very difficult. Now he tried to comprehend the American dialects. He assumed the American woman was offering him more coffee. "Oh, no, thank you. One cup is enough."

"Let's see, you were only on the Internet for ten minutes and had one cup. Let's say five dollahs," she said.

He paid the bill, with cash as he had been paying all of his bills, and walked out of the Java Net Cafe onto Exchange Street. Its bright aqua facade had been easy to find. He had used an iMac to check one of his Gmail accounts, but he had first connected to an anonymizing Web site so that Google's servers could not record the Internet IP address of the café. The Somali was to meet him when he walked out of the café.

On the sidewalk in front of the café, Bahadur saw the Somali and then looked to see that there was no one else within earshot. Bahadur spoke aloud the code words from the Hadith that were in the green moleskin notebook for this sleeper. "Give to a beggar even if he comes on a horse."

The Somali, who had looked nervous standing waiting on the sidewalk, seemed now suddenly calm. He bowed his head briefly. He knew that Bahadur was not from the FBI because this man knew a phrase to use with him that only two or three men in Pakistan knew, a personal phrase from the Prophet that had been assigned only to him when he had pledged *bayat,* allegiance to al Qaeda.

"Shall we walk down to the water?" Bahadur suggested. It was a chilly, late autumn day. There would be few people walking on the piers. They turned right on Commercial Street and looked out at the boats, then they strolled slowly out onto one of the docks. When they were far from anyone else, Bahadur began.

"Why do you want to do this?"

"Really, bro? For the money? I could tell you it's because my granddad got killed by the SEALs in Baidoa, but he didn't. He's still alive. Moved to Mog. I do hate the Americans, but truth is I am one, too, technically. I was born here. There's a bunch of Somalis live here. Here and in Minnesota. The Americans must have thought it was funny. Move the Somali refugees to the coldest-ass places in the country. Have them freak out when they see snow.

"But get it straight dude, I ain't no suicide guy. My cousin asked me if I had the balls to do this for a lot of money. He said he can't do it because he was born there. The FBI keeps an eye on them, the guys who came here, even when they were like two years old at the time they got to the U.S. of A. If I do it, I got to split some of the money with him. I'm okay with that."

Bahadur raised his hand to stop the Somali from talking. Otherwise, the Pakistani thought, the young man would have kept jabbering all day. He might look Somali, but he sounded very American. That was good.

The al Qaeda people he had met in Karachi had been right, this young man would raise few suspicions.

"We do not want suiciders. They are too crazy. They screw up. We want someone smart. You place the bomb in the tunnel then you leave. You have been to Boston before? Been on the T?" Bahadur asked.

"Sure, man. Done Beantown a shitload. Concert at the Garden last year. Then we took the trolley over to BU, Green Line. Still have the Charlie Card with money left on it."

Bahadur was unsure what all of that meant, but did not ask what a Charlie Card was. "You will have to go back and do some trial runs. See where you can leave the bomb. Check out the security. Look for the police, the cameras. Carry a backpack with books. Do nothing to raise suspicion. Do you have a car?"

"It's on the old side. Needs new snow tires, but it runs. Might be better if I got a new one."

"No, do nothing to attract attention. Do not spend money, especially after the job. Not here. Go to Europe after Christmas. We can show you a good time in Paris, girls, whatever. We will pay for all of that. Then we will give you the rest of the money and you can buy what you want, but in Europe, not here."

They were now standing outside of the Portland Lobster Company. The sign had a picture of a large red bug. Bahadur did not know how people could eat them. It was not just that, as bottom feeders, they were *haram*. They looked scary. How could they taste good? It would be like eating a scorpion.

"Do you eat lobsters?" he asked the Somali.

"I do, all the time. Get them off the boats. They're cheaper than anything else I can get. Like two and a quarter a pound on the docks. But the Somalis who came here from over there, they get all freaked out about us eating them. They say they're dirty. They ain't dirty, you wash all the sand out, get rid of all that yellow stuff inside. Over there, my mom says the beaches were full of them, but little ones without the claws. But the Somalis over there don't eat them even when they're starving. Crazy."

"Enough," Bahadur said. He extended his hand for the Somali to shake. In his palm there was a thumb drive. "On this are your instructions. It will not download. You can only open it and read it once. When you close the file, it will erase. Then drop it off the dock when no one is looking. There is a boat that leaves from this street and goes to Canada, yes?"

"The Blue Nose, yeah, every day, from up the street."

"Show me," Bahadur said. "Point it out and then walk away. If you do this work well, you do it exactly at the time I will give you. It must be precisely simultaneous. You will never have to work again, not for us, not for anyone. Understood?"

"I am down with that," the young man smiled. Sensing Bahadur's confusion, he added, "I get it, man, I understand. Rich man."

Bahadur smiled back as they walked together toward the Blue Nose. No, he thought, dead man. Just like the Yemeni in Philadelphia and the Nigerian in Chicago. They would probably all succeed in the missions. Some would die in the explosions because the timers were set differently than the boys were told. Some would survive, for a while. A few weeks later they would travel to France, to Mexico, to Jamaica to collect the rest of their money. There his men would meet them and wipe the trail clean.

# 23

MONDAY, NOVEMBER 23
FOUR MILE RUN
ARLINGTON, VIRGINIA

"I don't wear makeup," he said.

"Well, you will for this," Linda Greene told Raymond Bowman as she drove her Prius down the interstate. "I am your public affairs advisor for this, assigned by Winston Burrell. And I am not going to have you do badly or look badly. It would reflect poorly on the Administration, Dr. Burrell, and me. You are going to be persuasive. And you are going to wear makeup."

They were driving together to the PBS Washington studios, which were actually in Arlington, Virginia. And they were lost. "I know, we are late, but we will be there in time for the show. Just tell me again where we turn," Greene said into her iPhone as she drove. "No, I don't see the Weenie Beenie. What the hell is a Weenie Beenie? Yes, I know it's a live show and we have to be on time."

As they finally pulled up to the nondescript building

surrounded by high fencing, Linda Greene summed up one more time what Ray should say, "We have extensive checks and balances, a thorough review of every proposed mission. These missions are essential to the safety of the United States. They save American lives. Any Administration that had the capability to do this and failed to act would be guilty of dereliction of duty. Got it?"

"I know what to say," Ray replied as he stepped out of the car.

Raymond Bowman was about to defend the drone program on nationwide television, because the National Security Advisor had told him to do so. He was not looking forward to it. For over twenty years in government he had remained out of the public eye; now he was going to be cross-examined for twenty minutes by one of the nation's best-informed television personalities, Charlie Cross. After the opening introductions, Cross got right to it.

"Who decides who dies?" Cross began.

"I think our purpose is to prevent Americans from dying," Ray replied. "Terrorists may think they can decide on which Americans will die and when. It's our job to make sure that they don't succeed."

"That's not what I meant, and I think you know that," Cross countered. "Who decides who America kills with its drones?"

"American forces attack enemy forces based upon credible intelligence. When we use Unmanned Aerial Vehicles, UAVs, there is an extra process, involving lawyers, experts, and senior officials from five federal agencies. We have Rules of Engagement that require high confidence that the target is an active threat to American lives and America's national security interests."

"We'll get to that, but my question was who decides. Is it the President? What is his role?" Cross persisted. "Or is it you?"

The studio lights were so bright that Ray could see nothing in the room except his interrogator. It reminded him of one of the advanced interrogation techniques he had helped to put an end to. "The President approves the list of people designated as High Value Individuals. He is presented with the recommendations of the departments. He is given the dossiers, demonstrating that the individual is an active threat to Americans. These are people, Charlie, who are trying to kill Americans. Such people, regrettably, exist. They have to be stopped, before they kill," Ray said warming to his argument.

"So the President of the United States has become an executioner, deciding on who lives and who dies?"

"Charlie, the President is the head of the government. The government's first duty is to defend its people. He does that," Ray said, reaching for his glass of water. After taking a sip, he continued, "Another President might delegate this job, but he has chosen to be directly involved because, in his view, ultimately it is on his authority that these actions are being taken and he believes that he has a moral responsibility to ensure that we are acting ethically and responsibly."

"Ethically killing?" Cross asked.

"Ethically using force, including lethal force, in self-defense," Ray replied, "as Presidents have since George Washington."

"So what are the Rules of Engagement? How are we acting in self-defense when we surprise some group of Arabs in a small town in Yemen? What are we defending, the corrupt Yemeni government?" Cross pressed.

He felt sweat breaking through the makeup on his forehead, but decided to ignore it. "If we attack a target in Yemen, it is because we have very good reason to believe that those people are sitting there actively planning to kill Americans, training people to kill Americans," Ray answered.

"So we don't attack targets or people who threaten other governments? The attacks in Yemen aren't meant to prop up the regime there? You have never attacked a target there except to stop an attack on Americans?" Charlie Cross asked.

"I am unaware of any attack in Yemen except against AQAP, al Qaeda in the Arabian Peninsula, and they are committed to killing Americans," Ray hedged.

"Well, that's a little different from saying all the attacks were to prevent some imminent attack on Americans. We also used drones against Qadhafi's forces in Libya. Were they threatening America?" Cross asked. He had found a clear case when drones had been used when Americans were not in danger.

"In Libya, yes, back then we acted to enforce a UN Security Council resolution and under the authority of NATO. But now," Ray responded, "we are only acting to defend Americans. Sometimes the people we target simultaneously threaten Americans and others, but the determinative criterion, the ultimate question is 'Will these people kill Americans?' "

"Let's leave that. Let me ask you, you know the people who pull the trigger, the people who you call the pilots even though they never leave the ground. Doesn't it seem like a computer game to these guys after a while?" Cross probed.

"We call them pilots because they are. They have flown F-16s, F-18s in combat," Ray shot back. "They fly on average twenty-two hours on patrol or in transit for every hour that they are engaging a target. They know they are flying real planes, with real weapons. And it is not up to them to fire their weapons; they have to be given approval after an extensive review. They don't look at the target for seconds, the way other pilots do. They stare at the target for hours to be sure that they have the right target and that attacking will not endanger innocent people."

"And yet, you blew up an orphanage," Cross said.

Ray expected the orphanage question. "Charlie, we have flown over fifty thousand missions in the last five years. We do not want to make a mistake on any mission, but we have made rare mistakes. But we did not bomb an orphanage," he replied. "Orphans were kidnapped by terrorists and hidden in a target. We learned from that and we take even more elaborate steps now to be sure that there are no civilians in the target area."

"So how, then, did you kill an American, Wilhelm Stroeder, in Vienna, Austria?" Cross drilled. "Couldn't the Austrian police arrest any terrorists, and was the American a terrorist?"

Ray did not see that coming. "Charlie, I can't talk about specific operations. I can't confirm allegations that there was a U.S. drone flight over this or that specific country."

"Well, that sounded like an admission, but let's get back to whether this new kind of weapon is a good idea. Is it really fair? You fly so high overhead, the enemy may not even be able to know you are there. Isn't it like shooting fish in a barrel? The pilots are not at any risk, they can't be hurt. Doesn't it lower the barrier to lethal action?" Cross asked.

"It's not fair," Ray replied.

Cross was flummoxed for a moment. "So you agree with me?"

"The beauty of these weapon systems is that they defend American lives without risking American lives," Ray said. "Our pilots are invulnerable."

"What if drones were used against us?" Charlie Cross queried.

"We know that these weapons are not something that only the United States possesses. We would hope that any nation that uses them would use them with the care and high standards that we employ. If they are used against us, we will defend ourselves," he answered.

"Do you think the people the U.S. is targeting with drones should defend themselves?" Cross asked.

"I'm glad that they can't," Ray shot back.

"So far," Cross observed. "How long will these drone strikes go on, forever?"

"That's up to the President, of course," Ray answered. "But I think we all hope that the day would come when there is not an active terrorist threat to the United States."

"Indeed, but maybe, just maybe as long as you are killing people, and leaving behind their sons and brothers, you are creating more and more terrorists and this becomes a war without end. Thank you, Raymond Bowman, for being with us tonight. We will be right back." The bright lights faded.

Ray felt that he had been bettered by Cross, that he had not been as persuasive, as convincing as he wanted to be.

"You were great," Linda Greene said as he walked off the set. "Dr. Burrell said to tell you." She handed him a towelette to remove the makeup.

"I bet he says that to all the boys," Ray said as he smeared off the makeup.

"And Dr. Burrell said to tell you that a K Call is under way, whatever that is," Greene said as she dabbed his forehead. "They sent a car for you. It's outside. So I guess I don't get to drive you back."

"That's a shame," Ray said, as he moved toward the lobby, "but thanks for your help." Through the glass front door he could see a black Suburban sitting in front of the building. Nice, he thought, Burrell had sent the truck to rush him back to the PEG for the Kill Call. It probably had red and blue flashing lights in the grille, maybe a siren. As he approached the Suburban, the passenger door opened and an older African American woman emerged. "Are you Raymond Bowman?"

"You found me," he said, smiling. "Thanks for coming."

"This is a subpoena, Mr. Bowman. You have been served," she said as she jumped back into the Suburban.

He looked at the document. It had the name of a plantiff, Janet Stroeder. He noticed that the list of defendants included Sandra Vittonelli. Her employment by the Agency, her relationship to the program was classified. "Fucking O'Connell," he muttered.

"Mr. Bowman?" a pimply faced young man in an Army uniform said from inside a white Chevy Impala. "I'm your driver, sir. Where do you want to go?"

"Home," he sighed, "but let's go to Foggy Bottom."

## MONDAY, NOVEMBER 23
## ABOARD THE USS *ABRAHAM LINCOLN*
## THE GULF OF SIDRA, MEDITERRANEAN SEA

The large elevator reached the flight deck, ninety feet above the surface of the sea. It carried from the hangar below two men in blue vests and one thirty-eight-foot-long, matte gray Sea Ghost aircraft, its wings folded up above the smooth, rounded fuselage. The drone, designated Caspar Six Charlie today, was reporting for duty. A man in a yellow vest, holding a remote control box with a joystick, steered the Sea Ghost from the elevator, across the flight deck, by the two alert F-18s, past a Seahawk helicopter, to a fueling area. He hit a switch that caused the aircraft's wings to descend and lock into place. Its wingspan was now over sixty feet wide. Men in purple vests, known as grapes, leaped into action, running hoses and locking them onto each wing of the Sea Ghost.

Within minutes, the Sea Ghost's tanks were filled and the yellow-vested controller moved the joystick again, gliding the Sea Ghost to the steam catapults that would launch it. Men in green vests bent below the drone, locking the aircraft's wheels into the catapult's channels. Nearby on the flight deck men in red vests, the armorers, watched. They had no role in this aircraft's flight. It was flying unarmed, on a reconnaissance mission, patrolling the waters off Libya. Its bomb bay was filled with electronic spy gear instead of weapons. Two other Sea Ghosts sat below deck. If needed, they could be armed with air-to-air and air-to-ground missiles, fitted up inside a bomb bay in the smooth fuselage. When flying together the bat-shaped Sea Ghosts could swarm, flying in formation, communicating with each other with no human in the loop, deciding which of the drones should launch missiles against which of their assigned targets. If one were shot down, another would automatically assume its mission. If fired at, the aircraft could quickly pull such sharp turns that were there a human on board, he would quickly pass out. There were, of course, no humans on board. That would just have made the aircraft heavier, slower, and less effective.

Men in white vests did a last inspection of the Sea Ghost and then backed away, using hand signals to the yellow-vested controller. The controller looked one last time at his handheld device, checking the status of all onboard systems. Then he switched control to the aircraft itself. From now on it could fly a preprogrammed mission on its own, unless and until a human intervened. If none did, the Sea Ghost would patrol for four hours, then locate the *Lincoln,* signal for permission to land, and precisely set down on the rocking carrier flight deck, grabbing the arresting cable that would stop the aircraft's forward motion.

Now, in autonomous mode, the Sea Ghost waited for the catapult. A second yellow-vested man knelt near the aircraft. He gave a thumbs-up to the Sea Ghost's forward camera, then quickly dropped his arm, with his gloved hand pointing forward toward the sea. The forty-thousand-pound drone shot forward in a cloud of steam, left the deck, dropped briefly below the front of the *Lincoln,* then quickly rose as its one turbofan engine lifted the Sea Ghost up in a sharp climb toward the clouds.

There was no pilot assigned to that one drone, rather there was one flight supervisor below decks, monitoring the status of six Sea Ghosts aloft, some looking for aircraft, some looking for ships, others listening for electronic emissions. Two hours and fifteen minutes into the flight of Caspar Six Charlie something came up. Orders were received on the *Lincoln* and in minutes the flight "soup" got the kind of order he had been hoping to receive, an order to put a human in the loop. "Soup, take control of Six Charlie as its pilot and go feet dry. Set it on a vector to do photo recce of the Maaten al-Sarra air base."

Caspar Six Charlie was about to fly into Libyan airspace.

MONDAY, NOVEMBER 23
PEG HEADQUARTERS
NAVY HILL
WASHINGTON, DC

It took only fifteen minutes, driving against the last of the rush-hour traffic, for Bowman to get to his office. The Kill Call videoconference was already up on the ten flat screens on the wall of his conference room.

On the largest screen, he saw a single aircraft, a four-engine military cargo plane, sitting on an airstrip in a desert. "What have we got?" he asked as he sat down.

"We followed this AN-24 from Beirut International. CIA sources say it belongs to Hezbollah and is used to run guns throughout the region." It was Sandra's voice, coming from Las Vegas. "It's now on an airstrip in the Libyan desert. As you can see, it's being loaded from that storage bunker across the way. We believe that bunker is used to store chemical weapons, specifically VX nerve gas in artillery shells."

The NSA officer on screen chimed in. "We can confirm the aircraft is run by Hezbollah. And that Libyan military communications has in the past referred to Special Weapons being stored there. That is their jargon for their chemical weapons."

"Lovely," Ray said over the network connection.

"One more thing," Sandra added. "The Sea Ghost UAV we have giving us this image is a reconnaissance bird off the USS *Lincoln* in the Med. It's unarmed. No missiles."

"So what are our options?" Ray asked.

An Admiral at the Pentagon replied, "We recommend flying the Sea Ghost into the Antonov, ramming it, either on the runway or, better yet, in the air over the desert. The Sea Ghost has a jet engine. It can catch up with the Antonov once the cargo plane takes off. "

"Wouldn't that spill the nerve gas?" the Justice lawyer asked.

"Most of it would burn up," the Admiral answered.

"But not all of it?" the lawyer questioned.

"No, not all of it. Some would be vented, some would

be ejected beyond the thermal zone," the Admiral admitted.

"So what?" the State Department representative said. "Get real. The alternative is having the Hezbollah terrorist group getting its hands on nerve gas. They will use that against Israel, an American ally. The choice is between maybe killing a few camels in the middle of the desert or wiping out thousands of Israelis. That's a no-brainer."

"Legally, I don't think it's justified," the lawyer responded. "We do not know that Hezbollah will use the nerve gas. Doing so would trigger an enormous Israeli response. Hezbollah probably just wants it as a deterrent, to stop Israel from attacking it again. Moreover, we oppose using 'U.S. interests' as grounds for using the drones. It should be a group committed to killing Americans. Is Hezbollah?"

No one answered.

"Well, you are right about one thing," Ray finally said. "Our original guidance from the President was that we could use the UAV program to stop attacks against 'U.S. interests.' The proposed new guidance would drop that. We could only act against groups engaged in attacks on Americans. So, CIA, does Hezbollah engage in attacks on Americans?"

The image on the large screen showed the trucks driving away from the Antonov. The ramp from the rear clam doors was pulled back into the aircraft.

Ray could see the CIA officer on another, smaller screen talking to others off camera, but he could not hear their conversation. Their microphone was on mute. After a few minutes, the CIA man said, "Not in recent years. Hezbollah did kill Americans in the 1980s and was involved in the Khobar Towers attack on Americans in Saudi Arabia in 1996, but we have not seen an intentional attack aimed at Americans since then."

"Ray, that proposed new guidance is just that, proposed. It is under discussion, not adopted. State feels strongly that we have to act to defend U.S. interests, our allies, and not just ourselves," the woman from the Department of State explained.

Puffs of smoke rose from two of the propellers on the aircraft and then the rotors on two of the four engines began to spin. "All right. I am going to need the official, final view of each of your departments in the next very few minutes. Check up your tapes." He then muted his own microphone and stepped off camera. He picked up his drop line to the National Security Advisor, who answered it personally on the third ring. Ray quickly summarized the situation.

When he was done, Burrell answered quickly. "Ram the fucker."

"Winston, under the new guidance proposed by the Attorney General, he dropped protecting 'U.S. Interests.' He believes we should only attack those who pose an imminent threat to American citizens," Ray noted.

"Raymond, there are Americans all over Israel. Probably a million Israelis are also American citizens, hold U.S. passports," Burrell said. "Besides, whatever the President's guidance on UAVs might be, his orders to me on protecting Israel are very clear. He'd be crucified if he could have stopped Hezbollah from getting CW and failed to act. Ram the fucker. Understood?"

Raymond Bowman saw the third and fourth engine

start to spin and the aircraft begin to move slowly onto the runway. "All right, people. We have a decision. We will intercept the Antonov over the desert."

The Justice Department representative hit her Request to Speak button. "The Attorney General does not concur. Such a move would be outside our recommended legal parameters."

No one else spoke. "Noted for the record," Ray said. "GCC, you are instructed to fly the Sea Ghost into the Antonov in such a way that the Antonov crashes or explodes over the desert."

"Understood," Sandra replied.

The conversation on the conference call stopped. Everyone on the network watched silently as the Sea Ghost camera tracked the AN-22 taking off from the airstrip. The image on the large screen from the UAV's forward-looking camera showed the Antonov from behind, its four turbo-prop engines spinning as the aircraft climbed. The distance between the Sea Ghost and the AN-22 began to close.

"We're going to fly above the Antonov and then dive into it from about five thousand feet above it," Sandra said. "It should split in two and then explode. It's going to be over open desert, empty desert, for at least the next hour, but we should be in position to ram in about ten minutes."

The forward-looking camera no longer showed the AN-22, as the Sea Ghost climbed. The screen showed very bright blue, cloudless sky.

"We will have to tell the Libyans. This transfer of chemical weapons was probably not approved by the government in Tripoli, probably a rogue officer selling the stuff," the State Department officer commented. No one replied.

Then the image on the screen shifted, spun, and became a view of the desert below. "What the hell was that?" Ray asked.

"The Sea Ghost is in a sharp dive," Sandra said. That much was apparent. The ground was rushing up fast. Then the screen went black. "The Sea Ghost just flew straight into the ground."

"Why?" Ray asked. "How?"

"I don't know," Sandra replied softly.

"Holy shit," the Admiral said into an open microphone.

There was a long silence on the network.

"Admiral?" Ray called.

"Yes, sir?"

"Contact the Kirya op center directly," Ray ordered. "Give them an intercept vector."

"Roger that," the Admiral replied.

"What is the curio, or whatever you called it, if I may ask?" the Justice representative asked.

Ray stood up and began to walk out of the room. As he got to the door, he heard someone on the call answer the question. "Headquarters of the Israeli Defense Force."

# 24

TUESDAY, NOVEMBER 24TH
PARK STREET MBTA STATION
BOSTON, MASSACHUSETTS

The young Somali-American from Portland stepped off the Green Line trolley at Park Street Over, looking like another of the tens of thousands of students who went through that T station every morning. There were over twenty colleges and universities within two miles of that subway stop, in both Boston and Cambridge. There were a quarter of a million college students in the metropolitan area and it seemed like half of them were on the T headed out for Thanksgiving break.

He wore a backpack over his hoodie, had on a Patriots cap, and kept playing with his iPhone. He moved with the crowd toward Park Street Under and the Red Line trains to Harvard and Braintree. He took the stair that led to the middle platform, where he could get a train in either direction. He started walking behind the staircase to the end of the platform, where there were almost no people waiting. His mission for today was simple. Slip down into the tunnel and check it out for a place where, next time, he could leave his parcel.

A man from South Boston who had just turned eighty-two said to the young Portland man in the hoodie, "Trains don't stop that far down the platform. Only four-car trains this time a day."

"Fuck off, granddad," the young man replied and kept walking, disappearing behind the staircase.

The old man walked in the other direction, to the MBTA police officer who had just stepped out of the train from Ashmont. "The poster says 'If you see something, say something,' " he said to the officer and then he told him about the student.

As the officer walked around the staircase, he saw the young man holding a video camera and approaching the gate at the top of the ladder down from the platform to the tunnel. "Hey, hold up there," the officer called out.

The young man in the hoodie started to run toward the ladder. The officer bolted toward him. The student was over the gate and on the ladder before the officer could reach him. The old man, who had slowly followed them, saw both the student and then the officer jump over the gate and climb down into the dark subway tunnel.

In the tunnel, the officer moved quickly on the gravel path by the side of the track, on the opposite side of the railbed from the lethal third rail. As he approached the man in the hoodie, the officer reached out and grabbed the backpack, which came off in his hand. The officer lost his balance, staggering forward. The young man put his hands together and brought them swiftly down on the back of the officer's neck. The officer fell, hitting his head on the track. He did not get up.

Minutes later the old man saw the lights coming down the tunnel, the Red Line train from Harvard. As the lights grew close, the student climbed back over the gate onto the platform. His backpack was gone, as was his Patriots cap. His hood was hanging behind him. Once over the gate, he began to run up the platform.

"Hey, stop, where's the cop?" the old man yelled, grabbing onto the student.

The younger man pushed with both hands, knocking the old man down onto the hard concrete platform. "I told you to fuck off," the young man said as he ran off.

The driver on the Red Line train hit the horn and the brakes when he saw the body on the tracks in the tunnel, just a few meters outside of Park Street Station. When the alarm went off in the MBTA Operations Center at Arborway, the image from the surveillance camera on the platform showed the front car of the train stopped where the emergency brake had brought it to a halt, just inside the entrance to the station.

# 25

THURSDAY, NOVEMBER 26
NAVY HILL
WASHINGTON, DC

The heavy rains from earlier in the week were still moving down the creeks and into the streams that fed the Potomac, making it high, fast, and almost milk chocolate in color. Raymond Bowman sat on what he thought of as his bench, high above the rest of the Foggy Bottom neighborhood, on Navy Hill. His field of view included the green forest patch of Theodore Roosevelt Island in the middle of the river, with the high-rises in Virginia beyond. To the right was the giant Kleenex box that was the Kennedy Center and beyond it the riverside in Georgetown. To his left was what he thought of as an architectural travesty and an even more dubious use of money, the building housing the U.S. Institute for Peace.

It was where he came, behind Donovan Hall, a few hundred meters from his office, to think. The gray sky, the aroma from the black Dunkin's Bold, the breeze off the river all combined to relax him enough that he felt for the first time in months that his mind was clear, that for a moment his brain was not racing, processing, planning. And then Dugout sat down next to him.

"I think it was because the Navy guys were using the new Thuraya satellite over the Mediterranean," Dugout began, as he balanced his mug of green tea and his iPad on his lap.

"I was just sitting here quietly thinking about how George Washington and his friends lost money on the Potomac canal and locks. What the hell are you talking about, Thuraya, and by the way, hello," Ray replied. "Happy Dead Turkey Day. Shouldn't you be watching football or stuffing yourself while visiting family members?"

"Happy Thanksgiving, yourself. What I should be doing is having dinner with my band. Here, have a Cohiba. It's your Dead Turkey Day present. I know you will never buy these things for yourself. You wait for me to be your Enabler."

Ray unwrapped the cigar and smelled its freshness. "You, in a band?" he asked.

"Yeah, tenor sax in a jazz combo. My undergrad degree is in music, from Berklee. Anyway, you do realize that it's like drizzling out here? I saw you sitting in the rain on the video cam feed and thought, maybe I should come out and give you a weather report," Dugout said.

"You've hacked our own video cameras?" Ray asked. "Yes, I know it's drizzling. It's nice. You know Wild Bill Donovan created this complex up here in like '43? First real home of U.S. Intelligence."

"Yes, I knew that," Dugout replied and handed Bowman a box of wooden matches.

"You know that he had a drone program?" Ray asked. "He put little bombs on this species of really big bats and released them to fly behind Nazi lines."

"That work?" Dugout asked.

Bowman lit the Cohiba and tried to blow a smoke ring. He failed. "Shit no, of course, it didn't work. Now what was that you said about the Navy?"

"So, I've been working on how that Navy drone went down in Libya," Dugout replied. "The Navy uses a commercial satellite for its link from its drones in the Med, using X band frequencies. Sometimes when their bandwidth gets too thin, they drop the encryption. It's against policy, but the operators do it when they have to."

"So, that's what they did on the Sea Ghost op in Libya and somebody was waiting. The bad guys had probably seen it happen before and just kept a bot on that link looking for it to happen again. When it did, zap, they slipped into the data stream and nose-dived the bird into the sand. Just your luck it happened when you were trying to stop the Hezbollah guys from stealing some sarin."

Ray continued gazing out at the river. "The Antonov had engine trouble later. Crashed off Cyprus."

Dugout chuckled. "I heard. Engine trouble? Is that what you call it when an Israeli F-15 sends four, count them four, air to air missiles through your fuselage and you and your planeload of sarin plunge into the Med?"

"Don't eat the fish next time you are in Cyprus," Ray replied.

"I'll try to remember that for when I finally get my leave approved and I get to have last year's vacation," Dugout said.

"Suddenly everybody is messing with our drones. Hezbollah, Pakistanis," Ray said, turning to look at the man sitting next to him on the bench.

"Well, first off, I doubt it was Hezbollah who messed up the Sea Ghost. They just happened to have been the unplanned beneficiary," Dugout replied. "I think whoever put the bot out to look for when the Navy dropped sync on its encryption on the link to its drones is likely the same guy who stole the Pred in Pakistan," Dugout smiled.

"I would normally say you have gotten way too paranoid and are also making the analytical mistake of thinking all the jigsaw pieces are from the same puzzle, but I know that smile. You got something, don't you?" Ray asked.

"So, the digital master control system on the satellite over the Med and the one being used by the satellite over the Indian Ocean when they stole our Predator, turn out to be using the same operating system. And in both cases the hackers who took control used the same Oh-Day to exploit a vulnerability in the code. No one else, as far as I can tell, has ever used that Oh-Day. So, I would conclude that it's the same guy in both cases," Dugout said.

"I have no idea what you just said," Ray replied. "The only O'Day I know of is Anita O'Day, jazz singer. You should know her if you're a jazz guy. "

Dugout frowned. "Oh-Day as in Zero-Day. You drop the Zeer part and you get Oh-Day and besides lots of people call zero 'oh.' It's cyber speak for a new trick, a virgin hack, something that no one has known about until that first day when one guy uses it. Point is that the same guy hacked both satellites using a nifty exploit he developed. No one else seems to have used it yet, anywhere."

"Let's say I believe that for a minute about the satellites," Ray said. "It fits into your theory that the drone targets are fighting back. But explain to me how my getting sued fits in. Somehow the family of a victim from the Vienna operation got a video from the security camera across the street from the hotel. It shows the drone going in. As far as I knew, the only people who had that tape were the Austrian Security Service."

"I checked," Dugout said. "The Austrians didn't give it up intentionally. The reason that tape got into the hands of the family of the victim is that someone hacked the Austrian Security Service. Not all that easy. Maybe something Pak ISI could do, maybe. Then they mailed the video to the family's attorney."

"Okay, so it might be Pak ISI hacking into networks. But a lot of what is happening to us is on the ground out there, not in cyberspace." Ray said. "Somebody lures us to a house where they have stashed kids. No hacking there. Some of the targets are shooting back with Stingers; we've lost four Preds to that. No hacking there. The improvement in their defensive tactics with the use of cars in crowded areas for meets, the tunnels. Those are not technical solutions."

"Right," Dugout reacted. "So, I'd say one explanation is that you've got two groups maybe working together, the al Qaeda or maybe Taliban guys on the ground in

AfPak and then some hacker unit, like maybe in the Pakistani intelligence, the ISI, or maybe in the Iranian Rev Guards."

"Yeah, I think you're half right," Ray said. "I think it is two groups, but I'm not sure it's the Paks or Iranians. Could be the Russians just to mess with us. See if you can run with those theories, but add another. Look for a nonstate actor, a Wikileaks Collective on steroids, maybe a group of college kids in Boston or Palo Alto."

"Okay, I'll look at all those possibilities, but I am telling you now that it's no hacker collective or group in Boston or San Fran," Dugout said as he stood up from the bench and brushed raindrops from his windbreaker.

"Why not?" Ray asked.

" 'Cuz I know all those guys, what they're capable of, how they'd do it if they could. They're wicked smart, but the guys we're up against? They're a lot better than anyone I know."

# 26

MONDAY, NOVEMBER 30
GLOBAL COORDINATION CENTER,
OPERATIONS ROOM
CREECH AFB, NEVADA

"The compound that the Pakistani ISI source reported is in that valley up ahead," Bruce Dougherty said as he flew the Predator on a reconnaissance mission over Afghanistan. "If I fly in there, it would be a perfect place for them to shoot Manpads up at me from the hilltops."

"Good, then that's just what we will do, fly in there," Erik Parsons replied. He switched open his circuit to Sandra Vittonelli in her office twenty meters behind him. "Sandy, you may want to come out and watch this. I think you were right about that Pakistani ISI source. I think we are being lured into a Stinger kill box."

When Sandra joined them on the floor of the ops center, she could see the unarmed reconnaissance Predator flying toward the valley. That view was being provided by a stealthier drone, a Peregrine, flying in trail and higher up. "Good, this looks like another one of their traps," she said. "Make sure to turn off the chameleon skin on the Pred so that they can get a good look at it."

Time began to move slowly for the team on the Ops Room floor as they waited to see if there would be another Stingerlike missile attack, what could be the fifth shoot down of a UAV in a month. On the Big Board were images from both the Predator and the Peregrine above it.

On the hillsides on either side of the valley floor, men also waited, spotters and shooters. Their two SA-24 missile launchers were humming in standby mode. Like the U.S. Stinger, the SA-24 had to be drawing current from the battery pack to keep its highly sensitive infrared sensors warmed up and ready to move quickly to full active search. By flicking a switch next to the trigger, the operator could bring the launcher and the missile inside the tube to full readiness in thirty seconds. Then if the operator pointed the tube toward a target, as soon as the infrared seeker on the missile had locked on to the target's infrared signature, a high-piercing whine would come from the handgrip of the launcher holding the missile tube. Then, when the trigger was pulled and the missile launched from the tube, the SA-24 would seek that infrared source.

The spotter on the north ridge saw it first. "*Hamdullah,*" he cried and began hitting the Transmit button on his handheld two-way radio. The clicking sound from his hitting the button sent a warning across the valley to the team on the other ridge. The shooters on both teams moved their thumbs up on their grips, bringing both missile launchers into full active search. The shooters began to scan the sky through the optical tracker, looking for the drone. In less than a minute, both missile launchers were emitting an ear-piercing whine. They had locked on to their target, a Predator.

Two indicator lights linked to the Predator's onboard sensors turned red and began blinking on the pilot's dashboard, indicating that the Predator had detected that it was being lit up by an infrared seeker. "We've detected missile lock on. Two, one on either side of the valley," Bruce Dougherty said into his chin microphone. "Tallyho."

The slowly moving minutes with little happening were suddenly transformed into lightning quick seconds, with multiple simultaneous actions directed by sensors, not by humans. Two plumes of smoke could be seen on the video from the Peregrine as the SA-24s were launched toward the Predator. Almost simultaneously, red stars began shooting from the Predator, infrared heat sources with the same signature as the Predator itself had just seconds earlier. Near the rear of the Predator, two gray-white boxes began to emit new infrared signature patterns for the Predator, rapidly changing to prevent the upcoming missiles from switching to it and locking on.

To the sensors on the SA-24s, there were now dozens of objects with the infrared signature of the Predator and then there were other objects with different, new infrared signatures, constantly changing. The missiles were programmed to recognize that the many Predator signatures were probably flares designed to fool it.

Therefore, the missiles attempted to lock on the new signature source, but there were too many of them and they were too rapidly switching and transforming to permit target acquisition and lock on. Given that pattern, the missiles were programmed to fly to the general area of infrared activity and then to detonate, in the hope that some of the shrapnel from their explosion would strike the real target.

As the SA-24s streaked into the sky and the red star flares shot out from the Predator, the sensors aboard the Peregrine triangulated where the shooters were. Within two seconds of the Stingers leaving their launch tubes on the hillsides, four missiles with equal velocity leaped from the launch bay of the Peregrine, which was flying slightly above and behind the Predator. They raced toward the areas where the SA-24s had been fired. Once over the launch areas, the air-launched missiles exploded, spreading thousands of sharp, strong, antipersonnel razors out in a density such that anyone within two hundred meters would have been hit by a minimum of a dozen blades, each of which would be an artery-shredding, lethal attack.

The spotters and shooters stood watching their SA-24s climb through the air, but within seconds of their missiles being launched, just as they were beginning to see the red star flares come from the Predator, the eight men on the hillsides had become hundreds of shredded body parts. Almost simultaneously, the SA-24s erupted above in midair.

Bruce had programmed the Predator to go into a 12-g force turn and climb out as soon as it launched the red star flares and the Infrared Counter Measures pod began to light up. No onboard human pilot could withstand anything more than an 8-g turn. No human pilot could have executed such a fast maneuver by hand as quickly as the Predator executed the preprogrammed command. The machine was doing what no human pilot with a joystick could do. By moving so quickly, the Predator avoided most of the shrapnel from the SA-24s, picking up only small fragments of metal hitting its wings to no effect.

The op center floor broke into applause. Pilots stood in the cubicles and gave each other high fives. "Shoot at my birds, you little fuckers, and we will shred your asses," Erik Parsons yelled above the din.

Sandra Vittonelli shook hands with Bruce Dougherty when his aircraft were stabilized and returning to base. She turned to Erik, "You see this is basically a two-player game theory exercise in which every player-move generates a response. Anticipate theirs." She walked back to her office, off the operations room floor.

Erik Parsons looked at Bruce Dougherty. "What'd she say?"

# 27

TUESDAY, DECEMBER 1
30TH STREET AMTRAK STATION
PHILADELPHIA, PENNSYLVANIA

It was a giant angel, carrying a sleeping man. No one else was looking at it. The train station was filled with people, but no one looked at the giant sculpture that dominated the vast hall. It was such an odd country, so filled with religious symbols and so filled with sin, Bahadur thought.

It had been a long ride from Boston on the Acela train and the food had been awful. All of the seats had been taken, many by students returning from the Thanksgiving break. The rocking and swaying of the train car had made him almost ill. Bahadur knew that he should never go to any of the targets, but it would have been hard to arrange another way. He walked over to the map of the station. Yes, it was like New York's Penn Station, but smaller and less protected. On one level there were the city subway trains and the trolley cars. On another level were the suburban commuter lines. In the middle were the long-range Amtrak trains to other cities. It would work. Three men, three bombs. All rail traffic would be stopped. And none of the men would know that there were others, just in case one got caught or backed out.

He walked out of the station and across the street toward the Center City area. There was the man in the blue and gold Drexel University jacket. Bahadur approached him, stood next to him, and said the Hadith phrase the man hoped to hear, "Shall I not inform you about the inmates of Hell? It is every violent, impertinent, and proud person."

They began to walk together down Kennedy Boulevard. "You are a Saudi or a Yemeni?" Bahadur asked him after they had exchanged the meeting phrases.

"Both. My father is a Saudi, my mother is Yemeni. I was born here, in Philadelphia. I grew up in Lewisburg. My father taught at Bucknell," the man explained.

"And you are a good Muslim?"

"I practice Islam, maybe not the same way you do, but I am a Muslim."

"And you are willing to do this thing why?" Bahadur asked.

"Because all of my life, and especially since I was seven, since 9/11, they have taunted me because I am a Muslim, because I am a Saudi," he said.

"But you are not a Saudi, you are an American by birth, a citizen, correct?" Bahadur asked.

"Not to them. To them I am a raghead. The Americans are so arrogant. They did not learn the right lesson from 9/11. They are still killing Muslims. They need to be taught again. They need to be deterred from waging war on Islam. They need to pay a high price. I hope I am not all that you are doing," the student said. "I alone cannot make them hurt enough."

Bahadur stopped walking and faced the young man. "There are many more. It will all happen at once. That is why it is essential that you do not go early or late." Bahadur moved as close as he could to the student, their belts touching. "Once you are in this, you cannot back out or you, and your family, will pay the ultimate price for desertion. Do you understand? Not early, not late, no backing out."

"Yeah, I get it, I get it," the student said. "I am doing this."

"And the money, what will you do with the money?" Bahadur asked.

"When I graduate in May, I am going to move to Beirut. There are engineering jobs there. And with the money, I can get a nice apartment on the Corniche to start. And a Porsche."

"You will only get a little in cash now and when it happens. The rest will be in a bank in Beirut," Bahadur explained.

"Okay, as long as it's there."

"It will be, if you do the job right. This is a matter of Islamic honor between us. We will pay." Bahadur tried to sound convincing. "You will get the material that morning from the men who you know, from Lewisburg. You will have figured out how to leave it at the place on the plans and set the timer. You will be in a public place at the university when it happens. You can walk there easily from the train station. You will be shocked, horrified, by the attack. And then you will have only one more semester before you are living the good life in Beirut."

They had arrived at the end of the Boulevard. There was a giant clothes pin, soaring many stories high in front of a skyscraper. Bahadur didn't even bother to ask its religious significance.

"Now, there is another subway system that goes to New Jersey near here," Bahadur stated. "Can you walk me to near where the station is?"

"PATCO, it's this way."

# 28

SATURDAY, DECEMBER 5
DESERT HILLS
NORTH LAS VEGAS, NEVADA

"Did you buy the house because the street was called Wind Warrior Drive?" Sandra Vittonelli asked Jennifer Parsons. The two women lay poolside in the Parsons' backyard in North Las Vegas.

"I think it helped me to persuade Erik, seemed somehow job connected," Jen replied. "He says he is a Wind Warrior, but I think in the comics Wind Warrior was a woman. I haven't told him that yet. But the truth is that the house was not far from the base, and it was the right price, less than three hundred. It's a relatively small lot, but we do have the walled-in backyard with the pool, the hot tub, the big gas grill. Great for a quiet Saturday night like this. Glad you finally agreed to come over."

"I am, too. But beyond the great name of the street, why here? Why not get a ranch out in the desert?" Sandra asked.

"College. The girls went to Dartmouth and Brown,

not cheap," Jen said. "Erik transferred his GI Bill education benefits to the kids, but it still costs a lot. And they both want to go to med school, so we have invested in other things. Real estate just is not the growth ticket it used to be."

"That's great they wanted to go to med school like their mom," Sandra said as she reached for her beer. "Ray went to Brown."

"That's the third time today you have mentioned this Ray guy. Is there something I should know?"

Sandra laughed and choked on her beer. "Just because I am lying down on a chaise longue, doctor, does not mean you get to analyze me. No, Jen, you're right. I am thinking about him a lot."

"And he's your boss?" Jen asked.

"Not really, different outfit. But he is higher ranking. Younger, by three years, and higher by about four pay grades. Fucking overachiever, literally," Sandra laughed again. "It's the first time since the divorce that I—"

"Did I hear someone say overachiever? Talking about me again?" Erik said as he appeared carrying a platter from the grill. "Two Wagu steaks, rare, for us war fighters and one Copper River salmon for the doctor." The two women rose from their lounge chairs and followed Erik to the picnic table.

"Did you ever think you would be living in Las Vegas?" Jen asked Sandra.

"No, not in my line of work," she answered. "Not after Baghdad, Kabul, Dubai. But it's actually a lot like Dubai here. Desert, high-rises, fancy shopping malls, resorts, nobody's real home. Vegas just hasn't put in the Dubai indoor snow ski thing yet."

"Only a matter of time, boss," Erik said. "I can see it now, a scale replica of the Matterhorn just beyond the Wynn Encore, overlooking the golf course. They'll clean up."

"Speaking of cleaning up, honey," Jen began, "Did you—" The sudden noise sounded like a thunderclap on top of the house. The windows shook. The picture window shattered into spiderwebs. Erik jumped on top of the table to look around. Jennifer and Sandra turned around toward the direction of the blast in time to see the smoke begin to climb above a house farther down on the next street.

"Whoa," Erik said as he moved to the wall separating his yard from his neighbor's. "Four houses down on Loggers Mill," he yelled back to Jennifer and Sandra.

"Four?" Jennifer asked. "Honey, that's Patti and Bill's place." She turned to Sandra. "The Wongs. He's one of your pilots."

Erik vaulted over the six-foot-high stucco wall separating his house from the one on Loggers Mill Drive. He landed by the neighbor's pool and ran through their gate out onto the street. The houses on Loggers Mill were emptying out quickly, women and children standing in the street staring at the flames and smoke coming from the house at 2704. Several men were running toward the burning house. Erik sprinted up the street. "Calling 911?" he yelled at an older man who stood in a driveway with a mobile phone to his ear.

"Already did. They're on their way," the man screamed after Erik.

As he saw the flames coming out of the front window, Erik's heart sank. It was not the sort of fire that people would likely survive. It had engulfed the whole house in a few minutes and it was fierce. The heat created a force field out in the street beyond the end of the driveway. The Wongs had two little boys, he remembered, maybe aged six and four. There was no sign of any of the family in the group of people that had formed in the street next to the home.

"Did they get out?" Erik gasped as he ran up to the group. No one answered. Bill Wong's Grand Cherokee was in the driveway, the Creech Air Base sticker on the left rear bumper. Erik pulled off his T-shirt and held it over his face to protect himself from the wall of heat as he approached the Jeep. He used the balled up shirt to grab the doorknob of the Jeep, but still he felt the sting of the hot surface as he pulled the door open. Inside, like all Air Force pilots, Wong kept a fire extinguisher under the driver's seat. Erik ripped it from its mount and moved into the open garage. The flames had not yet reached the garage, but still it was like walking into a steel mill furnace. He knew immediately that his instinct to enter the house to search for the Wongs was insane. If he even tried to open the door from the garage into the house, he would be committing suicide.

Instead, he kicked open the rear door of the garage, and stepped into the backyard. A blackened body in a skirt was floating facedown in the pool. Patti Wong, he guessed. Near the brick grill was another form, charred and lifeless. There was no need to see if either body was still alive. They had been killed instantly by the blast and flame, then thrown several feet. He stood for a long moment looking at the blackened corpses, realizing that he had never seen the body of a victim up close before, only from the air or on the screen.

The stucco wall that demarcated the end of the Wong's property had almost disappeared, revealing what had been an empty lot behind them. Now that vacant land was a large crater, a hole that looked like it might have been made by the impact of a fiery meteor.

Erik felt powerless, ridiculous, as he stood there shirtless, in his bathing suit and bare feet, holding the little extinguisher. He heard sirens over the open-throated roar of the fire. He thought of the people whom he had seen on the Big Board, the ones who were always standing by the flaming houses that he had blown up. So this was what it felt like to be so close to the flames and not be able to do anything but watch.

Erik heard the loudest siren stop abruptly as the first fire truck braked outside the house.

# 29

SUNDAY, DECEMBER 6
DJIBOUTI-AMBOULI INTERNATIONAL AIRPORT
DJIBOUTI

France's Charles de Gaulle and Egypt's Gamal Abdel Nasser had little in common except the year of their death, 1970, and the corner in Djibouti where the streets named after them intersected. Nearby, the école was quiet early in the morning. In its courtyard, five men pulled the tarp off the back of the truck and went to work setting up the equipment.

The sound was a combination of a *whoosh* and a muffled thud. Then again. Then a third time.

As soon as the third mortar round jumped from the tube of the Ukrainian Sani 2B11M launcher, the five men ran from the big truck in the school courtyard to their motorbikes. In less than a minute, they were speeding down the narrow streets of the district, in three different directions. When he was three blocks away on the

Rue de Zeila, the fifth man stopped his bike, pulled the transmitter from his pocket, turned it on, and then hit the button that caused the fourth mortar round to explode inside the 120mm tube, destroying the launcher, the truck, and much of the empty schoolhouse.

By then the three GPS-equipped Gran bomblets that had flown out of their tubes had opened stabilizing fins, adjusted their trajectories, and fallen on the aircraft hangar that was two and a half miles from the school courtyard, inside what had been the old French Air Force Camp Lemonnier, at the far side of Djibouti-Ambouli International Airport. Two rounds exploded on contact with the roof. The third hit on the runway axis ramp outside of the hangar.

Three Predators and two of the larger Reapers that had been in the hangar were damaged beyond repair. None had been mated with Hellfire missiles or the new 250-pound laser-guided bombs. Missile and bomb mating with the aircraft occurred in the separate weaponization hangar, behind a berm at the end of the main runway. It was untouched by the mortar rounds. Four Reapers from the Djibouti base were flying missions when the attack took place. Three Predators were in a separate hangar undergoing electronics upgrades.

Of the seven men who died, all were American civilians. Six of them worked for General Avionics. The seventh was a CIA logistics officer. Twelve others, all Americans, were injured from the blasts.

SUNDAY, DECEMBER 6
PEG HEADQUARTERS
NAVY HILL
WASHINGTON, DC

Ray cherished his Sunday mornings. Sunday was the only day of the week when he could sleep in, when he could throw on gym shorts, grab the *Times* outside the town house door, brew coffee, toast English muffins, play Bach on his elaborate sound system, and ease into the day. Not this Sunday. The videoconference had started at seven. He sat sullenly, listening, watching, alone in the conference room at the Policy Evaluation Group. In silent protest, he had come in wearing the gym shorts and an old Brown sweatshirt. He had not bothered to comb his mop of hair.

"Coincidences do happen," Sandra was saying, "and Bagram Air Base has been hit with Taliban mortars hundreds of times. One mortar even hit the Chairman of the Joint Chiefs' aircraft a while back, but a direct hit on the Hellfire missile bunker the same morning that we get a mortar attack on our base in Djibouti?"

It occurred to Ray that it was only a little after five in the morning where Sandra was, outside Vegas. Maybe she had been up all night working on what had happened.

"Here's why we think it was coincidence," the CIA analyst replied in Virginia. "We have no evidence of any current, operational link between the Taliban in Afghanistan and anybody who might be operating a terrorist cell in Djibouti. So, it may just be that a hangar with our UAVs got hit in Djibouti and two thousand kilometers away at about the same time an ammo storage area with Hellfire missiles for our UAVs in Afghanistan also gets hit."

There was a Marine one-star General representing the Pentagon on the video link. Ray wondered what the Marine had done wrong to get the Sunday morning shift at the Pentagon. "We operate military forces all across the nation and all around the world," the General said. "And things happen simultaneously, or near simultaneously, all the time with us. A helicopter crashes at Twentynine Palms in California and a different kind of chopper off the USS *Inchon* in the Med goes down at the same time. No connection."

They began to discuss the operational effects of the losses at the two bases. Missions into Yemen and Somalia could still be run from Djibouti once replacement personnel arrived in forty-eight hours. Armament for missions over Afghanistan and Pakistan was also stored at Kandahar and some of that was being flown up to the huge Bagram base. A C-17 was already in the air from Diego Garcia in the Indian Ocean, loaded with Hellfire missiles for the UAVs in Afghanistan. Everything would be back to normal in a few days. The meeting on drones, Ray thought, was droning on. He chuckled to himself at that thought and took a gulp of the now cold coffee he had grabbed at the 7-Eleven on the way in.

"What's so funny?" Dugout asked as he walked into the conference room.

"What the hell are you doing here on a Sunday morning?" Ray asked. He checked to make sure his microphone was on mute and that the other participants in the conference could not hear him or see Dugout.

"I never left last night," Dugout replied. "I played a midnight set at the Hamilton, but then I came back afterward to see what was happening and just lost track of time. Pretty heavy shit, huh?"

Ray's reply was a combination of a sigh and a yawn. "I dunno. These guys all seem to think the two attacks were a coincidence and all will be well in no time, which does kind of cause me to wonder why I am here and not out jogging in Rock Creek."

"Remember that Minerva BDA software procurement you signed a few months back?" Dugout asked.

"Bomb Damage Assessment software?"

"No, Big Data Analysis. It's going to change the world, man. It's like artificial intelligence running naked through databases. The new Big Data program is called Minerva. You ask it plaintext questions and it queries structured and unstructured databases and makes correlations all on its own. It's the wave of the future for intel analysis," Dugout effused.

"So did I buy it for you already?" Ray asked.

"Yes, you signed the purchase order and here is what happens when you ask the program a fairly unstructured, plaintext question like 'What connections are there between the attacks on U.S. UAV assets in the last twenty-four hours?' " He handed Ray a stack of paper, the first page of which was a summary.

As he read, the discussion on the video link continued on. Ray flipped back and forth from the summary page to the tabbed detailed annexes. As he did, his eyes widened and he began looking back and forth at Dugout and the papers. What he read ended his lethargy. His synapses were now firing quickly, his blood flowing faster. While a State Department analyst was in midsentence, Ray unmuted his own microphone and interrupted.

"Can I go back to the Unified Coincidence Theory for a minute?" Not waiting for comment, he started. "I get that coincidences occur in life, but I didn't hear anybody comment on the fact that the three attacks all occurred within five minutes of each other. And that the forensics says that two of them involved Ukrainian mortar rounds with highly accurate GPS guidance systems. That suggests that the mortar targets were not random, but selected. And our databases show no prior use of those Ukrainian rounds by the Taliban or al Qaeda, by anyone in AfPak, Yemen, or East Africa."

The FBI representative was the first to reply. "Did you say three attacks? We have only been told about two."

"Yes, I did," Ray said. "And I bet that somewhere in the FBI you know about the third. You see part of the coincidence was that two minutes after the first mortar round hit in Djibouti and one minute before the first mortar hit in Afghanistan, the house of Lieutenant William Wong blew up outside of Creech Air Force Base in Nevada.

"Lieutenant Wong was a Predator pilot and his house exploded when the twenty-inch natural gas transit pipe running through his neighborhood coincidentally corroded and erupted, or so the gas pipeline company says. Also coincidentally, that gas pipeline company had a network breach about an hour earlier, a hack into its SCADA control system. Here's the really big coincidence. The hacker was using a laptop with a cyrillic keyboard, like they use in the Ukraine."

Ray waited a minute while it sank in. "Now then, there are some intelligence collection and analysis tasks I think we should set about fairly quickly. . . ."

With the videoconference meeting over, Ray looked at Dugout. "I'm not sure those agencies will find anything. I'm not even sure what I'm looking for."

"Well, this is no longer just about shit happening overseas to the drone program. They're here. So we look for them here," Dugout suggested.

"They're here because they blew up a gas pipeline? Couldn't they do that from anywhere by hacking into the SCADA system? You taught me that," Ray noted.

"Yes, but the fact that they figured out who Wong was, what he did for a living, where he lived, the fact that they knew a big gas pipeline was running through the yard next door, that has the feel of some on-the-ground presence, as well as hacking. Why Wong? How many others on the drone team did they look at before they found someone whom they could kill remotely?" Dugout asked.

"What did you just say?" Ray said.

"How many other . . . you mean the 'kill remotely' part. Yeah, it's like they are doing to us what we do to them," Dugout noted.

"If so, this could just be the start of a campaign here, in the U.S. And, yeah, I get it, they would probably want to be here or have some presence here to help." Ray Bowman suddenly looked up at the ceiling, as if he had just been hit by something falling on his head. "Damn it, Dug. Remember, way back during the summer when there was that report about somebody maybe doing attacks around Christmas? What if this is the start of it? What if they plan to attack the drone program like this and then maybe make other attacks around Christmas to blackmail us into stopping the drones?"

"Christmas isn't even a month off and we haven't seen any more about planned attacks since that one report last summer. That had everyone spun up then, but now they've forgotten about it," Dugout observed. "I can run the Minerva Big Data program to see if they've overlooked some leads, see if there is a Disturbance in the Force anywhere."

Ray sat quietly, running his own data analytics program in his head, his eyes darting back and forth as he thought through scenarios. Then he looked back up at Dugout. "Right. So let's start looking for anything unusual, anything that could be reconnaissance, planning for attacks here. And don't just look for typical AQ and Pakistani ISI types. What's the Ukrainian connection? This has the feel of something new. Start running your data searches, Minerva, big data. I have to go to my gym, to see a reporter."

"Not a good idea, Boss," Dugout said.

"Tell me about it," Ray replied.

SUNDAY, DECEMBER 6
SPORTS CLUB/LA
M STREET
WASHINGTON, DC

"Hi, I'm Bryce Duggan. If you don't mind my saying so, that looks like crankcase sludge." As had been suggested, he had shown up in gym attire. He was in a tank top and shorts. No notepad. No recorder. No place to hide one.

"It's called Green Machine and it's good for you, just like some other machines are good for you. Raymond Bowman. Sit down."

For a time neither man spoke. Finally, the younger man began. "I don't know which of our bosses asked for this meeting. I do know it is to be totally off the record."

"Doesn't matter who asked for it. You have questions for me. I have questions for you," Ray said.

Bryce indicated for Ray to start. "Okay, the dead kids in Afghanistan. You do know that wasn't an orphanage, right?"

"I tried to find out. They would only let me talk to certain people in the town. When I tried to get back later, the ANA troops wouldn't let me in. They stopped me at a roadblock outside of the town. I reported all of that. I said I couldn't confirm it was an orphanage," Bryce replied.

"And the guys who told you to go there, who handled you there?" Ray asked.

"Qazzani guys, I think. I mean that was what I was told. I had no way to verify that. It's not like the Qazzanis issue their men ID cards," Bryce said. "Look, I put around that I wanted to interview people about what it was like to be hunted by drones. These guys, who said they were Qazzani guys, got back to me."

Ray swallowed some of the green crankcase fluid. "And the drone they landed when you just happened to be in some little city in Pakistan. How'd that happen?"

"Same thing. Fares Sorhari, my cameraman and field

producer, he's an Emirati. From Dubai. Went to Georgetown. Hates the Islamists. He got a call when we were in Islamabad. 'Fly to Mashhad tomorrow. In the afternoon, go back to the airport. Big story. It will win you the prize.' So, we did."

"You're lucky you weren't kidnapped," Ray thought aloud.

"I know. We had GPS trackers hidden on us, but, yeah, we thought that could happen," Bryce admitted. "Remind me to tell you about roadblocks in Yemen."

"You know how much damage you have done to the program?" Ray asked.

"I know damage is being done. I'm not sure I'm the one who is doing it. We didn't shoot down your drones. We didn't hack the controls and hijack one. We reported on it," Bryce replied. "Look, kids did die in that town and they did die because a drone attacked that building. You don't deny that, you say it was a setup, but kids did die. That's a fact and we report the facts."

"The facts, Mr. Duggan, are that the terrorists kidnapped a bunch of little kids and they killed them by luring us into an attack. They wanted them to die and they killed them as surely as if they had put a bullet through each of their little heads. Did you report that?"

"We reported that you said that and that we were unable to prove who was right so far, because we can't, but we haven't given up trying to find out who was right," Bryce replied.

"Moral equivalence, huh? Equal credibility to the U.S. government and to a bunch of terrorists who would just as gladly kill you if they couldn't use you as their mouthpiece," Ray shot back.

Bryce wanted to cool the conversation down. "You went to the Kennedy School for a year, so did I. Did you take Brenda Williams's course on Government and the Media? She's been teaching it for years, keeps updating it because it keeps happening? There's a long record of the U.S. government lying to the media. So, yes, until we can independently verify something, all we can do is say that it is what the government tells us. And if their people say something else, we have to report that. If we can't say we know which one appears to be right, people can judge for themselves," Bryce said.

"Yes, I did take Williams's course and yes, I know that government officials have lied and covered up over the years, less here than in other countries, less in recent years than in the past. But I don't. I know you don't know me, but, off the record, I don't lie to the media. There are some things I don't volunteer, some things I won't talk about because doing so may get people killed, good people. But I do not lie, Bryce. Not to you, not to the Congress."

"Okay, I buy that," Bryce replied. As he said it, he wondered to himself if he really did buy it.

"What I am trying to do is stop a bunch of guys hopped up on some distorted version of Islam from continuing a wave of killing, to spread their control, to chop off hands and heads, to take girls out of schools, to burn down churches, and to blow up U.S. skyscrapers. That's what I do, Bryce. That's what I try to do and drones are one way I do it and there are not a lot of alternatives some times."

"I get that, I really do," Bryce replied. "I just got back from Nigeria. We were there last Sunday, by coincidence, no tip, when the Boko Haram guys, the local AQ types, set fire to a church with people in it and then shot at people fleeing. It's amazing video.

"Week before, we were in Mali. We got near Timbuktu. We paid some Tuareg tribesmen, not Ansar Dine the AQ affiliate, but local guys. We caught, on camera, a Reaper strike you guys did on an Ansar Dine compound. My Tuareg friends applauded. Both the Africa stories and some stuff we shot in Djibouti and Somalia are running on an hour-long special on terrorism in Africa in the near future. It's evenhanded, really."

"Can't wait," Ray replied. "Nigeria, Mali, what's happening across Africa is that radical Islamists are moving south, into what were moderate Islamic settlements, areas where Muslims lived side by side with Christians and others. And they are trying to drive the non-Muslims out and suppress the majority Muslims. They start by cutting off body parts. They smash gravestones because they say the stones are idols that people worship. This is really a case of a tiny percentage of people trying to impose some fourteenth-century version of a religion on a bunch of people who do not want it," Ray explained.

"I agree. It's awful. I know. I've been there," Bryce said. "But why is it our problem?"

"Because they made it our problem. They decided they were part of al Qaeda. They announced to everyone that they want to kill Americans and to spread this religious police state they set up when they take over anywhere, spread it to all parts of the world. One big caliphate. If they're not held in check, pushed back, they will move forward and eventually they will get around to their announced intention of killing Americans. First they will kill Americans to drive us out of 'their part of the world.' Then, they will kill to expand their part of the world, to Europe, to here. I know it sounds crazy, but Hitler and the Bolsheviks did at first, too. And these AQ guys have a track record."

Bryce had heard the arguments before. "I guess it's a question of where we choose to fight and who we choose to back in the process. When we back regimes like those in Mali, we get tarred with all of their sins," Bryce said. "The Mali government may not be as crazy as al Qaeda, but they are not people we would want to be associated with were it not for the fact that they are fighting, sort of, against AQ."

"We know that. America tried the 'enemy of my enemy' thing in the Cold War and we got into bed with a lot of Latin American sadists," Ray said. "We're trying to reform the people we are working with, when we can."

They both took a breath. And both scanned the few others in the little café off the gym to see if anyone appeared to be taking a special interest in them. Despite the ardor of what both men had been saying, they had kept the volume of the conversation level low.

"Collateral damage. There are a lot of independent observers who think that it has been much higher than you admit," Bryce noted. "Did you happen to see my piece on the village in Yemen?"

Ray smiled for the first time in the meeting. "Don't tell anyone, but yes, I have watched all of your drone stories. And yes, off the record, we probably did kill that guy's brother to get to an AQAP leader who was renting a room in the house. But notice that the attack took place when most of the women and children were out. We thought they were all out. That kind of intelligence collection is hard to get, but we try to do it."

"But the surviving brother. He wasn't AQAP before, but now he effectively is. He wants to kill Americans. What have you gained?" Bryce asked.

"With our attack in Yemen we took off the battlefield a hardened terrorist who had trained Americans of Yemeni and Saudi ethnic background and tried to send them back to the U.S. to do attacks," Ray said. "And because of where we had to get him, in that boardinghouse, which you think was so innocent, we pissed off an entire village and we now have one guy so mad he may join AQ. What lesson do I take from that personally? Lower the collateral damage even further. Wait till we can get the bad guy alone, preferably on the road."

"Why don't you want me to report that?" Bryce asked.

"Because the Yemeni government wants to keep the slight fiction that America is not using drones there. They judge that even as slight as that fiction is, it helps them. They want to say it was their Air Force, even though nobody really believes that."

"What happened to the American Yemenis this AQ guy had trained?" Bryce asked.

"Completely off the record? The Yemeni Army stopped them at a roadblock and a firefight erupted. They all bought it," Ray said. "Saved us from having to decide to do another drone strike on Americans."

Bryce felt a shiver at the thought of people dying at a Yemeni roadblock. "But would you have?" he asked. "Would you have killed the American citizens?"

"No, I was advocating for having them arrested in Dubai where they were going to get on a Delta flight to Atlanta and an Emirates flight to L.A." Ray finished the Green Machine. "But they never left Yemen and Americans did not kill them."

"But we might have been following them with a drone and told the Yemenis to set up a road block?" Bryce asked.

"As an old British TV show character used to say, 'You might think that. I could not possibly comment.' You see, you may report in color, but it's a world of grays. We fuck up. We learn. We try to fuck up less. The bad guys are definitely bad, in this struggle. Our motives are good and we try real hard not to become bad in the process. It's not always easy."

"I'm sure it's not," Bryce agreed.

"Where did you live when you were at the K School?" Ray asked.

"Somerville."

"Ah yes, Slumahvil. So did I. Shitty apartment in a three-decker, but there was a great bar on the corner. Lots of Bruins fans."

"I hope you think my Special Edition on Terrorism in Africa is fair," Bryce said as they stood up.

"I doubt I will, but keep trying." They shook hands. "And we will keep trying." Ray went downstairs and hit the weights.

# 30

MONDAY, DECEMBER 7
THE FERRY BUILDING, THE EMBARCADERO
SAN FRANCISCO, CALIFORNIA

"Can you tell me about the ferries? We're new to San Francisco," the taller young man asked.

"Fairies?" Ahmed Bahadur stared at the two young men. They were in white shirts with black ties and nametags. Bahadur wondered if this was some kind of trap. He did not want to say much, did not want to reveal his accent. "What is your role?" he said.

"We convert people," the other young man said.

Bahadur quickly turned his back on them and walked onto the boat to Sausalito, a man in a business suit, carrying a briefcase, perhaps taking the afternoon off, going home at midday.

"That is not what we are supposed to say," the taller young man said to his colleague. "You scared him. You keep that up and you will be sent back to Salt Lake."

Bahadur climbed to the aft deck and then farther up to the top open deck. "I don't know how you have lived among these kafirs," he said to the man in blue blazer. "They deserve what we are going to do."

Ghazi Nawarz did not turn to look at him. "You should wear sunglasses. They all wear sunglasses. You would blend in better."

"Two years ago when I was told to move to Australia and run things in that region for our organization, I shave my face and I wear their costume. That is enough," Bahadur replied. The boat jerked as it began to move away from the pier. The two men were alone on the upper deck, as Ghazi had hoped they would be. "You have done well. Qazzani must be very pleased with you," Bahadur said.

"Four drones have been shot down, one we crashed, and one we hijacked," Ghazi said, looking back at the Ferry Building as the boat moved into the Bay. "We will do more of that, but they have hundreds left, so we are using their media, their courts, their Congress. Indirectly, of course."

Bahadur snorted. "You are soft, you have lived among them too long, my friend. What we are going to do in their subways will hurt them much more. Then we tell them it will get worse unless they really leave Afghanistan, unless they stop the drones. They will understand pain. Pain will work. It always works."

A fourteen-meter sailboat crossed ahead of the ferry, pushed by the wind toward the Golden Gate Bridge. The wind served to muffle the conversation between the two men standing next to each other chatting and looking out at the view.

"You see that big fortress on the island over there? It's a prison. They say it's impossible to escape from it,"

Ghazi said. "How many prisoners do you think they have in it?"

Bahadur looked hard at Alcatraz. "If they have small cells like at Bagram, they must have ten thousand men in there. How many of them are Arabs? How many are our people? Maybe we should also demand their release?"

Ghazi laughed and turned to face Bahadur. "There are no Arabs, no Pushtuns, no prisoners at all. It's empty. It is for tourists." Bahadur frowned. "You see, Ahmed, you do not really understand these people. I do because, yes, I live in Canada, I live among them.

"But I also have a blood debt because of my father. And therefore I will help Qazzani kill them. And you and your boys will kill them. But killing them will not stop the drones. They will only send more. The only way to stop them is to use their media, their laws, their politicians. That way we make their own people stop the drones and decide to really leave Afghanistan. We make it their choice."

Bahadur shook his head. "I trust you because Qazzani trusts you, but you are not one of us anymore. You look like you belong here, you act like you belong here, you even sound like you are from here. But we must work together. We need to have our attacks happen at the same time. My bombs go off in the old subways. Your computer guys cause crashes in the new metros. We destroy their Christmas. Here, take my plans and the timing. Don't worry, it's on one of your special sticks. They will erase when you read them."

The man in the suit thrust out his hand as if to shake, but with the thumb drive in his palm. The two men shook hands without speaking and then Bahadur climbed down from the upper deck. Alone, looking out at the bridge, Ghazi fingered the thumb drive he had just put in his pants pocket.

He knew the attacks on the subways would infuriate the Americans again, just when they were getting used to the idea that they were invulnerable to any more terrorist attacks in their homeland. His attacks on their drone program would also make them know they were not invulnerable. But would it make them leave Muslim lands, would it make them stop the drones? Would even the political pressure from within America be enough to stop the drones? He wasn't sure.

And if it didn't work, should he continue? Or should he take his inheritance from his father and the matching money from Qazzani and just disappear, maybe to Brazil, South Africa, or New Zealand? It was a lot of money. He could live well. But he would always be looking over his shoulder and they would always be looking for him. Somehow they would find him, someday. They had taken forever to find Osama, but they finally did. And while Osama was waiting for them, he lived a horrid life, cooped up in that wretched house. I cannot live like that, Ghazi thought, waiting for them to come for me.

He had tried to be not just a Canadian, but a Global. It had worked, up to a point. He knew his way around in cities on every continent, where to get the best meal, the best wine, the best woman. Even without his father's money, he had stashed millions from the cyber crime in safe-deposit boxes all over the world. But no place was home, no cuisine, no traditions were his. He had never known a real emotion that drove him, until now. And that emotion did not have its roots in Vancouver, or Chelsea, or Saint-Tropez, or Hong Kong. It came from the Pushtun homeland and it was blood. It was not about Allah, or some myth about virgins waiting in an afterlife. No, it was about tribal duty, family duty. It was about vengeance.

So this, he knew now, was his fate. A short, but exciting life. Choice had been an illusion after all. There was no future, not for him, not now, just duty. This was going to be it, the vengeance, the statement, the accomplishment that would go down in history like 9/11, like 7/7 in London.

The boat shook as it docked in Sausalito, breaking his thoughts. He moved quickly to get off the boat. There was something he needed to buy in Marin.

# 31

TUESDAY, DECEMBER 8
GILGIT AIRPORT
GILGIT, PAKISTAN

"Zebra Roger Papa, requesting permission to take off."

"AP-ZRP, you are clear to take off," the man in the tower said. The aircraft had a civilian call sign, its tail number. The aircraft was painted white with blue trim. There was no logo, no livery.

It was the only aircraft at the field. Pakistan Airlines flew in twice a day, weather permitting, but for twenty-two hours a day Gilgit was usually an airport without aircraft. Gilgit was a small mountain town near Pakistan's border with China. It had been spared the presence of the Taliban and al Qaeda. It had been spared, therefore, the drones. For the last two weeks the unmarked, high wing, twin-engine aircraft had sat inside the old military hangar at Gilgit's little airport, out of sight.

"Roger, Gilgit Tower, ZRP rolling," the pilot said as the Chinese-made Y-11 began the full-powered run down the airstrip. He had flown the Y-11 when he was in the Pakistan Air Force. Now, he and the guys in the back of the plane were making more money in a month than they had made in a year in the military. Someone always wanted an unscheduled, off-the-books flight, with no questions about the cargo.

In the high, thin air of the Hindu Kush the twin-propellered aircraft would need every inch of the runway to lift off into the valley. The cargo, however, was light. Almost everything had been removed from the cabin, except for a table with computers and black boxes, and two men who sat watching them.

The aircraft banked and headed southwest, passing under the monstrous peak of Nanga Parbat. The pilot had the aircraft pointed toward the Swat Valley, an area of beauty once called the Switzerland of South Asia. For over a decade its resorts had seen few foreign tourists. Its morgue, however, had seen many victims of the fighting, some killed by the drones. Today, it was the drone that was being hunted.

In a short time, a drone was expected over the Swat Valley. The Pakistani ISI had passed word to the Americans, word that one of the few remaining leaders of al Qaeda Central was going to a meeting near the base of Tirch Mir, the 7,700-meter peak outside of Chitral. The Americans would likely come to look, perhaps to kill.

The men in the back watched their computers as the radios that had been added to the aircraft scanned the frequencies used by the drones. Other radios were standing by, not to receive, but to broadcast through the new antenna blister that had been added under the tail of the Y-11. One radio would overpower the satellite signal on which the drone's pilot was sending his commands to the aircraft. Another radio would send a loud noise onto the frequency the Americans used to transmit their encrypted GPS signal to their military receivers. Finally, a third radio would send a loud signal on the same frequency that was used for civilian navigation data, a false GPS signal. The result would be that the drone, unable to phone home, would fly home, or where it thought home was, based on the false GPS data. It would land at Mardan. There would be people there to meet it.

First, however, the Y-11 pilot needed to find the drone and fly his aircraft just a little higher, maybe at fifteen thousand feet, and just a little bit abeam, maybe one thousand meters. He had been told that the Americans could change the color of their drones to blend into the sky, but they could not do that on the top of the wings, just on the bottom. So, while you could not easily see the drone from below, from above it would stand out. He wished that his friends in the Pakistani Air Force, his former colleagues, could radio him when they saw the drone on their radar, but he knew they could not. The Americans were always listening, listening to everything. So he, and his copilot, scanned the sky below them as they approached the Swat Valley.

TUESDAY, DECEMBER 8
GLOBAL COORDINATION CENTER
CREECH AFB, NEVADA

"It was a gas leak. That little park, that lot next to his house, it had a big gas pipeline and a pump underground. That's why there was no house on the lot. The Wongs didn't know that. We all wondered who paid for the landscaping on that empty lot. But it was a gas leak, I asked the Clark County Sheriff's office. They're not treating it as a homicide. They say the pipe corroded," Erik Parsons told Sandra Vittonelli in her office.

"Erik, all I am saying is that Ray and Dugout think it was murder. They think someone hacked the control system for the long-distance pipeline and did something with the valve on that pump station. They say something like this happened in San Bruno, outside the San Francisco airport a few years ago," Sandra said, rising from behind her desk.

"Dugout? Now we're believing someone who calls himself Dugout, over the Sheriff and Air Force OSI?" Erik asked.

"Didn't know Office of Special Investigations is involved." Sandra said. "They run their own computer forensics?"

"I don't know. No, probably not. They told me to talk to the Sheriff. They kind of begged off doing anything of their own. This Dugout do some computer forensics?"

"Yes, he did. He works at the Policy Evaluation Group and he's good, real good. Ray gave the results to the Fibbies. They opened a case," Sandra replied.

"The FBI has opened a case to see if the Wongs were murdered?" Erik asked.

"Yes, they have," Sandra said as she approached the door to her office, "but keep that to yourself for now. Until we really know what happened, I don't want to freak out every pilot on that floor out there. Now, let's go take a look at this Swat Valley mission."

Sandra Vittonelli walked to a central area on the operations floor of the Global Coordination Center. Unlike the other cubicles, which were small and had a seat for only one pilot, this area was open, designed for complex, multibird missions. Major Bruce Dougherty sat in the middle of the three seats, supported by a civilian signals intelligence expert detailed from NSA and a senior enlisted officer who acted as a back-up pilot and communications expert.

"Okay, Major, what have we got?" she asked.

"Well, we're flying this specially configured Reaper. It's got the standard Ku-band satellite radio for my control links, just like all the other Preds and Reaps. That's off the commercial satellites, but it's encrypted. This Reap, however, has also got an X-band satellite radio and it's using a frequency that NRO let us use for a week only. NRO normally uses this freq for talking to its own secret satellites."

"So, we're also using a channel they normally use for their intelligence collection satellites, neat," Erik commented as he joined them.

"Right and we also have an X-band radio on the stealth bird, the Peregrine, that we're flying in trail at 22,000," Bruce Dougherty explained. "So we got back-up comms and using the two birds we can geolocate a signal source in the Ku band."

"Great. Let the games begin," Sandra said as she plunked down into one of the row of observer seats set behind and slightly above the operators.

"I'll throw the view from the Peregrine up on the Big Board," Bruce said as a scene of snow-covered mountains appeared at the front of the theaterlike operations center. The view then zoomed in on a gray-white Reaper drone, slowly flying ahead and below. Four missiles, but not Hellfires, were visible under its wings. The Reaper banked to the right and began a long, slow circle over the Swat Valley.

Halfway through the Peregrine's second time around the Valley an alarm sounded on the console next to Bruce Dougherty, taking Sandra out of her daydream. "Strong jamming on the Ku-band command link, Major," the sergeant read off of her computer screen.

"Roger that, switch command link to X band and continue circling," Bruce replied.

"The bird would have continued to circle anyway," Erik, seated in an observer chair, said to Sandra. "The guys in the jammer aircraft won't think that unusual."

"Triangulate on the jamming signal, slew the Peregrine's camera to the jammer," Bruce instructed.

The on-board computers on the two drones calculated where the jamming signal was originating. Their information was bounced up to a satellite, down to the GCC's computers, which correlated the data from both aircraft, computed the most likely point of origin, and then sent a signal to the higher-altitude stealth drone to point its camera.

The Y-11 aircraft suddenly appeared on the Big Board. "Two-engine prop job, tail number Alpha Poppa dash Zebra Romeo Poppa," Bruce read out.

"Chinese-made aircraft. Pakistani civilian aircraft designator," the NSA officer announced as she tapped into her computer. "And it's not in their database. It does not exist."

"Of course not," Sandra said.

The alarm sounded again. "Military GPS signal

being jammed. And, wait for it, it's the same source," the sergeant said.

"Okay, Bruce, bring the Peregrine alongside that Y-11. I want to look in the windows," Erik ordered.

"That should be fun, boss," Bruce replied. "Never done that before with a drone."

"No, but you and I have done it a few times when we flew F-16s. Same thing."

On the Big Board, the image of the Y-11 rolled about as the Peregrine drone came out of steady flight and moved into an intercept course. The screen split into two images. The new image was of three dots, one red, one blue, one green. It was a simulated radar screen, showing the location of the two drones and the Y-11 relative to each other. The blue dot, the Peregrine drone, was moving quickly toward the green dot, the jamming aircraft.

As the blue dot circled the green dot on the screen on the right, the screen on the left showed a camera feed from the Peregrine. The image zoomed into a side window on the Y-11. Then, as the Peregrine moved ahead, it looked back at the cockpit of the aircraft. Two astonished looking men sat in the Y-11's cockpit, pointing at the drone's front camera pod. As the Peregrine came around, the camera zoomed in on the newly installed antenna blister under the tail of the Y-11.

"Ms. Vittonelli, it is my professional opinion as a fighter pilot that the Y-11 aircraft is a hostile attempting to interfere with U.S. military operations and that it does not have onboard protected classes, such as women or children," Bruce said somewhat formally.

Erik stood up. "I concur."

"Very well, under the preapproved guidelines for handling hostile aircraft attempting to interfere with U.S. military operations," Sandra began, "Colonel Parsons, take out the hostile."

"Roger that," Erik replied. "Major, engage with two Sidewinders."

Bruce pulled the stick back, bringing the Peregrine quickly away from the Y-11, and then he handed off control. "Sarge, take over the Peregrine, keep it up at angels 25 and a klik off beam, keep its camera on the hostile."

Bruce then assumed control of the Reaper, bringing it out of its autopilot circling mode. The Reaper went into a tight turn, until it was pointed at the Y-11, which had been above and behind it. The Big Board image now split between the Reaper's view of the Y-11 from below and the Peregrine's view from above and off to the side.

A high-pitched beep came from Bruce's console. "I have a lock on the Y-11 with Fox two." A long two seconds passed. "And firing, one and two away."

The split screen showed on the left the smoke from contrails of two missiles leaving the Reaper and on the right a view of the Reaper itself and two darts, trailing smoke, streaking toward the Y-11.

"And impact," Bruce said softly. The two screens showed an orange flash, and then another, and then what looked something like an elaborate fireworks display as fingers of white smoke shot in every direction. There was no noise of an explosion in the GCC, no sound effects.

"Bruce, congratulations, you are the first drone ace. The first drone pilot with an air-to-air kill. Maybe we should tell the Pakistanis that one of our drones exploded, or got shot down, over the Swat Valley," Erik suggested.

"They'll know what happened," Sandra said, as she stood up. She shook hands with Bruce Dougherty and his two teammates. When she was ten feet away and moving toward her office, she spoke just loud enough to be heard by the team behind her. "Try to fucking steal my drones."

# 32

WEDNESDAY, DECEMBER 9
GLOBAL COORDINATION CENTER
CREECH AFB, NEVADA

The red capsule or the black capsule, he wondered. Erik Parsons had been working most of the day, but he had to stay at work for at least another six hours to oversee a sensitive flight over Syria. He needed a caffeine infusion. Black was intensity ten. He inserted the purple capsule in the Nespresso machine in the break room.

"Goddamn Mustangs." Bruce Dougherty had burst into the Break Room and thrown his car keys on the table.

"Some people like Mustangs, Major, my Jennifer for example," Erik responded. "Seriously, Bruce, chill. What's such a big deal?"

Bruce Dougherty collapsed into one of the plastic-molded chairs by the table. He held his left hand to his forehead, closed his eyes, and shook his head. "My car has another flat. I'm already driving on the little bitty spare. I can't get the Ford dealer's truck to come onto the base and they're closing the dealership for the night in half an hour. It's just everything is fucked, man, fucked."

Erik sat down next to Dougherty. "This isn't just about the car, Bruce, is it?"

"No, boss, it's not. I mean, everything was going so good after the problems I had at the beginning of the year with the divorce. You let me fly the Vienna op and then go after the guys with the Stingers. But then we find out that I killed that American guy in Vienna and Sandra gets sued for it. Then I fucking bomb an orphanage. Did you see the video of those little bodies all charred up? Somehow somebody steals one of our drones and there are all these special investigator guys from CIA crawling around the GCC trying to figure out how, like it was one of us who did it. Then Wong and his wife get killed by some freak gas pipeline explosion. Boss, sometimes I just don't know what I am doing here. I wanna fly, not play video games that kill real people, that kill little kids. I am like that freak who shot the kids in Connecticut, a baby killer, that's what they called the 'unknown pilot' on TV. It's me, I am the baby killer."

Erik Parsons looked at the younger pilot and wished Jennifer were there to help. She would know what to say. "Tell you what, Carrot Top. Take my car. No, seriously, take it. Jen can swing by and pick me up later. She has a base tag on the Edge."

"Boss, I can't just take—"

"Major, it's an order. Go home. Better yet, go to Caesar's, over by the roulette. Take one of the ladies who hang out there upstairs. Get drunk. Get laid. You're off the next two days anyway, right? Do it. You need it.

When was the last time you got laid? Don't answer that. Just go do it. Then we can talk on Friday. Here, take the fucking keys, I have to get back into the Ops Room." With that, Erik walked out of the Break Room.

Bruce looked at the two sets of keys on the table, picked up both, and walked out into the parking lot. He got into the black Camaro.

Forty minutes later he pulled up to the valet stand at Caesar's Palace. A Cadillac XTS pulled up behind him. Bruce headed for the casino floor, but not to roulette, to the blackjack tables. No sooner had he bought his chips and sat down at a table than the waitress asked him what he was drinking. "Scotch, but not the rail one, not the free one. A single malt, Glenfiddich neat. And make it a double." He handed her his AAFI MasterCard. "Run a tab."

At the valet stand outside, the Cadillac driver had returned. "Hey, I left my iPhone in the Caddy you guys just parked. I don't want you to pull it up here again. Can I just go down to the garage and get the phone out?"

"We're not supposed to let anyone down there, sir," the valet replied.

"I don't want to get you in trouble," Ghazi said, as he slipped the valet a twenty.

"No, sir, of course not. The cars are on level P4, in the back, spaces 400 to 600. The Caddy is probably like 480."

As he approached the Camaro, Ghazi reached under the back bumper and removed the small tracking device he had left there a week earlier. He had tracked Colonel Parsons's car, but the redheaded man who had walked out of it matched the description of Major Dougherty.

Strange, he thought. Then he removed a modified iPhone from his pocket and activated a custom app that the Ukrainians had created. It simulated an OnStar signal. The device interrogated the Camaro through the satellite antenna and then, *pop,* and the driver's side door unlocked. Inside, Ghazi found the USB connector and inserted a thumb drive. The OnStar signal had turned on one of the onboard computers, one of five. Now that computer had additional code running on it from the thumb drive. Ghazi removed the thumb drive and relocked the car.

Nine minutes later, back in the casino, still using his modified iPhone, Ghazi tracked Bruce's mobile to the blackjack table. Ghazi sat at the next table and watched. The Major drank for two hours and seldom won. Then, finally, he scored. To Ghazi's surprise, Dougherty then got up from the table and headed toward the teller window with his chips. Ghazi walked quickly to the valet stand and ordered up the Cadillac. As he was getting in, he noticed Dougherty giving his ticket to the valet. The Camaro would be pulled up soon.

Six minutes later, Bruce turned left on to Flamingo and then up the ramp on to I-15 North. He knew he was drunk, but he could still drive perfectly well. After all, he was a pilot, or used to be. The trick was not doing anything that would cause him to be pulled over by the Sheriff. There was no way he could blow the breathalyzer without getting arrested.

He took the left exit on to the Gragson Freeway west. He checked the side mirror as he merged into the flow of traffic. An 18-wheeler was coming fast in the right lane. No problem, Bruce thought, go to afterburners.

The Camaro SS, he knew, had great pick up, not great rear visibility, but a lot of power under the hood. He punched the accelerator.

Instead, the brakes came on. Bruce knew he had hit the correct pedal, but the Camaro shuddered to a stop. He heard the doors click, as they locked. He looked up into the mirror and saw the grille of the Mack truck.

The Mack rode up over the Camaro and dragged it for 150 feet, scraping and sparking, before the entire mass of metal slowed to a halt. The truck's driver was unhurt, the Sheriff's Deputy later noted in the highway fatality report. The body in the Camaro was badly mangled. Death had been instant when the neck had snapped from the spinal column.

# 33

SUNDAY, DECEMBER 13
PRADO PARK
CHINO, CALIFORNIA

The B-52 circled the field and then lined up with the runway for final approach. There was a slight crosswind, which caused the aircraft's nose to point a little to the left, but soon the pilot had righted the bomber as it descended and then touched down. It taxied down the runway and then pulled off to a parking apron. Then three men picked it up and carried it off to the grassy area where the other aircraft were on display.

"How long is that wingspan?" he asked the man who appeared to be the owner.

"Six feet on each side," the bomber's owner beamed. "You like it?"

"She's a beauty," Ghazi replied. "I've never seen a radio controlled plane this big. Is it the biggest?"

"One of the biggest. Was the biggest for a while, but newcomers, you know. Tom Harris over there, his C-17 is now the biggest, but Linda Cahill and her boy made that DC-3, or C-47 I should say. It's pretty huge."

"May I?" Ghazi asked, as he went to kneel down by the fuselage for a closer look. "So she has four engines that all work?"

"JetCat P120s. Course, the real B-52 have eight engines, four pairs, but they're little compared to what you would see on a real 777. You know, for ETOPS, those mothers are huge. A man can stand upright in one and still be dwarfed. Amazing."

"And this is all battery powered?" Ghazi asked.

"No, real Jet A-1 fuel. Plus a bunch of lithium batteries in sequence. The C-17 has four kerosene-fueled engines. That's why we have this new requirement that we all have to carry fire extinguishers. Just another expense."

Ghazi nodded, knowingly. He wandered down the flight line, amazed at the number and diversity of the model aircraft, and at their size. The owners were mostly middle-aged men, or older. They wore baseball hats with patches and buttons. Some wore old military-style jackets, but there were also teenagers in jeans and hoodies. The children, or maybe grandchildren, of the owners seemed just as enthusiastic as their elders. He stopped by one young man who was showing off to friends.

"Yeah, so I hacked the app for this Chinese RC model helicopter and made a few adjustments and, ta-da, now I can fly the Sukhoi from my iPad," the teenager was explaining. The Sukhoi Su-35 Flanker was one of the bigger fighters on the strip. Painted up in Russian Air Force livery, it looked so real that Ghazi caught himself thinking about *Gulliver's Travels.* Had he become a giant or had all the world's aircraft been shrunk?

"Mind if I ask you a question?" Ghazi said to the three teenagers with the Sukhoi. They nodded and mumbled agreement. "What is this airplane made out of? Is it aluminum?"

The boys shook their heads, no. "That would be way too heavy, dude. It's fiberglass mainly, some carbon fiber. And balsa wood. Got some metal parts, sure, but we try to keep the weight down so it can get off the ground and stay up for a while."

While these people all looked like the quintessential American patriots, Ghazi thought, their allegiance to the United States did not seem to extend to all of their aircraft. There were several British Spitfires, at least one Japanese Zero, the French Concorde, and a Chinese flagged MiG-21. Ghazi had been to the Air and Space Museum on the Mall in Washington. This field in Chino, California, looked like someone had stolen the museum's content and put it all in a miniaturizing machine.

As he walked down the line, aircraft continued to take off, perform aerobatics, and land. Speakers mounted on posts announced which aircraft was performing and who owned it. The crowd applauded often, although it was not altogether clear to him what prompted some of the clapping. From what he could gather from the announcer, there were to be prizes given out later in the day.

"Are you Tom Harris?" he asked the man standing by the C-17.

"Pleased to meet you."

"I heard that yours is the biggest aircraft here. Is that right?" Ghazi asked.

"For now. Jimmy Yang is working on an Airbus-380, you know, the one with the double deck. It'll be a monster, like the real one," Harris said.

"I was wondering, how long did it take you to build the C-17?" Ghazi asked.

"I call her the Globemaster II, that's the Air Force designator. Took me about ten months, start to finish. Why, you thinking of trying to build something?"

Ghazi lowered his chin, looking dejected. "Well, I was, but I assume that as a first timer it would take me at least twice as long, but I don't think we have two years."

"Why not? It's a great hobby. You can spend the nights out in the garage by yourself, with a little TV and a beer chiller. It's probably saved my marriage, I'll tell yah."

"I'm sure, but it's just that it's for my nephew, Sanjay. He loves these planes. But the doctors aren't sure how long he has. They told us one to three years, unless of course there is a breakthrough. Of course, we are all praying very hard to Jesus for a breakthrough. It would be a miracle of sorts," Ghazi said.

The C-17 owner looked at Ghazi for a long time, thinking, nodding his head. "You know, Jesus acts in all kind of ways, through all kinds of people. Maybe it's not always all that we pray for, but he knows best."

"Yes, it's true," Ghazi replied. He stared down at the C-17.

"Tell you what," the man said, "I've been thinking I need a new project. Thinking of building something bigger than Jimmy Yang's 380. Otherwise my wife has her Honey Do list, you know? You think you could scrape together ten thousand? That's about what it cost me, without the labor."

"You would sell me your Globemaster II?" Ghazi seemed incredulous. "Then, yes, I could pay cash. I had a very good year. I am in venture capital. In Palo Alto. I would give you twelve thousand for her. She is a beauty and Sanjay will love it. It will give him a new burst of energy."

The Globemaster pilot smiled broadly. "Have you got a pickup by any chance? May need that to pull the custom trailer."

"I have a Ford 150 here. And, I can go back into town to the Bank of America and get the money in cash," Ghazi offered.

"Now that's just icing on the cake. No need to involve the IRS. You know, sometimes it's little white lies that keep a marriage together. I may just tell Cynthia that the Globemaster crashed, otherwise she'll be wanting some of the proceeds for her damn landscaping. She wants an underground irrigation system. That woman never leaves her garden."

The men shook hands as red tri-winged aircraft flew low overhead. Now my squadron is complete, Ghazi thought, six beautiful, radio-controlled model planes, one of the best collections in the United States of America. "That's Joel Rubin, he calls himself the Red Baron. We call him Snoopy."

# 34

SUNDAY, DECEMBER 13
SOUTHWEST GATE, THE WHITE HOUSE
WASHINGTON, DC

Three large, green helicopters took off in sequence, headed south. It happened every Sunday afternoon. The First Family returning from Camp David, where the President and his wife liked to take the twins for the weekend. Ray Bowman was not allowed to enter until the "movement" was complete. As the three ships moved off, he inserted his badge into the card reader and punched in his PIN, nodded to the Uniformed Secret Service officer and walked up the snow-lined West Executive Avenue.

It was what one National Security Advisor had called the broadest narrow street in the world. On one side was more power than any one person had anywhere else, but also unrealistic expectation of what could be done with it. On the other side were the staff in the massive Eisenhower Executive Office Building, who knew the limits of power because they could never get everything done that the people across the alley wanted accomplished.

As he walked under the awning and into the ground floor of the West Wing, Ray thought about the job of the National Security Advisor. It had incredible scope and enormous influence, without all of the glare of media attention and the harassment of Congressional hearings. He wondered if, one day, he might be able to convince a President to let him have the job. To get there, he had to avoid disasters on his watch at the PEG. He knew that was not going to be easy.

Winston Burrell met him in a small conference room in the Situation Room. It seemed more like a private dining room for four, maybe six, except that in addition to all the dark wood there were lots of digital clocks and a very large flat screen. Burrell looked like an old city political boss, a rotund man in his early sixties, sitting in his little back room on a Sunday afternoon, receiving his ward leaders one at a time. In a way, Ray thought, that is what Winston Burrell was, more political than strategic, more boss than CEO. He saw his job as dealing with constituencies, here and abroad. For Burrell, Ray was an enforcer, someone he could trust to deal with difficult problems, discreetly, not someone he ever had to put on a State Dinner guest list.

"Some guardian angel you are," Burrell began.

"I know."

"Let's see, we have six hearings scheduled on the Hill on our drone policies. The UN has created a Special Rapporteur, whatever the fuck that is, to keep an eye on our use of drones. She's in Geneva, must be a cushy job. And the AG tells me there are now twelve distinct lawsuits filed in various courts around the country to stop us killing Americans with drones, to stop us from violating international law and Human Rights agreements we are party to, and to get all sorts of data on our use of flying killer robots under the Freedom of Information Act."

Ray poured himself a coffee from the decanter in the middle of the conference table. "To say nothing of the media frenzy. Especially WWN. It's a ratings thing for them. Now *60 Minutes* is piling on, planning an entire show on drones next week. And our best pilot just got flattened by a semi on the interstate. It's all going great, Win. Got anything else you want me to look after while I'm at it?"

"Is there any good news?" Burrell asked.

"Some. We seem to have scared the terrorists—at least, they haven't used a Stinger against us in a while, since we started firing back at the shooters. We foiled an attempt to hijack another drone and shot down the aircraft involved, linked it to ex-Pakistani intelligence by the way."

"I've been thinking of designating them, ISI, as a terrorist organization," Burrell observed. "What'd you think? State is bullshit with me for suggesting it."

Ray decided to let that question pass. "Drones are still the only game in town, Win. Without them Qadhafi would still be running around in the desert in Chad or someplace plotting a comeback. Al Qaeda would still have a Shura Council of experienced managers in Pakistan. The Taliban would be running even more of Afghanistan. Half a dozen Americans would still be hostage in Somalia and the President of Yemen would be toast, literally."

"You don't have to sell me, Ray. It's the only thing CIA can do. And the Pentagon says it's either drones or it's huge commando raids with SEALs, or better yet, plastering the countryside with B-2s. But there have been too many mistakes. You know what the President said when I told him drones were the only way we had to deal with al Qaeda in Yemen? He said drones were doing the recruiting for al Qaeda in Yemen. He'd heard it on television. It could be right, you know."

"I will get an analysis, but I doubt it's right," Ray replied.

"You remember that the Agency had a very sensitive human source who tipped them off about the gathering in Vienna? They won't even tell me anything about who the source is or how they got him. My guess is that the Jords or the Brits, maybe the Indians or the Emiratis developed the source, not CIA."

"Well, whoever it was, he was right about Vienna. The group we hit were Qazzani's men in Europe, but they were planning to do some contract work for al Qaeda, bombing German subways," Ray recalled. "What's that got to do with anything now?"

"The same source, whoever that may be, has reconnected and sent word that as a result of our attack in Vienna, there is a major plot afoot to seek revenge. Two groups are operating independently, but both will strike simultaneously, allegedly in the U.S. Two falcons, whatever that means. The source personally overheard that phrase 'two falcons.' That's all we've got, no where, when, how, who," Burrell said.

"That squares with another report we had last summer about something big happening around Christmas," Ray replied. "So, maybe, just maybe, something's going to happen somewhere, possibly someday in the next couple of weeks, but we don't know what it is or who is going to do it. Sounds like the summer of 2001. Nothing actionable, but be afraid. Be very afraid. Great." Ray replied.

"Yeah, well I am not telling the President or anybody else to deliver that message to the public, not yet. The FBI is chasing down all their informants, shaking all the trees. Maybe it will turn out to be nothing. Meanwhile, I want you to stay focused on saving the drone program. I assume you know about the latest Inspector General investigation, the Red Sea incident?" Burrell asked.

Ray shook his head. "No, what incident?"

"Seems like there were civilians, including kids, killed when we blew up that yacht with the AQAP and Shabab summit going on it. The Pentagon IG says there was a cover-up, focusing in on the Air Force pilot running the Vegas squadron. Was he the one that just got hit by the truck?"

"Wasn't him," Ray replied, "but it sounds like he is about to be."

Burrell slipped on his half glasses, balancing them near the tip of his nose. "We have to announce some changes, buy us some time."

"What have you got in mind?" Ray knew what was coming was not good. He stifled the obvious questions: Who wrote this paper you are reading from? Why wasn't

I involved in whatever process came up with the "changes?"

Winston Burrell read from the file. "So right now we have two kinds of targets, people who are called High Value Individuals, and places which have the signature of terrorist bases, which are put on a High Priority Target List. But we have used those two lists to provide close air support to the Yemeni Army, and the African Union troops in Somalia, and now the Nigerians and the fucking Mali government. You know we did an air strike in Timbuktu for Christ sakes? Who gives a shit about Timbuktu? I didn't even know it was a real place 'til we bombed it. We've become like Rent an Airstrike. Some of these guys we're flying in support of are not nice people. No peace prize candidates among them."

Raymond Bowman exhaled loudly. "Yes, but. We do not run those missions to support those governments as much as we fly them to stop al Qaeda and its affiliates from creating more failed states where they can set up terrorist training camps like bin Laden had in Afghanistan. You know what happens next in that scenario. They recruit thousands more nut jobs into being terrorists and then some of them start blowing up Americans abroad and, eventually, here. Has State or CIA got anywhere with their soft-power bullshit, preradicalization deradicalization? No, they haven't. So what are you going to do, ask USAID to dig wells in Mali? That won't stop AQIM."

"Who?" Burrell asked.

"Al Qaeda in the Magreb," Ray explained. "Used to call itself something like the movement for Preaching and Combat, bunch of Algerian misfits, but they affiliated with al Qaeda, changed their name, and now get money and training from the violent political Islamists all over the region. They are a potential threat to us."

"Preaching and combat?" Burrell mused. "I remember some Irish group, the Society for Marching and Chowder. I think Nixon horned his way into it. "

"Not quite the same thing," Raymond replied.

"No, I suppose not. But I am not going to take all of this heat so we can keep in power this President of Yemen or that potentate in Mali by using drones. Help them in other ways, quieter ways. And if some real terrorist camp pops up someday, that is really training people who are planning to attack Americans, then we send in the B-2s, fuck 'em dead."

"That's a policy," Ray replied. He knew that now was not the time to fight it.

"Damn right it's a policy. It's the President's policy as of this morning when he signed it," Burrell passed a document marked Top Secret across the table. "It will leak to the *Post* tomorrow. And, Ray, we may have to do more, raise the level of proof that an HVI is really planning to attack us. The signature strikes, places on the HVTL, they're a real problem. From now on we only do signature strikes when it is really a place where bad guys are getting ready to blow up shit in New York, or bomb some plane flying to JFK."

Bowman stood up from the conference table and picked up his briefcase. If this was the way Burrell treated his friends and supporters, what must it be like to be an enemy? he wondered.

"Where the hell are you going?" Burrell asked.

"Vegas. I guess I have a new Presidential policy to put into place. And I also want to find out what's going on."

"What is going on?"

"They're fighting back against the drone program, which means it's hurting them and yet we are about to engage in some sort of unilateral disarmament, hand them another success. Winston, the ways in which they are coming after the drone program are very sophisticated. I just need to figure out the full extent of it, and who is ultimately pulling the strings. Answering that may tell us who is the Master Puppeteer on a lot of things. Maybe if I can show the President, he'll rethink this new drone policy."

"In the meantime, Ray, can you make this work?" Burrell asked.

Raymond Bowman looked Winston Burrell in the eye and held the stare. "I suppose I can, until—"

"Until what?" Burrell demanded.

"Until something does blow up in New York, again." Ray headed for the door.

# 35

THURSDAY, DECEMBER 17
ONE CENTER PLAZA
BOSTON, MASSACHUSETTS

"Bobby, let's walk over to Dunkin Donuts," Judith Wolosky said, sticking her head into her deputy's office. It sounded more like an order than an idea.

"Okay, boss, always willing to uphold the stereotype of law enforcement officers, even federal ones," Robert Gallagher replied, reaching for his coat. Walking into the coffee shop without the coat on would have caused someone to complain about his gun. Some people in Boston, particularly those who lived on nearby Beacon Hill, did not like guns, he had noticed. Others, like his neighbors in Dorchester, did not seem to mind, but with home values rising there, too, he sensed the gun-tolerant attitude would fade.

The two walked across the vast expanse of red brick that was the plaza in front of City Hall. "The wind's off the water today. Smell the sea," Gallagher said.

"Yeah, I smell the sea, it's two blocks away and probably getting closer all the time if you believe the Global Warming people," Judith shot back. "And, by the way, I do believe them even if there has been a lot of snow so far this winter."

"Ah, you people from Washington don't know this city. If you did, you'd know that the water already was closer, but we filled it in about three hundred yards two centuries back," Gallager replied.

"Is that when you started with the Boston Field Office?" Judith Wolosky played with her slightly older deputy. He was now the ASAC, the Assistant Special Agent in Charge in Boston, really in all of New England because the Boston office ran most of the FBI activities in six states. He had started out with the FBI in the Boston office nineteen years earlier. The Marathon case had been the highlight of his career, but rather than getting him the SAC job, he was asked to help break in a new boss from Washington. If things worked out all right, in a year he would hit his twenty and walk across the Plaza to Fidelity to be their Chief Security Officer when the incumbent there retired.

"So what's up, Jude? What didn't you want to talk about in the office?" Bobby Gallagher asked.

"You know me too well already, Bobby. Remember that MBTA cop got hit by the Red Line train at Park Street a while back?"

"Yeah, BPD classified it as a homicide, blamed some unsub kid. Their theory is the kid got into a scuffle with the cop in the tunnel, kid knocked him down, he hit his head, couldn't get up, and then the cop got run over by the car from Ashmont. There was a witness from Southie, old guy, but he couldn't really describe him to the artist, so they never ID-ed the kid," Gallagher recounted. "So, why you asking?"

Judith Wolosky sat down on a bench, as two girls scattered the pigeons nearby. "So, I got a call from a friend in DC, not in the Bureau. Intelligence guy. Said he'd been running some regressions, using a new Big Data analytics software. Anyway, he wanted to know if anyone ever figured out what the kid was doing climbing down into the tunnel."

"Walking to the next station? I dunno, sometimes those trains take a long time to show up," Gallagher joked. "I don't know. It was suspicious. MBTA, BPD, the Staties all searched the tunnel. Used bomb dogs, brought in lights. They single tracked the Red Line for twelve hours. Glad I drove to work that day. Thing is that the surveillance camera never got a good look at the kid's face. He had a hoodie on most of the time. There were a few frames with the hood down, but the camera angles were bad. Why does DC care now?"

"There's some fear at the top about something happening before Christmas. They don't know what. Chatter, sensitive sources. They're pulling all the threads. They want us to Knock and Talk with every potential Jihadi in New England. Tap all our sources. See what we turn up," she replied.

"Yeah, I know all that, I got the briefing from the terrorism Task Force guys, too, but what's that got to do with the kid in the T? They think that he's connected to this chatter?"

"Dugout has been using this software looking for signs of a terrorist plot in the U.S. This is what he came up with," Judith replied. "The kid in the T. He has some video."

"Dugout? Sounds like some geezer bartender over near Fenway. Why do we care what he thinks?" Gallagher asked.

"Because he is real good, but look, this request did not come through Headquarters so it's kind of off the books." She took a DVD from her coat pocket and handed it to Gallagher. "He suggested that we take the video over to the MIT Media Lab to a woman named Dr. Joyce Fernandez. She has some project to extrapolate full frontal facials from side and top-down looks. If we get her to generate an image, we can run it through the Facial Recognition Data Base at DHS."

"You want me, the ASAC, personally to drive over to MIT and talk to this professor because some guy you know in DC, who is not even in the Bureau, has a hunch. Is that about right, boss?"

Judith Wolosky stood. "Bobby, it's what, a mile to MIT? Besides, Dr. Joyce is expecting you and she may be someone you might want to see again, who knows? Dugout said she is very nice. Now, let's get that coffee."

"Nah, you get your coffee. I gotta catch a cab to Cambridge."

THURSDAY, DECEMBER 17
ABOARD N44982
THIRTY-FIVE THOUSAND FEET ABOVE
KANSAS

"How many years I've been working at PEG and you never told me we had one of these," Dugout complained.

"One of what?" Ray asked.

"The Bat Plane, man. This is the way to travel. No lines. No pat downs. No taking your laptop out, your shoes off. No sit down and lock yourself in and don't touch electronics until Simon Says. What is this, a Gulfstream? And no markings, all vanilla. Phony tail number, too?"

"It's not mine, not PEG's. It's the Agency's. They weren't using it. And it's a Challenger, Canadian made. Do not get used to it. You rate coach. On Southwest. I only get Business and even that's usually on United," Ray said. "Doesn't really matter, they all suck." He took a long sip from his glass of scotch and stared at the white-covered land eight miles below.

"You're in a great mood. Let me see if I can cheer you up," Dugout said. "The latest Big Data Analysis run finds an interesting correlation. The mortars used in the attacks on the drone bases were Ukrainian. The keyboard used in the pipeline hack in Nevada was Cyrillic. Question, what do Ukrainians have to do with al Qaeda?"

"Answer, nothing," Ray shot back, still looking at the snow below.

"Right," Dugout admitted. "Modify question. What do Ukrainians have to do with a list of AQ associated groups? Answer?"

"Dunno," Ray mumbled.

"A Ukrainian mob runs drugs in southeast Europe, including heroin from Afghanistan, specifically, according to the DEA database, heroin distributed by . . . wait for it . . . the Qazzani clan."

Ray's eyes darted from the window to Dugout. "The Qazzanis do what again?"

"They move drugs to the Merezha, a Ukrainian mob involved in narcotics and, even better, cyber crime, including in the U.S. of A," Dugout read from his iPad.

"That's how they did it. That's how the Qazzanis hijacked the drone in Pakistan. It wasn't ISI, it was them," Ray said, pounding his fist on the folding table between them.

"How did we know that?" Dugout asked.

"The kid from WWN, Bruce something," Ray went for his notes on his laptop. "He said it was the Qazzanis who told him about the orphanage, correction the not-an-orphanage, and it was the Qazzanis who told him to go to Butthump, or wherever it was, to be there when the drone landed. Obviously the Qazzanis don't have sophisticated cyber capability, but they have more money than God, so they could rent it and, where else, from the Ukrainian guys they already do business with who have a sideline in hacking." Ray stopped for a minute to think it through. "Are those Ukrainians that good?"

"I'll find out. And I will ask Big Data Analysis for any further evidence of links between the two groups, any sign of unusual activity by the Ukrainian mob, especially in cyber space." Dugout was hitting his keyboard fast. "Now do I get to fly Business?"

"Did your Big Data Analysis software find anything to give credence to the idea that there might be a terrorist group preparing something for before Christmas?" Ray asked.

"I thought you told me Burrell said for you to focus on saving the drone program and let the Fibbies chase their tail on that rumor?" Dugout replied.

"I tell you too much. Yes, he did say that and yes I

did ask you to run your own traps to see if they missed anything."

Dugout swiped his fingers across the screen of his iPad, switching to another file. "Lots of rumors about plots, all the time. Lots of wannabees. The Fibbies are always out trying to entrap some poor, confused Muslim. But in terms of real plots, the indicators you'd look for of planning, not much. The software did find a report of something that could have been reconnaissance or planning."

"Where?" Ray asked.

"Boston."

"Not again. How credible?" Bowman pressed.

"Dunno yet. A friend of mine is running the FBI Field Office up there now. She's chasing it down." Dugout put down the iPad. "Now, about flying Business class."

"Not while you're a govie," Ray said, as he rose out of his seat and headed to the small kitchen in the rear of the Agency aircraft.

# 36

FRIDAY, DECEMBER 18
ONE CENTER PLAZA
BOSTON, MASSACHUSETTS

The sunlight had disappeared behind Beacon Hill two hours ago. Looking out on people hurrying home across the Plaza and the streets choked with traffic, Judith Wolosky calculated that she had another two hours of paperwork before she could walk home.

"What kind of name is Roble Adam?" Robert Gallagher asked as he walked into the spacious office of the Special Agent in Charge. "No *s* at the end."

"No *s* at the end? Well, I guess the answer is not that his great-great-great started the Revolution and then made beer down the street?" Judith replied.

"Get your coat, we're going flying," Gallagher instructed.

"You're planning on the usuals like where and why?" she said moving toward her coat closet.

"Portland. Staties got a chopper waiting for us at Logan," Gallagher said. "Mr. Roble Adam is the guy in the Park Street subway pictures. Turns out he lives in Maine."

They headed for the elevator to the parking garage. "Flying a State owned helicopter in the dark over water in winter. Sounds like a great idea so far. What about the why part?" she asked.

"So Roble is a Somali name. Means he was born in the rainy season. Who knew they had a rainy season? Joyce got back to me around eleven last night. She ran her new Facial Recognition app that can extrapolate a frontal image from a top down and some side shots. She got a pretty good full frontal facial off the images from the T. Made a composite," Gallagher said as the elevator descended to the garage. "I got it to DHS before midnight and they got me a name around noon from the Maine driver's licenses. Roble Adam. Portland."

"Thank God we didn't have to hold a press conference again and ask for Crowd Sourcing help," Judith said, thinking of the Marathon case. "Maybe this guy won't know we're coming and so he won't try to bolt."

"He wasn't at the address on the license. So our guys from the Portland office flashed his picture to some Somali community leaders. They dropped the dime on him right off. Living with some cousins in South Portland."

"Patriotic Somali-Americans. And we have him in custody?" Judith asked, getting into the waiting FBI Chevy Suburban, driven by a young, new Agent.

"L and S," Gallagher said to the driver. "No, under surveillance. He just got home to his fleabag apartment in South Portland. The Portland SWAT's going in with our guys now."

"Nice of them. Portland SWAT got lots of tanks like Boston? This going to be all over the TV?"

"I asked our guys in Portland to keep it low key, use encrypted channels on the police radio. Too many people listening to the scanners these days."

"So Dr. Fernandez, Joyce, was helpful then in creating an image that people could ID a guy from," she noted as the car pulled out onto Government Square, headed toward the Sumner Tunnel and the airport. "I told you she'd be good."

"She was, yes, she was." Gallagher looked out the window of the truck, which was now weaving its way through the rush-hour traffic with occasional *whoops* from its siren and the steady flashing of red and blue lights. The traffic nonetheless hardly moved for three blocks. "Yes, I told her the Bureau would take her to dinner at Locke-Ober as a way of saying thanks. Don't suppose the Bureau will pay?" The Suburban went up over a sidewalk and bounced down near the entrance of the tunnel.

"Was that a rhetorical question, Special Agent Gallagher?" Judith replied. "Or am I invited, too?"

"Rhetorical."

"What I thought," she replied. "Can we make a call while we're in the tunnel? I want to thank that old geezer bartender from Fenway, who is actually forty-five and a computer whiz in DC. Shall I tell him you want to take him to Locke-Ober, too?"

FRIDAY, DECEMBER 18
GLOBAL COORDINATION CENTER
CREECH AFB, NEVADA

"Send me back to Kabul," Sandra Vittonelli said loudly. "At least in Afghanistan, I usually knew who my enemies were. In Washington and with the job out here, I can never tell."

Ray had never seen her so out of control. He was beginning to think she might quit, in which case the program would really be at a loss.

"I get sued by some woman from Philadelphia for killing her son in Austria while I am supposedly in an undercover position here where nobody knows who I am. One of my pilots and his wife get killed when a gas pipeline bursts and you two tell me it's murder. Another pilot gets drunk and is run over by a Mack truck, literally. Then this," she threw the Presidential Directive limiting drone strikes onto her desk. "And now you tell me my chief pilot is under an IG investigation and will probably be suspended while they investigate. Fuck it. Honest to God, Ray, fuck it. Maybe Dugout would like to fly the Goddamn drones?"

Ray looked at Dugout in a way that made clear he should not answer that question.

"I'll do what I can to stop them from ordering his suspension, but the Inspector General is fairly independent," Ray offered. "What I gather is that they don't have a smoking gun, or they would already have done something. Just an anonymous tip, probably from someone on the staff here, probably someone who has a beef with Erik for whatever reason."

"But he's going to know he's under investigation?" she asked.

"The IG guys arrive late tomorrow. You probably want to tell him today," Ray suggested.

"Can't," Sandra said. "He's taking Major Dougherty's body back to his parents in Chicago. Finally got it out of the County Medical Examiner. Erik is really broken up about Dougherty's death. He thinks that somehow he should have done something more to help him. Instead, he told him go get drunk and gave him his car. Now it looks like maybe he got into the accident because he was drunk. Bruce was a really good pilot, really nice guy."

Ray glanced at Dugout in a way that said something. Dugout nodded as if he understood.

"I'd suggest maybe we want to let Dugout set up in Room 103, Spook Ops, to run traps on a few things. He might also look at the records from the Red Sea op, without leaving any traces that he has been looking."

Sandra stared at Ray. She knew not to ask. "It's already been set up for him. I ordered it when you called last night. Sergeant Miller will take you down there now, Dug."

When they were alone, Sandra and Ray sat down at her small conference table. "I know what you're thinking, but you can't quit," he began.

"The fuck I can't. It's a free country."

"I'd like to keep it that way," he said.

"Yeah and all that stands between tyranny and perdition is me and the program. Don't start with that crap, I've heard it all before and it's not true and you know it," she said. "It's just getting too hard and nobody gives a shit except us. Do you think those people out there on the Vegas Strip think the drone program is making them safer? They don't even think about it. They think they're perfectly safe, except maybe from whack job fellow Americans with assault guns every now and again, randomly."

Ray stood up and walked to the glass wall. He looked out at the Control Room, at the Big Board with video feeds coming from drones all over Africa and the Middle East. "They're not supposed to think about it. That's the whole point, Americans should not have to worry about terrorism here," Ray said softly, trying to lower the temperature in the conversation. "If there is another terrorist attack in the U.S. like 9/11, we will lose more of our freedoms in response, just like we did the first time. Warrantless wiretaps, throwing U.S. citizens in military prisons without trial, cameras everywhere, privacy out the window." He turned back to face Sandy. "We are what stops the next attack. We get them before they get here. That's what the people on the Vegas Strip want, that's what most Americans want."

Sandra walked to her desk and picked up a file. "We've been running Pattern of Life flights on a bunch of huts up in the mountains in Yemen. HUMINT says the AQAP bomb maker is up there. The flights show nothing but guys with guns up there for over a week now. No women. No children. Not even any unarmed men. The government in Sana'a says they can't go up there, too unsafe, terrorist territory. Can I still get a Kill Call?"

Ray took the file. "The AQAP bomb maker? The guy who keeps trying to get someone's undies to explode on a U.S. plane? I'd say he's a direct threat to Americans. Someday he's going to kill three hundred people, many of them Americans, in some 777 coming in from the Gulf and flying in over a U.S. city. Let's schedule the call."

FRIDAY, DECEMBER 18
FBI OFFICE
PORTLAND, MAINE

"The emphasis is on the second syllable, ah-dam," Roble Adam told Bobby Gallagher in the Portland FBI office's interview room.

"You don't want the coffee?" Gallagher asked. "It's getting late. You're tired. You need a little jolt to remember things?"

"I don't know what you put in it," Roble replied.

"It's black. You want milk and sugar?"

"I don't want your drugs. What drugs did you put in it?" Roble asked.

Gallagher put the two Starbucks cups next to each other in the middle of the table. "Pick either. I will drink the other one. After that, if you want, you can try drinking yours. Or not, I don't care." Roble didn't pick.

"All right, Roble, I want you to know where you stand right now. Even if you don't say another word, we already have enough evidence to charge you with murder of the police officer, possession of explosives, and terrorism," Gallagher noted.

"You know what this is, Roble?" Gallagher asked, as he put a key on the table between them.

Roble inhaled and blinked, but didn't answer.

"The Portland bomb squad is at the storage company now. They have a little robot. It's cute. You should see it. It's looking at your bomb right now. I just saw your bomb on the video feed. Is it RDX? That's not easy to get," Gallagher said.

Roble closed his eyes.

"Roble, in a little while they're going to take you away, to Virginia. There are CIA people and others waiting to interrogate you. You know how the CIA interrogates people, Roble? Did you see the movie about getting bin Laden?"

Roble quickly opened his eyes and stared at him. There was fear in his eyes, but also anger, rage.

"Look, I know you're just the lowest-level guy on the scrotum pole, the guy they got to carry the bomb. I can help you, but you have to tell me before they take you away. Then it will be too late," Gallagher said. "But there are still things that can happen here in the next few minutes that may change the rest of your life forever. And those things are up to you, but not for long.

"We did some research on you after we figured out it was you in the subway. Actually, you're not a bad guy and your family, they're good people. Your mom came here to this country from Somalia during the wars there, came with almost nothing, to make a place here that would be a better place to raise children. She worked hard, all for you, you and your sister."

Roble Adam glared at him. Gallagher continued, "And you, you made the football team here in high school, you helped out your mom, you protected your sister. Then these guys come along and recruit you, they use you, they spoil it all for you and your mom and your sister."

"They had nothing to do with it, my mother and my sister," Roble insisted.

"Actually, in some ways, Roble, you are the victim, the three of you. All of the Adam family has become victims because of what those guys, the recruiters, did to you. They're the bad guys in this whole thing, not you. I know you didn't mean for that cop to get hit by the train, he was—"

Roble interrupted, "He fell over, man, I didn't even push him. He fell and he hit his head or something."

"It was dark in there," Gallagher added, "I know, I know. We may not have to make it a murder charge. I just need your help to identify the people who did this to you and your family. That's all. And they don't deserve your protection, not after what they did to you and your mother and sister by getting you involved in all this. You just have to tell me, but now, before they take you to Virginia."

Roble sighed. "Tell you what?"

"Who recruited you?"

"They found me online. Then they came to our apartment one night. After a while, the big man came to town to meet me," Roble replied. "I thought they were you guys, some fucking FBI sting. But they said they would tell me just before something blew up, something they were going to blow up. And they did. They told me about that Marriott in Kuwait like an hour before it happened. Figured they weren't FBI after that."

"What were their names?"

"They didn't say, ever," Roble answered.

"We're going to need you to describe them to an artist," Gallagher said. "Tell me about the big man. Where did you meet?"

"On the street, he came out of a store," Roble said. "Like a light blue store, what you call it, aqua. On Exchange Street."

"And then what happened?" Gallagher asked.

"We talked while we walked down to the water. I left him by the boat, the one that goes to Canada."

"He got on the boat?" the FBI Agent asked.

"Not while I was there. He told me to walk away."

"What did he ask you to do?"

Roble waited a moment. "He asked me to do surveillance, a trial run he called it, then when he tells me to, to leave a bomb in the train tunnel in Boston. His guys showed up with the bomb the day after. We went together and rented the storage locker."

"When were you supposed to leave the bomb?"

"He said he would e-mail me. He created an e-mail account for me. I was supposed to check it every day," Roble said.

"We're going to need that account. Did you ever get an e-mail?" Gallagher asked.

"Not yet."

"All right, Roble. This has been good and I will do all that I can to make sure they don't hurt you, but what else can you tell me now, something valuable that I can use to get you a break," Gallagher said. "You know what's valuable."

Roble thought. "He said it was important that I not

go early or late because it had to go off simultaneous. Yeah, that was the word, *simultaneous.* He said before the end of the year, the Christian calendar, he called it."

"Don't worry. I won't let them torture you. It won't happen."

Gallagher stood and walked out of the room. Four other FBI men came in. Gallagher knew they would fly Roble Adam to Virginia, where the Special Interagency Interrogation Team awaited. He also knew that torture had stopped years earlier when the President took office.

FRIDAY, DECEMBER 18
COPPER HILL RANCH
KYLE CANYON, NEVADA

"No more hijacking drones," Yuri asserted as soon as Ghazi entered the room. "We lost two of our guys on that plane. I worked with one of them, Ivan, for twelve years. We lived together for almost three years before he got married."

"I'm sorry. Guys who worked with us a lot were the pilot and copilot. They died, too," Ghazi answered. "But people die in this business. It's not all sitting behind a computer for most of us. There's risk. Did you figure out what happened?"

"What happened is that they had another command frequency to talk to the bird. One we didn't know about," Yuri said, walking back to his bank of desktop and laptop computers. "And, obviously, they had an air-to-air missile on the bird. Something we also had not seen before."

"All right. Forget about hijacking drones. We did it

once. We got the publicity. Made them look like they couldn't control their own robots," Ghazi said. "Now let's worry about our Attack Day. We need to make sure everything will work."

"Our stuff will all work," Yuri said. "The guys who are attacking the older subways, that's your problem. When is A-Day?"

"It's coming," Ghazi replied. "And our drones? Remember, the drones are part of A-Day, too."

"They'll work fine."

"I may want to do a preliminary operation with one of them to see how much damage we get with one. When can you have one ready?" Ghazi asked.

"Give me a couple of days," the Ukrainian replied.

# 37

SATURDAY, DECEMBER 19
LE CROUPIER BAR AND GRILLE
NORTH LAS VEGAS, NEVADA

The restaurant staff seemed anxious to close up. Despite the name of the place, it did not keep Vegas casino hours. The big casinos on the strip were twelve miles away. By ten, the last diners had usually finished. The bar shut down at midnight on most days. It was in reality just another suburban office building bar and grill whose only connection to gambling was the few slot machines in the bar.

Ghazi had taken a table by the window, looking out at the parking lot, looking out at a reserved parking space at the front of the building. He called up the tracking app on his iPad. The beacon he had placed on her vehicle showed that she was only a minute away. When she parked the white Ford Edge, he asked for the check. He knew her pattern of life. It would only be half an hour before the first patient arrived. He hit the stopwatch function on his Humboldt.

The door to the third floor office was unlocked when he tried it. No one sat at the receptionist's desk. When she came around the corner from her office, she looked startled. And then he fired the Taser and she dropped to the floor, writhing in pain. He moved quickly, taping her mouth, binding her hands, injecting her with the sedative. Within two minutes she was in the portable trash bin and on the freight elevator headed toward the loading dock.

"Dr. Parsons?" the first patient called out upon entering the office for her late-night session. "Jennifer?"

SATURDAY, DECEMBER 19
SPECIAL OPERATIONS ROOM
CREECH AFB, NEVADA

"I have to have one of these," Dugout started.

"One of what?" Ray asked as he walked through the last of the three doors that led to the Sensitive Compartmented Information Facility, the SCIF. "You keep envying other people's stuff. First, it was the airplane. It's very unbecoming. Thou shalt not covet thy neighbor's tech gear."

"I covet the covert. I've been in dozens of SCIFs, but this one has great toys. I can do all sorts of things at once. I have enough diverse fiber connections and anonymizers to bring any country to its knees. And the databases they have direct access to. Amazing," Dugout said.

"I'm glad you like it. I'll ask Santa to see if he can afford to get you a littler one," Ray joked. "But what are you going to do with it?"

"No, not just what I am going to do, what have I already done. While you were sleeping, or whatever you two did last night in Sin City, your trusty sidekick here has been hard at work for the last bunch of hours, I don't even want to know what time it is," Dugout replied.

Ray let the implication pass. "And you found what?"

"The FBI arrested a guy in Maine who was going to bomb the subway in Boston. Somali-American. Turned in by other Somali-Americans after someone brilliantly figured out how to get his image and run it through the Facial Recognition Database, anyway, that's not the point," Dugout said. "Point is that this kid says the people who recruited him were planning simultaneous attacks sometime in the next few weeks."

"Shit, that squares with what Burrell told me," Ray thought aloud.

"Have you been holding back facts from me?" Dugout was reddening in the face. "You ask me to connect the dots and then you don't give me all the dots."

"Look, I'm not supposed to share this with you. Burrell told me. Let's just say there is a way that the CIA has of learning some things once in a while. It's a bit like a Magic Eight Ball. Its utterances are Delphic and you can't follow up right away and ask it what it means," Ray said.

"Most CIA reports are like that," Dugout observed.

"Yeah, but this particular Magic Eight Ball has a good track record. And recently it said that two big plots were afoot. Something about two falcons."

Dugout snorted. "That's really useful. So, the Agency has some hush-hush source, some agent in place, and they're not sharing the whole story even with you. So maybe now you think this stuff in Boston is one of the falcons. Well, I got a falcon feather for you.

"The FBI 302, the report on their interview with the kid they busted in Maine, says the big man behind the attack met him on the street in front of what turns out to be a cyber café. I got the date, went back to their logs for that day, around that time, and found a user who connected to three different anonymizer sites in twenty minutes, obviously a terrorist cloaking his identity," Dugout said.

"Or someone doing insider trading on Wall Street," Ray suggested. "Still, how does this help us?"

"Lots of ways. First, I checked on whom he was contacting. Whom. Found out he was hitting Virtual Private Network servers, as yet another way to hide his communication by using encryption and tunneling through the Internet. And I did a trace route on where he connected to using the VPNs. One guy was in Kiev. One some place in Pakistan. And one was in, drumroll, Texas."

"Wait, I didn't follow all of that, but if he was using anonymizer Web sites and then VPNs how could you go back and find what he did?' Ray asked.

"We've been worried about those anonymizer sites for a long time, been inside them a long time," Dugout explained. "The FBI can't do it because they could never get a search warrant. But I don't have that problem. Then again I don't want to use what I found out as evidence in court, because then we would have to reveal how we discovered it and that might not be strictly legal. So, don't ask, but for lead information, for stopping attacks. . . ."

Ray sat down, looking at the bank of computer screens. "So you have confirmed there is a Ukrainian and a Pakistani terrorist link and maybe they have somebody in Texas."

"As they say on the late-night television ads, 'but wait, there's more,'" Dugout said, hitting a keyboard. "The guy who used the cyber café is this guy, I got his picture enhanced by some nice people at MIT. The cyber café actually is very law-abiding and keeps a few hidden cameras running to stop kiddie pornsters and other pervs. So now we have his picture."

"Great job. Who is he?" Ray asked.

"Again, I used the Facial Recognition Database and, presto, his picture shows up in the Customs and Border Protection database. It's a ninety-nine percent probability that it's the same guy. When he landed at Logan Airport, here we see his CBP-taken photo there, he was using an Indian passport with a U.S. visa granted to him at our consular section at Embassy Delhi. Name on the Indian passport is Birbal Malhotra. I gave it to FBI and CIA.

"The CIA Station in Delhi is already talking to RAW, Indian intel, that's what they call it, RAW, to see who he really is.

"There is no record of this guy anywhere is the U.S., not with the name on the Indian passport. The FBI thinks he's using an alias. They also think he may have taken a boat from Portland to Canada. They are checking video, passenger manifests, talking to crew. We should know more soon, but meantime maybe the FBI should release his picture to the media."

Ray pursed his lips and squinted, a sign Dugout

recognized as his boss not liking an idea. "Maybe not yet. We don't want to cause him to go to ground, or, worse yet, launch some attack now before we can get him. I'll talk to Burrell and the FBI Director. Let's give it a day and see what turns up on who and where he is. Can you track down where in Texas the VPN server was and who it was connecting to?"

"Working on it, geez, always more he wants," Dugout said, turning his back on Ray and hitting another keyboard. " 'With whom it was connecting, by the way.' "

Raymond Bowman got up from his seat. As he was about to open the door to leave, Ray remembered something. "What about that Red Sea attack? Did Colonel Parsons do anything wrong?"

Dugout kept his back to him and kept hitting the keyboard. "There is no indication on any video file anywhere that there were any civilians killed in that attack."

"And no indication that Erik or anyone altered any database in any way?" Ray asked.

This time Dugout spun around on his chair to look at his boss.

"Please. When I do a file wipe, I never leave a trace."

# 38

SATURDAY, DECEMBER 19
CYRIL E. KING AIRPORT
ST. THOMAS, U.S. VIRGIN ISLANDS

"If you or your company ever needs to fly again, please think of us first," the copilot said as Bahadur stepped out of the Cessna Citation, onto the short flight of stairs from the cabin and into the bright Caribbean sun. "And have a happy holiday with your family down here."

The flight from Fort Lauderdale had been short. At no time had he seen a security official. There was no inspection or need to show identification at the Executive Jet terminal when he departed Florida and no need to go through Immigration upon landing in the U.S. Virgin Islands. Ghazi and his Ukrainians had leased the business jet for the flight and arranged for the onward transport. He took the ferry across from Red Hook to Cruz Bay on St. John, the run lasting twenty minutes at most. Then there was a scary taxi ride on too narrow and too twisting roads to near the other end of the island. There, half an hour late, the man with the speedboat arrived at the teetering dock. Half an hour more and he had left the United States and was in Britain, or at least the British Virgin Islands, landing on another ill-kept dock, this one a mile from the Immigration pier on Tortola.

At the back of a bar in Road Town, he met the courier, who gave him the identification documents. He was now neither the Pakistani Ahmed Bahadur, nor the Indian Birbal Malhotra. He was an Australian national who had arrived in Tortola two weeks earlier and was now booked on his return flight to St. Kitts and then on BA to Heathrow. One of Bahadur's men from Australia, one who looked something like him, had flown in to the Virgin Islands two weeks before. He had done little but sleep, drink, and fish since then. The Ukrainians had made the appropriate adjustments in the databases and the documents. Despite all the improvements in passports and facial recognition, fingerprints and iris scans, in the end, identity was only as good as the software running the databases and most of that was easily accessed and altered.

After the courier had left, Bahadur sat alone in the dark, sipping his rum drink. In a few hours he would be en route to London, where he would be a transit passenger scheduled first to Dubai and then on to Melbourne. He had no intentions of going to Melbourne. From Dubai he would catch a flight to Karachi and then take the long drive up to DG Khan. There he would wait with Rashid Qazzani to see how many of the bombs went off at the same time, how many of the more modern train systems had derailments and crashes from the Ukrainians' hacking, and how devastating Ghazi's attack would be. Then he would collect his reward from Qazzani. For him as a somewhat fallen Muslim, Bahadur thought, it might indeed be a Merry Christmas.

SATURDAY, DECEMBER 19
NEAR PAIUTE GOLF RESORT
NORTH LAS VEGAS, NEVADA

"Your life can go on for years. It can have meaning, it can be constructive," she said, still in a haze from the drugs.

"Oh, I am quite sure of that," Ghazi replied. He was wearing a ski mask and it was making him sweat and scratching at his stubble. "Do not worry, Dr. Parsons. You are not going to be raped. You are not going to be tortured like the prisoners at Abu Ghraib. We are not even going to kill you."

"Then what, why, who are you?" She struggled to see clearly in the darkened room. She thought she might be in an old mobile home.

"Why? We want you to be our witness. You will deliver our claim of responsibility. You can explain our motivation. You are a shrink. You are good at getting to motivation. You will watch videos of what the drones have done, killing innocent people. Later, after we get our revenge, you will go to news shows and explain what we want, why we did it, and how Americans can make it all stop from happening again. What we want is very easy to remember. Two things. U.S. out of all Muslim countries, beginning with Afghanistan. Your President said they would leave, but some are still there. Second, no more drones flying over our Muslim lands."

She coughed. Her mouth and throat were so dry. "Why me?"

"Because you know, Dr. Parsons, what the American government has done with drones, done to innocent people around the world, done in places where it has no business being. And you will get to see it on the video, over and over and over." He unbound her hands and gave her a bottle of water. "You know, Dr. Parsons, because your husband is one of the killers, one of the leaders of the drone warriors. He has much blood on his hands, doctor. And for his crimes, he will be punished. I thought I already had his punishment lined up, but it turned out to be one of his fellow criminals driving your husband's car. But I will get him. And you will watch."

He turned on the flat screen with a handheld remote. "This TV now will show you what the drones have done. The people they have left as widows and orphans. Later, on this TV, you will see what a drone sees, live."

He went to his backpack and removed an iPhone. "No, unlike your husband, I do not kill women. After our revenge is complete, that door will open. It will be on a timer lock. You will be free to walk outside. This is your iPhone. It is off now so they cannot track it, but it will be sitting outside on the steps. When you walk out, call 911. Because it will be like 9/11 that day, yes? The police will be busy, but they will come for you eventually. Then you tell them why we did it all. And you tell them what they must do to make us stop."

He left her in the old trailer, down a dirt road, a mile from the golf course. Feeling no guilt nor actually any emotion, he drove to the condo, a businessman, with his day's work complete. On the balcony of the condo, thirty-two stories above the street, he allowed himself a cigarette. The smoke felt good. It calmed him. There were no lights on in the apartment next to his. He took the matchbox-sized object from his jeans and threw it onto the next balcony. It landed perfectly in the dirt of the potted palm.

SATURDAY, DECEMBER 19
SPECIAL OPERATIONS ROOM
CREECH AFB, NEVADA

"Erik's on his way back now. He's missing Dougherty's funeral. He'll get into McCarran in a few hours. He's in a rage. Wants to know how his wife could go missing and no one knows how or where," Sandra said.

"Well, because somebody spray-painted several security cameras' lenses," Dugout said. "Otherwise I'd have video of her leaving the building. All the Sheriff can say is that her car is still out front of the building and there were signs of a struggle in her office."

"He also wants to know why somebody from the Inspector General's office contacted him seeking an appointment," Sandra added. "He's going to feel like the world is really closing in on him."

"I think that is what somebody has in mind," Ray suggested. "The problem is I don't know who that somebody is and all the leads we have suggest it's narcotraffickers, Ukrainians and Pakistanis. And that just makes no sense. Besides, what narcotrafficker is good enough to orchestrate all of this?"

"I don't know. It's all coming at me too quickly and I don't understand even what 'all of this' is," she said.

"I'm going to go home and shower, take a nap. Come by later, we can grab some dinner before we come back in for the Kill Call."

After she left, Ray and Dugout sat for a moment, each thinking, neither talking. Then Ray, his voice subdued, began what he was good at, asking questions. "So, have the FBI gotten anywhere further with the Portland-Boston case?"

"Not a lot," Dugout answered. "The RAW, the Indians, say that the guy who is on the CBP photo, the guy who our Embassy gave a visa to, doesn't really exist. He had one of those new foolproof Indian identity cards, but nobody knows how. They've stepped up security big time on the T in Boston, even checking people's bags."

"And the server you traced him using in Texas?"

"It's in Dallas, at a Colo, you know, colocation center, data center to you, but it's a cloud service provider and they allow anyone to establish an account online, with a credit card, and get a virtual server. Guess what? The credit card number comes back to an offshore bank account and a dead end. Everything on the server is encrypted with a mil grade code. I can't figure out where we go from here."

"Neither can I," Ray admitted. He was not used to being stumped, not for this long. The pieces of the jigsaw were on the table, at least some of them were, but he couldn't visualize how they came together. He closed his eyes and tried to clear his mind, but it kept racing, racing but going nowhere. "They shouldn't just be checking bags and adding cops on the subways in Boston. Simultaneous could be two or three cities. That was the old al Qaeda pattern. I'll call the Bureau."

"Simultaneous could also mean a train here, a plane there, a packed shopping mall days before Christmas," Dugout said.

"Yeah, it could mean almost anything, almost anywhere. So do we issue a national warning, 'It's Christmas and bad people are plotting to do something, somewhere'? That would be really helpful," Ray said. "If we still had the color-coded threat system, we could make it red for Christmas. Glad I don't have to make that call. How many more shopping days till Christmas?"

"Five. Can I ask you a philosophical question?" Dugout said.

"Oh, God, really? Now?" Ray replied. He dropped his head between his knees, ran his fingers through his thick hair, and then looked back up at Dugout. "Fire away."

"It's that old one about Ends and Means. How do you deal with it so well, all the time? I mean, without it changing who you are, without the line of what you are willing to do sliding too far off into the really bad side. How do you know when it has?" Dugout asked. "You seem to deal with it pretty well."

Ray looked at the flat screens for a moment, then back at Dugout. "It used to be the Front Page Rule: assume it will be on the front page of the *Post* someday and only do it if you could stand that level of exposure. But it's amazing what has been on the front page without any real consequences: torture, illegal wire taps, black sites. No one goes to jail. No one even gets fired. So I don't know anymore. I guess it's like art or porn, I know it when I see it. I know what I think is art. Others have to judge for themselves. Do you think I have been putting too much emphasis on the ends and playing a little too loose with the means? Because if so, tell me."

Dugout shook his head, "No, no I don't. I think we are pretty well still inside the Good Zone. I just think we need to step back every once in a while and reset the compass, keep things in perspective."

Ray looked at the flat screens and out, through the one-way window, to the floor of the GCC, with its row upon row of drone pilots. "The data bases, the drones, these are really powerful tools. You're right, we shouldn't get too jaded about using them. They're for special situations. In the wrong hands . . ." He stood up and walked to the door.

"They're the only tools we have that work," Dugout said. "Where are you going?"

"To the airport to meet Erik when he comes in. He's going to need some more help," Ray noted.

# 39

SUNDAY, DECEMBER 20
36TH STREET AND RACE STREET
WEST PHILADELPHIA, PENNSYLVANIA

"Are you alone in the apartment?" the voice on the phone asked.

"Shit, yah. Alone in the building. Everybody has gone home for the semester, but me," the Drexel student said. "Where are you?"

"Outside your door. Please open it."

The two men put on ski masks just before the door opened. They carried a box, gift-wrapped for Christmas. "Here is your present," the taller man said when the door opened. "Let us come in and explain how to use it."

The three men sat at the small table in the living room–dining area. The taller man in the ski mask explained. "You sit on a bench in the station. In the main hall, but over by the food stands on the Market Street side. You unwrap the gift, like you can't wait until you get home. Inside is a remote controlled racecar in a lot of packaging. Take the toy, just the car. Throw everything else and the packaging in the waste bin. The plastic explosives are in the packaging. As you walk away, hit the horn on the car and you will start the timer. You will have twenty minutes to be somewhere in public, somewhere on a surveillance tape when it goes off. Do not let on that you know what happened. Be confused looking."

"That's not much explosive," the student said.

"It's concentrated, compacted. Feel how heavy it is," the man suggested. "And here is the first part of the money. Untraceable bills, all one hundreds. Count it out."

"It's good," the student said after several minutes of counting. "When?"

"Not tonight. Maybe tomorrow. Maybe the next day. Very soon. We will give you two hours' notice. Now, we have to get going."

"More Christmas presents for Santa to deliver tonight?" the student asked as he walked them to the door.

"Exactly," the shorter man said as they walked out.

SUNDAY, DECEMBER 20
TERMINAL FIVE, LONDON HEATHROW AIRPORT
LONDON, UK

He followed the signs for passengers in transit. There were too many passengers, he thought. Even the newer Terminal 5 was too crowded. He had designed his flights so that he did not need to change terminals. He had taken a puddle jumper from Tortola to St. Kitts and then a BA flight nonstop to Heathrow. Now he would take a BA flight out to Dubai, never leaving the In Transit area in Terminal 5.

Within the vast BA Terminal, he took the train from Concourse C over to Concourse A, following the purple Transit Passengers signs. Then he saw the security checkpoint.

"But I am just in transit," he said to the woman in the information booth. "And I am staying on British, staying in Terminal Five. Why do I need to wait in line?"

"Sorry, sir, everyone in transit has to go through security," she said in a singsong voice. "It's the rules, love."

He felt the sweat again. British security was good and they probably had data ties to the Americans and maybe even the Australians. He knew that his Australian identity was solid. He had used it many times. He told himself to relax, again, and exhale. The line was mercifully short.

"Where are you coming from?"

"St. Kitts."

"Going where?"

"Back home, Melbourne, via Dubai."

The Immigration man in the cubicle typed into his computer. Now was the moment of truth, Bahadur knew.

"Thank you. Next," the officer yelled out and handed him back his boarding pass and passport.

Bahadur moved quickly to the Duty Free Shopping area in the main part of the Terminal. Concourse A was just a walk away. He walked in and sat down at a bar off the main hall and ordered a scotch, neat. He had two hours to kill.

It was forty minutes later that the officer at the booth Bahadur had gone through was handed the picture on a "look out" flyer. As his supervisor began to move along, the officer called him back.

"Are you absolutely certain?" the supervisor asked.

"Positive, sir. Within the hour," the officer explained. "Said he was going home to Australia, via Dubai."

"But this man they want has an Indian passport," the supervisor noted.

"Your flyer says it's a false Indian document, sir."

"When does the BA flight to Dubai leave?" the supervisor asked into his microphone. "Right. Switch me over to the Armed Police desk."

Bahadur was still at the bar, reading a two-day-old *Times of India* when he sensed something happening. He looked halfway up from his paper and saw two pairs of police with automatic weapons standing about ten feet apart in the passageway beyond the bar.

At almost the same instant, he felt a strong hand grabbing his left arm. Bahadur used the bar stool to swing around quickly, and his boot to push up between the plainclothes policeman's legs. He leaped from the stool and drove his head straight into the second detective's stomach, causing him to drop his handgun. Bahadur grabbed the weapon and fired two rounds at the first officer's head. He rolled on the floor and let off another round at the second man, the man whose gun he was using, hitting him in the stomach. The three shots sounded like explosions in the low-ceilinged airport bar. He heard screaming in the hall and a man yelling, "I have it."

Then there was a much louder noise as the armed

police sergeant fired six shots from the hallway into the bar, into the man on the floor with the gun, moving the shots up from the bottom of his torso and ending at the top of Bahadur's head. The screaming grew louder in the hallway and in the bar, and the stampeding away from the shooting turned Heathrow Terminal 5 into chaos.

"How did he think he could ever get away, Sarge?" the younger armed policeman asked as he and the three other men with assault weapons entered the bar.

"He didn't think he could get away, Jeremy, but he also didn't want to be taken alive," the sergeant said. "You've just seen suicide by police, he made me become a killer, but he didn't give me much choice."

# 40

SUNDAY, DECEMBER 20
SPECIAL OPERATIONS ROOM
GLOBAL COORDINATION CENTER
CREECH AFB, NEVADA

"Did you get any sleep?" Sandra Vittonelli asked Colonel Erik Parsons as she, Ray, and Dugout entered her office.

"How could I," he replied. "Not with Jen out there, somewhere. And we don't even know if she's alive or dead."

"The FBI profiler believes she is alive," Ray offered. "She thinks the kidnappers plan to use Dr. Parsons in some way to get to you. Killing her would serve little purpose."

"The FBI guys are nice, but they don't have a clue about what to do next, not a single lead," Erik said.

"I read their reports," Dugout commented. "Seems Jen's cell is missing. What kind of mobile did she have?"

"The new iPhone," Erik answered. "I got it for her birthday."

"Yes!" Dugout said, punching the air. "But you guys never added the remote activation antenna and software to some of the Predators."

"We didn't do what?" Sandra asked.

"You can't remove the battery from the iPhone like you can on most mobiles," Dugout explained. "So it's never fully dead, even when it's off. It still leaks a little juice from the battery to keep the clock going and on the new iPhone it also powers the Find My iPhone app when the phone can link to an open WiFi network. It's a fix from earlier versions of the app. It's designed to find stolen iPhones even if the thief never turns the device on. It doesn't search for a cell tower because that would drain the battery, but every hour it looks briefly for a WiFi network and when one sends out a ping to the Finder app, it will send back an ack packet, an acknowledgment, with its coordinates."

"So, how does that help us?" Erik asked.

"Simple, we add the new antenna and software to a bunch of Preds over Vegas and establish open WiFi networks from them. We activate her Find My iPhone app and broadcast that out over the WiFi nets. If her device is still in one piece, it will get the message and will beep back its location. If we have two Preds up that can get the signal, we can triangulate to within a few feet."

"Let's get going," Erik said.

Ray held up his hand, gesturing to slow down. "It's very unlikely that the phone is still where she is."

Sandra was picking up the drop line to Flight Ops. "Maybe, but it could give us a lead, like maybe some fingerprints." She looked up at the aircraft status screen. "I need techs to work on the four Pred trainers, add an antenna and download some software updates. How long will that take?"

"I'm piloting," Erik insisted.

She hung up the landline. "They're calling in the ground tech guys. If they push it, we could have them ready to launch around sundown."

SUNDAY, DECEMBER 20
ONE CENTER PLAZA
BOSTON, MASSACHUSETTS

"Got him," Bobby Gallagher yelled as he burst into Judith Wolosky's office.

"Who, Mister Big? The Indian guy? Where?"

"London, in the airport. He'd just flown in from the Virgin Islands and he was carrying an Australian passport," Gallagher said.

"We sure it's the same guy?" she asked.

"Yeah, they found the Indian passport and ID sewn into his carry-on, same guy."

"Well, who gets to go to London to interrogate him? I'll call Headquarters. It's our case," she said.

"Don't bother. He's dead. Resisting arrest. Grabbed a cop's gun, killed him, wounded another one. Scotland Yard guy I talked to said it was like he didn't want to be taken alive."

"Shit," Wolosky said. "That ain't good. Means he was afraid of revealing information, like what the other things are that are supposed to happen simultaneously."

"Yeah, I see what you mean," Gallagher added. "That probably means they will go off without needing him. Autopilot."

Judith Wolosky walked to the big window looking out on the city. "Besides the Indian ID in the lining, anything interesting? Any pocket litter?"

"Nada."

"Of course not," Wolosky said. "If you were going to bomb the T, maybe other cities' subways, too, maybe other things, when would you do it?"

"The busiest shopping day is probably tomorrow, or maybe the day before Christmas," Gallagher offered.

"We have to get them to go back into the tunnels with the dogs, with lights. Double-check that no one has planted anything. Red Line, Blue Line, Green Line, Orange Line, the works," she said. "I think I should call the Governor."

SUNDAY, DECEMBER 20
SPECIAL OPERATIONS ROOM
GLOBAL COORDINATION CENTER
CREECH AFB, NEVADA

After a fruitless hour and a quarter of flying the drones over Las Vegas, Ray said to Erik Parsons, "Well, we didn't think they would have her near the Strip or in Henderson. Let's expand the search areas, two north toward Creech, two east toward Nellis. Good thing is, now, we got Clark County SWAT ready to go if we get a location. FBI got Nellis Air Force Base to give them four Blackhawks to fly SWAT in."

Erik instructed two Air Force sergeants where to move the two pairs of Predators that were circling low over Clark County, Nevada, transmitting an open WiFi network signal.

"Got it," Dugout cried out.

"You found her phone?" Erik said, moving quickly down the line to Dugout's desk.

"No, not yet, sorry I didn't mean to, uh . . ." Dugout said, looking up at the Air Force officer. "But I did find the flaw in their encryption algo."

"Good for you," Erik said sarcastically. "Dug, I'm sorry, too, man, no sleep. What does that do for us?"

"Means in a few hours or so, if I'm lucky, I can crack the three servers we've been looking at and maybe get the IP addresses of where these guys are. Maybe run a trace route that will tell me which buildings, maybe which hotel room or office suite," Dugout said. "They may have her at the U.S. location, the one that's connected to the server in Dallas."

"No need to wait for that, sir," Sergeant Miller said, standing up at his screens. "I got her iPhone pinging back up north of the city, near the golf course. Getting visual now on the area." He adjusted the camera. "Nothing around up there but that old trailer home. Looks abandoned."

Erik looked at Ray. "Let's go." The two men ran to the Chevy Suburbans parked outside, where a team of FBI agents had been waiting, hoping that the Predators would find a signal. As the three black trucks drove off the base, the lead Agent radioed ahead to the SWAT team.

"Do you hit the house right away? The bad guys might kill her if they see us coming." Erik asked the lead Agent.

"We'll sneak up to the building, they won't see us in the dark," the FBI man explained.

"But they may have perimeter sensors," Ray said. The FBI man frowned, but said nothing.

"Wait a minute. Patch me through on your radio to the GCC," Erik said to him. "Miller, don't we have the IR human form sensors on those Preds? Good, image the house through each of the windows. Also scan multispec for tunnels."

In a few minutes Miller called back to Erik Parsons. "Right, you're one hundred percent sure?" Erik looked at Ray and the Bureau lead. "We assess one live body in the trailer home. No tunnels."

"You willing to risk your wife's life on that, Colonel?" the FBI man asked.

Erik inhaled, exhaled, thought a long moment. "Yes."

The FBI Agent talked into his radio. "All right, tell SWAT to land two of the helos at the house and go in. We think there is one person in the house. Could be the vic or the perp. Don't shoot till you are sure which. Watch out for booby traps." The Agent looked at Erik. The black Suburbans were racing up the Interstate, pushing traffic out of the left-hand lane. Ray saw the speed indicator go to three digits.

Ray and Erik exchanged nods, hoping they had done the right thing. The FBI Agent put the tactical commander's radio bridge on speaker.

"Hawk one landed."

"Hawk two landed."

"Two other Blackhawks are circling the site, throwing down light."

Then there were three very long minutes of static.

"Going in, going in."

Erik's eyes were closed, his head down, his hands squeezing the back of the seat in front of him.

For five more minutes they raced up the highway listening to static. Silence.

Then, "Building cleared, no traps. Victim recovered. Reports she is thirsty, hungry. Should we chopper her to the ER for a checkup?"

A cheer went up in the Suburban. Tears ran down the Air Force pilot's face. "No, no. Wait till we get there." Erik began to choke up. "If she's hungry, she's fine. Can I talk with her?"

"That might be hard to patch together, Colonel, but at this speed, we're less than five mics out," the lead FBI Agent replied.

He was out of the Suburban before it stopped, running toward his wife, who sat in the open side door of one of the Blackhawks. He embraced her and then lifted her high in the air before the two collapsed in the dirt together, crying and laughing.

After they had settled down and were holding hands, staring up at the stars, Ray knelt next to them in the dirt. "Dr. Parsons, I know this is not the time for the debrief, but time is important right now. You are a trained observer. Is there anything you can tell us that would help us right now?"

Both Jennifer and Erik sat up. She began, "One man," she began. "Thirties. Sounded American. Ski mask, couldn't see the face. Made me watch video of drone strikes. Said he was going to get Erik. Said he tried once already, but got the wrong guy. Maybe I'll remember more, but . . ."

Ray thanked her and walked away. He pulled out his mobile and called Sandra Vittonelli. "I heard, it's great news," she said before Ray could talk. "I was just about to hop in the shower. Come on over. Did you talk with her?"

"Yeah, not much to add yet, but the kidnap was definitely about drones. It wasn't some former patient."

Sandra adjusted her terry cloth robe with one hand, her mobile in the other. "What did they do to her?" she asked Ray Bowman.

"One bad guy that she saw. Made her watch video of drone damage and said—"

Sandra cut him off. Thirty-three floors above the Vegas Strip, Sandra Vittonelli walked past the floor-to-ceiling windows in her living room. She paused at the door out on to the tiny balcony she used to grow some herbs. The peripheral vision in her left eye saw movement and she turned. "What the fuck? There's a B-52 coming straight for my—"

At first it seemed like the B-52 was some distance away, but her brain quickly flashed to the conclusion that it was just outside the window, a miniature B-52. In the nanosecond that her conscious mind understood what was happening, she saw a metal rod extending from the nose of the aircraft smash through the floor-to-ceiling glass window. As glass crashed into her suite, the B-52 erupted into a fireball that chased the glass inside, flash-burning everything in the room.

Raymond Bowman heard her say "B-52" followed by a loud noise. Then the line went dead. He redialed, but the call went to voice mail. He tried again with the same result. He got the number of her condo building and tried to call the concierge desk, but it just kept ringing. He called Dugout back at the Global Coordination Center. "Ask Miller to fly one of the drones over to the intersection of Flamingo and Wynn, scan the big new condo on the corner, the blue glass one, see if anything looks odd. Also scan the sky en route for a B-52 flying low."

"You got it, boss, and by the way I think I'll have the geocoordinates of those servers in an hour or so," Dugout added.

Ray walked back to the Suburban. The driver was standing outside with the door open, listening to radio chatter. "Anything else going on tonight on the frequencies?" Ray asked the driver.

"Nah, not really. Lots of assault and batteries, but that's normal. Explosion and fire in some high-rise."

Ray's mobile rang. It was Dugout. "There's a fire in an upper floor in that building. Looks contained to one or two apartments."

"Thirty-third floor?" Ray asked.

"Could be, yah? What's in that building?"

Ray ended the call and found the lead FBI Agent. "We need to get one of those Blackhawks and fly downtown now. We can land in the street."

Ten minutes later they could see the smoke pouring from the upper floors of the condominium tower. Ray's heart sank. He knew Sandra's apartment was in flames. His mind flashed to images of her there, standing naked in the dark looking out on the flashing lights of the Strip before he dragged her back into bed. As the helicopter neared the Strip, the smoke was already diminishing. He knew it was futile to hope that she had survived, but she was special, tough, creative. Maybe she had found a way.

The Blackhawk touched down in an empty, dirt parking lot across the street from her building, kicking up a dust cloud that blinded the Las Vegas police who were there waiting for them. The helicopter lifted off almost immediately, as Ray was running across the lot to the nearest police car. A uniformed officer moved to greet him. "I'm Captain Robinson, LVPD. I just got told by headquarters that you're from Washington and I'm supposed to cooperate with you. What's this all about?"

Ray flashed his credentials to the police captain. "There's an important federal official who lives in this building," he yelled over the noise of the ascending helicopter. "I have reason to believe this fire is from an explosion targeting her, maybe an aircraft of some kind."

The captain indicated for Ray to follow and they began moving quickly toward the tower. "Well, I don't know what happened yet, but I don't think an airplane hit the building. The explosion was fairly contained and the FD has got the fire almost out," Robinson said. Ray's optimism was rising again.

The police car pulled up to a Fire Department Mobile Command Post in the middle of the street below the smoking condominium building. Ray and Captain Robinson both quickly jumped out of the car. The policeman introduced Bowman to the fire chief who was the on scene commander. "Yeah, it's under control now. It was some sort of explosion on thirty-three. We've only found one fatality so far, but there may be others."

Although he could barely get out the words, Ray Bowman asked, "Do you have an ID on the victim?"

"No, not yet, the ME just rolled with the body a few minutes ago." The fireman consulted his iPad. "Female, badly burned. Found in the probable bedroom area in 3304. The concierge guy told us 3304 belongs to a Janet Sutherland." Ray knew that was Sandra Vittonelli's cover name for her life in Las Vegas. He turned away from the Fire Chief, hung his head, and pounded his fist hard onto the hood of a patrol car.

Then, slowly, he regained control. He walked back to the Chief. "I will need to see the body," he found himself saying. The words had come out of his mouth, but his mind had frozen up. He felt himself shutting down.

He was aware that the policeman was talking to him. "I can take you over to the Medical Examiner's building."

With effort, he formed the words of a reply. "Yes, please."

# 41

MONDAY, DECEMBER 21
SPECIAL OPERATIONS ROOM
GLOBAL COORDINATION CENTER
CREECH AFB, NEVADA

None of them had slept. Ray had identified Sandy's body at the Medical Examiner's building. She had been burned badly, but was recognizable. He did not stay there looking at the charred remains, did not stand by her side and think. He left quickly before the image of her that way froze in his mind. With all of his self-control, he had decided to lock his emotions away in a corner of his brain, a corner he would revisit later when he could deal with it. Now, he told himself, he had work to do. If he let himself go, let himself feel, he would not be able to work, to finish the job. She would want him to finish it. He had to find her killers. He had to kill them.

Erik Parsons had taken his wife to the Emergency Room, where she had been examined and found to be dehydrated, but otherwise fine. They had urged her to spend a day under observation in the hospital. Her hospital room was protected by an FBI Agent and a local policeman. She asked for an Ambien and told Erik to go get some rest. He went back to the GCC.

Dugout had never left the drone operations center. When Ray reappeared at the Operations Room it was three thirty in the morning. His suit had ash and dust on it. His pants were dirty at the knees. His tie was off and his hair was unkempt. He carried a coffee.

"Don't say anything about her. Not yet," he said to Dugout and Erik. "Ask your Big Data Analysis thing to find connections between what we have been looking for and model airplanes, radio controlled, big ones, custom. Add model B-52s as a subset."

He then placed a secure call to White House Signal, the Army-run communications room for the classified networks serving the President and his staff. He asked to be put through to the National Security Advisor. Before Winston Burrell could say anything about Sandra Vittonelli, Ray got down to business.

"Win, we have a tough decision to make and we have to make it now. We have every reason to believe that there is an active plot to conduct bombings in the U.S. in the next forty-eight hours. We don't know where, but we believe it could involve subways, possibly including Boston's. If we issue a vague national warning, some people will panic needlessly, but if we say nothing and it happens . . ." He let the implications of that course go unsaid.

"Right. This is your government advising you to stop your holiday shopping and hunker down because we think something may happen somewhere," Burrell replied. "The Governor of Massachusetts called the President last night. The FBI has the Gov all spun up. He wanted to issue some sort of Red Alert."

"What did you tell him?"

"Told him we don't do colors anymore and for now he should just massively step up police presence and searches, keep hospital ERs fully staffed, but no announcement yet," Burrell replied. "Told him we hoped to have more information on the plot today. Will we?"

"Maybe, but if we don't, I would advise that some sort of announcement is going to be necessary later today. It may scare them away for now, give us more time. Or it may panic them into going early. No way to tell," Ray admitted.

Hanging up the secure line, he turned to see Colonel Parsons busily running several drone missions. "You should be with your wife," he said to Erik.

"She'll be asleep for hours. Besides, I got work to do here," Erik replied.

"Like what?" Ray asked.

Dugout looked at Erik. "Better tell him."

"All right, but do not try to stop me," Erik said to Ray. "I have a Global Reach on the way to Kiev and a Reaper en route to this place in Pakistan, DG Khan."

Ray frowned at Dugout. "I geolocated the servers at the user ends of those VPNs," Dug said. "The Kiev one is a complex that the CIA and FBI databases show as the warehouse headquarters of the Merezha cyber/narco cartel. It's heavily guarded and they appear to have bought off the local police."

"And the other place?" Ray asked.

"A villa outside of a city known as DG Khan. CIA carries it as the headquarters of the Qazzani clan. We did a Pattern of Life a few times before and it was all bad guys, but we never got the political clearance. State objected to hitting anything that deep into Pakistan."

"Isn't there also one in the U.S.?" Ray asked.

"It's routed through Texas, but it's really just north of Vegas, about five miles from where they were holding Jen. The Bureau and the SWAT guys are going to hit it right after dawn." Dugout paused. "I asked them if I could go in after they cleared the place to do a first line exploitation on their computers. I'm already in the ones that are online, but they probably have some that aren't always connected, or are never connected. Anyway, I got into the online ones."

"Of course you did," Ray said, sitting down.

"So, can I do it?" Dugout asked. "Can I go with the SWAT guys, I mean after the SWAT guys?"

Ray ran his hand through his hair. "Sure, why the fuck not, we're about to break all sorts of rules." He looked at Erik. "Colonel, did you know there's already an IG investigation of you?"

"Yeah, but I understand they haven't got anything on me. They asked me to take a voluntary polygraph," Erik said.

"What'd you say?" Ray asked.

"I told them to get fucked. And then I figured I might as well do something they could actually investigate."

Ray stared at the Big Board. He saw the Global Reach and the Reaper en route to their targets. "I don't suppose anyone in Washington has approved those two flights?" No one answered.

"Didn't think so," he said to no one in particular.

"The ranch we're going to hit at dawn?" Dugout said, changing the subject. "We just got this: there's a mobile phone there that's been calling another mobile about three miles from here. Narrowed it down to a high school, or near it."

Ray stood up. "Gimme those coordinates and the number. We still have FBI guys out front. Maybe I'll drive over there with them. Dugout, you go get out to that ranch and exploit the computers after the SWAT guys hit it.

"Erik, you moved up when Sandy died. You're in charge here now. Do what you have to do. You're familiar with the emergency protocol, right? It gives the GCC Director the authority to act in exigent circumstances. With Sandy gone that would be you. You just have to check with the most senior National Security official available. That would be me. And I judge that there is an imminent threat to the lives of Americans who could be killed in a series of terrorist attacks planned by the Qazzani cartel, working with the Merezha gang."

Ray and Dugout walked to the exit together. "Take 'em out, Colonel, take the bastards out," Ray said in a loud voice that everyone on the Ops Floor could hear. Then in a quiet voice he said to Dugout, "And let's hope they haven't already sent the go signal to their attack cells."

# 42

TUESDAY, DECEMBER 22
COPPER HILLS RANCH
KYLE CANYON, NEVADA

"You're up early, Mykola," Yuri Poderev said as he stumbled into their computer room in his underwear. "Did you make the coffee yet?"

"I talked to Ghazi. He's coming over later. This is probably A-Day," Mykola replied. "I bet when he comes today, he tells us it's time. Then I play with the DC Metro, and BART, and MARTA in Atlanta. Big day."

Yuri stretched. "Did you make the coffee?" he repeated, as he walked into the dirty kitchen and found a fresh pot already made. As he began to pour the coffee, a loud alarm sounded, "Intruder! Intruder!" and then a series of loud blurts. Yuri poured the coffee on the floor, and on himself. He moved quickly back into the living room they had converted into their computer room.

"All the intruder sensors are going crazy," Mykola said. "And the perimeter ones. Look at the cameras, there are SUVs on the road."

"Pull out the hard drives. Smash them," Yuri yelled, but by then they could both hear the loud rotors of a helicopter directly above the house. As a blindingly bright light shone through the window, there was a blast and the front door flew across the room, quickly followed by two, then four men in dark blue helmets and body armor, swinging automatic weapons with lights on them, wildly from left to right.

"Do not move, if you move you die!" one of the stormtroopers yelled. "All right now, arms out to your sides. Show me your palms. Open hands facing me. Now, slowly, down on your knees. Slowly, facedown on the floor. Do not breathe." In seconds, Yuri and Mykola had their hands tied behind their backs and then their ankles laced together by a strong plastic belt. They heard a helicopter landing, but the light from another hovering aircraft still darted in and out of the window.

"It's clear, bring him in," one of the blue men said into a microphone on his helmet.

Dugout, wearing some of the blue body armor suit, walked gingerly through the blasted doorframe and struggled to take off his helmet. "Next time, I want the white suit. Which one of you guys is Vader?" he said to what were by then twelve body-armored blue men crowding the living room.

"I'm the senior FBI Special Agent on site," one of the assault team members said dryly. "I am supposed to 'facilitate your exploitation of the computers' for an hour or so. Then we start ripping them out and taking them to our computer forensic lab."

"I'll tell you when they get ripped out," Dugout said,

sitting down at one of the chairs in front of a bank of three screens.

Two FBI agents in body armor were lifting Yuri off the floor and dragging him out of the house. Dugout spun around in his chair and pointed at two more agents about to drag Mykola out. "Hang on a minute." He looked at Mykola. "I know you. *Dovgo ne bachīlīs. Berlin, dah?*"

"I speak English," Mykola replied. "Yes, it was Chaos Communication Congress, two years ago in Berlin. You spoke on finding flaws in encryption routines. Is that what you did? Is that how you found us?"

"Next time when I submit a paper at Chaos, maybe you should read it," Dugout replied. "Listen, you're hosed, so all you can do now is buy yourself a better prison roommate. I can get you a safe one, or your own private room, but you better talk to me now. Passwords, the attack plans, you know what I need. No tricks. Trick me and you get shot resisting arrest. Shot dead, man, fatal, right, Darth?"

TUESDAY, DECEMBER 22
LEGACY HIGH SCHOOL
NORTH LAS VEGAS

Ray was not supposed to do tactical missions. There was a bright red line against that in his job description. It had taken him years to stop people from saying he should not be "operational." The advent of drones had made him very operational and no one could argue against that, at least not successfully. The PEG Director, however, was supposed to do analysis, not race through the suburbs in a convoy of Chevy Suburbans. As they drove, he noticed the streetlights go out and the sky turn a pinkish orange. He wasn't supposed to be with the gun toters and, he thought with a smile, Dugout certainly wasn't either.

He held on to the door handle as the big truck cornered without slowing down and began speeding down the straightway, past the high school campus, over the rise, and into the open desert. Then he saw the 747 above.

"Stop," he yelled. "Everyone out, out of the truck. Incoming. Get away from the truck!" He opened the door and leaped while the vehicle was just starting to slow down. He hit the dirt hard, but curled and rolled in the military parachute landing style, keeping his head off the ground. He scrambled to get up and ran into the sand and rock at the side of the road as he heard the second Suburban rear-end the first with a metal on metal crunch.

Then the explosion knocked him down, face first into the dirt. He felt a rock cut into his left cheekbone just below the eye. Facedown, he could still see the light from the blast and the fire. He felt the heat.

Ray forced himself up. He knew there was blood coming from somewhere, or maybe a couple of places, his cheek, his nose, his left ear. He saw the FBI men trying to make sure that everyone had made it out of the first two vehicles. Their windows were shattered into giant spiderwebs. He staggered ahead, away from the wreck. Was this what a concussion felt like? There was a ringing in his ears and he was squinting, trying to focus. Then he saw the C-17 model lifting off at the end of the long flat, dirt road. Three models waited for takeoff, a B-17, an A-380, and a B-29. Ray tried to yell back to the agents, but he couldn't get the words out, coughing, choking.

But the large model C-17 banked left after lifting off, flying its programmed flight path, seeking a homing beacon.

"You okay, sir?" It was an agent from the third vehicle, one of three men in body armor who were now standing with him.

"Hey, there's a guy down there in the middle of the road," one of the agents called out, raising his HK33 assault weapon.

"Don't shoot," Ray said. "Let's take him."

"We'll give that a try, sir, but we have our rules," the Special Agent replied.

The four men walked slowly down the road toward Ghazi, who had placed a flight controller module on the ground and was walking toward them with his arms hanging by his sides, his hands empty.

"Stop there," the Agent yelled. And then in low voice to Ray, he said, "Could have a suicide belt on."

"Take off your coat and drop it on the ground," another Agent yelled.

Ghazi stopped, but kept the coat on. "You thought you were invulnerable here, didn't you? No one could get your drone pilots here. You could kill innocent people everywhere in the world, but no one could kill you, no one could get their revenge? Never be any payback? Thought you were the only ones with drones, didn't you?" His right hand darted into his North Face windbreaker. "Vengeance!" he yelled and started to run toward them.

"Gun!" one of the agents cried out. All three FBI agents fired their HK33s in short bursts of a few bullets each.

Ghazi had no gun. Instead, he held a detonator and as soon as he hit its switch, the three large model radio controlled aircraft on the road behind him blew up in what seemed like a single, massive explosion.

The blast knocked the FBI agents and Ray to the ground again. Ghazi's lifeless body lay bleeding out on the pavement.

TUESDAY, DECEMBER 22
SPECIAL OPERATIONS ROOM
GLOBAL COORDINATION CENTER
CREECH AFB, NEVADA

First, the Global Reach drone got to the target outside of Kiev.

"Five SUVs, one pickup in the yard. Guards inside at the gate. Guards outside. Guard on the roof. No signs of civilians. Getting multiple, human life forms readings through the windows. Laser is having trouble getting the conversation, but the voices are all male," Major Jaimie Hernandez was calling out. It was his first day at the GCC, but he had flown birds from Eglin Air Base in Florida. Now he was stepping up to the big time, to the place where the important national missions were flown and on his initial shift there, he realized, he was already part of a mission like none he had ever heard about.

"Weapons check?" Erik asked.

"We've got two laser-guided 250-pound bombs, Mark 82s, and four Hellfire missiles, two with high explosives and two with fragmentation warheads."

"Let's drop the two bombs on the first pass, ten-second interval. On my mark, and fire."

The warehouse erupted on the Big Board and then disappeared as the Global Reach banked to avoid the explosion it had created. There was no second bird to provide a video feed. Erik had been lucky to find a Global Reach already over eastern Turkey, looking for PKK terrorists and arms being smuggled into Syria.

"Okay, Jaimie, finish them off and set course for home. Do you have enough fuel to get back to CONUS?" Erik asked.

"No way, sir, I was going to bring it back to Turkey, to Incirlik," Major Hernandez replied.

"The Turks may get a little touchy about our blowing shit up in the Ukraine and then landing in Turkey. If you can't get to Sicily, Sigonella, bring it in to Ramat David and I'll let the Israelis know not to shoot it down," Erik said.

Looking at the Big Board, at the missiles ripping into the flaming warehouse complex, Erik walked down the line of flight controllers to Sergeant Rod Miller's cubicle. Miller was flying a Reaper over the target in Pakistan. As Colonel Erik Parsons looked over Miller's shoulder at the images from Pakistan, Communications switched a call from the Pentagon for Parsons to a red phone in Miller's cubicle. It was Admiral Johnston.

"Colonel, are you the acting Officer in Charge?" the Admiral yelled down the line.

"Yes, sir. Under the Continuity of Ops plan, I took over when the Director was . . . was no longer available."

"Well, what the shit did you guys just do in the Ukraine? There's been no authorization to fly in there, let alone bomb in there. You trying to start a war there, son?"

"Admiral, I am operating a mission today under the Intelligence chain of command, not military. And, with all due respect, sir, I am still in the middle of that mission, so if you will forgive me, sir, I need to get back to work. I'm sure the White House will—"

"Colonel, you are to stand down. Now. You are relieved of any billet you have in any Intelligence outfit. Let the Agency do that stuff. I will not have a serving officer starting a Goddamn war. You get in your car and you drive over to Nellis Air Base and report to the Inspector General. Colonel?"

"Sir, I think you may be mistaken. I am not in your chain of command, sir." Colonel Parsons hung up the red phone and looked at Sergeant Rod Miller.

"You get to DG Khan city yet?"

"Be there about thirty mics, sir. Nice villa Qazzani's got there, but it's no family manse. This is clearly the workplace, lots of guys with guns. No kiddie toys. No clothesline. Last time we profiled this place it came up clean for collateral then, too."

"How do we know Qazzani himself is there, the big guy?" Erik asked.

"That step van out front is his personal war wagon, we know the plates," Miller replied. "We've also been listening to his bodyguard's mobile. He ordered up two boys to be delivered to the villa. Then Qazzani's step van showed up about two hours ago."

"Boys?" Erik asked.

"Intel says that's what he likes," Miller replied. "He didn't take too long with them. We saw the two kids walked to a car and driven away about twenty minutes ago. The bodyguard's mobile was on again. Looks like he is the one driving the car away from the compound with the kids. I think in the compound now is just Qazzani himself and some other bad guys."

"Wonder how we got the bodyguard's cell phone number?" Erik mused aloud to no one in particular. He then switched the image on the Big Board to the target in Pakistan. It was a nice, clear High Definition image from the Reaper.

"Colonel, two questions," Miller began. "First, aren't the Paks going to be rip-shit about us hitting down there, long way from the kill box they approved up in Waziristan? And, two, would you like to fly this, because rules are we need an officer flying when we pull the trigger."

"Different rules today, Rod, different rules. Imminent threat to Americans, exigent circumstances," Erik explained. "Yes, the Paks will be pissed. Think what the Ukrainians will be saying once they figure out it wasn't a meth lab that blew itself up out at that gang's compound. Are you willing to fly this one, Sarge?"

"Yes, sir," Sergeant Miller replied and looked back at his controls.

"Hit the main building with two now," Erik ordered. "Wait fifteen minutes and see who shows up to rescue and then hit it again with the last two, the frag warheads, so we get the rest of them, too."

Erik looked down at Miller's hands as the sergeant flipped switches and moved the joystick, causing weapons to release thousands of miles away a fraction of a second later. He noticed the pack of Marlboros next to Miller's wallet in the cubicle. Then his eyes moved to the HD explosion on the Big Board and then the same view from a Predator higher up. There were secondary explosions, bombs or ordnance cooking off inside the building.

"You can't smoke in here, Sergeant," Erik said as he took the Marlboros and the lighter. "Major Hernandez, you're in Control. I'll be back in ten."

The last of the night sky was disappearing and the sun beginning to brighten the day as he stood in the parking lot and lit up. He had stopped smoking eight years ago, but the smoke felt so good just now as he leaned against Jen's white Ford Edge. It was a nice crossover, but he missed his Camaro. He missed Bruce Dougherty, who had died in that Camaro. And he was still trying to come to grips with losing Sandra Vittonelli. So many good friends, fellow war fighters. The fun had gone out of this job a long time ago, he thought. Too much killing, maybe time for him and Jen to find that place on the islands in the Juan de Fuca.

As he was thinking of Jen, his mobile vibrated. The caller ID said it was Ray Bowman phoning him.

That's when he saw the C-17 diving for the Edge. He had no time to react. It hit the Edge in the middle of its large moon roof, bursting into an orange sunburstlike flash flame. Colonel Erik Parsons's last thought was half formed when his brain was shattered by the blast. He had seen scores of attacks from the perspective of the attacking aircraft. For a second, he thought he was seeing one from the other side, and then he thought no more. The explosion was big enough to blow in the front doors of the GCC and channel a blast down the corridor, cracking interior glass walls, but the center survived the aircraft attack.

A few miles away, a B-17, an A-380, and a B-29, laden with explosives, destined for the GCC, were now in little pieces on the ground near Ghazi's dead body. Ray Bowman, still dazzled by the concussive effect of their explosion, dusted off the dirt on his clothes. He had tried Erik on his landline in the GCC, then on his mobile. Nothing. Now he tried Dugout at the North Vegas ranch scene and got through. "How's the exploitation coming?" he asked Dug.

"I think I stopped the preprogrammed cyber attacks on the subways in DC, San Fran, and Atlanta. Got good leads on guys in Boston, Chicago, and Philly. The Fibbies think they can set those guys up for meets and then bag them before any attacks," Dugout explained. "How's things at your end?"

"Guy had huge model planes with some high explosive in them. He launched one. Don't know where it went. I guess we will find out. He tried to kill us by blowing up the three others. The Bureau guys dropped him. They're going to go through what's left of him and his car. I'm not going to wait around. Thought I'd go by the ER and get some nicks tended to," Ray said walking toward a waiting Sheriff's car. "I guess I'll advise

Burrell to hold off issuing a public warning. Let the Christmas shopping go on."

"Who was the guy piloting the RC models?" Dugout asked.

Ray used one hand to shield his eyes from the bright morning sun coming up over the mountains, and with the other hand held his mobile. "Dunno. Was yelling something about our not being invulnerable here, something about payback. Vengeance. Sounded American." Ray sounded tired, his mind seemed focused elsewhere. "We'll try to figure out who he was. See where in the never-ending circle of retaliations this guy fits in."

As he walked away from the smoking wreckage of the radio controlled model aircraft, past the dead body of the terrorist, Ray heard a buzz and looked up. The white drone circling above the scene had large block letters in blue that read SHERIFF.

# 43

TUESDAY, DECEMBER 22
NAVY HILL
WASHINGTON, DC

It was warm for Christmas, he thought. Climate Change was going to be the big issue from now on, not terrorism. It would do what the terrorists never could, bankrupt us and kill millions. So if the entire world was going to hell, why not smoke the Havana? What was there to lose? Sandra was dead, as was Erik. The drone program was in a legal straitjacket and the Ukrainian and Pakistani governments were demanding investigations, arrests, UN meetings, INTERPOL red notices.

Maybe it wasn't too late to escape town for the week between the holidays. Maybe fly down to Anguilla. Get a room at that high-end resort. Blow some of the small savings he had left.

Raymond Bowman sat on what he thought of as his bench above the Potomac, wearing the leather flight jacket that had been Erik Parsons's. His widow had insisted that he have it. She didn't blame him for Erik's death, or Sandra's, or Bruce's. But he blamed himself. Failure sat on his shoulders like twenty-pound weights. It ate at his gut like an acid. It kept him awake like that damn Provigil pill. It caused him to think that nothing was worthwhile, especially him.

Sandra had been the first woman whom he had really connected with in years. She was so good at everything she did, and all that she asked for were tougher missions, harder jobs, and a chance to do good for her country. Between him and her, Ray thought, there was mutual understanding and real mutual respect. While he had never admitted it to himself before, he had hoped at some subliminal level that it might go somewhere, might lead to the next several chapters of his life. Now he had no idea what those next chapters would be and, worse yet, at this moment, he did not care.

"You should shave. How long's it been? You look like a park bench bum, even if the park bench is inside a highly guarded facility." Dugout sat down next to him, holding a half lit cigar.

"Privacy. I know it's a concept that's foreign to you hackers, but . . ." Ray said to him. "And theft. Even theft of a Havana. It's theft. Four days and I think I may not shave again for quite a few more."

"The Bureau thinks they got the last guy this morning," Dugout said. "He was a Yemeni American student at Temple. He was supposed to set off a bomb in Reading Terminal in Philly."

"So it's over?" Raymond Bowman asked.

"For now. Just in case I missed something, Metro, MARTA, BART, the T are all on manual. Their digital control networks are severed from the Internet. From what we found on a trick thumb drive at the ranch in Nevada, the FBI tracked down the facilitators in Philly and Chicago. None of them had ever gotten the go signal. Seems like the guy that got shot in Heathrow was going to send out the go code from Dubai or Karachi."

"We think the guy in Heathrow was the guy that got on the boat to Canada? Doesn't make sense," Ray noted.

"He never got on the boat. He kept leaving false trails, just in case we got to any of the bombers. CIA thinks now that he was one of the two falcons. The guy you got in Vegas was the other," Dugout explained. "Lived in Canada, but originally Pakistani, one Ghazi Nawarz."

"Probably some facilitators in the U.S. the Bureau hasn't identified yet," Ray thought aloud. "Did you see the BDA on Kiev and DG Khan?"

Dugout shook his head in the affirmative as he sucked on his cigar, trying to keep it lit. "Bomb Damage Assessment, not Big Data Analysis? It's pretty good. Those drone attacks fried both places. Also HUMINT says that the heads of both the Qazzani and the Merezha bought it, along with lots of underlings. Apparently some friendly country, I think the Brits, had a guy in the Qazzani compound and the Agency signaled him to leave just before we hit it."

"Ah, the falcon watcher," Ray said. "But this won't be the end of the Qazzani enterprise. Too much money on the table. Where there are drugs to be moved, there will be movers."

"Right, but now there will be a scramble among the deputies and lieutenants to see who gets to take over both groups. Probably end up killing each other in the succession struggle, as number fours become number threes, and number twos go after each other."

"I'm sure the Kill Committee will update the target list," Ray replied.

A white drone with a red stripe on it was headed south above the river. On its side, Ray could make out the words COAST GUARD.

Ray stood and looked down on the river. "Winston Burrell called this morning. Wants me to come up to Camp David. President wants to give me some bullshit award."

"When?" Dugout asked, standing next to him and looking down at the river.

"Tomorrow. But I think I'm headed to the beach instead. Maybe Anguilla."

"You do know it's Christmas in three days?" Dugout said.

"So?"

"So, it's happening without the attacks. You saved a lot of lives. You should accept the Goddamn medal," Dugout said.

"I saved a lot of lives, except for the ones I knew, the ones I cared about most. There's no great feeling of accomplishment when you kill the bad guys, knowing that there will just be more of them and you or someone else will have to do it again, and again. There's just a feeling of emptiness."

Ray turned to face Dugout and put his left hand on his friend's shoulder. "Jennifer said there is a PTSD syndrome that happens when you survive and everyone else in the Humvee buys it. She said the best cure is to change your environment completely and chill out as much as possible, beer, sun, sand, waves."

"And then what? When are you coming back? After New Year's?" Dugout asked. "There are a lot more bad guys out there we haven't gotten yet."

"There will always be bad guys out there." Ray pulled his right arm back behind him to gain leverage and then threw his cigar out as far as he could, toward the Potomac.

# Author's Note

Readers of two of my earlier books may recall that I have some personal responsibility for the use of drones against terrorists. In full disclosure, here is that story. I served in the White House for over a decade beginning in 1992, for three successive Presidents. My job for many of those years was National Coordinator for Security and Counter-terrorism. In that capacity, I came to believe that we needed to capture or kill the leadership of a group that few people in the United States had ever heard of, al Qaeda.

The CIA was instructed to get bin Ladin, but proved incapable of doing so. They were then asked to locate him reliably in a place where he would be staying for at least four hours, so that we could launch cruise missiles at the site. That did not work either. Frustrated, I asked for an independent review by Charlie Allen, a legendary intelligence officer and iconoclast. Charlie suggested we deploy Predators to the region and fly them over Afghanistan. Predators were only available as unarmed aircraft in those days, but we thought that they might be better than past efforts to find bin Ladin. CIA and the Pentagon, however, opposed the use of Predators for this purpose.

Eventually, the White House had to order the CIA to do a test deployment of the unarmed Predators. I still recall my amazement, sitting in a darkened room well after midnight Washington time, watching the video feed live from Afghanistan, following a truck, zooming in on a camp. On the fourth flight, bin Ladin was located. Then the winter set in and the winds were such that we could not fly the Predator over the mountains into Afghanistan from its base in Central Asia. We would not be able to fly again until spring. It was the fall of 2000 and the Clinton administration was coming to a close.

During the winter, I tried to get the Air Force to arm the Predator with missiles. They had thought about it, but had no plans to try it for several years. With the help of USAF General John Jumper, we compressed that timeline into a few months. Predator, armed with Hellfire missiles, worked well in the experimental flights. We then sought approval from the new Bush administration to deploy this armed Predator to get bin Ladin. Once again, the CIA and the Pentagon opposed the mission. I pressed for a decision to override them again, but National Security Advisor Condoleezza Rice delayed a decision for months.

Finally, on September 4, 2001, the Principals' Committee met in the White House Situation Room. CIA Director George Tenet and the DOD leadership both spoke out against the use of armed Predators to get bin Ladin and the al Qaeda leadership. They were not overruled.

A week later we were attacked.

On September 12, 2001, CIA proposed deploying armed Predators to attack al Qaeda in Afghanistan. On November 14, 2001, in Afghanistan, Mohammed Atef, the head of al Qaeda's military forces, became the first person to be killed by a Predator. Since then the United States has killed at least two thousand people in five countries using armed drones. And the killing continues.

Read on for an excerpt from
Richard A. Clarke's next book

# PINNACLE EVENT

Available in hardcover from Thomas Dunne Books/
St. Martin's Press

# Prologue

TUESDAY, AUGUST 9

INDIAN OCEAN

Alone in the water, below the gray rain clouds, *Octavius* crept forward at barely five knots. Had the captain still stood on her deck, scanning the horizons, he would have seen nothing but the waters of the Indian Ocean stretching away, empty under the low sky. Abandoned by her crew the night before, the ghost ship moved in a broad circular path, her death spiral. There was no one to hear the engine thumping below, the computer humming in the deckhouse, the flag of the Comoros snapping from the stern in the stiff breeze. Silently a stream of data moved up from the computer to the satellite dish and then into space. Images from the cameras, the readings from the engine room, automated pilot data, all shot the thirty-three thousand kilometers to the Thuraya satellite in encrypted packets that took a quarter second to travel that distance.

Data packets came down, as well. Automatically

decrypted on arrival in the laptop in the deckhouse, the final message was brief. It was routed down a fiber optic cable to the device in the hold. The 512-bit code caused the device to activate the detonation sequence, beginning with an electrical charge to the high-intensity conventional explosive. That explosion caused a bright flash and sent a large, bullet-shaped package of highly enriched uranium shooting down a tube into a hole in the uranium mass.

The presence of the added uranium in the mass caused it to reach criticality.

The intense light and heat were instant and immeasurable.

The iron and steel that was the MV *Octavius* vaporized first, as X-rays, gamma rays, and neutrons rushed out. Oranges, yellows, purples, greens, and a bright white leaped, twisted, churned, and fled the nuclei of the uranium like a mob let loose from imprisonment.

In less than a second, the surface water for a half a mile around underwent molecular transformation and some of it was ejected eight miles up as steam. The waters beyond the blast zone were sucked up and then thrown down, sending a small tsunami out in all directions. At the center of the eruption, a giant toadstool stood roiling, poisonous as the fungi it resembled. The sound waves traveled slower, for hundreds of kilometers, simultaneously deep, sharp, and growling.

In the complete silence of space, twelve hundred kilometers from the Thuraya satellite, another communications satellite was at work. The AEHF-2 rested in a geosynchronous orbit. The Advanced Extremely High Frequency satellite of the U.S. Space Command's 4th

Space Operations Squadron picked up signals from American forces throughout the Indian Ocean area and nearby, from Bahrain, Bagram, and Brisbane. It converted their electronic packets into laser beams and shot them to its sister, the AEHF-1, which then sent them down to Arizona.

The AEHF-2 was just a big router in the sky for the world's largest Internet provider, the Defense Information Systems Agency, but on the bottom of the American satellite sat a small dome, covering a series of specialized sensors. In the 1960s similar sensors had been so large that they had filled a satellite, which had been code named Vela. Although the sensors had officially been known by an ever-changing series of Pentagon acronyms, unofficially the original name Vela had stuck.

Any report related to a nuclear weapon being detonated, lost, or stolen moved across the Defense Department communications network with the highest precedence, knocking all other message traffic back in the cue. Such messages were tagged on the subject line: PINNACLE EVENT. When a message with that caption arrived at a command post, audio alarms sounded.

While the cloud was still rushing skyward from where the MV *Octavius* had been, the Vela sensors on the bottom of the AEHF-2 sent a series of data packets from space on a circuitous path to the Pentagon's National Military Command Center and seven other command centers. At one of them, on Patrick Air Force Base in Florida, the message packets caused a red light to begin spinning in the Operations Room of the Air Force Technical Applications Center. As the duty officers at AFTAC looked up, they heard a prerecorded female voice speaking slowly, calmly, as though she were informing them that the airport shuttle train doors were about to close.

"Attention, attention. There has been a Pinnacle Event. Repeat, Pinnacle." The red light spun its beam across the room. "An atmospheric nuclear detonation has been detected. Repeat, nuclear detonation."

# 1

MONDAY, AUGUST 15
GRINZING
VIENNA, AUSTRIA

Herman Strodmann rang the bell as he drove the first trolley of the day out of the little, end-of-the-line station at 0600. He loved driving the number 38 route because he could walk to work from his cottage, at the edge of the Vienna Woods, on the hill above the village of Grinzing. He walked by the house where Beethoven had written the Second Symphony. He thought of the 38 tram as a time machine, taking him in half an hour from the quaint, traditional wine *stubels* and *heurigers* of eighteenth-century Grinzing to the hectic modernity of downtown Vienna. He especially liked the first kilometer of the route, when the tram had its own railbed to the right of the road. On that stretch he did not have to share the street with cars.

There he could get the two-car trolley up to a decent speed. As he was doing just that, he noticed a blue BMW in his rear mirror.

The car was accelerating quickly up the Grinzinger Alle behind the tram. It was going to overtake him quickly, Strodmann thought. What was the rush so early in the morning? As the tram approached the corner of Hungerbergstrasse, the exclusive railbed ended and Strodmann guided the trolley on to the street. As he did, for a second he lost sight of the BMW. Then, suddenly, it was veering right in front of the tram, aiming into the Daringergasse. Herman Strodmann hit the brakes just as the trolley smashed into the BMW and rode up over it, crushing the passenger compartment.

In seconds, the BMW 525 erupted into an orange ball of flame shooting twenty-five feet in the air. The flame scorched the windows around the trolley driver's seat and leaped in the small, open side window, giving Herman Strodmann second-degree burns on his left arm. He quickly threw open all the doors for the few passengers to get out and then he leaped from the crippled tram. He could see that the flames instantly incinerated the man driving the BMW.

Karl Potgeiter had known when he bought the car that it was a younger man's vehicle. Although he was seventy-two, partially retired, and now working as a consultant to the UN's Vienna-based, International Atomic Energy Agency (IAEA), he was fit and looked much younger than his years. A nuclear physicist, he was a South African citizen, but had lived in Austria for twenty-two years. Every weekday morning, he drove himself into Vienna for an early *Frühstück*, breakfast, at his favorite haunt, the Café Lantman next to the Burgtheater on the Ringstrasse.

That morning, his usual waitress, Maria, wondered

where he was. She learned about the crash a few hours later. Word spread quickly as to why the 38 tram route was closed. Later, Maria would read that poor Dr. Potgeiter's body was burned beyond all recognition and was only identified by dental records. It did not help her calm down to see the picture of the flaming car dominating the front page of *Kronen Zeitung* the next day. Maria knew he had been such a nice man, such a good tipper. She also knew that it was such bad luck. There were so few fatal accidents with the trolleys.

### HERZLIYA, ISRAEL

Dawid Steyn and his wife, Rachel, enjoyed living in Herzliya Pituah, near the beach. It was an expensive neighborhood, but the house was big enough for her mother to live with them and take care of the girls. It was also close to Israel's Silicon Valley. Rachel could drive to work at Google in ten minutes, including the time it took to drop Dawid off at the train station. For Dawid, the train ride into Tel Aviv gave him just enough time to scan *The Jerusalem Post*. He usually tried to get a seat on the upper level of the double-decker train that ran from Binyamina through Tel Aviv to Ashkelon. On the 0708 train, that was usually not a problem. If he waited for a later departure, the upper deck filled up before the train got to Herzliya, but Rachel was an early riser and Dawid had adjusted to her ways long ago, so making the early train was easy.

His eighteen-minute commute, from Herzliya, a town named after the father of Zionism, to a train station named for the original Israeli military, the Haganah, reminded him every day of the origins of his adopted country. He and his father had moved to Israel after his mother died, when Dawid was ten. His mother had been Jewish, so Dawid gained Israeli citizenship automatically through the Right of Return. Now, with his father dead, Dawid Steyn carried on the family's international investment business from a small office in Tel Aviv. No one could tell from the Steyn office suite's modest size that the firm managed over two billion dollars in assets, and as of this week it was two and a half billion.

He looked up as the train stopped at Tel Aviv University, watching the students disembarking. They looked so young, but he reminded himself that it was almost fifteen years ago that he had graduated from that school. In less than a decade, his own girls could be riding this train to University, if Rachel's mother could ever let go of them.

At 0726 the big, red, double-decker train from Binyamina pulled into track three at Tel Aviv Haganah Station, from which Dawid would normally catch the line 16 Dan bus to his office near the beach promenade. He was among the last to get off the train, at the rear of the crowd making its way up the platform to the escalator, his head still in the *Post* as he walked. There was a push, then a shove. Startled, Dawid looked up as the man hit against him hard, sending him off the platform and on to Track 4 just as the express from Nahariya pulled into the station.

Dawid Steyn, thirty-five, was the first person to die on the tracks at the Haganah Station. It was almost

0830 when the Tel Aviv Police reached Rachel at her desk at Google. Her first emotion was guilt, that she had been wrong to mock Dawid's paranoia, his theory that people were following him.

### THE ADDRESS HOTEL, MALL OF THE EMIRATES
### DUBAI, UNITED ARAB EMIRATES

"Room service," he heard from outside his door. Marius Plessis thought room service was the best part of his condo-apartment in the hotel, that and the fact that he could walk to all the restaurants and stores in the Mall. It was also a five-minute taxi ride to his office and a fifteen-minute drive to the marina where he kept his boat.

He threw on his robe, tying it closed as he made his way to the door. He had set the time for breakfast delivery at 0900. Was it nine already? He had gotten in late from the airport the night before. His flight from Zürich had not landed until after midnight. Rubbing his eyes, he opened the door. "Please, set it up on the balcony," he said to the waiter. Half the year, the weather in Dubai was delightful and he enjoyed being outside as much as possible. The other half it was so hot that, if he had to be in Dubai then, he tried never to leave the air-conditioned environments.

Marius stepped into the bathroom as the waiter pushed the food dolly cart to the balcony. When he emerged, the polite, young Indian stood waiting for him on the balcony, holding the morning papers. "The

*Khaleej Times,* sir, and your *Financial Times,* as usual," the waiter said. Marius added a tip and signed for the breakfast.

He regretted that they did not serve "real" bacon. It was one of the few things that he missed, living in Dubai. As he devoured the scrambled eggs, Marius Plessis folded the salmon-colored *Financial Times* so he could read the story on the rise in the price of natural gas. He wondered if it was too late to invest in the new Australian shale fields. He would have to find somewhere new to invest soon, now that the money had hit the accounts he managed. His advisors at the Dubai International Financial Center had been at the office for hours already, straddling the Asian and European markets. He thought he should call them after breakfast, or maybe he would just go over there after lunch at La Petite Maison. It was a better restaurant, he thought, than the London original, behind Claridge's.

Finishing breakfast, he rose and stretched, looking north toward Iran. It may be a troubled neighborhood, he thought, but there could be few better places to live than in Dubai. You could get anything here, anything, and nowhere was the standard of living higher. With a modern, high-rise, luxury condominium here and another in Vancouver for the summer months, what more could he ask for in life? He never missed the land of his birth, let them have it. They were destroying it, as he knew they would. His two daughters were happily married and living in Toronto and San Diego. He saw them and their babies just enough. They would never approve of the female friends he had here, some of them younger than his daughters, but what was money for if you did not get enjoyment from it. At seventy-one, he was still in great shape, with a little assistance from the pills.

Perhaps, he thought, he would visit the gym after going over to the DIFC. His trainer would be there today, at the hotel's marvelous spa. He heard the waiter entering the suite to collect the food cart. Marius looked down at the dancing fountains, forty-six floors below, and smiled, contented with his life now, after all of the earlier strife. Then he felt his legs being grabbed at the ankles, his head was over the railing and he was in the air, off the building, falling toward the fountains.

The *Khaleej Times* would not carry the story of Marius Plessis's death. Suicides, like his, did not fit in with the themes that the Ruler wanted reported in his papers and, in reality, there were hardly any suicides in the emirate except among the guest workers on the construction projects. White men like Plessis almost never killed themselves in Dubai.

CLARKE QUAY
SINGAPORE

"I don't think you need me anymore, Dr. Coetzee," the attractive Asian woman said, dabbing her mouth with her napkin. "Your Chinese is almost flawless, but I do enjoy our lunches and tutorials, so I will not complain if you wish to continue." The couple sat at an outside restaurant on the water, enjoying a late and long lunch, in a modern complex of bars, restaurants, and shops where once the old freighters had docked. Now the ships were so large that only the giant cranes could handle their container cargo, at the computerized terminals across the harbor. The current cargo piers were like conveyor belts for the containers, with hundreds of ships lined up just beyond the harbor, waiting their turns to offload and load up.

"Weemin, my Chinese is only fair. When my associates drop the English and start talking rapidly in Chinese, I only pick up about half of what they are saying to each other."

"That may be, sir, because they do not want you to know what they are saying. They may suspect that you have been taking Chinese lessons for years now. After all, they are all spies at the Security and Intelligence Division, the SID, they must know about me," she said, smiling at the older man.

Cornelius Coetzee looked slightly embarrassed. "I may have led them to believe that our relationship is less than platonic. I don't think they know I speak and read Chinese. There is never a Chinese language document in the office. English is the government language, the business language. Chinese is only spoken at home, and, as you say, when they want to keep things from me."

"How do you know, Dr. Coetzee, that I do not work for your colleagues at the SID? I may report everything to them," Weemin said, laughing.

"Because you work for my employers' archrival, the internal security boys, ISD. My dear, I have known that for years and I must say that your reports to them about me must be very boring indeed."

"Cornelius, how can you think that?" she protested, mildly. "And if I did work for ISD, why after all these years of having nothing to report about you would they keep sending me out to meet you?"

Coetzee chuckled. "Because they hate the SID so much that any chance they could learn some inside tidbit is worth it to them, however silly that is."

"I think there is another reason that you want to improve your Chinese," she suggested.

The check came and Cornelius Coetzee produced a credit card. "Oh, really. And what, please tell, might that be, my little spook?"

"You advise the SID only one day a week now, not because they do not want you to spend more time with them, but because your investments take more and more of your time." She was dropping all pretense now of being only a Chinese tutor. "You have been investing heavily in China and doing very well where others have not. And just this week you received a great deal more money to invest. They may ask you where that money came from?"

Coetzee, too, had ceased to play the part of the doddering, old, retired spy. "Who might ask me, Weemin?"

"The Internal Security Division, or even your friends at the SID. They must know, too," she said.

He signed the credit card bill and punched his PIN into the handheld machine the waiter brought to the table. When the waiter was gone, Dr. Cornelius Coetzee looked Weemin Zhu in the eyes and said, very softly, "You know, Weemin, I think you are right. My Chinese has gotten to the point where I don't need you anymore. May you live a long and happy life." He rose from the table and walked toward the street, leaving her sitting, somewhat stunned, by the waterside.

He strode quickly toward River Valley Road, past the modern chain stores and bars, ignoring the sign that read THE PARTY NEVER STOPS AT CLARKE QUAY. The anger was rising up inside him. He had worked for this little city-state country for more than two decades, helping their fledgling foreign intelligence service in tradecraft, talent spotting, and agent handling, everything he had done so well in his own country. His advice had helped them penetrate the U.S. Navy, the Australian Army, the Indonesian President's office, and the Malaysian police. And what gratitude do they show? When the money entrusted to him by his old colleagues suddenly increases, they think he's been paid off for spying on Singapore? He had been completely loyal to his new home. Furthermore, who would pay him half a billion dollars U.S. for spying on Singapore? He would have to sell their giant casino complex, that ugly monstrosity, to get paid that kind of money.

He knew that getting mad like this was not good for his blood pressure, so he exhaled and tried to calm down. He reached the road and thrust up his arm to hail one of the ubiquitous blue taxis. As he did, a 9mm bullet pierced his forehead just above his nose. Cornelius Coetzee leaned backward and then folded like a Macy's parade balloon, falling to his knees and then forward, his head hitting the sidewalk and covering it with a quickly expanding pool of bright red blood.

Hearing the shot, Weemin Zhu ran toward him, pulling a handgun from her purse, but there was no one to shoot at, no indication of the shot's origin. She looked down at Coetzee and knew that the single bullet had been fatal. She replaced the gun in her handbag and removed her mobile. She called the Watch Command at the Internal Security Division and identified herself. "I need a response unit immediately at Clarke Quay. There has been a murder of my subject. The police will be here soon. Do you want me to tell them that this is my case?"

They did want her to. The Internal Security Division thought the police would never be able to figure it out and, besides, maybe Coetzee's murder would reflect badly on their rival, his employer, the SID. After all, they said to Weemin, a murder in Singapore had to be an espionage-related event. There was no street crime in the city.

THE ROCKS, SYDNEY
NEW SOUTH WALES, AUSTRALIA

"I'm taking the rest of the day off. Got some chums in town, going to go do the Manly thing with them," Willem Merwe announced to his staff as he bounded out of the office of Merwe-Wyk-Roux in the restored brick building in the old part of town. "See you all in the morning."

His small team was used to him disappearing for rugby, or volleyball on Bondi Beach. It was clear to them that the younger Mr. Merwe was nothing like his late father, who had spent long hours poring over investments and accounts. They should have known that he would be different as soon as he moved them from the downtown office tower to the funky town house in the Rocks district. "Roux in the Rocks," Willy had jokingly proclaimed, his only attempt at a rationale to the staff for moving. The real reason, his staff knew, was that he wanted to abandon the staid old image and become more hip. He never wore a tie and he biked to work. Despite his youth, his investment strategies, which included Chinese computer components, media and real estate, had paid off. One of them must have just hit big, the staff assumed, because he had told them that morning that there was a substantial amount more to invest and he wanted "transformational" ideas.

At twenty-nine, Willy Merwe looked like the All Australian Male—tall, blond, broad shouldered, with the muscled legs of a champion bicyclist. No one on Bondi would have guessed he was an immigrant and, if they had, no one would have cared. He was cool and Australia was a nation of immigrants.

Merwe locked his bike on the rack at Circular Quay Ferry Terminal and ran for the 0315 boat from Pier 3 to Manly Beach, across Sydney Harbor. He made his way upstairs to the bar, got a KB Lager, and then climbed higher up to the top deck, which was open to the sky and the breeze.

He looked back at the Sydney skyline and smiled. It was a view that always made him happy, the Opera House, the Bridge, the skyscrapers. He never understood why so few people came up to the top deck, like now, when he was the only one there. Why also did people live in these crowded financial centers like New York, Tokyo, or London, he wondered, when you could bloody well do the same bit of business in a city that was livable and liked to have fun?

He knew his team at the office thought he was going over to Manly Beach for a good time. He did not want to disabuse them of that idea, because it was actually to meet up with some people from his father's organization who had showed up in town without notice and suggested a get-together where they might all look like old buddies doing the tourist thing. His dad's old organization was now his, he supposed. The role was something that he inherited, something he had been trained to do because he had been designated as his father's successor. There was always a designated successor. Even he had one now, a guy about his age in New Zealand, Paul Wyk.

Willy Merwe, however, planned to do the job for the next twenty years. He would manage the funds, hidden in various safe havens, grow the principal, pay the families on a regular basis, and make emergency disbursements when he thought that one of the families had a legitimate need for more. If any family did not like his decision, they could appeal to the four others, but no one ever did. He was fair and he was generous. He was also more successful with his Discretionary Investment Fund than any of the other four had been in the last two years. Now that they had made the Deacquisition Decision, as he and Karl Potgeiter had advocated, there was a real opportunity to put some big money to work. Willy Merwe never forgot what he had learned in his finance class at Wharton: there are opportunities only open to big money, opportunities to get IRRs in the forties. "It takes big money to make big money," Professor Meitzinger had said. Now, Willy thought, I am going to do just that.

Instead, he felt a sharp, overwhelming pain in the back of his skull, so dominating his consciousness that he never felt the fall until he hit the water. His brain was so jarred by the impact of the strike to his head that it was unable to send messages to his arms and legs. His body was swept up in the spinning water of the ferry's propeller wash. No one would be too surprised that another drunken passenger had fallen off a Sydney ferry and drowned. Unfortunately, it happened a lot.